PRAISE FOR ADRIAN PHOENIX AND

A RUSH OF WINGS

"Phoenix slings the reader into an intense world of dizzying passion, tremendous heart, and arresting originality. Sharp, wicked, and hot as sin."

   —*New York Times* bestselling author Marjorie M. Liu

"This one pulled me in from the first page. Heather and Dante are among those rare characters readers so often look for and seldom find."

   —Barb Hendee, bestselling coauthor of *Traitor to the Blood*

"For far too long, Adrian Phoenix has been one of fantastic literature's best kept secrets. Finally, she has fulfilled all the promise of her brilliant but infrequent short stories with *A Rush of Wings*. The novel is a fast-paced ride, its New Orleans setting appropriately rich and gothic, its characters both real and surprising. If you read only one debut novel this season, make it this one."

   —*New York Times* bestselling author Kristine Kathryn Rusch

"A goth urban fantasy that moves as fast as its otherworldly characters. A bit like *The Crow* crossed with *The Silence of the Lambs* crossed with a voice that is Phoenix's own, *A Rush of Wings* is decadent, glittering fun, wrapped up in leather and latex."

   —Justine Musk, author of *BloodAngel*

"*A Rush of Wings* is a dark, rich, sensual treat, where heroes and villains alike are fascinating and three-dimensional. Adrian

A Rush of Wings

Adrian Phoenix

POCKET BOOKS
New York   London   Toronto   Sydney

Pocket Books
A Division of Simon & Schuster, Inc.
1230 Avenue of the Americas
New York, NY 10020

First Pocket Books trade paperback edition January 2008

POCKET and colophon are registered trademarks of Simon & Schuster, Inc.

For information about special discounts for bulk purchases, please contact Simon & Schuster Special Sales at 1-800-456-6798 or business@simonandschuster.com

Designed by Carla Jayne Little

Manufactured in the United States of America

10   9   8   7   6   5   4   3   2   1

Library of Congress Cataloging-in-Publication Data

Phoenix, Adrian.
    A rush of wings / Adrian Phoenix.—1st Pocket Books trade pbk. ed.
       p. cm.
    1. Vampires—Fiction. I. Title.
    PS3616.H6R87 2008
    813'.6—dc22
                                                     2007023302

ISBN-13: 978-1-4165-4144-8
ISBN- 10:   1-4165-4144-6

DEDICATED TO SEAN PRESCOTT

DUUUDE.

ACKNOWLEDGMENTS

Special thanks to: Kris Rusch and Dean Smith for their friendship, guidance and support; to my agent, Matt Bialer, and to my editor, Jen Heddle, for believing in me—this has been a fun, kick-ass journey.

Thanks to: My son Matt Jensen, and his lovely partner, Sherri Lyons; to my son Sebastian Phoenix, and his equally lovely partner, Jen Phoenix; and to my own sweet Kylah; thanks to Rose Prescott, Karen Abrahamson, Louisa Swann (for crying), Jamie Whittaker, Tawnia Seward, Joe Cummings, and the rest of the OWN gang for all the support and encouragement.

Thanks also to: Lynn Adams, D.T. Steiner, Marty and Sharon Embertson, and Hunter Kennedy for always being there.

And last, but not least, thanks to: New Orleans, my soul-city; to Dark Cloud 9 of Portland, and Trent Reznor, for all the work and sweat and love he pours into his music and kick-ass live NIN shows, providing music that is both a source of inspiration and an emotional soundscape.

And thanks to you, the reader, for picking this book up and plunging into my world. *Merci beaucoup*!

1

VOICE FOR THE DEAD

THE SWEET, CLOYING ODOR of blood and honeysuckle hung in the rain-misted courtyard like rancid smoke. A nude figure was curled against the courtyard's ivy-draped stone wall, his bound hands tucked beneath his face like those of a sleeping child, a stark counterpoint to his swollen and battered face. A dark mesh shirt was twisted around his throat and night-blackened blood pooled around his body. Gleamed upon skin and stone.

And on the wall above scrawled in blood—

WAKE UP

HEATHER WALLACE'S MUSCLES, KNOTTED from her long flight from Seattle, kinked even tighter. The message was a disturbing addition if this was the work of the Cross-Country Killer. A warning? A command? A dark, ironic joke aimed at his dying victim?

Drawing in a careful breath, Heather stepped from the back door of DaVinci's Pizza and walked into the shadowed courtyard. She skirted the numbered evidence placards dotting the old stone floor.

"Daniel Spurrell, age nineteen," Detective Collins said from the doorway. "From Lafayette. LSU student. Disappeared three days ago. Discovered in the courtyard about noon by an employee."

Tortured somewhere else, then dumped, Heather thought. Why *here*?

Old-fashioned gaslit lanterns cast pale, flickering light across the courtyard. Beneath the blood stink, Heather caught a whiff of jasmine and ivy, thick and wintergreen, a white-flowered bouquet unable to mask the smell of death.

Three years she'd been tracking the CCK. And dealing with his victims never got any easier.

She knelt beside all that remained of Daniel Spurrell. Tortured. Raped. Slaughtered. Posed. Latest victim of a wandering sexual sadist.

A deep, thudding vibration emanated from next door, snaked up her spine. "What's on the other side of the wall?" she said, her gaze on Daniel's bruised face.

"Club Hell," Collins answered. "Music venue. Bar." He paused, then added, "And a vampire hangout. Pretend, y'know?"

"Do you mean Goths? Or gamers?"

Collins chuckled. "Shit, you tell me. Sounds like you're more in the know."

"My sister fronted a band," Heather said. "I met all kinds at her gigs."

Long, midnight-blue hair veiled the boy's face. NightGlo, Heather mused. A hair color Annie'd often used when she and WMD hit the stage in all their hard-edged punk glory. Before Annie'd flamed out in a spectacular bipolar meltdown and sliced her wrists onstage.

Heather focused on a mark on the boy's chest—something

cut or scorched into the flesh. She leaned in closer. Blackened skin. Blistered. A series of circles—burned with a *car lighter?*

The anarchy symbol.

Cold frosted Heather's veins. The symbol was also new. Like the blood message. If this was the work of the Cross-Country Killer, then his signature, his *reason*, his drive for the kill had changed from an insular intimacy, his victim's final desperate moments his and his alone, to an overt act inviting attention. Impossible. Theoretically. But if it *had* changed, what then?

Then she needed to find out why.

Heather studied Daniel's face, the midnight-blue hair, the twist of cloth embedded into his throat, knotted around it. Breathed in the lingering smell of death and tasted it.

Why you? Chosen? Or wrong place, wrong time? Why here?

She heard her father's voice, deep and low, his tone reverential: *The dead speak* only *through evidence. Through evidence alone are you a voice for the dead.*

Heather stood. S.A. James William Wallace—the Bureau's leading forensic specialist and world's lousiest father.

The dead aren't the only ones seeking a voice, Dad.

Ah, Pumpkin, they *found their voices the moment they picked up a gun, a knife, a rope, or a baseball bat, the moment they killed. Through evidence you will silence them.*

Heather turned away from Daniel's curled body. She pushed rain-damp strands of hair back from her face, listened to the pounding bass beat coming from Club Hell.

Daniel's killer spoke loud and clear. He was an organized killer, deliberate. So it was no accident that he chose the wall next to the club. Had Daniel met his killer in there? So why leave his body here and not in the club's courtyard, on the other side of the wall?

And if this was the work of a copycat?

Then the Cross-Country Killer was still out there, enjoying his little jaunt across the States, casually selecting victims—male *and* female—like a Bermuda shorts–wearing tourist picking out postcards.

Still out there. Still needing to be silenced.

As Heather crossed the courtyard, a familiar truth burned bright in her mind: She'd never allow a case to go cold to protect the reputation of a loved one; never bury evidence no matter how much it hurt.

Unlike the famous James William Wallace.

Heather joined Collins at the threshold leading into DaVinci's. She read the unasked question in the detective's eyes: *Is the Cross-Country Killer in New Orleans?*

"Signature's different," she said. "The message . . . I'll know more once we have the autopsy report and the DNA workup."

"What's your gut say?"

Heather glanced at the body. Huddled. Praying hands. Naked in the rain. Stabbed over and over. Strangled. Young and pretty, once.

Heather looked at Collins. Six one, she judged, and lean. Midthirties. She noted the tension in his shoulders, his jaw. "How deep in the shit did you get buried for calling in a fed?"

A flicker of surprise crossed his eyes. "They made you special agent for a reason. Neck deep and it's still piling up."

"I'll do what I can to dig you out," Heather said. "I appreciate your call."

Collins regarded her for a long moment, his hazel eyes weighing, considering. He nodded. "Thanks. But I'll dig myself out."

"Fair enough." Heather met his gaze. "My gut tells me this *is* the CCK's work. But that's off the record."

A faint smile touched Collins's lips. "Fair enough."

"He's probably long gone."

Collins nodded, face bleak. "Traveling man."

Shrieks of laughter and sharp jazz riffs drifted in from the street. And underneath it all, the steady thump-thump-thump of music from Club Hell.

"Mardi Gras," Collins said. "Well, almost. Still three days out and it's crazy." He shook his head. "Y'ever been?"

"No, this is my first trip to New Orleans."

"Let me thank your gut by treating you to a N'awlins-style dinner." Collins pushed away from the doorway. His clean, spicy cologne cut through the courtyard's thickening smell of death and blood.

"Thanks, but I'll take a rain check. I want to look into a few things, maybe catch a little sleep." Heather offered her hand. "I appreciate your time and help, Detective."

Collins grasped her hand and shook it. Strong grip. An honest man. "Call me Trent. Or Collins, if you're old-school. I'll contact you soon as I hear anything."

"Sounds good, Trent."

Releasing Collins's hand, Heather walked back into the pizzeria, headed for the front door. A thought circled around the anarchy symbol burning in her mind.

The pattern has changed. He's communicating. But with whom, and why now?

SITTING AT THE SMALL, lacquered desk in her room, Heather connected her laptop to the hotel's Internet service. She tabbed open a can of Dr Pepper and took a long swallow of the cold, sweet plum–flavored soda. It hit her empty stomach like a chunk of ice.

WAKE UP.

A challenge? To law enforcement? The Bureau? Her? None of the above?

Drunken laughter and shouts—*"Dude! Wanna get a bite? Duuuude!"*—boomed past her door and down the corridor, fading as the revelers found their rooms.

Heather worked her iPod's headphones into her ears and thumbed the volume down low so she'd hear it if anyone called.

Knocking back another long swallow of Dr Pepper, she typed in an online search of Club Hell.

The Leigh Stanz bootleg she'd downloaded into her iPod curled into her ears and focused her thoughts. Low and intense, accompanied by acoustic guitar, Stanz's voice was husky and worn, like the voice of a man emptying his heart out for the last time.

I long to drift like an empty boat on a calm sea / I don't need light / I don't fear darkness . . .

Checking the links pulled up on her search page, Heather learned that the *very* hip Club Hell had opened nearly four years earlier and was frequented by a Goth/punk/wannabe-vampires crowd. The kind of place Annie would've gigged at with WMD.

A lot of local bands and underground acts performed at the club, especially Inferno, an industrial/Goth band fronted by a young man rumored to also be the owner of Club Hell. He appeared to be known only as Dante.

Heather shook her head. Dante's Inferno. Cute. Good for marketing, no doubt. Hoping to find out more about the club's possible owner, she Googled Inferno and received a trillion hits. Scrolling down to the band's official Web site, she clicked on tour dates—none in the last year; albums—two, with the third due to be released in a few days; photos. She paused, studying the captured images.

Three men in their early to midtwenties—dreads, faux hawks, hard bodies pierced and tattooed—stood in one of New Orleans's cities of the dead, each of them looking in a different direction. Behind them stood a fourth figure in black jeans and baggy sweatshirt, hood pulled up. Head bowed, fingers holding the hood's edges, his face unseen, he seemed to be contemplating the seashell and gravel path beneath his boots.

But what caught Heather's attention was the pendant hanging at his throat. The anarchy symbol. She sat up straighter and enlarged the photo. Stared at a circled letter *A* fashioned out of what looked like barbed wire and strung on a black cord.

Heart pounding, Heather checked the photo's caption. The figure was Dante. She clicked on the next photo. Dante's back was to the camera. No visible anarchy symbol. In the next photo, she caught a glimpse of the barbed-wire pendant dangling like a charm from a twist of wire around his wrist.

Heather scrutinized each photo. The anarchy symbol wasn't always present or visible. But she did notice one thing: Inferno's front man was never the focus of the photos. Dante stood behind the other members or off to the side or knelt in front, head bowed. Not once did she see his face. A flash of black hair in one, a pale cheek in another, but that was all.

Another marketing ploy? The oh-so-mysterious front man? Or genuine reluctance to be front and center—except when onstage?

Heather scrolled through online band interviews and wasn't surprised to discover nearly all were conducted with the other members of Inferno. "In the studio" was the usual reason given for Dante's absence.

Heather finished her can of Dr Pepper, then lined down to the last article and opened it. This time, Dante wasn't "in the studio"; he sat, alone, for the interview. Clunking the empty can onto the desk, Heather leaned forward to read.

Dante spoke intelligently about music and the state of the music industry, French or Cajun words spicing his comments, his tone often dark and humorous.

DANTE: It's time to return to the days of the guillotine. If you don't have passion for music, if you don't have *le coeur*, and you're only in it for the money, the fame, or the chicks, then off with your head.

AP: Are you serious?

DANTE:	Yeah. At least that'd be honest entertainment. You need to bleed for your audience one way or another.
AP:	Why don't you give more interviews?
DANTE:	I want the focus to be on the music. Not me.
AP:	But people want to know more about you. You *are* the music. Why did you open Club Hell?
DANTE:	(Tense) To showcase musicians, new talent.
AP:	How do you address the rumors that you're a vampire?
DANTE:	(Standing) Wrong focus. We're done.

VAMPIRE? WAS THAT A joke? More marketing? Heather suddenly remembered Collins saying: *And a vampire hangout. Pretend, y'know?*

Using Bureau ID codes, Heather tapped into city records and looked up all pertinent info on Club Hell. The owner was listed as one Lucien De Noir, a French entrepreneur. All licenses and deeds were in his name, but based on that last interview and her own gut feeling, Heather believed De Noir was only the money man. Club Hell was Dante's baby.

Heather plugged into the NOPD's system with her guest security code and searched for Dante, though with no last name, she didn't hold a lot of hope for a hit. The search spat up a list of Dantes as first names and last names and she worked her way through them quickly. She came to a halt on Dante Prejean. No social security number. No driver's license. Age estimated to be twenty-one. Refused to give a birth date. No legal surname. Prejean was a name tacked on from the family who'd fostered him as a kid in Lafayette.

Lafayette. Daniel Spurrell's hometown. Connections clicked

and whirled through her mind like a slot machine. The bars all snapped to a stop in a line.

Anarchy symbol. Lafayette. Club Hell.

Heather skimmed Dante Prejean's file—criminal mischief, vandalism, trespassing, loitering—all misdemeanors. She scanned for a mug shot, but didn't find one posted. Frowning, she scrolled through case notes and arrest records. Camera malfunction was usually listed as the reason for no mug shot being taken, but one officer had jotted a different reason altogether:

> *Little shit won't hold still. He moves so goddamned fast, every time we snap his picture, he's fucking gone. This happens every freaking time with this asshole. This is the only picture he's ever stood still for.*

HEATHER CLICKED ON THE photo. A bowed, hooded head. And a hand in front of the hidden face, middle finger extended. Defiant, even under arrest, playing games. She stared at the photo for a long time. The only mug shot Dante ever stood *still* for? Were the arresting officers plain inept?

Let me go, bro, let me go . . .

Leigh Stanz's hoarse voice and sad, yearning words ended. In the ensuing silence the unasked question in Collins's eyes looped through Heather's thoughts: *Is the Cross-Country Killer in New Orleans?*

And is he . . . what? . . . identifying with Dante Prejean?

Now? Suddenly? After three years?

An instant message from her SAC, Craig Stearns, blipped onto the laptop's screen: *Wallace, consultation progress?*

Heather typed: *Consultation continuing. Looks like the CCK, but not positive.* She stopped, fingers poised over the keyboard.

Should she mention the records glitch she'd run into on the flight from Seattle? The inability to access ViCAP and NCAVC files on the CCK's victims? A problem she'd never experienced before in working this case?

Heather rubbed her face. She glanced at the window. Rain poured outside, streaking the glass with ribbons of neon-lit color. Maybe she was being paranoid. Human error. Server malfunction. Shit happens. Maybe she needed to upgrade her computer.

And yet. A change in the CCK's pattern. A computer glitch.

Heather returned her gaze to the monitor and the blipping cursor. A knot of unease nestled in her belly.

And if the glitch *was* deliberate? Could it have been Stearns?

She shook her head. Her SAC was a stand-up guy, hard but honest. He'd even helped her with Annie when Dad refused. That kind of deception wasn't Stearns's way.

Heather's fingers dropped onto the keys: *Checking leads. Nearly finished. Will contact you tomorrow.* She hit send.

Scooting her chair back from the desk, she shut the laptop down and switched off her iPod. Heather shrugged on her trenchcoat. Scooping her Colt .38 up from the desk, she slipped it into the trench's specially designed inside breast pocket.

Time to go to Hell.

2

CLUB HELL

"Fuck your money. Go to the back of the line."

Heather squeezed free of a knot of people clustered in the crowded, narrow street and, grabbing hold of one of the brass horse head hitching posts, pulled herself up onto the teeming sidewalk.

She glanced at the speaker. He stood at the club's entrance behind a velvet and barbed-wire rope barrier, eyes hidden behind shades. Reflections of neon light winked and edged the dark lenses and lit up the silver crescent moon inked below his right eye. Tall and lean, he wore jeans, road-weathered leather chaps, and a leather jacket marked with nomad colors, which surprised her. She'd never seen a member of one of the family-oriented gypsy-style clans *working* before, let alone for in-town squatters. At least, not at something legal. Long dark hair tied back, a mustache framing his mouth, he grinned at the fetish-dressed-but-slumming tourist slinking to the back of the line.

Heather paused. Had she seen *fangs* when the bouncer grinned? Maybe so. She'd learned at one of Annie's gigs that for a few thousand dollars a person could get customized fangs implanted.

And given that this was Club Hell . . .

People fought their way onto the sidewalk, elbows and shoulders jostling Heather. A sharp jab to the ribs made her pull her arms in tight against her sides. She locked one hand around the purse strap looped over her shoulder. Her gaze skipped along the swollen line of people waiting to gain admittance.

The majority were Goth—dyed black hair, pale makeup, black lipstick and eyeliner, male and female. Some of the young men seemed to think they were Brad Pitt or Tom Cruise in that old vampire movie: long hair, lace ruffled shirts, velvet jackets, and silver-headed canes. The young women squeezed into form-fitting rubber or latex dresses, or dark velvet minis with tights and fishnet stockings.

Splashing the line with odd bits of color were kids in torn jeans and Ts, their hair buzz-cut or knotted into dreads. Some, like the admonished tourist, were simply curious.

Looking up the three-storied, black iron balconied building, Heather saw curtains fluttering in the night breeze from opened French windows on the third floor. Light flickered inside, like from a candle, and beckoned, like a curved finger.

Heather edged her way through the crowd, slipping between partiers reeking of beer and patchouli and sweat, to the bouncer. She glanced at the unmarked door beyond him—nothing identi-fied the club.

The rain shifted into a cool drizzle, beading on Heather's face, in her hair, and on her trench. Like Seattle, she mused. She reached into her purse and palmed her badge.

A punk queen in plaid trousers with bondage straps and a torn, black EATS YOUR DEAD tee safety-pinned up the sides submitted to the bouncer's search. His skimming, fight-scarred hands paused at the cuff of her left trouser. Reaching under and into her boot, he slipped free a secreted switch-blade.

"Naughty, naughty," the bouncer said, one eyebrow arched. He held the gleaming blade like a pro, spinning it between his fingers before sliding it into a pocket of his leather jacket.

The punk queen smacked her forehead with a tattooed hand. A sheepish smile touched her lips. "Fuck, Von. Forgot."

"I'll bet," he said. "You can have it back when you leave. Go in."

Heather noted the name. She stood on the sidewalk, maybe a yard from him. She knew he was aware of her presence; saw it in the deceptive ease of his body, the deliberate refusal to look her way. That was fine. For now, she was content to observe.

After a couple of minutes, the bouncer turned and, head tilted to one side, regarded Heather for a long moment. "Okay, little girl," he said, flashing another fanged grin. "What can I do for you?"

"I'm Special Agent Wallace," Heather said, stepping beside him. She flipped open her badge so only he could see it. "I'm investigating the murder next door."

The bouncer shook his head. "Cops already been here, dar-lin'."

Palming her badge, Heather looked up into the nomad's shaded eyes. Her twinned reflection looked back: face wet, hair pulled back, rain glistening on her black trench. "I'm looking for Dante Prejean."

Shrugging, the bouncer shifted his attention to the Goth princess swinging her weight from one foot to the next, a pout on her red-lipsticked lips. "Might be in, might not," he said. "No tellin'."

His hands skimmed the Goth princess's velvet-clad curves. "Go on in, darlin'," he said to the girl. He glanced at Heather. "You, too. Doubt it's your kinda scene, but—"

"What's your last name, Von?"

Arching an eyebrow, he murmured, "Sharp ears." He shrugged again. "Smith. Or maybe Jones. Mama lost track. But if you get it figured out, doll," he said, looking at Heather from over the tops of his shades. His green eyes seemed to glow. "Call me."

"Count on it," Heather said.

VON WATCHED THE FED disappear into the club.

<Law coming in. Pretty trenchcoat with no-nonsense eyes.>

As always, Lucien's mind felt busy, structured, somehow alien. But receptive. Von felt the activity pause, then his thought was allowed in. *<She wants Dante.>*

Lucien's thought arrowed into Von's mind with an intensity that sometimes unnerved him, especially when he reflected on the fact that Lucien's reply was *gentle*.

<She'll have to settle for me.>

Good enough. Two surprises so far and the night was young. The fed had been *numero dos*. A nightkind stranger—a bearded black dude wearing jeans, untucked pearl-buttoned blue shirt and snakeskin boots, and trailed by a geeky-looking mortal—had been *numero uno*.

An honor, llygad, the stranger had said as Von patted him down. But his rigid body language had totally disagreed with that statement.

As had his mortal buddy's amused grin.

Von's attention returned to the line. He smiled at two pretty young things clutching each other, laughing and peering at him with drug-dilated pupils. He smelled them—sandalwood, vanilla, and chemical tang. He listened to the blood pulsing through their veins.

With a half bow, he unhooked the rope barrier and gestured them through. The first one, honey-haired and dark-eyed, grasped his hand, then kissed it. Her soft lips lingered, warm against Von's skin. Her kiss tingled up his arm and down the length of his spine.

She looked at him with adoring eyes. "Nightkind," she sighed, blowing him a kiss as her giggling girlfriend grabbed her hand and led her into the club.

Hunger unwound within Von. The honey-haired mortal's warm vanilla scent tugged at him. Sucking in a deep breath, he slid his hands over the next person in line. He scanned the bobbing crowd, looking and sensing for someone else who was out of place. Feds rarely worked alone. He tamped down his hunger. He had to stay sharp. Tonight was not a night to dream of warm flesh and hot blood and sexy giggles. Not with a fed inside.

And a nightkind stranger.

GINA'S HEAD RESTED AGAINST Dante's shoulder as he bit into her pale throat. Blood, hot, rich, and laced with cocaine, trickled into his mouth. He drank her in carefully, in measured swallows. He slid his hand into her unlaced bodice, caressing and cupping her firm, warm breast. Her nipple stiffened against his palm. She moaned, then gasped. Dante slipped his arm around her waist, holding her even tighter.

Gina arched her hips, and Dante glanced down the length of her reclining body to where Jay, kneeling on the floor at the edge of the bed, eased his hands under Gina's bare ass and buried his face between her thighs.

Dante felt himself stir, harden. He closed his eyes and drank. Gina's moans increased in frequency and urgency. He listened to the rasp of her thigh-high stockings against the chenille bedspread, listened to Jay's muffled breathing, listened to Gina's pounding heart, listened to the creak of his own leather pants as he shifted on the bed.

A soundless voice—a wordless song—touched his burning

thoughts, rousing him from the heady flavor of Gina's cocaine-laden blood. Concern whispered into his mind.

Dante opened his eyes and stared into the candle-and-neon-lit room.

<Lucien?>

<Stay put, child. Feed. Play with your tayeaux.>

Dante lifted his head from Gina's throat. She glanced up at him, her heavy-lidded eyes puzzled. Then she gasped as Jay slid a finger inside of her. Her eyes closed again.

<What's wrong?>

<Nothing,> Lucien sent. <Just business.>

Sudden pain needled Dante's left temple. His breath caught in his throat as the pain intensified, then faded. Muscles knotted, he held Gina tight, closing his eyes and listening to her uneven breathing as Jay brought her ever closer to climax. He listened to Gina and ignored everything else.

Including the whispers left behind in the pain's wake.

HEATHER WALKED DOWN A crowded hall with black-painted walls scrawled with graffiti in fluorescent paint. Her gaze skipped over a few of the messages: INFERNO RULES! and RANDY SUKS DIK and WE DIE YOUNG.

People lined either side of the passageway, holding drinks, smoking—embers glowing as they breathed in—kissing, feeling each other up. The sweet odors of clove, pot, and wine mingled uneasily with the smells of vomit and warring perfumes.

Black lights glowed purple from bared male torsos and from nude, glitter-dusted breasts; shimmered from nipple piercings, NightGlo tattoos, and fluorescent body paint.

Music pounded like a sledgehammer and Heather regretted leaving her earplugs at home in Seattle. *Didn't think I'd be clubbing.*

Looking from face to face and wondering if a killer was among them, Heather worked her way through the crowd to the entrance proper. A glowing red neon sign hung above the entrance.

BURN

HEATHER PAUSED BENEATH THE flickering sign as dry ice mist swirled around her legs. What if she was wrong? What if DaVinci's courtyard being chosen, that particular wall being written on, had been coincidence?

Heather didn't believe in coincidence. She passed the sign and stepped into Hell.

STANDING BEHIND DANTE'S STONE bat-winged throne, Lucien shifted his gaze from the black, bearded nightkind stranger at the bar and his sallow-skinned mortal companion, to keep a watch on the entrance.

Silver and Simone sat on the stairs leading to the throne, their heads close together, talking and laughing. The crowd beyond them bobbed and jumped, dancing to the music blasting from the Cage.

Why was the law asking for Dante again? They'd already been here regarding the murder next door. His hands curled over the top edge of the throne, the stone gritty beneath his fingers.

Even more disturbing was the piercing pain he'd felt from Dante a few minutes ago. But there was no time to go to him now. No time to cool the hurt away—even temporarily.

Stone dust fell from beneath Lucien's fingers, powdering the black velvet cushion. He yanked his hands away from the throne. As he did, his gaze locked onto a woman standing in the entrance, one hand holding onto the strap of the purse looped over her shoulder. Lucien noticed that one side of her trench-coat hung just a little lower than the other. Gun, he mused.

Pretty trenchcoat with no-nonsense eyes. Apt description. Lucien took in her rain-darkened auburn hair, her petite frame, her confident posture. Apt, indeed.

Now to get her out of here.

Lucien stepped from around the throne and started down the stairs.

THE DANCING, THRASHING CROWD filling the dance floor held Heather's attention. A band played inside a steel-barred cage while the audience stalked them, seeking ways inside. Some climbed the cage, reaching in as they did, trying to grab a sleeve, a lock of hair. Without missing a note, the band kept playing as they dodged and skipped out of reach.

A young woman standing on the mesh top of the cage held out her arms, threw back her head and stepped off. The crowd caught her. As she was passed from one set of arms to another, hands slipped under her dress, inside her top, feeling her up as she was passed to safety.

Heather forced her tensed muscles to relax. She looked away from the thrashing dancers. Small circular tables lit by candles dotted the other side of the club. Immediately to her left was a long polished bar and directly in front of her a . . . throne.

The bat-winged throne stood on a dais reached by four stairs. A couple perched on the uppermost stair. They both suddenly looked her way, fixing on her as though synchronized.

The boy was pretty, punked out, and way too young to be in the club. A half-empty glass of wine rested beside him on the step. *Sixteen?* Heather wondered. The woman wrapped her arms around her upraised knees. Her long, spiraled hair gleamed like gold against her black tights. Both her eyes and the boy's seemed to catch and reflect the club's low light.

Movement above them caught Heather's eye. A tall, broad-shouldered man in a white long-sleeved shirt and black trousers stepped out from behind the throne and took the steps in two strides. Light winked from a pendant or chain at his throat. As he walked through the crowd, people parted for him without prompting, following his progress across the floor with gazes that Heather could only describe as awed.

Heather stepped aside from the entrance and waited for him, certain he was Lucien De Noir. As he drew nearer, she realized he was unusually tall. *Six seven? Six eight?* She straightened, determined to make every inch of her five feet four count.

"Good evening," he said, stopping before her. "I'm Lucien De Noir, club owner. May I help you?"

Heather met his gaze. His black hair was tied back, his clothing neat and crisp. A sterling-silver, rough-edged X on a black cord hung just below the hollow of his throat. He radiated power, oozed strength. A slight smile curved his lips. A handsome man, she realized, one, no doubt, who knew when to turn on the charm.

Flipping open her badge for De Noir, Heather returned his smile. "I'm Special Agent Wallace. I'd like to see Dante Prejean. I understood this was *his* club."

De Noir scrutinized her badge for a long moment before motioning for her to put it away. "His name is simply Dante," he said, his voice a low rumble. "And I'm afraid your information is mistaken. But, in any case, Dante isn't here tonight." De Noir's smile widened, warmed. Gold glinted in the depths of his eyes. "Perhaps I can help you."

"Do you know anything about the murder next door? Or the victim?"

De Noir shook his head. "Only what I've heard from the police and on the street." The gold lights in his eyes vanished. "And I'd imagine that Dante would know even less. He doesn't keep up with the news."

"It looks like it hasn't hurt business, anyway," Heather said, offering another smile. "Is there somewhere quieter we can talk?"

"The courtyard outside," De Noir said, turning away and stepping into the crowd. His tied-back hair, black and gleaming, reached to his waist.

Knowing there had to be an office on either the second or third floor of the building, Heather wondered why she was being ushered out the back. So to speak. But, for once, she didn't have a problem with that; she *wanted* to see the courtyard that adjoined DaVinci's.

Slipping her badge back into her purse, Heather followed De Noir onto the dance floor and through the parting crowd.

DANTE EASED OUT FROM behind Gina and slid to the edge of the rumpled bed. The black lace curtains framing the opened French windows twisted in the cool night breeze. The smell of rain and Mississippi mud filled the room. Dante trailed his fingers through his hair.

Still kneeling beside the bed, his hands resting on Gina's thighs, Jay watched him with interest.

"What's wrong, sugar?" Gina said, sitting up.

Dante didn't have to look at Gina to see the pout on her lips. "I've gotta go," he said. Candlelight flickered orange across the shadowed walls, across his leather pants, his boots. Pain flickered in his mind.

Gina's fingers wrapped around Dante's belt. She tugged. "Looks to me like you're all hot and bothered. Looks to me like you need to stay," she murmured. "Just lie down and we'll—"

Gently plucking Gina's fingers free from his belt, Dante stood. He shook his head. "Later. Play without me for now."

"Dante, *mon cher* . . . " Jay's hand slid from Gina's thigh, reached for Dante.

Dante pushed away Jay's hand, then seized a handful of the

mortal's blond hair and yanked his head back. Jay's breathing became rough, uneven. Bending down, Dante kissed him deeply. The honey, musk, and salt taste of Gina on Jay's tongue and lips damn near changed Dante's mind. But a familiar, dangerous restlessness burned within him. He *couldn't* stay.

Finishing the kiss, Dante released Jay's hair and trailed a finger along his jawline, then straightened and strode from the room. He heard Gina advising Jay to let him be.

Out in the hallway, Dante leaned against the wall. Eyes closed, he thumped his head lightly against the plaster. He waited for his hard-on to subside, wishing the dark, writhing things inside would subside as well. But knew they wouldn't. Pain prickled at his temple.

Fuck! Focus, dammit. Something's troubling Lucien. Zero in on that.

But Lucien's shields were up and he couldn't get through. In fact, it almost seemed as though Lucien was keeping him out deliberately. Dante opened his eyes and shoved himself away from the wall.

HEATHER GLANCED AT THE people sitting on the stairs as she weaved through the crowd behind De Noir. They watched her progress with something close to envy or maybe disbelief on their powder-pale faces. De Noir edged past them, seemingly oblivious to the shining gazes, the half-parted lips, and the whispers:

"Lucien. Will *he* see us?"

"Is *he* coming down?"

"Lucien Nightbringer. Lucien . . ."

Earnest, desperate, hungry.

Heather stepped past their outstretched fingers, disturbed by De Noir's silence. She wondered why he didn't say anything, why he didn't even glance at them.

De Noir stood aside and opened the door to the courtyard, gestured for Heather to enter. She looked into the ivy-draped clearing. Protected within gargoyle sconces, candles cast eerie windblown shadows across the stone walls. Her gaze was drawn to the wall where a killer's message had been smeared in blood on the other side. For a moment, she saw the blood seeping through the stone, letters forming in reverse. Her gut told her: Not by chance or coincidence. This wall had been *chosen*.

She was about to step out of the club when a sudden whisper rushed through the crowd like wind through tall grass. She stopped as the yearning voices abruptly fell silent. The air seemed to thicken, to crackle with anticipation.

She glanced at De Noir. His face was still, his eyes unreadable. But tension tightened his muscles. He met her gaze, seemed to be willing her into the courtyard. Slowly, Heather turned and looked back the way she'd come.

Someone walked down the stairs, stepping out of the shadows on the second-floor landing. It seemed to Heather as though every single person in the club sucked in a breath at the same time.

Then the figure crossed into the light and glanced with gleaming eyes over the heads of the crowd at Heather or maybe past her to De Noir, she couldn't be sure. She stood frozen, unable to move or breathe, then the collective pent-up breath in the club released. Voices clamored:

"Dante! Dante! *Mon ange!*"

"Yeah! Fuckin' hope he gets in the Cage tonight!"

Heather stared, dizzied and stunned, as he descended, overwhelmed by what she'd seen in the moment he'd looked her way—

Dark, light-filled eyes looking into her, drawing her in—

Slender, hard body, five nine or five ten, moving with dangerous and unself-conscious grace, all coiled muscles and knife-sharp reflexes—

Tousled black hair spilling past his shoulders, dressed in mesh and leather and steel-ringed bondage collar, a sexuality that scorched—

She wrenched her gaze from him and watched the faces of those who called his name, witnessed their smiles and tears as he stroked a jawline there, touched a cheek here, kissed a pair of lips there.

Then . . . he stepped into the crowd and out of sight, and Heather gasped for air, able to breathe again.

If that was Dante Prejean, then he was literally breathtaking. She'd never seen anyone so gorgeous. It also meant that De Noir had lied about Dante's not being here tonight. She turned to face De Noir and caught him rubbing the bridge of his nose, gaze on the floor. He looked like a man who'd suddenly felt the pain of Murphy's Law kicking him in the ass.

"Strange, I was sure you'd said that Dante wasn't here," Heather said. "Must've just arrived, then."

Dropping his hand, De Noir said, "So it would seem." Lifting his eyes, he met Heather's gaze. "The police have already spoken to him, Agent Wallace. I see no need to—"

"I'm sorry," Heather interrupted. "But I do."

She glanced over her shoulder. Dante climbed the steps leading to the cheesy Kingdom-of-Hell themed throne. Kneeling between the pretty underage punk and the earthy blonde, Dante stroked the boy's purple spiked hair. He leaned in close to the blonde, seemed to speak into her ear. Several Goth princesses at the foot of the steps bounced and squealed.

Why was De Noir so protective of Dante Prejean? What was he hiding?

Heather spun away from De Noir's strange black, gold-edged eyes and slipped into the crowd. She intended to find out.

3

WITHOUT A WORD

DANTE GLANCED OVER HIS shoulder. He didn't see the red-haired, trenchcoated woman who'd been standing beside Lucien, but he *felt* her pushing through the crowd, resolve and authority radiating from her like sunshine; bright, piercing, and deadly.

<*What's going on,* mon ami?>

Dante returned his attention to Simone. "Dunno." He slid his fingers along the silky length of her hair, pushed it behind her ear. "But I'm gonna find out soon. Whether I wanna or not." He smiled.

Simone watched him carefully, searched his eyes. He shook his head.

She sighed. "If you're sure."

Lowering his head, he kissed her, drinking in her magnolias and blood scent. *"Merci beaucoup, chérie,"* he whispered against her lips.

Simone sighed again. She glanced past him to Silver. "Come, *petit.*" She stretched a hand to Silver and wriggled her fingers. The boy took her hand and pulled her to her feet. They headed down the few steps to the dance floor.

Dante rose to his feet and climbed onto the dais. Under Pressure slammed and raged in the Cage, their music a fist—punching, punching, knockout. Dante closed his eyes. Every chord, every screamed word, every drum strike vibrated into him, thrummed along his spine.

A gentle nudge from Lucien opened the link between them. <*She's FBI. Tried to get rid of her.*>

Dante smiled at the chiding tone. <*Yeah, yeah. I didn't stay put. I know.* Merci.>

Opening his eyes, Dante spun around. The crowd howled. Several of his *tayeaux* squeezed from the crowd to curl on the steps below. The tiny bat tattoos at the hollows of their throats shimmered in the overheads, visible only to nightkind, marking them off-limits. Dark emotions oozed from the crowd at the sight of them—envy, bitterness, resentment—and lapped against the edges of Dante's consciousness. He looked into each pale face, each set of kohl-rimmed eyes, curving his lips into a smile but thinking, as always, *What do they want from me?*

Pain flickered and Dante shook his head, one hand to his temple. Drawing in a deep breath of the clove, cinnamon, and sweat scented air, he turned his thoughts outward.

Silver and Simone danced and shimmied on the floor, beautiful and graceful, nearly luminous with inner light—moon-blooded and hungry. Mortal watchers circled them. Hoping to be chosen, dreaming of a smooth, cool hand locking around a wrist and pulling them into the dance.

Beyond them, the crowd parted for Lucien, murmuring as he passed.

The FBI agent stepped out of the crowd and onto the first step leading to the dais, Lucien right behind her. He looked up at Dante, a warning in his eyes. Dante shrugged. He studied the woman climbing the steps. Slender in a black trenchcoat and slacks, trendy black Skechers, dark red hair twisted back in a French braid, stray wisps curling beside her smooth cheeks and forehead, generous lips. Her blue eyes burned with intelligence and determination.

<*Cute,*> Dante sent.

Lucien's warning darkened to a glare as he stepped past the woman to stand behind the throne. <*Dangerous,*> he arrowed back.

Dante grinned.

The agent stepped onto the dais. "Dante?" she shouted.

Despite the music, Dante heard her just fine, but was content to let her shout. He nodded. She reached into her purse, withdrew a slim wallet, and flipped it open.

"Special Agent Wallace," she shouted. "FBI."

Leaning closer, Dante touched the badge, looked from the photo ID to the agent's solemn face, back to the photo, back to her. She smelled clean and sharp, like sage, like the city after a hard rain.

"Good picture." Releasing the badge, he shifted his gaze back to her face. "I've already talked to the cops, though."

Agent Wallace dropped the badge back into her purse. "I realize that. This is a separate inquiry," she shouted. "I find it—"

Under Pressure ended their set with a long feedback squeal and a final tribal-style pounding on the drums, then the club plunged into darkness so the band could slip unnoticed from the Cage. The noise from the packed club—squeals, shouts, the buzz of a hundred conversations—swelled in the darkness. The low-wattage house lights switched back on to reveal an empty Cage.

Agent Wallace resumed speaking in a more normal tone of voice. "I find it *curious* that Mister De Noir led me to believe you weren't here." Her gaze held his.

Dante shrugged. "I'm hard to keep track of. I come and go a lot."

"Is there some place more private where we can talk?"

"Probably," Dante said. "But I don't want to, so, no."

One eyebrow arched up. "Is there a problem?" she asked, voice low, taut.

"You mean aside from you being here?" Dante said. "No."

<*Caution, child. This is a game you should* not *play.*>

Dante ignored Lucien, ignored the heat of his gaze, focused on the flash of anger in Agent Wallace's blue eyes. His pulse raced.

"This is a *murder* investigation," Agent Wallace said, stepping in close, *too* close. "I don't understand why you're refusing to cooperate."

"Yeah, that whole cooperation with the law thing? Just ain't me," Dante said, standing his ground, refusing to step back after she'd thought he would by invading his personal space.

He listened to the rapid beat of the fed's heart, heard the rush of blood through her veins, smelled it, rich and sweet.

"I won't take much of your time. I just need to verify a few things."

Dante ran his fingers through his hair. "Everything I had to say is in the police report." He sprawled onto the throne, stretched his legs out before him. "Read it."

"I'll do that," Wallace said, meeting Dante's gaze. "But I'd like your permission to look around the premises, the courtyard in particular."

"Not without a warrant," Dante said, voice low.

<*Child . . .*>

She looked at him for a long moment, head tilted, her gaze considering. "Look, we don't have to do this the hard way."

"It's the only way I know," Dante said.

"Did you know the victim was from Lafayette?" Wallace asked, voice tight.

Drawing his legs in, Dante sat up. *Lafayette.* Pain strobed, spasmed. He touched his fingers to his left temple and rubbed until the pain faded. "Fuck," he whispered.

"Is something wrong?" Wallace said.

"Yes," Lucien rumbled from behind the throne. "He suffers from migraines. I'm afraid you'll have to resume your questions at another time."

<*Trouble,*> Von sent. <*Étienne's on his way in.*>

"No, I–" Wallace's words ended abruptly as excited whispers buzzed and echoed throughout the club.

Dante watched as Étienne's Armani-clad form sliced through the crowd. His chicory-and-cream-colored skin seemed lit from within; he bristled with hate. A step behind, Von strode along the now silent path Étienne had cut.

Étienne stopped at the bottom of the steps. A fringe of cobalt-beaded braids framed his cold, chiseled face. Von stood to the visiting vampire's right, taking up his duties as *llygad* on the floor instead of on the dais at Dante's side.

Dante sat forward, hands on the throne's armrests, muscles coiled.

"You've been ordered to present yourself before Guy Mauvais," Étienne said.

"You're fucking kidding," Dante said, half laughing.

Étienne tensed. "The Council is conducting an inquiry."

"The Council has no authority over Dante," Lucien said.

"*Je regrette*, Nightbringer," Étienne said, inclining his head respectfully. "But this doesn't concern the Fallen."

"Willing to stake your life on that?" Lucien's deep voice rang through the club.

FBI investigations. Council inquiries. Goody. "Nothing like being popular," Dante murmured. To Étienne, he said, "If this is about the fire *again*, tell 'em not to waste their time. *Sa vaut pas la peine.* I don't know–"

Étienne flew up the steps, only stopping on the third when Von, in a nightkind blur of speed, leapt behind him and seized his arm.

"Arrogant lying prick!" Étienne hissed, his narrowed gaze

dark and seething. "You need to be leashed! Brought to your knees!"

Cool air fluttered Dante's hair as Lucien rushed from behind the throne. Dante flung out an arm, blocking his passage. "You calling me out, Étienne?" he asked quietly.

Étienne yanked free of Von's grasp and smoothed the front of his suit. He touched fingers to the carved ivory rose cuff link at each Armani-sleeved wrist. "No," he said, his hands knotting into fists. "Not yet."

"Too bad." Dante lowered his arm.

"But one night," Étienne added, a smile stretching his lips, "I'll be waiting."

Dante stood. "Bring it on," he said.

"I delivered the order," Étienne said. "I hope you ignore it, *marmot*." Whirling, he stalked into the silent, staring crowd, Von on his heels. The mortals melted away from him as though he were on fire.

Dante sank down onto the throne. Pain throbbed at his temples and behind his eyes. His stomach knotted. He gripped the armrest with white-knuckled fingers.

"What was that all about?"

Dante looked up to see Agent Wallace down on one knee beside him. She scanned his face. He had the feeling she missed very little. "Nothing much," he sighed. "Ass-kissing denied. Harsh punishment threatened. The usual."

"Funny," Wallace murmured, her tone sounding as though he was anything *but*. "De Noir told the truth about the headaches, didn't he?"

"Indeed, Agent Wallace," Lucien said dryly. "I *am* right here."

Wallace's gaze flicked from Dante to Lucien, then back. "I'm sorry," she said, her voice low, no longer official. "My sister suffers from migraines, too."

Dante glanced at her. The FBI mask had slipped from her

face. She met his gaze, her expression open and her blue eyes steady. For a moment, he thought he saw into the heart of her, warm and compassionate and tough, edged in flame and steel.

"Yeah?" he said.

Wallace nodded. "Dante, listen, I can save us both a lot of time and trouble. Just give me your permission—"

"No," Dante said. Her mask was back in place. Maybe that was all there was to her; maybe what he'd thought he'd seen within her was an illusion. White light edged his vision. Hurt his eyes.

Wallace's smile faded. She stared at him in frustration. Standing, she said, "This is pointless. I can get a search warrant in an hour."

Unhooking his shades from his belt, Dante slipped them on. "Get it. I'll be waiting."

"I'll do that," Wallace said. She strode down the steps and into the crowd.

Wallace's clean, fresh rain scent lingered, as did the heated aroma of her blood. But her spiky rays of authority receded with every step she took, and Dante found himself breathing a little easier. She was strong, persistent, and gorgeous. Too bad she was a fucking cop.

A hand, cool and soothing, brushed against the hair at Dante's temple, icing the pain for a moment. He closed his eyes.

<Don't make me sleep.>

<You need rest. You need blood.> Lucien's thought curled past the pain. *<I'll take you home before the pain gets worse.>*

"No." Dante pushed Lucien's hand from his temple. "I'm gonna get in the Cage."

Lucien stepped around in front of him. Dante looked up into golden eyes. "Not tonight," Lucien said. "You're in no shape—"

"I'm in *exactly* the right shape," Dante cut in.

"Hey, sugar."

Lucien turned, and Dante saw Gina and Jay standing on the

step behind him, holding hands, satiated smiles on their lips. Gina's bodice was still unlaced. The cleavage created by her corset, fragrant with black cherry perfume, reawakened his hunger and twisted around the pain, braiding the two together.

Releasing Jay's hand, Gina stepped past Lucien and settled herself in Dante's lap. She cupped his face, bent her head, and kissed him. He tasted Jay on her lips and tongue; tasted her, too—pungent and rich. He bit her lip, sucked at the blood oozing from the wound. She gasped, then moaned.

Burning. Restless. Dangerous.

<Child . . . >

Trembling, Dante ended the kiss. He licked her lower lip until the bleeding stopped and the wound healed. Gina looked at him with half-lidded eyes. Sleepy. Happy. He caressed her jawline with shaking fingers. Sweat trickled along his temple.

Gina touched a finger to his lips. "We gotta go, sexy," she whispered, sliding from his lap. "Tomorrow night?"

The pain was an ice pick through his brain and his control was slipping. He released her without a word. Jay leaned over and kissed him.

"Tomorrow," Jay murmured. Grasping Gina's hand, he led her down the steps. Gina waved, an impish smile on her lips.

Tomorrow night.

Dante watched them walk away.

4

STILL FALLING

Bourbon splashed into Thomas Ronin's shot glass, dark amber under the low lights. The bartender swiped the debit spike Ronin had left on the counter, then sauntered on to the next customer bellied up to the long, polished bar. Ronin picked up his glass and turned around.

"Looks like you fucked up," E drawled. Shaking a cigarette from the partially crumpled pack of Marlboro, he stuck it between his lips and lit it with a silver Zippo.

Ronin plucked E's cigarette from between his fingers, and dropped it onto the floor. Twisted out the embers with the toe of his snakeskin boot. "Amuse me," he said. "Tell me how."

E glanced at Ronin, his eyes hidden behind shades, a stretched-out grin on his face. He shook another cigarette from the pack, jammed it between his lips, then lit it. He exhaled gray smoke into Ronin's face. "Think you know everything, dontcha, Tommy-boy?"

Ronin nodded, sipped his bourbon. "Most things."

"Yeah?" E's grin widened. "Didcha know the chick talking to Dante is Special Agent Heather Wallace?"

Ronin's hand hesitated in the act of fanning away the cigarette smoke. Lifting his shades, he stared at the trenchcoated woman on the dais. Yes, it *was* her—the profiler working the Cross-Country Killer case.

"Even changing MO and signature and shit didn't fool her," E said, his gin-scented words smug. "I knew it wouldn't. Heather's in the house."

The admiring tone in E's voice drew Ronin's gaze. E stared at Wallace, his face lit with love. Or what passed for love in a twisted and stunted thing like E.

Ronin finished his bourbon. It burned through his veins, awakening another kind of hunger. He watched Dante and the woman. The boy was exquisite. His assessment went beyond Dante's stunning exterior. Ronin had read the files. He knew what the boy was and what he *could* be.

De Noir stood behind the cheesy throne like one of the statues guarding the mausoleums in St. Louis No. 3. And what was De Noir? Not vampire, no. Something else entirely. Something Ronin suspected to be far older and far darker.

Her lovely face composed despite the anger tightening her movements, Wallace whirled and trotted down the steps to the dance floor. She disappeared into the crowd.

Ronin turned to face the bar again. Nudged the bartender with a gentle flick from his mind. The bartender refilled Ronin's glass. Ronin's pulse quickened. *In all my centuries. I've never seen or felt anyone like Dante. Not once.* He tossed back the bourbon. It burned, untasted, down his throat to his gut.

E remembers his past. Dante doesn't. Why is that? Was Johanna harder on Dante because of his bloodline? Did she push him over edges a mortal could never endure?

Ronin watched as Dante dropped back onto his throne, fingers at his temple, caressing his pale skin.

Or maybe he hasn't endured, after all. Maybe he fell further than anyone else. And is falling still.

Ronin turned to face his companion. "Anyone catch your fancy yet?"

"Maybe the purple-haired kid or the blonde vamp with him." E continued to look straight ahead, scanning the crowd. Red telltales shone from the edges of his shades. Infra, thermal, name it, E most likely had it installed.

Ronin shook his head. "Too much for you to handle."

"I've got an idea," E said, voice cheerful. He turned to look at Ronin. "What about Dante? He's fucking gorgeous *and* fucking dangerous. I bet he'd be a *shitload* of fun." The grin vanished from E's face. "Whaddaya say? Can I play with Dante?"

Metal whispered against denim as E slipped free one of his shivs, smuggled in past the *llygad* who'd let them into the club. Ronin's hand snapped out and seized E's wrist, locking it at hip level. He squeezed. Sweat beaded E's forehead. Ronin twisted. E grimaced, baring his teeth. The smell of his pain, hot and bitter like bile, rushed into Ronin's nostrils. The shiv *tink-tunk*ed onto the mist-shrouded floor.

"You do and I'll feed you your own guts," Ronin snapped. "Touch him before it's time and see if I don't."

E stared at him, his eyes hidden behind his shades, but his hatred shimmered in the dim light like radiation from a leaking nuke. Ronin twisted E's wrist a little more, then released him.

"Have you forgotten what he is?"

"No, asshole, I haven't. Fucking bloodsuckers." E rubbed his wrist.

He bent and scooped his shiv from the floor. Then, like a magician at a cheap Las Vegas dinner show, he made it disappear. Jaw clenched, he turned and stabbed a finger at the bartender, then down at his glass in case the bartender was an idiot.

"Are we clear?" Ronin said.

E spun around. "Like a two-way mirror," he muttered.

A pretty dark-haired girl plopped down onto Dante's lap,

while a blond youth in lace, velvet, and black eyeliner stood on the steps, watching as they kissed.

"Keep our goal in mind," Ronin murmured. "Remember who truly deserves your . . . *artistic* . . . touch."

Hand in hand, the dark-haired girl and the blond youth walked down the steps and into the crowd.

"Tag. They're it." Tossing back the last of his gin and tonic, E slammed the glass onto the bar. A smile crawled onto his lips. He glanced at Ronin. "See ya later, Tom-Tom." He shoved away from the bar and into the crowd.

"Have fun," Ronin said, voice dry. When he couldn't see E any longer, he shifted his attention back to the dais.

E didn't seem to get that Dante was more than just a "bloodsucker." He'd been *born* vampire—a rare True Blood. A fact even Dante seemed unaware of; an ignorance Ronin hoped to use to his advantage.

Ronin watched as De Noir brushed his fingers against Dante's temples. The boy closed his eyes, but only for a moment. Twisting free of De Noir's caress, he stood. Strode down the steps and disappeared into the sweating, adoring, grasping crowd. The house lights dimmed twice, then went out.

Ronin worked his earplugs back into his ears. The crowd buzzed and chattered. He shivered as the crowd's sense of anticipation splashed over him like a wave of warm seawater. He stared through the darkness and into the Cage. Stark-white bone, red feather, and leather fetishes hung from its steel bars.

"Dante! Beautiful angel!" a pining female voice cried out.

"Mon beau diable," a male shouted.

A low growl rumbled through the crowd as voices took up the chant of: "Inferno! Inferno! Inferno!"

The fetishes swung and twisted as heat-radiating bodies climbed into the Cage. An aura of bluish-silver light surrounded one slender figure.

True Blood. Ronin drew in a deep breath of the club's reeking, heady air. *When our paths join, only one of us shall walk away into the night.*

The lights switched back on. The crowd roared.

"Can't believe I wanted it," Dante whispered into the microphone, dark eyes hidden behind shades. His hands cupped the mike like a lover's face. "Needed it. Tied to the bed. Unable to reach myself."

The overhead lights sparked silver fire from the rings on Dante's fingers and thumbs and glinted from the rows of hoops piercing each ear. Dante rocked the microphone back and forth, leaning it over, straddling it, then stepping back and jerking it up again. Ronin noticed Dante's fingers trembling as he yanked the mike free of the stand, caught the gleam of sweat at his temples.

He's hurting, Ronin thought, sipping at his bourbon. *And he's using it.*

Behind Dante, the rest of Inferno flailed and slammed at their instruments—braids, dreads, and 'hawks swinging through the air, their frenzied movement a blur of tattoos, piercings, leather, steel, and races—almond eyes; toffee-colored skin; strong noses; and hard, wiry muscles.

Kicking the mike stand to the floor of the Cage, Dante turned his back to the screaming crowd. "Your promises squirm like worms in my soul . . . sweet parasite . . ." Spinning around, he dropped to one knee and crossed his arms over his face. The mike dangled seemingly forgotten from one white-knuckled fist. "I want more . . . more . . ."

Several people had climbed the Cage to its steel-meshed top and had lain facedown, spread-eagled, offerings to their dark, beautiful god. They screamed his name, slicing at their wrists and forearms, even nicking their throats with quick flicks of razors and box knives. Blood dripped down, spattering the Cage's floor and Dante's pale face.

Hands reached through the bars, grasping, fingers flexed,

poised to grab clothing, flesh, hair, anything within reach. The other three members of Inferno sidestepped and kicked, and kept pounding their instruments without missing a beat.

Dante, however, was precariously close to the bars and the greedy hands.

Had he positioned himself deliberately? Ronin wondered. Punishment? Or distraction?

"I want more . . ." Dante half sang, half growled, his voice low and strained, simmering with rage. He stood. And Ronin witnessed pain blossoming full flower as Dante suddenly stumbled. Eyes squeezed shut, head thrown back, neck muscles corded, he screamed, *"More of your fucking lies!"*

Hands seized him, yanked him against the Cage's steel bars. Dante hit hard, shoulder first, his back to the surging crowd. The microphone tumbled from his fingers, thudding onto the floor with a piercing feedback squeal. The crowd screamed, wild, hungry. Fingers latched around Dante, grabbing his arms, his hands, his thighs; clutched at his clothing, yanked at his hair. Imprisoned him within manacles of flesh.

Knocked loose, Dante's shades bounced onto the floor and under the boots of the keyboard player. Dark bits of plastic and glass scattered across the Cage. The other members of Inferno kept playing, frenzied and thrashing, the music hard and angry.

Ronin leaned forward, muscles coiled, shades lowered below the bridge of his nose. Why was Dante allowing them to hold him? Was he *that* lost to the pain? A blur of movement captured Ronin's attention. De Noir rushed from the dais to the Cage with a speed that Ronin doubted any mortal eye could perceive.

Drinking in Dante's rage and anguish, the crowd pulsed like a huge tribal heart, its fierce and primal rhythm beating against Ronin, drumming up his own hunger.

His need sliced into him like one of E's shivs. He stepped into the crowd. Hot, sweaty bodies moshed against him, blood thundering through their veins, hearts jackhammering. Not here. He'd feed in some dank back alley, feasting on the forgotten and unwanted. As a stranger in a claimed city, Ronin had no desire to draw attention to himself. Sliding through the crowd, he stepped outside into the cool, rain-misted night.

The *llygad* nodded at him, his shaded eyes no doubt observing every detail, his body language wary. Ronin nodded in return. Another marvel. Why had an *llygad* abandoned his impartiality and aligned himself to one House? *And* worked as a fucking bouncer?

"Dante," Ronin whispered. True Blood.

Strolling along the wet cobblestone streets, Ronin headed for Canal Street. With every wasted soul he fed on this night, he'd be sure to thank Dante for rousing an intensity of hunger that had slumbered for years.

5

THE HARD WAY

HEATHER SIPPED AT HER café au lait, the Styrofoam cup finally cool enough to hold. Dawn edged the gray horizon with orange and peach and gilded the undersides of the clouds. She yawned and rubbed at her face. The search warrant fluttered on the rented Subaru Legacy's dashboard vents. She switched off the heat. The car's engine clicked and tinked as it cooled.

She was parked across the street from Dante's plantation house, some miles from New Orleans. Old river rock and black iron walls surrounded the house. On paper the house belonged to Lucien De Noir, but Heather suspected that, as with the club, the house was actually Dante's. Thick greenery and fragrant flowers twisted along the walls. Huge oak trees shaded the property. The black iron gate hung open. In the circular drive a black van, a chopped Harley, and a little black MG were parked.

Heather glanced at her watch. Six thirty. About an hour ago, she'd seen the van pull into the drive, followed by Von on the Harley. The blonde and the pretty punk boy had climbed out of the van. De Noir had carried Dante in his arms like a child.

Drunk? Migraine sick? They'd all gone inside the house. The door had closed. Nothing had stirred since.

A twinge of guilt pricked Heather. Migraines. She remembered Annie's pain-dilated eyes, her desperation. Shaking her head, she looked down at the coffee cup in her hand, then glanced out the window. Dante was *not* Annie and it couldn't be helped. He'd given her no other choice.

There was something strange about the relationship between De Noir and Dante. Could they be lovers? She replayed the events at Club Hell through her mind, looking for clues. Remembered De Noir lying about Dante's presence, remembered De Noir flying from behind that ridiculous throne when Armani Suit had charged up the steps. Remembered De Noir saying, *He suffers from migraines*, heard the sheltering tone in his deep voice.

No, Heather finally decided. Not lovers. De Noir had been protective and caring, but she hadn't felt any underlying sexual tension or erotic chemistry between the two. Instead, they'd seemed comfortable with each other. Old friends, then.

Heather sighed, then took a long sip of her rapidly cooling coffee. No, there was something else between De Noir and Dante. Unrequited love? Something like that, hidden and secret, but only on De Noir's part. He'd watched Dante every moment they were together. At least, he had last night.

Finishing her coffee, Heather tossed the cup onto the passenger-side floor. It had cost her a lot of time and considerable charm to convince a judge to agree to a search warrant. In truth, she believed Detective Collins had had more to do with it than any amount of personal charm. Despite all that, the warrant was for the courtyard only.

Heather looked at the silent plantation house. Dark curtains blinded every window. Must be sound asleep by now. Time to serve the warrant. Dante wanted to be difficult, fine. Gravel crunched beneath her Skechers as she got out of the car and crossed the road to the yawning gate.

Heather followed the broken, tree-root-uplifted path alongside the house to the front porch. The steps creaked under her weight as she climbed onto the wide porch. Grabbing the black iron gargoyle knocker bolted to the door's center, she thunked it repeatedly against the solid oak. The sound echoed throughout the silent house.

Wrapping her fingers around the cold iron knocker again, Heather pounded it against the door three more times. The sound rippled through the plantation house, then faded into silence.

Heather was reaching for the knocker again when the door's inside locks clicked and the door cracked open. De Noir looked down at Heather, his face cold. Still dressed in his clothes from last night. Not asleep yet, then, she mused. The rough-edged X pendant around his throat caught rosy light from the rising sun.

"What can I do for you?" De Noir said, his deep voice level and controlled.

Heather held up the search warrant. "Get Dante up."

De Noir frowned. "Can't your warrant be served at a more convenient time? In the evening, perhaps?"

"No."

Golden light sparked to life in De Noir's narrowed eyes. He slammed the door shut. Twisted the locks.

Smiling, Heather relaxed against the door frame. She glanced at her watch. She'd give him fifteen minutes to rouse Dante, then put the gargoyle knocker back to use. She'd wake up everyone in the goddamned house, if necessary.

Look, we don't have to do this the hard way.

It's the only way I know.

His choice. Heather tucked the search warrant into her purse. His words.

Fifteen minutes passed and Heather thumped the gargoyle against the door. In another fifteen minutes, she'd give another twenty whacks, she thought as she leaned back against the door frame once more. The sky brightened, turned the dew-laden grass into a sea of jeweled fire.

Just as Heather was about to grab the gargoyle again, the locks clicked and the door opened. Dante slipped out of the house and onto the porch, still fastening his belt. Definitely dragged out of bed.

Heather stared, suddenly breathless, her gaze lingering on his pale face—dark eyes, last night's eyeliner smudged underneath, high cheekbones, full lower lip. . . . She was disgusted with herself for being sucker punched by good looks.

"Lucien doesn't think very much of you," Dante said, walking past her and down the front steps. He pulled up the gray hood of a sweatshirt worn under his leather jacket, shadowing his face.

Heather followed him onto the buckled flagstones. "Sorry to hear that. Good morning, by the way," she said. "Got that search warrant."

Dante raised a gloved hand; his index finger circled whoop-de-do. He kept walking.

"My car's across the street," Heather said.

Dante strode through the wrought-iron gate.

Heather shook her head, bemused. Even at this hour, Dante looked as though he'd dressed for a Goth convention: stylish shades, leather gloves, leather pants, and black long-sleeved mesh shirt under a black T, both shirts only half-tucked, and black, silver-buckled biker boots. The back of his leather jacket read MAD EDGAR, the safety-pinned letters looking like they'd been cut out of magazines: a walking ransom note.

Lengthening her stride, she passed Dante, crossing the street to the Subaru. She unlocked both doors, then waited until Dante had slouched into the passenger seat before seating herself.

"Seat belt," she said, strapping her own shut.

"Got a warrant for that too?"

"No," Heather said, voice low. "Is this how it's going to be with you?"

"Most likely."

Heather stared at him for a long moment. Opened her mouth. Shut it again. *Pick your battles. This one isn't worth it.*

"Good to know," she said finally.

Keying on the ignition, Heather slammed the gearshift into drive and peeled out onto the street, the Subaru's tires spitting gravel. Dante pulled the sun visor down.

Heather drove in silence until her anger and irritation were under control. *He's tired. I'm tired. Cranky is the word for the day.* She loosened her grip on the steering wheel. She eased the Subaru onto the interstate and aimed it for New Orleans.

She wrinkled her nose, puzzled by the buttery, suntan oil kind of odor filling the car. "Is that *sunscreen* I smell?"

"Mmm."

Heather glanced at her passenger. "You playing up those vampire rumors?"

"Not playing," Dante murmured.

"Right."

Heather stared straight ahead, attention focused on the road. She had a feeling Dante wasn't kidding. His sleepy voice had sounded sincere.

She'd dealt with this type at the psychiatric hospital outside Boise where she'd done volunteer work in an effort to better understand the difference between *mentally ill* and *sociopath*. And in hopes of better understanding Annie. Goth, wannabe undead. Yearning to be special. He probably had dental implants and kept bagged blood in his refrigerator, all part of the delusion.

Heather glanced at Dante. He slept, his head back against the seat and turned to one side, the hoodie hiding his face, gloved hands relaxed and open on his thighs.

"Hey, Dante, wake up!" He didn't stir. Seemed dead to the

world. Keeping her gaze on the road, she smacked him lightly on the shoulder. "C'mon, wake up."

"*Tais toi,*" Dante murmured, turning his face away and folding his arms against his chest, snuggled up tight for sleep.

And he speaks French. Or was it Cajun? He *was* from Lafayette, Cajun territory, had a bit of an accent.

Rain began to spatter the windshield, nothing serious, just a dawn sprinkle. Heather switched on the wipers. What *was* it with this city? Vampires. Voodoo. Cities of the dead. She glanced at Dante. He was still curled up, his breathing low, hard to perceive.

"Do you actually believe you're a vampire?"

To her surprise, Dante stirred, sat up. He tugged the hood's edges farther over his face. "Nightkind," he said, yawning. "Belief's got nothing to do with it. Are you mortal just because you believe you are?"

"*Mortal?* Of course not," Heather said, looking at him, trying to see his hidden face. "I was *born* human. Just like everyone else."

Slouched down in the seat again, arms folded across his chest, Dante turned his hooded head to look out the passenger window. "Mmm. Glad you cleared *that* up."

Heather lapsed into silence. She was failing with him. Maybe he really believed the vampire stuff or maybe he wanted her to see through it. And maybe, just maybe, it was all a rocker prank, a mindfuck for the fun of it and nothing to get worked up over.

She was tired, and it was affecting her judgment. A quick look at Dante revealed that he slept again—or pretended to, at least.

Once in the city, Heather steered the car to Canal Street, then from Canal down Royal, finally turning onto St. Peter. Bits and pieces from last night were strewn across the rain-dampened cobblestones: bright paper, beads, empty plastic cups, a black bra. After the madness and frenzy of the night before, the Quarter looked desolate and abandoned.

Heather parked in front of the club. She leaned over and was about to shake Dante's shoulder when he suddenly sat up, his shaded gaze on one of the upper floors. Scrunching down, Heather looked through the passenger window to see what had drawn his attention. On the third floor, an open pair of French windows.

Heather remembered curtains dancing in the night breeze, the orange flicker of candlelight. "Something wrong?"

"Hope not." Dante yanked at the door handle.

Heather blinked. Dante stood on the sidewalk, gaze on the windows. She hadn't seen him actually open the door or even get out. All she'd seen was his gloved fingers pulling the door latch and then she'd heard the thunk as the door closed after him.

What the hell? Heather rubbed at her eyes. Had she dozed off for a second? Was she *that* tired? She joined Dante on the sidewalk and followed his gaze up. The curtains hung limp.

"Who was up there last night?"

"I was," Dante replied—but his voice was further away.

Looking down, Heather realized that Dante was already at the club entrance, working keys in the locks.

Wake up, Wallace, Jesus Christ. She hurried to join him as he pulled open the heavy door and stepped inside.

The stale smell of smoke, old beer, and sex lingered in the dark hallway. Dante stood next to the security panel of the club's alarm system. Red light from the BURN sign down the hall flickered across the back of his hood. Frowning, he pushed the hood back and slid his shades to the top of his head. Green telltales glowed on the security panel. He no longer looked sleepy.

"What's wrong?" Heather asked, stepping up beside him.

"The alarm's not on," he said. He glanced back over his

shoulder at the buzzing neon sign. Red light jittered across his pale face. "I don't think Lucien woulda forgot."

Heather straightened, adrenaline pumping into her bloodstream. Her heart beat faster. Reaching into the trench's inside pocket, she pulled free her .38.

"Stay here," she said.

"Fuck that," Dante said. Then he was gone.

"Dante, no!" she hissed into the red-lit darkness, but he was long gone. How had he moved so fast? Reflex boost? Enhancement?

Sliding the .38's safety off, Heather ran the length of the hall, her back close to the wall, and into the club. Across an eerie red-lit wasteland of tables, chairs, Cage, and throne, she saw Dante on the staircase, rounding the corner onto the third-floor landing.

Easing her way between tables, her gaze flicking from shadow to shadow, she hurried to the stairs. The icy sense of wrongness that had seized her at the security panel hadn't diminished. Something was *very* wrong. And Dante was about to walk right into it. Walk, hell. Teleport was more like it. But he *was* a civilian in her custody; her responsibility.

Heather started up the stairs, her back to the wall, her .38 held in a two-handed grip. Her own dim shadow scouted ahead of her, and she winced every time a stair creaked beneath her foot. Stepping onto the second-floor landing, she brought her gun up as she dropped down into a crouch, checking right, then left, before straightening again. She listened. The old building creaked around her. Soft footsteps pattered above her on the third floor, then stopped.

She climbed the next flight of stairs, her gaze shifting from the dark third-floor landing to the red-lit club beyond and beneath the wrought-iron railings. Nothing moved in the shadows below.

On the landing, she dropped into a crouch and cleared right, then turned to the left. Dante stood in a doorway, one gloved hand braced against the threshold. Heather straightened. Gargoyle candle sconces guarded the framed art lining the walls. An old-fashioned Oriental hall carpet cushioned her footsteps. Dante didn't move, did nothing to indicate that he heard her or knew she was there.

A thick, coppery smell filled Heather's nostrils, a smell she knew all too well. Her gut knotted. The steady plop-plop of dripping became more distinct as she drew nearer. She stepped beside Dante, gun still held in both hands, and looked into the room.

It was worse than she could've imagined.

Much worse.

6

MAGIC AND MYSTERY

JOHANNA MOORE STOOD AT her office window, watching the snow fall. Snow always made her think of Christmas and of her youth; she remembered the magic and mystery of the tiny glittered windows of the Advent calendar and the surprises they revealed when opened. February in D.C. lacked magic or mystery and held only ice-slicked sidewalks and stark tree limbs.

"E is in New Orleans," she said finally.

"A coincidence," Gifford replied.

"I don't think so," Johanna said. "And I don't like it one bit." She turned away from the window and the snow and her memories.

Gifford sat in the plush leather chair in front of Johanna's cherrywood desk, a frown on his face as he thumbed through the thick file in his lap. He reached a hand into his suit jacket's inside pocket and withdrew a slim brown cigarillo.

He shook his head, his gaze still on the file. "He can't *possibly* know about S. Or Bad Seed." Flicking open his lighter, he touched flame to the cigarillo.

Johanna heard the crackle of the tobacco as it withered and burned. A sweet cherry-vanilla scent curled into the air.

"I wonder," she said, crossing to her desk. Several more files and CDs were scattered across its polished surface, all marked: TOP SECRET and RESEARCH—SPECIAL OPS ONLY.

"The last victim had met S." Johanna sat on the edge of her desk and fixed her gaze on Gifford. "And was slaughtered in the courtyard next to the club."

He looked up, gray eyes thoughtful. "Again, coincidence."

"And, again, I don't think so. E burned S's logo into the victim's chest." Reaching over, Johanna plucked the cigarillo from between Gifford's fingers. Brought it up to her lips. Inhaled.

Amusement lit Gifford's eyes. "Maybe E is a music lover," he said. "Hell, maybe he's a fan of Inferno. Even serial killers have their favorite bands."

Johanna blew out a stream of scented smoke, savoring its tobacco-and-vanilla taste. She shook her head. "No. He's communicating."

She extended the cigarillo to Gifford. He took it back from her, his fingers lingering for a moment against hers, warm and smooth.

"It scares the crap out of me to think he might actually have an agenda."

"Communicating?" Gifford asked. He glanced down at the file in his lap again. His brows knitted together as he flipped through several pages. "With who?"

"I don't know," Johanna said quietly. "S, maybe."

"If that's the case, we don't have to worry," Gifford said. Paper rustled. "S doesn't know *shit*, right?"

"Not after the way his memory was torn apart. No." Standing, Johanna brushed past Gifford's knees and returned to the window.

The snow continued to fall. The sky lightened from dark gray to light gray as the dawn deepened into a winter morning. A thick white silence, like the one insulating her heart, encased the world beyond her window.

The sound of flipping paper suddenly stopped. "*Blocked* and *fragmented*," Gifford said. "According to the history."

Johanna heard Gifford's finger sliding from line to line in the report. "I was there, Dan, from start to finish," she said. "Torn apart is *far* more accurate."

An image slipped past her guard, her silent white barricade:

A slender twelve-year-old boy in a blood-spattered straitjacket suspended upside down from the ceiling, chains wrapped around his ankles. Long black hair streams past his face except for a few sweat-and-blood-dampened tendrils clinging to his forehead, his pale cheeks. He hangs motionless, the fight, rage, and grief drained from him like blood from a corpse.

His punishment ended, no one wants to bring him down—the blood-sprayed walls and the bodies crumpled on the cement floor keep them on the safe side of the steel door.

Johanna enters alone and alone stabs a hypo full of tranks into the boy's neck. Alone, she eases the boy's chains from the butcher's hook and lowers him to the floor. Doped and dreaming, this beautiful vampire child, lost to the madness of puberty.

Gathering him into her arms, she carries him to another cell. She trembles, magic and mystery pulsing once again through her veins, glittering like Christmas in her mind. The boy's psyche is, for her, an Advent calendar; with each compartment she opens or twists or triggers, a wonderful surprise is revealed.

Johanna ran her fingers through her short-cropped hair, glancing at her faint reflection in the window. Attractive, early thirties, blonde and blue-eyed Nordic, tall and fit. The very opposite of her *père de sang* in physical appearance. But she and Ronin shared a deep hunger for knowledge. In that they were very much alike.

Weariness surged through her. She needed blood, then Sleep.

She was pushing the pills' limits too far. She could only postpone Sleep so long.

"What was done to S's memory isn't the problem," she said, turning to face Gifford. "E's cross-country killing spree and the Bureau's involvement in the case is the problem. I don't know how, but E's led them, more or less, straight to S."

"Do you want E stopped?"

Johanna shook her head. "I'd like to keep studying his progress. But it's making me nervous that the Bureau's so close."

"I see," Gifford said. He leaned forward in the chair. His composed gaze met and held Johanna's. "What do you want done?"

LUCIEN SAT IN THE darkened living room, back straight, eyes closed as he guarded those who Slept in the rooms upstairs. Slept deeply. Except for one. Dante's Sleep-addled thoughts brushed against Lucien's mind. He felt Dante's struggle to remain conscious, alert. Damned woman and her damned search warrant. Lucien's fingers flexed and gripped the easy chair's armrests. He drew in a deep breath and carefully lifted his fingers. *Calm.*

He knew how difficult and contrary Dante could be—the child had often tested his own considerable patience—and Wallace had simply reacted to Dante's refusal to cooperate.

But . . . why did Wallace even wish to search the courtyard? What did she hope to find? And what did *any* of it have to do with Dante?

Lucien opened his eyes and stared into the curtained gloom. Shadows draped the sofa, bookcases, and standing lamps, hiding all color. Outside, birds twittered and sang, busy with morning tasks.

For a moment, Lucien longed to take to the air, to feel the dawn warm against his face, to warble his *wybrcathl* into the golden sunrise, to await the answering aria of another of the Elohim.

But his *wybrcathl* needed to remain unvoiced. The child he guarded needed to remain hidden from the Elohim, undiscovered. Lucien touched the pendant hanging at his throat. Ran his fingers along the edges of the X, the metal smooth and warm.

The rune for partnership—given to him four years before by Dante, a warm and unexpected token of their friendship. Lucien's fingers tightened around the pendant. The rough edges bit into his flesh. He bowed his head and closed his eyes. Remembered the wild, rough *anhrefncathl* he'd answered five years before . . . remembered landing on a wharf beside the Mississippi River.

A youth in worn leather pants, scuffed-up boots, and a T-shirt sits cross-legged on the wharf's warped and weathered wood, something wriggling between his hands caught in a bluish glow.

Lucien lands lightly on the wharf, his wings expanding in a last flutter of air before folding behind him. Water laps and splashes against the wharf pilings. The strong odor of fish, muddy water, and rank mud layers the air.

The youth doesn't look up. Black hair hides his face, his head bowed as he concentrates on the thing squirming in his hands.

Lucien steps forward, the wood still sun-warm against his bare feet. Pain and power radiate from the youth, sharp and spiky and fevered. Blood drips from his nose and splashes onto the back of his hand.

The blue light glowing from the youth's hands, the chaos song swirling up from him, anguished and yearning and heartbroken—draw Lucien closer. His muscles tighten; fire burns through his veins. The last time he saw that blue glow or heard an anhrefncathl *was thousands of years ago from a* creawdwr *now long dead.*

Has another finally *been born? Hidden in the mortal world?*

Lucien's wings tuck into their pouches on his back as he crouches in front of the youth. Pain pierces him. Drawing his shields tight, Lucien flexes away the youth's unwanted agony.

"Child."

The night-haired youth doesn't respond. His hands open, trembling, and the blue glow fades, then vanishes, like a snuffed flame. The thing he held scampers away, bright black eyes gleaming in the moonlight.

A wharf rat, Lucien realizes in surprise. Or, at least what used to be a wharf rat. The former rat scurries to the edge of the wharf and off. Its many pairs of translucent and delicate dragonfly-like wings lift it uncertainly into the night. It flies away.

Forever altered by a creawdwr's *touch.*

"Child," Lucien says again, and tips the youth's face up with a taloned finger.

He is too stunned by recognition—the dark, intelligent eyes, the cheekbones, the curve of the lips—to even fend the boy off as he uncoils from the wharf. Lucien falls back as the boy wraps strong, slender arms around him and sinks his fangs into Lucien's throat.

Heat radiates from the boy as he gulps down Lucien's blood, heat and hunger and a deep, deep grief. Lucien holds him for a moment, allowing him to feed, allowing the youth to pin him to the wharf's old wood with a leather-clad thigh. He smells of smoky autumn fires and November frost, sharp and clean and intoxicating. The youth's pain and near madness batters at Lucien's shields like an unrelenting sledgehammer.

He looks just like her.

Not possible.

Her son . . .

Gently, Lucien breaks the boy's steel-muscled grip and rests a hand against his fevered temple. He pours healing energy into the boy, dousing the fire ravaging his mind and easing him into sleep. The youth slumps against Lucien, his bloodied face smearing a red trail along Lucien's shoulder and chest.

Lucien pushes aside the tangled black hair and gazes into the boy's white face. He stares in wonder. Trails a finger along the boy's jawline. Pushes his lip up and looks at the slender fangs. Cold seeps into Lucien.

Where is his mother?

Genevieve . . .

Lucien opened his eyes, fingers still locked around his pendant. So much unknown and unsaid. He should've told Dante the truth when they met. Now he feared it was too late. The moment had long passed. Sighing, Lucien released the pendant with a final caress.

He listened to the still house—the tick-tock of the pendulum clock in the hall, the creak of old wood and old foundations, the sunny buzz of life beyond the shaded windows.

Lucien relaxed into the easy chair, allowing himself to doze/meditate. Several minutes passed. A half hour. The rosy light of dawn faded to gray. The curtains darkened. Rain clicked against the roof tiles, spattered the stone walk.

A prickle of rage, the deep ache of an old hurt reopened, roused Lucien. His head lifted. Apprehension twisted like barbed wire around the length of his spine.

His child no longer struggled with Sleep. He was wide-awake.

7

CLOSER THAN SHE'D EVER BEEN

HER NUDE BODY LAY face-up on the rumpled bed, her hands cuffed to the bedposts, legs spread, a black stocking wrapped and knotted around her throat. Stab wounds punctured her breasts and stomach. Long dark hair partially veiled her face, which was turned toward the door. Blood and foam flecked her lips and her tongue protruded slightly. Mascara and eyeliner and dried tears streaked her face. Her half-lidded gaze seemed to stare straight at Heather.

Carved into each milky-white inner thigh was the anarchy symbol.

Blood dripped onto the carpet. Heather's gaze followed the blood up to the soaked sheets, then up blood-streaked forearms to the vertically slit wrists. Her vision narrowed down to the falling drops of blood. *Just died. Minutes? A half hour—tops?*

On the wall behind the bed, a message had been scrawled in

blood, the uneven, slanting letters smeared across most of the wall.

WAKE UP S

"Gina," Dante whispered.

Heather looked at him sharply. "You *knew* her?"

Dante nodded, disbelief, shock, and something Heather couldn't quite name shadowing his face. He fumbled for the sunglasses on top of his head, slipped them on.

Shifting her .38 to her left hand, Heather retrieved her cell phone from her purse and thumbed in the number for the Eighth District. "Agent Wallace," she said into the phone. "There's been a homicide at 666 St. Peter. Club Hell."

Switching off the phone, Heather slid it back into her purse, her gaze fixed on the rain-damp curtains beside the open French windows.

Maybe the killer had left as they'd entered the club. Or—

Heather shoved Dante against the door frame. "Stay there."

Or maybe he'd never had the chance.

.38 extended in both hands, Heather crossed the room, edging past the bed, to the French windows. Stepping out onto the balcony, she slid low and to the left, gun aimed at the opposite end of the rain-slick balcony. Empty. She leaned against the black iron railing, gun lowered.

She looked down into the street below. A few pre–Mardi Gras revelers staggered along the wet sidewalk. Laughter drifted up like smoke.

Wiping rain from her face, Heather closed her eyes for a moment. Two deaths in one location. *Another* broken pattern. The violence was escalating. Why now? And why here?

The sound of a car engine opened Heather's eyes. Two squad cars raced down the narrow street, followed by a blue-light blinking unmarked. All three screeched to a halt in front of the club. As the uniforms climbed out of the squad cars, Heather waved.

"Upstairs," she called. "Door's open."

Looking up, one of the cops waved back.

Heather pushed aside the curtains and stepped back into the room. Dante hadn't stayed put. He sat on the blood-soaked bed beside the girl's body, his leather jacket spread over the victim's— *Gina, he said her name was Gina—* body.

Heather couldn't see Dante's face; his attention was fixed on the victim's slashed wrists. His hands knotted into fists. The blood stench, the lingering echoes of violence and fear, the girl's stark, glazing stare; none of it frightened Dante. Most people wouldn't be able to stay in the same room with a friend's body, let alone sit beside it on a blood-soaked bed.

But Dante had put aside whatever he was feeling in order to cover her, to give her back some dignity.

"She's still warm," he said.

Squatting beside the bed, Heather touched Dante's arm. "I know this is hard," she said. "I *know*. But you have to remove the jacket. I need to secure the scene—"

Dante turned to look at her, his gaze hidden behind his shades. "He took everything from her," he said, voice low and harsh. "The jacket stays."

"I understand," Heather said. Had anyone done the same for her mother? Or even *wanted* to? "And I wish I *could* leave it with her. But you might be destroying evidence."

From the hall, she heard New Orleans's finest pounding their way up the stairs. Dante stood. Heather reached over and plucked his jacket from the body.

"I'm sorry," she said.

Dante took the jacket from her. "Y'know, I believe you are."

Heather touched his elbow. "Let's talk out in the hall," she said, voice level and, she hoped, soothing. "You can't be in here and I have some questions to ask."

She wished he'd take off the shades. Unable to read his eyes, his expression was lost to her. But his tight jaw and tense, agitated body language spoke volumes. She didn't want to force him out of the room, but would, if necessary.

With a curt nod, Dante stepped out into the hall. He glanced down the hall toward the stairs. Breathing in relief, Heather followed.

"What questions?"

"When did you see Gina last?"

"Last night."

Heather stared at Dante, feeling as though someone had just dumped a bucket of ice over her head. "Last night? You sure?"

Another broken pattern. The CCK—*if* it was the CCK—always kept his victims for several days. Intuition whispered, *It's him, all right.*

"Yeah, I'm sure," Dante said. "We were even in this room."

No coincidence. *Dante* was meant to find her. Heather glanced at the blood-smeared wall behind the bed. WAKE UP S. Last time, it had simply read Wake Up. What did the *S* stand for?

Could an obsession with Dante be the reason for the broken pattern? The messages meant for him? Lafayette. The cigarette-lighter-burned symbol on Daniel Spurrell's chest. The images of a hooded Dante wearing the anarchy symbol around his throat, then around his wrist. If he'd been meant to find the body . . . her pulse raced.

He's communicating. With Dante.

She was close to the killer. Closer than she'd ever been.

"Does 'Wake Up S' mean anything—"

Heather turned as two uniformed officers rounded the corner from the landing. "Special Agent Wallace, FBI," she said. "I'm reaching for my identification." As she slid a hand into her purse, the first cop, flushed with excitement and adrenaline, zeroed in on Dante and dropped a hand to his holster.

"You!" he barked at Dante. "On the floor! Now!"

"Tell your partner to back off," Heather said, displaying her badge to the second officer, a man older, thicker, and more certain than the one yapping like a terrier at Dante. "He's the club owner. He knows the victim."

"Jefferson," the cop sighed. "Enough. Leave off." Shaking his head, he stopped in front of Heather. "Manning," he said. Nodded toward his partner. "Rookie and still green as a gator's hind end."

Heather smiled. "No kidding."

She glanced at Dante. He stood at ease, pretending to ignore the now-silenced rookie. He even yawned. She wasn't fooled, however; she read the tension in his shoulders and noted the wound-up-ready-to-spring tautness of his muscles.

"Oh, Jesus."

Heather looked over at Jefferson. He stood frozen in the doorway, staring at the bound body, the message on the wall, his mouth open as he sucked in the reek of blood and death and shit. Jefferson blanched. Swallowed hard.

"Don't puke in here, asshole."

Two men stepped from the landing and into the hall. The speaker pushed past Jefferson and walked into the room. His low-voiced rebuke, rumpled suit, and easy, confident stride told Heather the newcomer was a detective, as was the man following him. Partners, no doubt. His bored gaze scanned the scene, his lids shuttering like a camera lens, capturing every detail, etching every shadow and blood trail into memory.

His partner nodded at Heather, an unlit cigarette between his lips, a camera in his hands. He stepped into the room, stopping just inside the door. The camera whined as he snapped shots of the scene.

Manning and his rookie partner stood at either side of the door, guarding the scene. Jefferson's complexion was greenish and he kept his gaze on the floor.

"You must be the fed Collins told me about," the first detective said.

"That's right," Heather said. She walked into the room, edging past the cameraman. "Special Agent Heather Wallace. And you are . . . ?"

"LaRousse," he said, turning to face Heather. "Homicide." He tilted his head in the direction of his partner. "That's Davis, over there."

"Hey," Davis said, tucking the cigarette behind his ear. He slipped the camera strap around his neck. Reaching inside his jacket, he withdrew a notepad with a pen clipped to it. He began taking notes, his pen scratching across the pad.

LaRousse's gaze slid the length of Heather's body, his lids shuttering several times. "Collins never mentioned that you were a looker." He winked. "Guess he was keeping that info to himself." Smiling, he shook his head, brown hair falling over his eyes in an aw-shucks kind of way.

"Must be the professional in him," Heather said, voice level. "Could be he's a little more interested in collaring bad guys than hooking up."

LaRousse's smile vanished. He jerked a thumb in Dante's direction. "Is the rock god over there good for it?"

Heather glanced at Dante. He stood in the doorway, jacket hanging from one hand, his shaded gaze on her and LaRousse. *Could* he have killed the girl before De Noir had brought him home in the van? Could that be the reason De Noir had lied about his presence in the club?

She's still warm.

Blood dripping onto carpet.

The stunned look on his pale, pale face.

Too much time had passed between Dante's arrival at the plantation house and their return to the club. The windows had been left open. Cold air would've chilled the body; the blood would've congealed in the hours between. No, Gina'd been killed as Heather drove Dante into New Orleans.

Heather's gaze shifted to LaRousse and his wintry eyes. All

his down-home friendliness had frozen over, his gaze pale-blue ice. "No," she said. "But I *do* want a statement from him."

Digging out a microrecorder from her purse, Heather clipped it to the collar of her trench. "Dante, why don't you wait downstairs? I want—"

"Let's go one better," LaRousse interrupted, jabbing a finger at Dante. "Manning, run Prejean to headquarters. I think we can dig up a couple of old warrants."

"What the hell are you doing?" Heather stared at LaRousse in disbelief.

"Criminal mischief. Vandalism," LaRousse said, gaze fixed on Dante. A hard smile twisted his lips. "Spray paints that damned anarchy symbol everywhere."

Dante dropped his jacket. It hit the carpet with a muffled jingle. "Nothing like having your priorities straight," he said. His gloved hands curled into fists.

"Hold on a minute—" Heather began, but LaRousse nodded at Manning. The uniformed cop unhooked the cuffs from his belt and reached for Dante.

Dante *moved*.

At least, Heather had a glimpse of movement; then Manning flew across the room and slammed into the wall. His head cracked against the plaster, denting it. The handcuffs tumbled from his grasp. Expression pained, dazed, Manning pawed at his holstered pistol.

Dante stood in the doorway, one hand still lifted, body tensed.

"Freeze, motherfucker!" Jefferson screamed, swinging his pistol up.

Dante's shaded gaze locked on Jefferson. He lowered his hand, then knotted both into fists. His head ducked down just slightly. Heather'd seen enough street fights to know he was going to rush the rookie.

Stretching out a hand, Heather cried, "No! Wait!" Not sure if she spoke to Jefferson, Dante, or both.

She hurtled forward, but everything slowed down. Her vision narrowed into a long, dark tunnel ending in Jefferson's gun. His finger spasmed against the trigger. Pulled it back. Catching peripheral movement—Davis and LaRousse helping? hindering?—Heather lunged for the gun.

She knew the moment she did that she'd never make it.

Jefferson fired.

E TOOK ANOTHER SIP of whiskey, then set the chilled glass down on the nightstand beside the half-empty bottle of Canadian Hunter. Ice clinked. He stretched out on the bed, worrying his head and shoulders against the piled pillows until he'd made a comfortable hollow.

E crossed his ankles and picked up his bloodstained book of poetry, *Inside the Monster's Heart and Other Poems* by Juan Alejandro Navarro, and resumed reading. He read the same stanzas over and over without taking anything in. After a few more minutes of staring at the page without turning it, E slammed the book shut and tossed it onto the bed.

He needed sleep, but couldn't. He was too wired. He burned to create. He kept hearing her voice, begging him to keep reading to her, and he had. In a gentle voice.

> *. . . frost-scorched and time-withered, this heart*
> *its black edges curling in*
> *like a dead spider's legs . . .*

AND STILL SHE'D SOBBED.

E reached into the pocket of his cords and slipped out his latest souvenir. Closing his eyes, he rubbed the silky black stocking against his face. It whispered against the beard stubble on his face. He smelled her, cherries and musky sweat. He opened his eyes and stared into a world tinted black.

Had she begged him to keep reading just to prevent him from reaching into his satchel full of sharp tricks? Or had she truly wanted the sound of his voice, the music of the written word?

Please, no, no, read to me, please . . . keep reading.

Staring into the black-smudged light, E heard her whispers again; he listened to her voice—low and shaky and seductive.

Read to me, please . . . please . . .

For a moment, as he'd read to Gina, he'd felt a sudden warmth in his chest. Looking up from the page, he'd seen a golden bond stretching from her heart to his own. The golden bond had shivered and shifted into a pale mist of light spilling between them, pouring like heated honey between Gina's lips. When she'd opened her eyes again, they were golden.

Please . . . read to me . . .

Be my god . . .

Okay, maybe she'd never said that last part. All the same, he'd seen it in her transformed eyes.

Setting the book aside, unmarked, E kneels beside the bed, and kisses her bare shoulder. She shudders, her breath hitching. And, looking in, he sees a hard, crafty smile beneath the golden light, falsely curving those honeyed lips and dimming the radiance of her gaze.

Ice hardens in his belly, frosts his guts, and quenches the fire raging in his veins.

"Name the one you love," he says, sitting back on his heels to watch her face.

Her eyes flick back and forth, searching his face for clues. He goes still and gives her nothing.

"He'll come for me," she finally breathes. "He's nightkind."

E slides a shaking hand into his satchel; cold steel sticks to his icy skin. Wraps his fingers around the shiv's hilt.

"Say his name."

She sobs. Closes her eyes. Knows, maybe, that he can look in and see her lies. Her betrayal. "He'll come—"

"For you?" E finishes. "No, he won't." He lifts the shiv out of the satchel; dawn light sparks along the blade. "Dante doesn't care about you. Why would he? You're just a piece of ass."

Her eyes fly open at the sound of the name she hadn't spoken. At the same moment, E plunges the knife into her belly.

E rolled over onto his side, Gina's stocking locked within his hand, a rosary for meditating upon the mysteries of lying bitches.

She'd offered him love with her golden gaze, tempted him with adoration in the shape of her pleas. But he'd been smarter and stronger. He'd seen the lies squirming beneath her smooth skin. And beneath her black cherry scent, he'd smelled deceit, ripe and rank.

He could've given her so much. He could've been her god.

Which brought up an interesting point—being a god, why would he need a fucking bloodsucker like Ronin to guide him . . . *control* him?

He'd awaken S all by himself.

THE BULLET EXPLODED FROM the gun's muzzle, the sharp retort cracking through the air, rebounding from the walls and shattering the narrow tunnel obstructing Heather's vision. Her heart stopped for a split second, then everything zoomed forward in a blinding rush of speed.

She slammed Jefferson into the wall with a body block. She seized his wrist and jerked his gun hand up. Davis wrenched the pistol from Jefferson's fingers.

"Holy shit, asshole," he said, voice harsh. "You wanna fuck us all?"

"Nothing to worry about," LaRousse said. "He missed the bastard."

Heather looked at the doorway. Dante wasn't there. Instead, he stood in the center of the room. As she watched, he walked back to the doorway, bracing his gloved hands against either side. He looked ready to launch himself at Jefferson. Again.

Heather felt herself unknot. She drew in a deep breath, then slowly released it as relief leeched her strength and left her weak-limbed.

She caught Dante's shaded gaze, or thought she did, anyway, and shook her head. *Don't move. No more stupidity.* He remained braced in the doorway, body coiled. She could almost smell the adrenaline and fury that radiated from him. And testosterone. *Don't forget that.* With all the males in the room, the air crackled with it.

Heather turned to Jefferson. "What the hell were you doing?"

Jefferson met her gaze, opened his mouth, then shut it again. He looked down.

"Protecting his partner, Agent Wallace," LaRousse cut in. "Or don't y'all do that in the Bureau? Here, we do whatever's necessary."

Heather closed her eyes for a second, then turned. LaRousse knelt beside Manning, one hand on the cop's shoulder.

"Prejean was unarmed," she said, voice tight. "There was *no* need for deadly force. And you know it."

LaRousse snorted. Shook his head. He helped Manning to his feet.

"Take him to the emergency room," LaRousse said to Jefferson. "And write a detailed report."

"I'm fine," Manning said, face flushed. "Christ!"

Jefferson slipped an arm around his partner and walked the protesting Manning to the doorway. Dante still stood there, hands braced. A wry smile tilted up one corner of Dante's mouth. Lowering his hands, he stepped inside the room.

"Je va te voir plus tard," he said to Jefferson.

All color drained from Jefferson's face. "I don't know none of that Cajun talk," he stammered. Pushing Manning through the doorway, Jefferson hurried into the hall.

Heather blew loose strands of her hair from her face and glared at Dante. "You weren't kidding about that problem with cooperation, were you?"

"He told Jefferson he'd see him later," LaRousse said. "Sounds like a threat."

"No threat," Dante said. "Just bound to happen."

Swiveling to face LaRousse, Heather said, "Prejean is *not* a player. I think he needs to be placed in protective custody."

"No thanks," Dante said. "And my name ain't Prejean."

"Shut up," Heather said. "You're not helping."

"Oh, he'll be placed in protective custody, all right," LaRousse said, a tight smile thinning his lips. "In jail. For assaulting an officer and resisting arrest."

"Let's get things straight right now, LaRousse," Heather said, stepping closer to the detective, muscles tight, hands clenched. "*I'm* in charge of this investigation—"

LaRousse leaned in and met her head-on. "That's where you're wrong, Agent Wallace," he said. "You're *not* in charge. You're *consulting*. Hell, you haven't told us whether or not the damned Cross-Country Killer is even here."

LaRousse's words hit Heather like an open-handed slap. Her cheeks burned, but she didn't look away or back down. Her nails dug into her palms.

"I'm waiting for DNA confirmation," she said, keeping her voice level.

"Even if he is here and you're put in charge, I wouldn't give a flying fuck," LaRousse said. "That *prick*"—he stabbed a finger in Dante's direction—"assaulted one of my officers."

Still holding Heather's gaze, LaRousse called, "Davis, cuff that piece of street trash and hand him over to the uniforms downstairs."

"We're not finished," Heather said, voice low, and turned around.

Davis approached Dante cautiously, handcuffs held loose in one hand. "Take it easy," he murmured, a man gentling a growling dog. "Don't have to be hard. We can do this easy."

Dante's wary face and coiled body spelled hard in a big way.

Look, we don't have to do this the hard way.

It's the only way I know.

"Wait. Back off," Heather said. "*I'll* cuff him."

Hands lifted in a gesture of surrender, his gaze still locked on Dante, Davis said, "Fine. He's all yours."

Well aware that LaRousse watched her every move, Heather took the handcuffs from Davis's outstretched hand and crossed the carpeted floor. Dante watched her, expression guarded, hands clenched at his sides.

"What'd you do?" Heather murmured as she stopped in front of him. "Stand LaRousse up at the prom? What a hard-ass."

A smile quirked up the corners of Dante's mouth. His hands unclenched, relaxed. But his gloved fingers curled in slightly, on the verge of closing into fists again.

Heather realized in that moment that it had been *need* she'd seen on Dante's face as he'd looked at Gina's body, need mingled with the shock and disbelief.

The room reeked of blood, the bed drenched in it. He believed he was a vampire. . . . Had it been a vampire's need she'd seen? Or something darker yet?

"Just relax, okay?" Heather said. "Trust me. I'll get this all straightened out."

Sweat trickled along Dante's temple and his jaw was clenched. Migraine? Annie had often looked the same just before a headache.

"I've never trusted a cop," Dante said, voice husky.

"I'm not asking you to trust a cop," Heather said. "I'm asking you to trust *me*."

Dante looked at her for a long moment. Sudden dizziness swirled through Heather, spinning from her head to the base of her spine. Just as panic touched her, the sensation vanished.

Without another word, Dante tugged off his gloves, tossing them into the easy chair. Then he turned around, hands behind his back.

8

THE UNMAKER

WITH SHARP METALLIC CLICKS, the cuffs ratcheted shut around Dante's wrists. Old demons he couldn't even name awakened. Hot, arid whispers seared his thoughts. *Break the cuffs. Snuff them. All of them. You'll be out the window long before their blood finishes splashing the floor. Wantitneeditdoit-wantitneed—*

Muscles knotted, Dante bowed his head, struggling not to listen.

Beneath the thick smell of Gina's blood, he caught a whiff of gasoline and charred flesh. Heard the crackle of flames. *But not here. Another time. Another place.* He shuddered. Pain unfurled. His vision blurred.

"Hey," Wallace said. "Breathe. Just breathe. C'mon, in. Out. In."

Listening to the smooth, calming tone of Wallace's lowered voice, Dante reached for Lucien, and touched his waiting mind through their link.

<*Gina's dead. Bail me out after the others wake.*>

"Breathe, Dante. Do you have any medication?"

<Bail you out . . . ? Child, why allow yourself to be arrested?>

<Wantitneeditdoitwantitneeditwantitburnit–> escaped before he could stop it.

<Shhhhh . . . >

Cool light suddenly bathed Dante's mind, icing his pain and silencing the voices. He jumped when Wallace reached up and gently lowered his shades. He turned his head away, dazed by the gray morning light. She gripped his chin, turned his head around to face her.

"Medication? Do you take any?"

"Morphine. Opium sometimes," he said, looking through his lashes into her eyes. Twilight blue, he thought, just as the stars come out.

She held his gaze, brows knitted. Wisps of red hair framed her face and curled against her temples. "Couldn't you name something legal, at least?" she whispered, shoving the shades back onto the bridge of his nose. "Christ."

Dante shrugged. "You asked. I don't lie."

"Maybe you should." Wallace shook her head.

"Take him in," Dickhead–LaRousse–said. "Lock him up. He'll be asleep in no time, I guarantee."

Dante glanced over his shoulder. Dickhead winked.

He knows I'm nightkind.

"Hold on." Wallace pulled Dante's hood up, tugged the edges past his face. "Don't want you bursting into flames or anything," she whispered. A quick smile curved her lips.

"Merci beaucoup," he murmured.

Wallace's actions surprised Dante. Hell, *bewildered* him. She didn't act like a cop–at least, not all the time–even when she was busy rousting nightkind from Sleep with search warrants. He saw nothing cynical or mocking in her gaze. He watched as she turned away and crossed the room to the bed.

The cool morning breeze ruffled Gina's hair, fluttered the

stocking knotted around her throat. Dante looked at her for the last time.

We gotta go, sexy. Tomorrow night?

He hadn't said a word. Now it was a little late. "Yeah," he whispered. "Tomorrow night."

He followed Sidekick out into the hall and down the stairs. Ice melted and pain sparked anew. Sweat beaded his forehead.

We . . .

Where was Jay?

THE NEED TO SLEEP rolled through Dante, a need that put him on the nod despite his determination to stay awake. He sat knees up in a corner of the holding cell, drifting as he listened to his fellow lawbreakers.

"So this hoodoo lady sez, watch out, ya know—" said Geeky-Sweaty Dude sitting on the bench across the cell, his voice fast and high; a caffeinated Ping-Pong ball.

"Shut the fuck up," growled Unfriendly Dude hunched on the bench beside him.

And the drunk Bayou Boy clutching the toilet puked . . . again . . . retching hard enough to earn a grunt of semi-sympathy from Unfriendly Dude. Geeky Dude gagged at the violent splashing sound echoing from the bowl and the sour, vile smell wafting through the cell.

Since his shades and hoodie had been confiscated along with his belt and jewelry, Dante was grateful that the cell was windowless, though a little fresh air would've been welcome. His eyes closed and his head nodded.

Dante thumped his head back against the wall, forced his eyes open. He squinted against the fluorescent lighting. *Stay awake!*

Geeky Dude, undeterred by the interruptions from Bayou

Boy and Unfriendly Dude, picked up right where he'd left off. "For the reshaper, the unmaker, she sez."

"Who gives a fuck, shithead?"

A little brown cockroach scuttled from a crack in the wall, hauling ass for the shadow cast by Dante's knees. Snatching it up from the floor, he cupped it between his hands. The cockroach's delicate legs and antennae brushed against his palms.

Concentrate. C'mon . . . stay awake.

A faint blue glow emanated from his palms and, despite his effort, his eyes closed. A song lured him in: the cockroach's genetic song, an undulating wave, backed by DNA rhythm. Dante plucked at the rhythm's strings and altered the song. Sleep still beckoned. For a moment, he drifted and the strings went slack, then knotted, and another song entirely blasted through his mind—chaos rhythms of nightmare and rage.

An image flashed through his mind; a little girl, a plushie orca—black and white and red-spotted . . . deep red . . .

Gone.

Renewed pain snaked through Dante's mind. So *much* he didn't remember. Each time he tried, a fucking migraine laid him out.

Opening his eyes, Dante lowered his cupped hands between his boots. Blue light gleamed against his bootstraps and buckles and glittered on the hard, black surface of the thing he released from trembling hands. What used to be a cockroach slithered away from its maker, mewling.

Dante thumped his head against the wall once, twice. Did it all *fucking* wrong. He squeezed his eyes shut. Hand shaking, he touched his temple. Sweat slicked his fingers.

"What the hell is *that*?!"

"Gah! Kill it!"

The pounding vibration of several pairs of stomping feet jackhammered up Dante's spine to his skull. Pain flared like a supernova—white-hot and vast. Sleep sucker punched him and shoved him down into inner night.

"So . . . death by strangulation?" Heather asked.

"Unofficially, yes," Adams said. "I'll know for certain after the autopsy." He slid Gina's sheet-covered body back into the cold storage body bank. The door closed with a solid *ka-chunk* that echoed throughout the room.

Heather noticed fatigue shadowing the medical examiner's eyes and lining the corners of his mouth. Tension corded his neck muscles. A busy week in the Big Easy for the coroner's office, what with Mardi Gras *and* a serial killer. She didn't envy the man.

"When will you have the results on the semen samples?" Heather said, shifting her attention to the square steel door Gina rested beyond.

The CCK is edging ever closer to Dante. Why is he playing games?

"Midweek, most likely. I'll keep you informed." Adams's voice was low and strained, heated.

Heather jerked her gaze up. Adams's brows were furrowed, his jaw tight. "Which is a sight more courtesy than you showed us," he continued.

"Pardon me?" Heather regarded the M.E. warily, caught off guard by the hostility in his gaze.

"Why didn't you let us know? We could've issued alerts, warnings. A serial killer is in New Orleans, Agent Wallace," Adams said. "You knew it. And said nothing."

Weariness swept through Heather. "I apologize. But I *have* to be certain."

"Tell *her* that," Adams said, nodding at the body bank. He crossed the tile floor, then stepped out into the hall, the door swinging shut behind him.

Heather stood alone in the morgue, surrounded by the voiceless dead. She touched a hand to the cold metal door. Pictured Gina beneath the sheet. Remembered Dante saying: *He took everything from her.*

Heather's throat tightened. True. Everything. But once she nailed this bastard, Gina would have one last opportunity to speak.

Small comfort.

After three long years, she finally had a link to the Cross-Country Killer: Dante.

But at what cost?

Dropping her hand from the cold storage door, Heather walked across the room, cold pinching the nape of her neck. She refused to look back. She slipped out the morgue's door, pausing as the door clicked shut behind her.

Forgive me, Gina.

LUCIEN STOOD IN THE center of the living room, gaze directed at the ceiling. The old floorboards creaked as a foot touched them. His fists opened. His talons pulled free of his palms, the wounds already healing as he did so. He hurried to the front door and wrenched it open. Fading gray light spilled into the room. The day was dying.

Lucien arrowed a message to the waking minds above, sending, in a single thought/image, news of Gina's murder and Dante's arrest. The replies slammed against Lucien's shield, stunned, perplexed. He shut them all out and strode into the rose-and-rain scented evening.

RONIN'S EYES OPENED. COLOR—ORANGE and violet—bled into the room from beneath the curtained window. Sunset.

A sharp beep ruined the silence and drew Ronin's gaze to the nightstand beside the bed. A yellow message light glowed on his cell phone. Rolling onto his side, he grabbed the cell, flipped it open, and thumbed up the text message. It was from his contact in the department.

PREJEAN HELD AT 8th PRECINCT.

Ronin smiled.

A SOUND PULLED DANTE from Sleep. He opened his eyes and pushed his hair back from his face. A cop whapped the holding cell's bars with his nightstick. The steel sang.

"Yo, sleeping beauty," the cop drawled. "Your bail's been posted."

"Groovy." Dante stretched, muscles unkinking, then eased to his feet. Hunger awakened and uncurled within him. He needed to feed.

Bayou Boy and Unfriendly Dude were gone, long sprung, but Geeky Dude squatted on the bench, his feet tucked under him. He eyed the floor nervously. "Down there somewhere . . . watch out—"

"Shut up, Wilson," the cop said, shaking his head. "Ain't you slept it off yet, fer chrissakes?" He keyed open the cell.

Geeky Dude—*Wilson*—glanced up at Dante. His eyes widened. He wrapped his arms around himself, hugging tight like he could make himself smaller; a little garden gnome perched on a steel bench. "The reshaper is here. The unmaker."

Dante halted, his gaze locking on Wilson. "What are you talking about?"

The cell door slid open with a loud clang.

Wilson peered at Dante from between his arm and his knees. "Beautiful."

"Looks like you got a fan there, rock boy," the cop said with a malicious grin.

"Unmaker," Wilson repeated.

Shaking his head, Dante stepped out of the cell. The door

clanged shut. He followed the cop down the hall, Wilson's words chilling his blood.

"WHERE IS HE?" HEATHER halted in front of LaRousse's cluttered desk.

"His bail was posted," LaRousse said. He kept typing on the keyboard, his attention on the monitor. "We had to release him."

Heather leaned across the desk and pressed her hand onto the keyboard. The computer made several odd sounds. LaRousse looked up, eyes flashing. She held his gaze, hoped hers made him pause. This went beyond the usual passive-aggressive bullshit she put up with when stepping into an ongoing homicide investigation; it even went beyond the bristling-alpha-male-refusing-to-submit-to-female-authority thing. This was between her and LaRousse—as individuals.

"I wanted a statement from him," Heather said. "You *knew* that."

"So call him at home and make a date."

"Asshole." Heather lifted her hand from the keyboard. "Did you even bother to interview him? He *knew* the victim."

The chatter stopped in the other cubicles. The clicking of fingers across keyboards slowed.

"We *tried* to get a statement from him," LaRousse said, leaning back in his chair and propping his feet on the desk. "All we got was an hour's worth of 'Fuck off.'"

"As charming as you are?" Heather snorted, crossing her arms over her chest.

"LaRousse? Charming?"

Heather glanced toward the speaker. Collins stood in the squad room doorway, a Styrofoam cup of coffee in each hand. Just coming on duty, then. She nodded. "Trent."

"Agent Wallace was just leaving," LaRousse said, dropping

his feet to the floor and sitting up. He switched off his computer, looked at Collins. "Unless you want your pet fed to keep you company."

"Like I said, charming." Collins sauntered over to stand beside Heather. A deep vertical line creased the skin on his forehead—what Heather's mother used to call the *thinking deep* line. "What's up?"

"I have reason to believe Dante Prejean is the CCK's next target," Heather said.

"Yeah?" LaRousse said. "Well, he can have Prejean, far as I'm concerned."

"Why Prejean?" Collins questioned. He handed Heather one of the cups.

Heather accepted the coffee, smiling. The sharp, fresh-brewed aroma cleared her head. "Well, the last two victims have had contact with Prejean, one intimately. The first was from Lafayette—same as Prejean."

Collins nodded. "Just heard about this morning's call."

Heather paused to take a sip of the coffee. "The CCK—if it's the CCK—has added Prejean's anarchy logo to his signature. One vic was killed *next* to Club Hell, the other *in* Club Hell. I think the killer's circling in, closer and closer. Sooner or later, he'll decide to take Prejean."

LaRousse said, "You sure it ain't Prejean himself?"

"I was watching his house during the time frame of the last victim's death," Heather said. *Gina. Her name was Gina. She was breathing just a few hours ago.*

"Positive he was there?" LaRousse said, a slight smirk on his lips.

"Yeah," Heather said, voice even. "I saw him arrive and go inside. And he came out when I served the warrant."

"You must enjoy watching him, Wallace," LaRousse said, leaning back in his chair again. "A good-looking rock star like that."

"Kinda sounds like *you're* the one hung up on him, and he's not a rock star," Heather replied. "He's an underground cult figure. And yeah, he's good-looking, so what?"

"Good-looking *street* trash, y'mean," LaRousse muttered. "Wouldn't know an honest day's work if it kicked him in the ass."

Collins groaned. "Spare us, Reverend."

Heather couldn't believe her ears. The bastard was *envious* of Dante. Whether LaRousse wanted the so-called fame, the so-called money, or the groupies; whether he wanted Dante's looks, his life, none of that mattered. The only thing that mattered was that he had refused to offer protection to a killer's potential victim, had allowed Dante to walk.

Pulse pounding in her temples, Heather grabbed the arms of LaRousse's chair and swung it around so he faced her. "Hear this," she said. "I'll hold *you* accountable if anything happens to him."

LaRousse met her gaze, dark seething emotions shadowing his face. After a moment, he looked away, lips thinned into a white line.

Heather released the chair, then turned her back on the detective. Collins met her gaze, eyebrow arched, vertical crease smoothed away. A warning glimmered in his eyes. *Careful. Very thin ice.*

"I know," Heather murmured. "I need you to contact the Prejeans and the Spurrells in Lafayette, see if the families had any connections."

"Will do. Where you headed?"

"To find Prejean."

9

UNWALKED PATHS

THE BLONDE WITH THE long spiraled hair answered the door. *"Oui?"* she said, scanning the dark yard behind Heather before focusing on her face. A slight smile brushed across her lips.

"I need to speak to Dante," Heather said.

The blonde shook her head and Heather caught a whiff of flowers—roses, maybe magnolias. "Dante's not at home," she said, starting to close the door.

Heather stopped the door with her hand. "I intend to wait," she said, holding her badge up at eye level.

The blonde regarded the badge with thoughtful brown eyes, then she stepped back, opening the door wide. *"S'il te plaît,"* she said, gesturing Heather inside with a graceful wave of her hand.

"Thank you."

The blonde led Heather to the front room. "Make yourself at home," she said, stopping beside a sofa.

Heather sat, perching on the edge, muscles knotted. She needed sleep, a meal. She glanced at her hands. They trembled ever so slightly. She curled her hands into fists. The last twenty-four hours—not to mention all the damned coffee—were catching up with her.

"Are you all right, *M'selle* Wallace?"

Heather looked up. The blonde studied her, expression neutral, but her brown eyes sharp. "I'm sorry," Heather said, managing a smile. "You know my name, but I don't know yours."

"Simone," she answered, returning Heather's smile. "You look tired. Would you like some coffee?"

"Oh, yeah, that'd be great." Heather unknotted her hands and pressed her fingers flat against her slacks.

Nodding, Simone walked across the room. She paused at the archway and looked back at Heather, her long blonde hair swinging against her denim-skirted hips. "I'll be right back," she said.

Heather smiled in acknowledgment of her statement and what was implied: *Don't go anywhere.*

Once Simone had left the room, Heather slumped back into the sofa and closed her eyes. The last thing she needed was more caffeine, but she was afraid she'd fall asleep without it. Kind of difficult to protect someone while snoozing on their sofa.

She shook her head. She was losing focus. And she hadn't checked in with Stearns . . . oh . . . since seven o'clock last night and it was now—Opening her eyes, she peered at her watch. Eight fourteen p.m. Sunday. She sighed.

Well, she *was* the one who decided to forego sleep so she could serve her warrant to Dante at the most inconvenient moment possible.

But she gut-knew that the man who'd murdered Gina was the same one she'd been pursuing for the last three years.

His first known kill had been in Seattle. Serial killers *always* started where they were the most comfortable, and then expanded outward from that point as they grew more confident.

So, did Dante have any ties to Seattle?

"Not really," a low voice said. "Just some music contacts."

"What?" Heather looked up sharply. She straightened, her gaze lighting on the speaker—the wine-drinking minor from the club. Had she been thinking out loud?

He leaned against the wall just inside the archway, purple hair gelled into a disheveled rock star/bedhead look. His startling silver eyes seemed lit from within, his face pensive as he chewed on his lower lip. He looked no older than sixteen.

"I'm sorry," Heather said. "What did you say?"

He wore black jeans studded with metal, zippered and looped with chains. A wide, low-slung belt circled his narrow hips and his slashed and faded black SINENGINE T was so tight it looked like it'd been airbrushed on over his lean torso.

Simone stepped into the room. She glanced at the boy for a moment, then shifted her gaze to Heather. "This is Silver," she said, squeezing the boy's shoulder. "Silver, this is *Agent* Wallace."

Heather noted Simone's emphasis on the word *agent*. Silver had just been warned or perhaps reminded. Why?

"The coffee will be ready in a few minutes," Simone said, releasing Silver's shoulder. "Would you like to freshen up?" Without a backward glance, the boy slipped from the room.

Heather met Simone's gaze and smiled. "I'd like that, thank you."

Simone led her into a narrow hall lined with framed artwork and old-fashioned candleholders. A dark brown carpet etched with leaves in gold and scarlet stretched the length of the hall. Heather caught a glimpse of stairs spiraling up at the hall's opposite end. Faint blue light edged beneath a partially opened door beside the stairs.

Simone gestured toward the bathroom and began to walk away. Heather said, "Did you know Gina?"

Simone halted. "*Oui*, she was Dante's friend."

"Do you know of anyone who'd want to harm her?" Heather said. "Maybe something you heard?"

Simone shook her head. "No."

"What about Étienne?" Heather asked. "He was pretty pissed off at Dante last night at the club. Do you think he might be capable of—"

"Having Gina murdered?" Simone finished. "Capable, *oui*." Her gaze drifted past Heather and up. "What do you think, *llygad*?"

Heather stiffened as she realized someone stood behind her. Worse, she had a feeling he'd been standing there for a while. Turning, she put her back to the wall and glanced to the right.

The nomad bouncer stood at the foot of the stairs, dressed in faded jeans and a button-down black shirt, his deep brown hair brushing his shoulders. His green eyes, no longer hidden behind shades, seemed to look beyond Heather. He stroked the sides of his mustache thoughtfully.

"Nah," he said finally. "Not Étienne's style. He'd hurt Dante, sure. But not through a mortal—not unless he could make Dante watch."

Heather glanced from Von to Simone. Their gazes held for a heartbeat longer, then Simone glanced down, a smile on her lips.

Grinning wolfishly, fangs showing, Von strode down the hall in long-legged, confident strides. He winked at Heather as he passed. His scent was frosty and clear, the first chilly breath of autumn. He brushed the backs of his fingers against Simone's pale cheek as he passed. Then he was gone.

"There it was again," Heather said. "That word. *Mortals.* Dante believes he's a vampire. Von has fangs. What about you?"

Simone regarded her for a long moment, all amusement gone from her dark eyes. "What you need to remember, *m'selle*, is that Dante never tells or forgives a lie." Swiveling around, Simone walked away, hips swinging. "I'll fetch your coffee."

"Everyone lies," Heather said under her breath. That was

the universal truth of detective work, one she'd had drilled into her since before her days at the Academy. *Everyone* lies. Guilty people lie. Innocent people lie. Cops lie. Bad guys definitely lie. The reasons differ—to hide, to protect another, to cover up—but everyone lies.

Heather stepped into the bathroom and shut the door. She regarded her weary reflection in the mirror. Tendrils of hair clung to her face and neck. Shadows smudged her eyes. She turned on the faucet, splashed cold water onto her face.

So . . . Dante had a reputation for not lying.

Heather patted her face dry with a plush blue towel, then looked into the mirror again. All that meant was that Dante *believed* he was a vampire. If his friends, hell, even his enemies encouraged his delusional thinking, then to him, he spoke the truth.

Reaching behind her head, Heather unpinned and unwound her French braid. Her hair, frizzy with humidity, tumbled past her shoulders.

What if he *was* a vampire? What if everyone in this house were *exactly* what they pretended to be—sun-shunning vampires? What was the word Dante had used? *Nightkind.*

Heather fumbled her brush and makeup bag out of her purse and onto the counter.

But she'd picked Dante up shortly after dawn.

It was overcast. He wore sunscreen and shades and gloves. He hid his face within a hood.

His mind-dazzling speed. Jackson pulled the trigger. No way that bullet could've missed Dante. But it had.

The need on his face. The blood, still dripping, the air reeking with it.

Then why had he allowed himself to be arrested? Weren't vampires strong enough to snap handcuffs?

Heather tugged the brush through her hair. She didn't like the path her thoughts were taking, but it was a path she needed to walk. She'd learned over the years to examine every angle, no matter how absurd.

What about the scene at the club? Étienne and his dark promises?

Leaning against the counter, Heather touched up her lipstick. She conceded it could've all been a game. Some live-action roleplayers took their games *very* seriously, especially the vampire and werewolf groups. She'd seen it in Seattle more than once.

But what if it hadn't been a game?

What had Étienne said to De Noir?

This doesn't concern the Fallen.

Suddenly cold, Heather tucked her lipstick back into her makeup bag, then dropped it back into her purse. She stared into the mirror; her reflection stared back, eyes dilated and nearly black in the low light, rimmed with cornflower blue.

She dropped her gaze to her hands. They trembled once again. Fallen. As in angels? *Nightbringer.* Everything about De Noir seemed unearthly: his powerful presence, the gleam of gold in his black eyes, his speed as he rushed toward Étienne.

Heather shrugged out of her trench, then draped it over her arm so that she had easy access to her .38. She smoothed her sweater. Opening the door, she stepped out into the empty hall. The front door opened as she walked into the front room. De Noir stepped through, closing the door behind him.

Apprehension iced her spine. "Where's Dante?" she asked.

SAC CRAIG STEARNS SIPPED at his coffee, his zillionth of the day, as he looked out his office window into the rainy Seattle night. He'd been trying to reach Wallace since morning, without luck. She hadn't responded to his e-mail messages or to his calls.

Wallace had never gone this long without checking in. Her

last message had stated that she was checking leads and would contact him today.

Returning to his desk, he sank into his chair. He flipped through some of the field reports stacked on his desk. He'd already read each several times.

If anything had ... *happened* ... to Wallace, he would've heard by now. Unless it was the kind of *happened* no one knew about yet.

Stearns swallowed the last of his coffee. He'd call that detective Wallace was consulting with in New Orleans—Collins. As he reached for the phone, it rang and he jerked his hand back, heart pounding. Chagrined, he switched on the speaker and tabbed on the vid-mon. Maybe he *should* cut down on the caffeine.

But the face that took shape on the monitor reassured him that his instincts were as sharp as ever: Blonde hair stylishly razor-cut, almond-shaped blue eyes, and a deceptively warm smile. He knew from experience that if a heart beat within her curvaceous chest, it'd been carved from glacial ice.

"I knew I'd find you at the office, Craig," ADIC Johanna Moore said.

"What's shaking, Moore?"

"Good news, I hope," she said, her smile widening. "We've got a dead perp in Pensacola that we've reason to believe is the Cross-Country Killer."

"What makes you think that?"

"You name it, we got it. We're waiting on DNA results, but, really, that's just a formality." Moore shook her head. "It's finally over, Craig. Call your agent home."

Stearns smiled despite the sudden cold icing his bones. Something was *way* hinky here. "How'd it happen?"

"One of my agents caught the perp in action. Made a good kill." Moore's smile faded. "Unfortunately, the perp's victim didn't make it."

"A shame," Stearns said. "I think I'll send my agent on to Pensacola to get those DNA results. Since this isn't exactly your department." Especially for the ADIC of Special Ops and Research, an ADIC rumored to have ties to the "non-existant" shadow branch.

"Not necessary," Moore replied, another warm smile on her lips. "I've got an agent there now."

"Well, hell, then I'll tell my agent to hang out and enjoy Mardi Gras."

"Recall Wallace," Moore said, smile gone.

"So that's it." Stearns's mind raced, flipping through possible courses of action. "What are you hiding in New Orleans?"

"You're fencing with the wrong person. Get your agent out."

"One of your *projects* must be down there. That it?"

A rueful smile brushed over Moore's lips. "You know better than to ask that, Craig, you of all people."

It hit Stearns, then, like a fist to the gut. One of Moore's projects and the CCK were one and the same. Why had Moore even allowed them to work the case? Maybe it hadn't mattered before because they were never close, but now they were. Wallace was *on* the bad guy's ass. Closing in.

"Wallace had better be all right," he said, voice tight.

"Bring her in," Moore said softly, "and she will be." She switched off, the vid-mon going slate-gray with static.

Stearns jumped to his feet, kicked his chair. It rolled across the polished hardwood floor and thunked into the wall. He paced from the rain-misted window to the door and back again. Think! Wallace would never buy it if he just called her in. She'd want to go to Pensacola, check the evidence for herself. Moore probably expected that.

Let Wallace know that the case was officially closed. The CCK was dead. End of story.

Bracing his hands on either side of the window, Stearns stared out into the black night. His stomach churned. Neon flashed on the streets below; car headlights streaked along the wet pavement. Moore's request was simple.

All he had to do was bring an agent in. And let a killer walk. Again.

10

UNFORESEEN

Ronin pulled his Camaro over to the curb and switched off the engine. He glanced at the handheld GPS receiver. Dante's movement had stopped, then resumed, but at a much slower pace. So . . . the boy was now on foot.

Getting out of his car, Ronin stepped onto the sidewalk and tabbed his debit spike into the parking meter, then set it for two hours. He checked the GPS receiver, then started walking down neon-lit Canal Street, toward the Mississippi. Even here tourists and vendors crowded the sidewalks, and the four lanes of traffic gleamed with headlights. Horns honked as drivers warned strolling pedestrians as they hung rights or lefts across crosswalks.

Ronin kept his pace at a deliberate mortal-paced stride. He walked with a small herd of pedestrians, not wishing to call attention to himself. Blend, meld, become ordinary and therefore invisible. He didn't want Dante to see him. At least, not yet. The GPS receiver marked the young vampire just a few blocks ahead of him.

Another thing E didn't know—microchip-size GPS transmitters had been implanted at the base of the skull of each Bad Seed subject. Johanna had wanted to keep tabs on her experiments once they'd been unleashed.

Of course, most of the subjects—all ignorant of each other and Bad Seed's existence, let alone their own participation—were now dead or entombed in prisons. E and Dante were the only two still roaming free.

Ronin looked up and over the heads of some of the people encircling him. He saw Dante a block ahead of him, stopped in front of the light-filled and glittering Harrah's, next to the black iron fence near the entrance.

Muscles tightening in anticipation, Ronin slowed his pace, allowing his camouflage group to trundle across the street without him. A vendor sat on a metal folding chair next to a streetlight, his wares—colorful MARDI GRAS! T-shirts, plastic beads, and other bits of cheap jewelry—displayed on a sheet spread out on the sidewalk.

Ronin stopped and looked over the vendor's goods, pretending a mild interest. What was Dante doing? he wondered, his gaze skipping from DRUNK ON BOURBON STREET Ts to 'gator charm bracelets. Meeting someone? Planning to play the slots?

"This one be real pop'lar," the vendor, a black man in his midtwenties, said eagerly. He held up a shirt reading SHOW ME YOUR TITTIES! "Fresh batch. I keep sellin' out of 'em."

"Ah," Ronin murmured. "No doubt." He glanced up the street.

Dante leaned against the fence, his hands gripping the railing behind him. He stood near the double-globed streetlight, but not directly beneath it, his face hood-hidden. Light danced across his leather pants and winked from his rings and hoops and bracelets. His head was bowed, his shaded gaze on the sidewalk.

People flowing in, out, and past Harrah's glanced at him. More than a few paused and stared until nudged into motion by a less-dazzled companion.

"Maybe this one's more to your liking? Sir?"

Ronin forced his gaze away from Dante. The vendor held up a shirt proclaiming LAISSEZ LES BONS TEMPS ROULLER. *Let the good times roll.* Ronin nodded.

"That one. How much?"

"Ten, sir. Cash only."

As Ronin tugged his wallet free of his hip pocket, he darted another glance up the street. Two men in jeans and Saints sweat-shirts paused near Dante. They leaned in close to one another, hands gesturing, their conversation intense. One pointed across Canal street toward the French Quarter. The other shook his head, then looked toward the casino.

Dante lifted his head, his pale hands pushing his hood back. He slid his shades off and looped them through his studded belt. The mortal froze, mouth open. A smile tilted Dante's lips, wicked and oh-so-inviting. The man gripped his friend's forearm and squeezed. Swinging his head around, the friend looked and went still also, mesmerized by the moonlit slice of sexual fantasy leaning against the fence.

Ronin looked away. Excitement shook his hands as he slid a ten out of his wallet and handed it to the vendor.

Dante was hunting.

Snatching the T-shirt from the vendor's hands, Ronin tucked one end of it into his hip pocket and started up the sidewalk. He forced himself to walk slowly. He still couldn't afford to call attention to himself, especially near a hyper-alert and, undoubt-edly, territorial vampire on the hunt.

Both mortals had recovered enough from their first glimpse of Dante's breath-stealing beauty to sidle in on either side of him, their bodies nearly touching. Their hungry, somewhat predatory, stance amused Ronin. They spoke to Dante, smiling, their gestures friendly. One displayed a wad of cash.

Ronin paused at a store window. He was close enough now that Dante would feel his presence if he wasn't careful. He tamped his aura down tight, stilled his questing mind. Blood surged through his veins electrified, adrenalized. For a moment, his thoughts spun, and he shook his head, perplexed. What had come over him? He prized control—the essence of strength and self-rule.

Dante. True Blood. Vampire aristocracy.

He looked up the street again. Dante walked away with the mortals, one still on either side of him. The men glanced at each other. Winked. One squeezed a hand into a fist. Ronin watched as the threesome turned the corner onto Tchopitoulas Street. The mortals no doubt planned bad things for the young Goth hustler walking between them; planned to use him, then hurt him. And not necessarily in that order.

Ronin now knew why Dante had lifted his head and allowed those two to look at him and fall under his spell.

He'd smelled their filthy little hearts jittering away inside their chests. Had heard their fevered whispers. Seen their twisted thoughts.

Ronin grinned. Dante hunted the *evil-doer*. Or, at the very least, he preyed on predators. Ironic? Yes. Fascinating? Yes. Something Johanna and her squad of behavioral scientists had foreseen? Hell, no.

Ronin paused at another store window, allowing Dante and his new friends time to get ahead. One thing troubled him—S.A. Heather Wallace. Why was she investigating Dante? Was it possible she'd understood what Dante hadn't so far? That the messages were for him?

Ronin glanced at the GPS receiver. Dante had stopped. Looking up the street, he realized that Dante and the two Saints fans were no longer in view. Ronin dropped the mortal pretense and *moved*. He breezed through the sidewalk throngs with the ease of a man walking a deserted street. He touched no one and perhaps only a few mortals felt a cool rush of air as he passed.

The receiver showed Dante halfway down an alley just ahead

and to the right. Ronin slowed to a walk. His heart pounded hard in his chest. He *felt* Dante, felt his hunger sharp as a double-edged sword. But underneath that he felt rage, unvoiced and wordless; a red-hot torrent rushing through Dante's veins.

Shielding himself with steel thought and glass illusion—*No one here. Look past. No one here. Look past*—Ronin dared a glance down the shadow-filled alley.

One Saints fan stood in front of Dante, pressing a pocket-knife against his pale throat while his buddy handcuffed Dante's hands behind his back. A dark smile crossed Dante's lips as the knife nicked his throat. Blood oozed from the tiny cut, trickling down his white skin and onto the collar of his mesh shirt.

Ronin breathed in the blood's fragrance, sucked it down into his lungs: rich and thick with pheromones and ripe-berry sweet. Hunger seized him. He hugged the building's edge, his fingers curling around weather-worn brick, and watched.

"Viens ici," Dante said to the mortal holding the knife to his throat. *"J'ai faim."*

The Saints fan narrowed his eyes, his smile turning brittle. "What the hell did you just say?"

His buddy grasped Dante's hips and pressed hard against him. "Who gives a fuck what he said? Talking isn't on the menu."

"Can you take as good as you give?" Dante murmured.

He leaned forward and nuzzled the mortal's throat, licked the flesh over the fast-pulsing artery. The pocketknife slid away from Dante's throat, blood trailing from its point. The mortal closed his eyes. Dante sank his fangs into the man's throat.

Groaning, the Saints fan stumbled back into the wall. The knife tumbled from his fingers and hit the concrete with a sharp *ting*. Dante pressed against him, snugging one leather-clad leg between his, pinning him.

The other mortal had moved with them, one hand still clutching Dante's hip, the other wriggling between his buddy and Dante in an effort to unbuckle Dante's belt.

Ronin's muscles tightened, his breath coming hard and fast. His lips parted. He felt the whisker-stubbled flesh beneath his lips, tasted the hot blood gushing into his mouth. He closed his eyes. Listened to his own thundering heart.

True Blood. Destiny.

Opening his eyes, Ronin smiled, then hunkered down. *Let's see how the True Blood, child that he is, gets himself out of this alley . . . alone.*

The mortal Dante feasted on suddenly started to struggle. His eyes flew open. He lifted a trembling hand, seized Dante's shoulder, and shoved. But Dante didn't budge.

"Andy," he slurred, his voice thick and panicked. "Help me. Andy . . ."

With a casual shrug, Dante snapped the handcuffs. Metal *tink*ed off brick and stone. His hands latched onto the mortal's shoulders and held him still, burrowing his face deeper into the mortal's throat, ripping into the flesh.

The other mortal, Andy, jumped back when Dante snapped the handcuffs, astonishment on his face. "What the . . ."

Dante released the Saints fan, who slumped to the ground in a boneless heap, his eyes already glazing. Licking the blood from his lips, Dante swiveled around and looked at Andy. He lifted his arms and glanced pointedly at the handcuff bracelets on his wrists.

With a tiny shriek, Andy whirled around, and ran—

Right into Dante.

Ronin shook his head, marveling at Dante's speed. He wondered if the boy had any other surprises.

Dante embraced Andy, locking his arms around him as his fangs pierced his throat. Andy's legs gave out and they both went down, the mortal sprawling on the rain-puddled alley floor. Dante straddled him, sitting on his belly and pinning his arms to the concrete. Dante fed, swallowing mouthful after mouthful of hot blood.

Ronin realized he'd stood at some point and had moved into the alley without being aware of it, his gaze locked on Dante's slender coiled form, his thoughts hunger-fevered, craving only the blood burning through Dante's veins.

Sliding to a sudden halt, dirt gritted beneath Ronin's snake-skin boots. He held his breath hoping the boy hadn't heard—

But he had. Dante looked up, his dark-eyed gaze locking onto Ronin. Wiping blood from his mouth with the back of his hand, he uncurled from the mortal's body and stood. Behind him, Andy twitched, then lay still.

Ronin held Dante's gleaming, hostile gaze for a single time-stretching moment, then the boy *moved*.

Ronin danced aside using a change-body technique, sucking in as he whirled. Dante passed so close mesh whispered against denim, and heat radiated against Ronin's night-cooled flesh. Dante's scent swirled through the night air—blood and deep, dark earth, heady and sharp. And dangerous. Ronin forced himself to focus. His aikido-trained muscles relaxed, ready for Dante's next charge.

"Hey," said a low, husky voice to Ronin's right.

Turning, Ronin met Dante's dark gaze again. The boy stood not five feet from him at the alley mouth's other edge. He watched Ronin through his lashes, his hands curled into fists, his muscles taut. He had a street fighter's posture; deceptively still. His fighting style would be down, dirty, and vicious, but easy to handle with the calm focus of aikido.

"Who the fuck are you?" Dante tilted his head and sudden knowledge lit his eyes. "You were in the club last night—you're the one Lucien and Von told me about."

Ronin smiled and nodded his head in acknowledgment. "That I was."

"Where's your mortal buddy?"

"My assistant, you mean?" Ronin asked. Dante's fists hadn't relaxed. "I gave him the evening off."

"Assistant?" A half smile tilted Dante's lips. "That's a new one."

"I'm a journalist," Ronin said. "Crime journalist, actually."

Tugging his wallet free, he looked up into Dante's dark, red-streaked eyes. He now stood only a foot away. Ronin hadn't heard him move, hadn't felt him. He slid a black card from his wallet, extended it to Dante between two fingers.

Dante plucked it free and read its silver-lettered surface. "Thomas Ronin," he murmured. "So, what are you doing here, Peeping Tom?" He flicked the card into the rain-filled gutter.

Ronin watched the sodden card float to a sewer grate not half a block down. He met Dante's sardonic gaze and held it. In that moment, he had one regret—that Johanna had discovered this child, born of unwilling vampire mother, and he hadn't.

How he could've shaped him.

Was it too late? Possibility raged through his mind with hurricane force.

"Yo, Peeping Tom, you awake?" Dante's voice now came from behind.

Ronin swiveled around. Still only a foot away, Dante studied him, dark eyes missing little.

"Sorry," Ronin said, shaking his head. "I've been working the Cross-Country Killer case. And I've wanted to talk to you since the body was discovered in the pizza parlor's courtyard and now—"

"How'd you find me here?" Dante said, voice flat.

"Pure coincidence," Ronin said. "I went to the club, but it was closed. I decided to check out Harrah's for fun and I happened to see you." Ronin spread his arms out in a half shrug, palms open. "What the fuck, you know? I decided to follow."

Dante's hands remained knotted at his sides, his gaze wary. "You wasted your time, *M'sieu* Peeping Tom," he said. He glanced away for a moment, but before he did, Ronin saw something flash in his eyes—hurt, grief, maybe both.

"I know we're not off to the best start," Ronin said. "And I completely understand you not wanting to talk to me . . . now. But in a day or two, you may feel differently. I really want to see this son of a bitch nailed."

"We're not off to *any* start," Dante said. "And I'm not gonna talk to you in a day or two or five or ever." He backed up, half turned, his gaze still on Ronin. *"Foute ton quant d'ici."*

"You running me out of town?" Ronin asked, eyebrow arched, voice hard.

Dante laughed. "Fuck, no! Go where you want. You can even go to Hell. But stay away from me."

Ronin took several long-legged strides after him, then stopped. "Need a ride home?" he called. "No strings attached, I promise."

Dante turned completely and walked up the sidewalk. He didn't answer. When he reached the corner, he stopped, then about-faced.

"Hey, what mag you writing for?"

"Freelance. But I'll probably let *Rolling Stone* have first shot at the story."

Dante laughed again, then rounded the corner.

Ronin waited for a few moments, listening to the city's pulse, the traffic noise, the streetcar clacking along the rails, chattering tourists—all bound to an earth-deep rhythm that lured musicians from around the world.

Dante was gone.

The entire encounter had gone south with breathtaking speed.

Ronin glanced down the alley. The first Saints fan still lay sprawled on the concrete, his body heat dissipating into the night. Andy, however—Andy was pulling himself by his fingernails down the alley.

Closing his eyes, Ronin remembered the smell of Dante's blood, felt him hot and restless; saw again his mocking smile and smoldering dark eyes.

Ronin opened his eyes and strode down the alley. He seized the mortal by the scruff of his neck and lifted him up. Sank his fangs into the wounds left by Dante's sharp teeth. Andy sobbed and kicked weakly. Ronin drank what remained of him down, savoring every hot spurt, every last drop.

With a squeeze of his hand, Ronin crushed what remained of Andy's throat. He dropped the lifeless body and stretched as new blood coursed through his veins. He pulled from his hip pocket the T-shirt he'd bought from the street vendor and dropped it onto the cooling corpse. It draped across the mortal's face.

Let the good times roll.

E SAT UP STRAIGHT when the yellow cab pulled to a stop at the plantation house's gates. A black-clad, hooded figure slid out of the backseat, shut the door, and walked to the gates with a lithe, graceful motion E found arousing. Dante. And minus Tom-Tom. The cab drove away, taillights glowing red in the night.

E grinned. Things must not have gone according to plan for ol' Tommy, then. E was pretty sure Ronin had said he'd come back *with* Dante, their friendship off to a solid beginning. E's grin widened.

Gosh. Guess not.

Dante slipped through the partially opened gates and disappeared into the night-drenched yard. The only light illuminating the overgrown grounds was the pale yellow light spilling from several windows.

Touching the rim of his shades, E toggled from night-view to infrared. Bluish-silver light outlined Dante as he pushed open the front door and stepped inside the house.

E flipped the shades back to night-view. He drummed his

fingers against the Jeep's steering wheel. Why was it that he saw bluish-silver light around only Dante? The other bloodsuckers usually showed up yellow/orange or vibrant red, depending on how long since they'd fed. Ronin showed up gold and E had a feeling that had more to do with Tom-Tom's age than anything else.

But Dante . . . that boy gleamed like the winter moon on snow—sparkling blue-silver edged with purple. Kinda funny, considering how damned *hot* he looked.

Even for a bloodsucker.

Pulling the keys from the ignition, E hopped out of the Jeep. Gravel crunched beneath his Nikes. Pocketing the keys, he leaned against the Jeep for a moment, scanning the quiet yard across the road.

Vampires. Whatta *fucking* revelation. When Ronin had showed up at his kill site in New York, E had stabbed him to death. But the bastard hadn't dropped. Blood had spread across his fancy shirt in a deep red stain, then . . .

The bastard grins.

Something loosens inside E at the sight of those curving white fangs, something that curdles in his belly and freezes his thoughts. He catches a whiff of something rank, like maybe he'd stepped in dogshit somewhere along the line. But the heavy warmth in his drawers reveals the truth: E has crapped his pants. And then he's attacking the grinning black bastard with his shivs again—

And finds himself sprawled on the floor, his shivs no longer in his hands, but in the vampire's, whirling between his long fingers like sharpened shards of moonlight.

Yep. A revelation. Once E had calmed down and cleaned himself of his own stink, he and the vampire had a *very* long talk.

E shoved away from the Jeep and ambled toward the road. *Vampires walk among us. Hell, they always have and, according to Tommy-boy, they always will. And they'll keep feeding on us until the end of time. Amen.*

E loped across the dark road. He edged up carefully to the black iron gate, then ghosted through, sidling along the stone wall to the back of the house. He stepped carefully, avoiding any fallen leaves, gravel paths, or old gnarled roots. His heart raced a little, excited. He *loved* night-crawling. He paused beside a twisted old oak, sliding his hand along the rough bark.

Ronin had explained to him just how special he truly was—something E had known all along, that he had a special purpose; he hadn't been born just to mill among the sheep. He'd been born to *cull* them.

Hunching, E scurried across the untended yard to the nearest light-filled window, then squatted alongside it.

Tommy-boy had also told him that he'd been *programmed*; programmed, charted, graphed, and predicted, then turned loose.

E's jaw clenched. *Predicted? Programmed? Fuck, no!* Tommy-boy had then offered him the opportunity to return to the one who'd been stupid enough to think *she* controlled him. The opportunity to stand before her, shivs in hand.

The opportunity to say, *I'm home. Did you fucking foresee that?*

Stretching up, E turned his head and looked in the window. Glowing blue light from a thin monitor shimmered upon the face of a figure reclining in a black leather chair, goggled eyes aimed at the ceiling. Information flashed across the monitor with mind-numbing speed. Metal-capped fingers flicked and danced through the air. Data blurred across the monitor. The figure's waist-length dreads nearly brushed the floor, twisting like tentacles with his motion. A thin cable extended from the computer to the base of his skull, the jack hidden beneath his dreads.

Holy shit! Dante not only had a web-runner, he had a *vampire* web-runner. With his reflexes and—according to Tom-Tom, but E still wasn't convinced—superior brain power, this bloodsucker could rule the fucking world. Or burn out computers at an astonishing rate. E voted for the latter.

The blonde vamp from the club slipped in through the partially opened door and crouched beside the web-runner's chair. Her mini-skirt hugged her ass and black tights stretched along her legs. She touched the web-runner's arm and spoke, her words indistinct, although E could hear enough to know she spoke in French or Cajun or some goddamned thing. The only thing he heard clearly was the web-runner's name: Trey.

Trey continued to ignore the blonde, his fingers flickering through the air. Exasperation highlighted the blonde's face.

E pulled away from the window, then dropped down to the grass on his belly. Pretty stupid of ol' Trey to ignore such a hot chick. With her lovely, pale face and slender curves, she was a shiny in a world of dull. He collected shinies. Gina was shiny. Or had been. E pressed his hot face into the night-dewed grass, his heart pounding against his ribs so hard he half expected worms to vibrate up out of the soil.

With the scent of wild mint and wet grass in his nostrils, E bellied through the grass toward the next patch of yellow light, hoping to catch a glimpse of the single human in a houseful of bloodsuckers—his lovely Heather, the brightest of the sheep.

Tucking up against the house again, his back against the wood, E stretched up and peeked in the window. And lo, there *she* was, sitting at a kitchen table, hands wrapped around a coffee mug, gaze lost in the coffee's depths. Her red hair coiled past her shoulders. Her skin seemed almost luminous in the dim light, her lips flushed with deep color. Her violet sweater clung to her curves and her fitted black slacks revealed her trim, athletic figure.

E touched a finger to the window for a split second, then pulled it away. Was she thinking of him? Did he haunt her dreams? Did he lurk faceless in the ragged edges of nightmare, shivs gleaming? Did he make her pulse race?

Did she, like E, hope the chase would never end?

The kitchen door swung open and Dante stepped into the kitchen. Heather lifted her head and looked at him. He paused for a moment, meeting her gaze. She said something, her voice a low murmur. He answered, his voice also low and indistinct, then opened a cupboard and pulled down a black mug. As he poured coffee into it, Heather leaned forward against the table, speaking to him in an urgent but level voice.

Dante set the coffeepot back on its hot plate, then stood still, his head cocked as though listening.

E couldn't make out everything Heather said, but he did catch the words "danger," "stalked," and "serial killer." Proof that she was, indeed, thinking of him; a fact that would normally slather a sloppy grin across his face.

But not this time. E ducked down from the window, plastering himself against the house. His heart banged away in a frantic, disjointed rhythm. An image seared itself into his mind, an image that scorched and blackened his self-control:

Heather looks up, her gaze sliding the length of the fucking bloodsucker's lean, hard body, lingering for a long moment on his pale face. A smile curves her lips. She seems lit from within, vibrant, alive—then she composes her face, dims the light, and becomes Ms. FBI again.

Heather had fucking fallen for a goddamned bloodsucker.

E's muscles tightened. His knuckles rapped against his thighs. He stared into the night. A shadow suddenly divided the puddle of light on the grass, and E held his breath.

He just *knew* Dante stood at the window. Knew that he'd sensed something raging outside, right under his fucking nose.

The shadow vanished.

E sprang to his feet and ran. Thighs pumping. Breath burning. Adrenaline flooding. Heart hammering. The stone wall jittered closer with every step across the dew-slick grass.

Then a tree stepped into his path and E slammed into it. Pain grated his consciousness like cheese. The world whirled. His vision grayed. His legs, suddenly boneless, dumped him onto the ground. Nausea clutched his belly.

A deep voice rumbled, "He knew you'd spotted him." Ah. The big guy. Also the unexpected tree.

"I *felt* him," said a low voice—Dante. "I didn't see him."

From further away, Heather's voice, sharp and clear and protective. "Get away from him," she called. "He might be armed."

"Peeping Tom's assistant," Dante murmured. "So *this* is how he spends his evenings off. Figures."

Fingers brushed over his face. Little electric bursts sparked beneath his skin; sizzled blue and cool along his spine. The world whirled even faster. His vision darkened.

Hands patted him down—De Noir's, he thought. Fingers plucked. Once. Twice. Three times. Nah, nah. Didn't find 'em all.

"Are knives required equipment for a journalist's assistant?" De Noir rumbled.

"Depends on the journalist," Dante said.

The cheese-grating-world-spinning-nausea-lurching-head-aching suddenly torqued. E spun off the world into a starless void.

11

A BREATHING
CONNECTION

LUCIEN DUMPED THE UNCONSCIOUS assistant onto the sofa in the front room. A huge purple and blue lump had knotted up on the man's forehead. Dante knelt beside the sofa and searched through the man's pockets, his hands sure and fast.

Done this before, Heather mused. *Looks like more than once.*

Dante tossed a small ring of keys to the floor, along with a cell phone, several coins, and a tinfoil-wrapped stick of gum. Another sharp knife *tunk*ed onto the pile.

De Noir sucked in his breath. Heather glanced at him. He shook his head, jaw tight, clearly angry that he'd missed the weapon.

When she returned her attention to Dante, he held a slim black wallet in his hand. Flipping it open, he pulled up several credit spikes and a few bills.

"Elroy Jordan," Dante said. "According to his ID, anyway."

"Where from?" Heather said, kneeling beside him to read over his shoulder.

"New York."

Dante scooped up the assistant's cell phone. "Let's see who Elroy spoke to last," he said, punching the redial button.

Heather scanned Jordan's photo. Thinning hair, loopy grin—classic DMV shot.

Dante held up a finger, then a grin lit his face. "If it ain't Peeping Tom," he said into the cell. "I met your assistant, Elroy the Perv." Dante listened a moment, his grin widening.

Heather stared at his fangs, which she told herself had to be implants. Didn't they?

"I don't think so," Dante said, grin vanishing. "He's a little unconscious right now. Since he had the night off, he must be a voyeur on his own time, huh?"

Dante listened again, running a hand through his hair. He glanced at Heather and smiled. Then he laughed, a low, smooth sound full of dark humor.

"Don't worry. I'll turn him loose when he wakes up." Dante thumbed the end button. He tossed the cell back onto Jordan's pile of stuff.

"What's the journalist's name?" Heather asked.

"Ronin. Thomas Ronin."

Heather stared at Dante. "*Ronin?* That bastard's here?"

"Apparently you weren't impressed by his cool black business card either," Dante said, a smile tugging up one corner of his mouth. "What gives?"

"He turns up at crime scenes before we even have a chance to process them," Heather said, voice hard. "He takes pictures of the victims and sells them to tabloid rags or Internet death-porn sites. He's a good writer, I'll give him that, but he's always accusing the police and the Bureau of being incompetent. Or worse, claiming that we plant evidence and arrest the innocent. His articles always end with him knowing who the 'real' killer is."

Heather stood, brushing off the knees of her slacks. "Where'd you run into him?"

"On the street," Dante said, easing to his feet with a fluid, unconscious grace. "Said he wanted to interview me."

He slipped the driver's license from the wallet and tucked it into his back pocket. He tossed the wallet onto the pile of stuff on the floor.

"You didn't agree to that, did you?" Heather asked.

"Fuck, no," Dante snorted. Striding across the room, he pushed open the kitchen door and stepped inside.

Heather sighed and rubbed the bridge of her nose. *Great. Insult the man.*

A small crowd had gathered around them in the front room. Silver sprawled in the easy chair beside the sofa, his legs draped over the arm of the chair. Simone stood near the hall entrance beside a man with waist-length dreads, goggles pushed on top of his head. Simone nodded at Heather. "My brother, Trey," she said touching his arm.

"Trey," Heather murmured.

"Would someone be willing to keep an eye on this creep while I talk to Dante?" Her gaze skipped from Simone to De Noir.

"I will," De Noir said. "Just keep it short, Agent Wallace."

"Let me know the instant this guy comes to," Heather said. She walked from the room.

Dante sat at the kitchen table, coffee mug and a bottle of brandy in front of him.

"Look," Heather said. "I know you don't give a lot of interviews to the music mags and I didn't mean to question your integrity, I—"

"Forget it," Dante said, shrugging. "I have."

Heather sat at the table across from him. Steam curled up from her cup and she suspected that Dante might've reheated her coffee in the microwave. She smiled.

"So . . . you said that I'm being stalked by a . . . *serial* killer?" Dante splashed brandy into his coffee cup. He glanced at Heather and lifted the bottle.

She shook her head. "I believe so. Somewhere along the line he fixated on you. Maybe he's a fan."

Heather took a sip of the cream-and-sugared chicory coffee. She studied Dante as he stirred brandy into his mug, noting the tension in his shoulders. He seemed very aware that she was watching him and his expression was guarded.

"Did you know Daniel Spurrell?" she asked. "The victim from the pizza parlor's courtyard," she clarified when Dante frowned.

"That his name? Daniel?" Dante shook his head. "I'd seen him at the club and he'd talked to me about Inferno's last album, but I didn't know him."

"How long had you known Gina?"

Dante looked away. His fingers squeezed the coffee cup. "*Had* known? I can't get used to thinking of her in past tense."

"I know this is difficult, but I have to ask."

Trailing his fingers through his hair, Dante leaned back in his chair, tipping it. "We'd been hanging out for . . . oh . . . maybe six months or so." He glanced up. "I suck at dates and times. Always have."

"So . . . you and Gina were an item? A couple?"

Dante took a long swallow of the brandy-laced coffee. "No. We were friends. She has . . . *had*—fuck!—a boyfriend."

"Does the phrase 'Wake Up S' mean anything to you?"

Dante's muscles tensed and his hands locked around his cup. He shut his eyes. "No," he whispered.

Heather set her coffee cup on the table. She *hated* this part, poking and prodding the grief, stirring up the pain. She knew just how much it hurt when you realized a loved one had been murdered. Hadn't died in their sleep or even in a tragic car accident. They'd been *murdered*, their life deliberately stolen, and they were never, ever coming back.

Just like her mother.

She reached across the table for Dante's hand. He glanced

up and she froze, her breath caught in her throat. She felt drawn into his dark eyes like blood into a needle. Heart fluttering hummingbird fast, Heather wrenched her gaze away and pulled her hand back to her coffee cup, wrapped her shaking fingers around it.

What *was* it about him? He was gorgeous, sure, but she was no schoolgirl; in fact, she was pretty sure she was a handful of years older than him. Why the hell did he leave her tongue-tied and flustered?

Heather reached for the brandy. Dante handed it to her. His fingers brushed against hers and an electric tingle zipped from Heather's hand to her belly. She nearly dropped the bottle.

"You mentioned that Gina had a boyfriend," Heather said, carefully pouring a little brandy into her coffee. "Do you think *he* . . . what's his name? . . . could've—"

"Fuck, no! Jay loves . . . loved her."

Heather looked up from her cup and set the bottle of brandy down on the table. Dante's expression remained guarded and his body language—averted gaze, white-knuckled grip on his mug—revealed his tension.

Softening her voice, Heather continued, "Maybe out of jealousy? You *were* spending time with *his* girlfriend."

"Nothing to be jealous of." Dante met Heather's gaze. "He was always included."

"In everything?"

"Everything. Yeah."

Scooting back his chair, Dante stood. He walked to the counter, gripped the edge.

Heather swiveled in her chair. "Where can I find Jay? What's his last name?"

"As far as I know Jay's missing," Dante said. He turned around, his back to the counter, arms crossed over his chest. "He left with Gina last night. I plan to look for him. As soon as we're done here."

"He *left* with her? How do you know he's not dead? Or even the killer? Do you need me to spell this out for you?" Heather said, finger stabbing the table for emphasis. "A killer is studying you. He knows who is close to you. Give me Jay's last name."

Dante held her gaze, but said nothing. Heather sighed. Good-looking, sexy, but pigheaded. "*You* can't go looking for him. Let me help. I can get cops—"

"Fuck the cops."

"I've tracked this psycho for three years," she said, voice low, "and you're my only breathing connection to him."

Dante stepped beside the table. He reached for the brandy. As his fingers wrapped around the brandy bottle's neck, Heather locked a hand around his wrist. His skin was velvet-smooth and warm. "I want to keep you that way," she said. "So you're stuck with me for the time being."

Dante looked at her, his face less guarded, his eyes thoughtful, serious.

"You trusted me at the club this morning," she said. "What's different now?"

Dante gently pulled free of her hold. Bottle in hand, he leaned against the counter. Light sparked from the hoops in his ears. "Shit, I don't know. Everything. Nothing. What do I call you, anyway? Special Agent Wallace? Lady Law? Mistress? What?"

Scooting her chair back on the linoleum, Heather stood and joined him at the counter, hands braced behind her. "I have a feeling you're not half the asshole you pretend to be."

A brief smile touched Dante's lips. "How accurate are your feelings?" He took another quick drink from the brandy bottle.

"Good enough," Heather replied. "Let's do first names, since that's the only name I have for you. Mine's Heather."

"Fair enough. Heather."

"You know, I can't find any legal surname for you," she said, holding Dante's gaze. "Just one tacked on from your foster family in Lafayette—Prejean. Daniel Spurrell was from Lafayette, too."

Dante remained silent, expression wary, muscles tight.

"You have a local rap sheet," Heather continued. She knew she was pushing him, but maybe the reason for the messages rested in Dante's unrecorded past. "Aside from a sealed juvenile record, I can't find *anything* on you—no driver's license, no social security number, no credit history—nothing. Why is that?"

Dante winced and touched a hand to his temple. Sweat suddenly beaded his forehead. Heather touched his shoulder, alarmed. *Another* migraine? Triggered by her questions? How was that possible?

"Hey. You okay?"

Dante stumbled away from her, then leaned against the refrigerator, his body tensed, almost shaking with strain. "If your psycho wants me," he said, voice ragged, "let him have me."

"Are you nuts?" Heather stepped toward him. "You need to be placed in protective custody."

"Fuck that. Bait the hook, okay? Bait the hook. I'm nightkind, remember?"

The bottle of brandy slipped from Dante's fingers and shattered on the floor. Amber liquid sprayed the cabinets and Heather's feet. Dante dropped to his knees, one hand still at his temple, the other braced against the refrigerator. Racing around in front of him, Heather knelt and grabbed his shoulders. Blood trickled from his nose. His eyes rolled up white.

The kitchen door *whang*ed open, hitting the wall and punching a hole in the plaster as De Noir flew into the room.

Dante slumped in Heather's grasp, head lolling. She sat down hard on the linoleum, holding him tight, her pulse roaring in her ears. Blood streamed from his nose and spattered on her arms, her hands, her trousers.

De Noir reached for Dante, something close to fear on his face.

12

AN UNREMEMBERED PAST

D ANTE IN HIS ARMS, De Noir walked with innate grace across the darkened bedroom, stepping around and over the CD cases, clothes and books cluttering the floor. The bed, a futon, was unmade and rumpled, the bedding and sheets all black—or maybe dark blue, Heather thought, following De Noir into the room.

He knelt beside the bed and eased Dante onto the sheets, then tipped Dante's head back against the pillows and wiped at the blood trickling from his nose with a dish towel he'd scooped up in the kitchen. Moonlight softened De Noir's angular features, changed his grim expression to one of sorrow.

Heather tilted her head, studying De Noir as he tended to Dante, watched his large hand skim delicately against Dante's hair, brushing it back from his face. What *was* it between them?

"Is he going to be all right?" she asked. "Does he have medication for his headaches? A doctor?"

"All he needs is rest," De Noir said.

"Didcha ask him about his past?" a voice said from the doorway. "That's usually when he gets 'em real bad like this."

Heather glanced over at Silver. He leaned in the doorway, one foot braced on the threshold behind him, his silver eyes gleaming in the moonlight.

"I only asked a few basic questions," Heather said.

"Dante was raised by the State of Louisiana, Agent Wallace," De Noir murmured. He held out the bloodied dish towel.

"Yeah, yeah," Silver muttered. Uncoiling from the doorway, he slouched into the room and took the dish towel. Then he was gone.

Heather blinked, startled. Superhuman speed seemed to be a common thing in this household. Taking a deep breath, she refocused on De Noir.

"Yes, I know," she said. "He was raised in a foster home by the Prejeans."

Lucien shook his head. "That was only the *last* one. He was shuffled from foster home to foster home for years."

Heather went still. De Noir had just given her information that hadn't been in Dante's file. Why had only the last foster home been listed?

"The past is something Dante does not remember well," De Noir said quietly. "And perhaps it's best that way." He held out his hand.

A cool rush of air blew past Heather, fluttering her hair. Silver appeared in front of her and placed the dampened dish towel in De Noir's waiting hand. With a quick, sharp-toothed grin, the boy disappeared again.

"Maybe he *needs* to remember," Heather said. "Maybe that's what causes the migraines."

"No," De Noir whispered. He daubed at the slowing trickle of blood beneath Dante's nose with the damp towel. "No."

A sudden pang of sympathy sliced through Heather's weariness and she realized in that moment that De Noir loved Dante, and that it was *regret* that shadowed his face and roughened his voice.

Regret. For what? An unremembered past that needed to remain unremembered? No matter the cost?

"Dante told me he was a vampire," she said.

De Noir closed his eyes. A muscle in his jaw jumped. "Do you believe vampires exist, Agent Wallace?"

"No. But I've got a feeling Dante does."

De Noir's eyes opened. Gold light flecked his eyes. "Indeed," he murmured. He unbuckled Dante's boots, then tugged them off his feet. Each hit the floor with a dull thud.

"He thinks he's invulnerable and that's gonna get him killed," Heather said, crossing to the futon.

De Noir said nothing. The hand at Dante's temple trailed back through his tousled black hair, then away. De Noir unfolded from the floor and stood.

"I won't let that happen," De Noir said. He turned away from her.

She stared at him, stunned by his dismissive attitude. Stepping forward, she seized De Noir's forearm. It felt hard and cool as marble beneath her fingers. But fire flared within her, tightening her muscles.

"There's a man out there who wants . . . who's looking *forward* to torturing him," she said, voice low and hard. "Rape. Mutilate. Kill. It's not a thing you can control. *You* don't have a say in it." She released his arm.

De Noir stood still for a long moment, tendrils of his long hair snaking into the air. Barely visible blue light sparked around his body. Heather's skin tingled. The sharp smell of ozone cut through the air. Dante stirred on the futon, suddenly restless, pale face troubled. Silver straightened in the doorway, gleaming eyes wary.

Then, like a sudden clap of thunder or an implosion sucking all the air from the room, it was gone. No blue light. No snaky hair. Just a tall man standing motionless beside a bed. Étienne's voice whispered through Heather's memory: *Fallen.*

"I won't let it happen," De Noir said again. Bending, he pulled the blankets up over Dante, then sat on the futon's edge. He touched a hand to Dante's temple.

"Good night, Agent Wallace," De Noir rumbled.

Heather stalked from the room, brushing past Silver, her body as tight as her fists. She'd told Dante she'd stick with him. She meant it. De Noir could cram his good night up his ass. She trotted down the stairs, one hand gliding along the polished wood banister.

When Heather walked into the front room, Simone looked up from the easy chair, a book in her lap. Jordan was still sprawled on the sofa, one hand dangling on the floor, his mouth slightly open.

"Thank you for keeping an eye on him," Heather said.

Simone closed her book, then stood. "I've been looking for time to read," she said with a shrug. "How's Dante?"

Heather shook her head. "He's out cold, but at least the nosebleed stopped. De Noir seems to think all he needs is rest."

"Ah," Simone breathed. Concern tightened her face. "It's not rest he needs," she murmured. She walked toward the hall.

"How long have you known Dante?" Heather asked.

"Three, four years."

"Are his headaches getting worse?"

Simone paused at the threshold. "*Oui.* Why do you ask?" She glanced over her shoulder, her face watchful and closed.

"He needs help—"

"*We* will help him," Simone said. "*You* can't. He told you true, *m'selle.* He's nightkind." Simone walked from the room.

Sighing, Heather sank into the chair opposite the sofa and buried her face in her hands. They were all mad. Delusional.

Or they were all vampires. How would she even write that up on a report?

The subject refuses to submit to protective custody because he's a vampire. When I informed the subject that serial killers are quite capable of pounding a stake through his heart, he laughed. "Bait the hook," he said.

Heather's hands dropped from her face. She stared at the floor, pulse racing. *Bait the hook.* Vampire or not—and she wasn't ready to admit to anything but the *possibility*—would it work? After three years, could she lure the bastard in? Reel him in and net him? If it worked . . .

And if it didn't work? If her perp wiggled through the net with Dante in his jaws? She rose to her feet and headed for the kitchen. She pushed the door open, then paused, her gaze on the brandy-and-blood spattered floor. Dante's strained voice curled through her memory: *Let him have me.*

What if her bad guy believed Dante was a vampire?

Most of Inferno's fan sites seemed to adhere to that belief. Interviewers asked and Dante walked away, the question unanswered.

Wake up. Wake up S.

What did *he* want Dante to wake up to? And what was *S*—the first letter of Dante's true surname? Did he think it time Dante lived up to his vampiric reputation? Did he want the answer the interviewers never received?

Edging around the blood stains out of habit, Heather hurried to the table and her purse. She pulled out her cell phone. As she returned to the living room, she flipped the cell open. No bars. And her charger was at the hotel. Maybe someone here had a charger she could use—

Her gaze fell on the snoozing Jordan's cell phone on the floor beside his wallet. Crossing to it, she bent and scooped the cell phone up. Four bars. She plopped back into the chair and tapped in Collins's number.

Collins picked up on the second ring. "Collins," he said, voice curt. "Who's this?" Heather realized that his phone would've IDed the incoming call as Elroy Jordan.

"Collins, it's Wallace. I had to borrow a phone."

"Goddamn, Wallace," he replied, relief evident in his voice. "I've been trying to reach you—"

"Listen," Heather bulldozed right over the detective's words, eager to share her discoveries. "I found Dante Prejean and I'm staying close to him in case our perp puts in an appearance."

"But—"

"No, listen, did you go to Lafayette and talk to the Prejeans—get some history on Dante? Did the Prejeans and the Spurrells ever come into contact with each other?"

"Didn't need to," Collins said. "Our perp won't be targeting anyone ever again."

"What?" Heather sat up straight.

"I take it you haven't talked to your supervisor," Collins said. "The bastard was nailed in Pensacola."

"Pensacola?" Heather repeated. "That's impossible. He's here. At least he was this morning when he murdered—"

"Traveling man, Wallace," Collins said. "That's why he was called the Cross-Country Killer, right?"

"Right, right. You said he'd been nailed. Do you mean as in dead?"

"Yeah. Another agent happened to catch him in the act." Collins paused a moment, paper rustled in the background. "Victim didn't make it, though."

"Was there another message?"

More paper rustling. "No, but he never finished, ya know?"

Dead. And in Florida. How could she have been so *wrong*? Her thoughts spun—Lafayette, anarchy, Club Hell, Dante—all of the connections felt true.

"Are they positive it's him? I mean, they wouldn't have the all the lab work back yet and—"

"I'm flying to Pensacola in the morning," Collins said. "I figured you'd want to go too, so I reserved a seat for you."

Heather smiled. "Good man," she murmured. "I'll meet you at the airport. What time?"

"Eight in the a.m., sunshine," Collins said. "See you there." He ended the call.

Heather thumbed the cell off, then switched it back on. Punching in more numbers, she called Stearns. No answer. Just voice mail. Maybe the damned caller ID had screwed her again. "It's Wallace, sir," she said after the beep. "I'm heading to Pensacola in the morning to check out the dead suspect and look over their evidence. I'll be in touch soon after."

Heather slumped down in the chair, placing the cell on the armrest. She ran a hand through her hair. She wanted to tell Dante the turn of events. She also wanted to have a little chat with Mr. Jordan about the dangers of window-peeping for prime tabloid shots.

She closed her eyes. Weariness weighed her down like concrete overshoes. Pensacola. After murdering Gina shortly before dawn? Killing another woman the same day?

Jack the Ripper had done two in one night—a double event— not even an hour apart. Jack had never been caught—at least officially.

She strongly suspected that the Cross-Country Killer hadn't been caught either. Officially or otherwise.

Heather sank into a black ocean, her concrete overshoes dragging her to the bottom. Somewhere in the darkness, Leigh Stanz sang, his husky voice rippling beneath the waves.

I long to drift like an empty boat on a calm sea / I don't need light / I don't fear darkness . . .

You should, Heather thought, sinking and sinking and sinking—

She staggers along the highway's edge, thumb out, peering into the darkness. Her car won't start and she's left it in the tavern parking lot. She really has to get home. She only stopped in for a few drinks while out on errands. The kids were at soccer practice or guitar lessons or Scouts and she had a few moments to herself.

The next thing she knows, it's dark and the moon's high in the sky.

Her new friends try to talk her into staying and, for a moment, she considers it. But she pulls free of her friends' beseeching hands and escapes into the chilly October night. She can't find her cell phone. Did she leave it at work? In the tavern?

She abandons the car and decides to thumb a ride home. She stumbles, her heel catching on the asphalt's ragged edge. She giggles. Good thing she isn't driving. Point in her favor. She licks the tip of a finger and strokes an imaginary line in the air. Sliding off her shoe, she peers at the heel.

Headlights pierce the night. She sticks out her shoe instead of her thumb, cocking her weight onto one hip and smiling. The car pulls over, tires crunching on gravel, the muffler streaming a plume of exhaust, the heady smell of gasoline in the air.

She wobbles as she tries to put her shoe back on. She hops backward before sprawling onto her ass. She throws her head back and laughs. Good thing she isn't walking the line for a cop. Another point in her favor. She draws another imaginary line in the air. Slipping off her other shoe, she climbs to her feet, stumbling only a little. She's brushing the dirt off her hind end when the driver's door opens.

A man slips out of the purring car. Something gleams in his hand.

Dante stood in the doorway, hands braced against either side of the threshold. Wallace—*Heather*—slept slumped in the easy chair, her head turned to the left. Her red hair tumbled across her cheek, edged her half-parted lips. Her breathing was slow and easy. Candlelight flickered orange and gold across her face.

Beautiful, he thought. Easy to forget she was a cop.

He padded barefoot into the front room. Scooping a folded blanket up from the back of the empty sofa, he shook it out, then spread it over her. His bracelets clinked against each other with the movement, but she didn't stir.

Dante sat cross-legged in front of the chair. She'd stood up for him—in front of other cops. Had even tackled the chickenshit bastard with the gun. *Why would she stand up for me? What gives?* He breathed in her fresh rain scent, detecting a hint of lilac and sage laced beneath. He listened to the deep, steady beat of her heart.

Asleep, she looked even younger than the twenty-eight or thirty years he pegged her at. Asleep, curled and warm, she wasn't a cop or an FBI agent, but a woman with heart; a woman with steel for a spine. A woman, so far, true to her word.

Trust me. I'm asking you to trust me.

How many times had he heard those words? Spoken by mortals and nightkind alike, the words empty, void: *Trust me.*

But not with Heather. He'd looked into her and she'd met his gaze, her own open and steady, hiding nothing. For a moment, as he'd looked into her blue eyes, the voices raging inside had hushed.

And so he'd put his hands behind his back and let her handcuff him.

The ceiling creaked. Lucien stirred on his rooftop perch, watching the night. Listening to a rhythm that Dante heard at times, felt it pulsing in sync with the blood in his veins.

Heather shifted in the chair, a slight frown on her lips. Her heart rate picked up speed. Bad dream? Rising to his knees, Dante leaned in and brushed her hair back from her face. Adrenaline spiked her scent. Her brows drew together, face troubled, maybe scared. Beads of sweat sprang up along her hairline.

"Heather." Dante gently shook her shoulder. "Heather, wake up."

She jerked awake, eyes wide. She sat bolt upright, knocking Dante's hand aside, the blanket sliding from her lap and puddling on the floor. She brought up both hands together as though she held her gun.

"Don't," she whispered. "Don't get in the car. . . ."

"Hey," Dante said. "It's okay."

At the sound of his voice, Heather shuddered, then leaned forward, elbows to knees, head to hands. She drew in a long breath. The frantic pounding of her heart gradually slowed.

After a moment, she lowered her hands. Her face was night-kind-white, her eyes dilated and rimmed with brilliant blue.

"*T'est blême comme un mort.*" Dante said. "Nightmare?"

Heather glanced at him. Her heart double-thumped. Her breath caught in her throat. Dante tensed, his fingers curving in toward his palms. He almost looked away, not wanting to see the frustrating mix of adoration, lust, and wonder that lit the eyes of most who looked at him. But she held his gaze, her heart calming, her breathing evening out. She looked *in*.

"Yes," she whispered. "Nightmare."

"I know about nightmares."

Heather tilted her head and looked at him intently. "I bet you do," she said. "How's your head?" She touched a finger to her own temple.

"I'm good," he murmured, shrugging.

Heather glanced about the room, her gaze stopping at the sofa. "Where is he?" she said, jumping to her feet.

"Peeping Tom's perv assistant?" Dante asked, looking up at her. She nodded. "He was gone when I came downstairs."

"So are his things," she said. "The stuff you took from his pockets."

Heather searched the chair she'd been sleeping in, sliding her hands between the cushion and the chair, kneeling to look underneath. "So's his cell phone," she said, pushing her hair back from her face. Color flushed her cheeks. "I had it on the arm of the chair."

Dante caught her meaning. "So he stood over you while you slept."

Lips pressed together, Heather nodded. Frustration and renewed weariness tightened her face. "I was going to recommend that he find a less sleazy boss, but . . ."

"*Bon à rien*, both of 'em," Dante said, standing. "A perfect match."

Heather smiled, then it faded from her lips. Her mind was

unshielded, wide open, and he could go in and snag every single thought—if he wanted.

But if someone were to go into *his* mind unwelcomed—force their way in or seduce their way in—and take what *they* wanted . . . he tensed. He had no desire to look into Heather's unguarded mind.

"I need to talk to you," she said. "Can we go somewhere private?"

Dante nodded. "Sure."

"Looks like you're recovering from that cooperation problem."

He snorted. "Keep thinking that."

She smiled again.

Dante led Heather out of the front room and down the hall to his studio. Just as he opened the door, Trey rushed out of the web room, goggles swinging from his hand. He stopped in front of Dante, reeking of adrenaline.

Sudden fear spiked into Dante when he saw the look on Trey's face.

"Bad news, *mon ami*," Trey said, his voice even more Cajun-spiced than his sister's. "They pulled Jay from the river. Throat slit."

Dante leaned against the wall, stunned. "Fuck," he whispered.

"That's not all," Trey said. He hesitated, his gaze on Dante, his mind fluttering against Dante's shields.

"I'm okay," Dante said.

Trey nodded, but he looked unhappy. He swallowed. "The cops think you're good for both murders."

HEATHER STEPPED BACK WHEN Dante, dark eyes blazing, whirled and punched his fist through the wall. Plaster and dry-wall tumbled to the floor in chunks and ragged pieces.

"Did you hack into the NOPD's system?" she asked Trey.

He shrugged, then nodded. *"Oui."*

Like she'd been conjured, Simone suddenly appeared beside her brother, her troubled gaze on Dante. Above them all, the ceiling creaked and groaned, then fell silent. Heather heard what sounded like the powerful rush of wings. Very large wings.

She looked at Dante. He stood motionless, every muscle taut, his fist still inside the hole he'd punched, his other hand braced against the wall. Head bowed, face veiled by his black hair, he seemed to vibrate with rage.

"I'm sorry about Jay." Heather touched his shoulder. "They've got nothing. You didn't do it. And they know it. That's what I want to talk to you about."

A blizzard of plaster fell to the floor when Dante pulled his fist free of the wall. Lifting his head and tossing back his hair, he looked at her. Fury and anguish mingled within his dark eyes. His muscles flexed beneath her fingers. She stared into his eyes, unable to look away, drawn in and sucked down, caught in a whirlpool of emotion.

Dante looked *into* her, his dark gleaming gaze as warm as a wanted caress. Releasing him, she looked down, face burning.

"Then talk to me," he said.

The front door opened, then clicked shut. De Noir. "Alone," Heather said, stepping into the room he'd led her to. Dante followed, closing the door behind him.

Heather's gaze skipped around the room—*studio*, she amended. Several different keyboards, a synthesizer, a mixing board, amps, computer, and monitor crowded the space. A black guitar was propped in one corner. A half-empty bottle of French absinthe stood on the computer table surrounded by headphones, scattered papers, and lyric sheets.

Her gaze fixed on the opposite wall. Spray-painted on the wall in the color of dried blood was the anarchy symbol.

The image of the symbol scorched into Daniel Spurrell's

flesh flared to life in Heather's mind. The killer—whether it was the CCK or not—was trying to prove that he and Dante were kindred souls sharing the same beliefs. But instead of painting the symbol on walls, buildings or squad cars, the killer etched it into unwilling flesh.

Gina's murder was meant as a slap in the face to Dante. A challenge. *Look how far I'm willing to go. Can you top this? Have you got the guts to live up to that symbol?* If the killer now felt *superior* to Dante, if he felt like *he* was in control, then it meant he'd also feel comfortable enough—strong enough—to claim Dante and make him his own.

But, if he was dead . . . then, no threat. Wrenching her gaze away from the wall, Heather glanced at her watch. 4:34 a.m. Pushing her hair back from her face, she turned to face Dante.

"I found out a few hours ago that our suspect's been killed in Pensacola," she said. "I don't understand it, but—"

"You don't think it's him, do you?"

"I'm on my way to Florida to find out."

Dante stepped past Heather, his body brushing against hers. "You don't know what he looks like," Dante said, picking up a pair of shades from the computer console. He slid them on. "How will—"

"I've studied his . . . *work* . . . for three years," she said. "I'll know."

Dante stepped closer. "Is *that* what you dream of?"

Caught off guard, Heather looked away. *Too close. Way too close.* Lifting her head, she met Dante's shaded gaze. "What does that anarchy symbol mean to you?"

Dante shrugged. "Besides a general 'fuck you' to society?"

Heather shook her head. "You can do better than that."

Dante lifted his shades. Streaks of red slashed his dark irises. His gaze, intense, direct, and dead serious, locked with hers. "Okay then. Rage. Firestorm. Truth."

"Truth?"

"Yeah. Freedom is the result of rage."

Heather stared at him, throat tight. Spoken like a true survivor of any state-run foster home system. Spoken with intelligence and conviction. And that planted a seed of doubt in her belly.

What had created that rage? Fueled it?

Dante lowered the shades back over his eyes. "So now what?"

She sighed, trailing a hand through her hair. "I want you to play it safe until you hear from me."

A smile quirked up one corner of Dante's mouth. "That'd be a first."

"Try," Heather said. "I'd like you to keep breathing." Her gaze shifted to the anarchy symbol behind him. For one heartbeat, he was a part of the symbol—a sharp black dagger piercing the heart of chaos, night-wrapped and unpredictable.

No way the killer would've left New Orleans without Dante dead or beside him. Whoever lay on that tray in the Pensacola morgue wasn't her perp. But she had to be sure. Collins would be expecting her at the airport and she still had to stop at her hotel.

"Walk with me," she said, turning and opening the studio door.

She felt Dante behind her in the hall; his silence unnerved her, even with bare feet and carpet, he should've made *some* sound.

"What happens if it ain't your guy in Pensacola?"

"Then I'll be back."

HEATHER UNLOCKED THE SUBARU, then slid inside. Starting the engine, she turned the defroster and heater up to high. Dante stood beside the open driver's side window, barefoot in the late-February chill, sunglasses perched on top his head.

He's got to be cold. Heather thought. *I know I'd be freezing.*

"I'll call you as soon as I know something," she said.

Dante bent down and held out a piece of paper. Heather took it, pulling it free from between his fingers. She glanced at it. Phone numbers. Written with a lefty's slant; one marked CLUB, one marked HOME. She looked up at him.

Arms folded over his chest, Dante shrugged. "In case," he said. His gaze skipped past her. "That's my jacket."

"Huh?" Heather shifted in her seat and glanced in the direction he was looking. Dante's leather jacket was crumpled in the passenger seat. "Oh! Yes." She picked up the jacket, then passed it through the window to Dante. "I've been holding it since you were arrested."

Dante shrugged on the jacket. Metal jingled. *"Merci,"* he said. "Did you go through the pockets?"

Heather smiled. "What do you think?"

"I think . . ." He paused and looked at her for a moment. "Yeah. I know *I* would."

Heather's smile widened. "You seem pretty experienced in rifling pockets."

He grinned, and Heather caught a flash of slender, curving canines. He was either delusional or undead, so why did he make her feel like a teenager swooning over her first sullen and leather-jacketed bad boy?

"Look, when this is over . . ."

"Yeah?" Dante leaned in even closer. Faint green light from the dash streaked the steel ring on his bondage collar.

She could smell him, crisp autumn leaves and dark earth—a warm bed, the scent of sex. Her cheeks burned as heat fluttered through her belly. "Uh . . . I'll call you as soon as I know anything." Forcing a smile onto her lips, she rolled up the window.

He straightened, then backed up a pace as she stepped on the gas.

She followed the curving driveway carefully, passing the van and the MG. The Harley was gone. *I was going to ask if I could see him again.* So much for objectivity. So much for professionalism. She glanced into the rearview mirror. Dante still stood in the driveway, watching as she drove away. A breeze blew strands of hair across his night-shadowed face.

A figure suddenly appeared beside Dante. Heather hit the brakes. The Subaru screeched to a stop. The red glow from her taillights wasn't enough to see well by, and she was on the verge of throwing the car into reverse or stepping out and drawing her .38, when Dante slipped his arm around the other figure's shoulders.

A cloud drifted free of the moon. Southern-winter moonlight frosted the trees, the iron gates, the looming mansion, and Silver's gel- spiked hair and shining silver eyes. Moonlight gilded the boy's smile. He snuggled an arm around Dante's waist.

Releasing her breath, Heather wrenched her gaze away from the rearview. Too much adrenaline and too little sleep had left her feeling shaky and weak-limbed. She stepped on the gas and drove through the opened gates.

Maybe she'd baited the hook simply by leaving.

In that bleak moment, she truly wished Dante *was* a vampire.

Maybe then he'd have a chance of surviving if the killer took the bait.

13

KEEPSAKES

Ronin unlocked the padlock looped through the metal door's hasp. The door screeched when he yanked it open, the sound reverberating through the empty warehouse. He flicked on the light switch beside the door and stepped inside.

Huddled on the cot, arms wrapped around his legs, the shivering youth looked up, blinking in the sudden harsh light. The fluorescent overheads buzzed, marring the silence. At the sight of Ronin, the youth scooted into the corner, his back to the wall.

Smiling, Ronin shook his head. "It's not me you need to fear," he said. "It's my companion—the one who brought you here. Do you remember him?"

The boy shook his head, kept his eyeliner-smudged gaze on Ronin. He pressed himself harder against the wall, like he could seep into it and vanish. Ronin's smile widened. The boy's gaze locked onto his revealed fangs. He went still.

Ronin sat on the edge of the cot. The youth's fast-pounding heart intrigued him. He smelled the adrenaline-laden blood pulsing hot through his veins. He glanced at the youth's lace-edged throat. An iridescent bat tattoo nestled at its hollow. How often had Dante kissed that white flesh? Pierced it with his fangs? Drank the dark blood that poured through those veins?

Leaning over, Ronin brushed a strand of blond hair from the boy's face. The boy's muscles—knotted and tensed—trembled. His green eyes never left Ronin's face.

"I hear your every thought, boy," Ronin said. "You might as well speak them."

The youth closed his eyes for a moment. He drew in a deep breath, trying to calm himself and order his mind, but he remained pressed up against the concrete wall, his heart hammering against his ribs.

"Let me help you," Ronin said. "Gina's dead. Yes, I know you have Dante's mark. And you *will* die at the hands of a serial killer—*if* I leave you here."

The boy turned his face to one side as though sucker punched by the blunt words.

"Oh, and as for *why* all this is happening, call it destiny."

"I don't believe you," the youth said, voice low and strained. Opening his eyes, he turned to face Ronin. "Gina's not dead. Dante'd find her, he—"

"He *did* find her," Ronin said, pleased by the sudden spark of fire lighting the boy's eyes. "*After* my companion had finished with her."

The youth blinked away unshed tears. Swallowed. "You're full of shit."

Seizing the boy's slender throat with one hand, Ronin jerked him away from the wall and against himself. "Am I?" he whispered. "Dante's looking for *you*, now. It's up to you whether he finds you *before* my companion returns or *after*."

The youth struggled to get free, pulling at Ronin's wrist with one hand while shoving against Ronin's chest with the other. Eyes half-closed, Ronin listened to the youth's triple-timing heart. Smelled anger, fear, and desperation in equal measures. His blood would be a heady brew of natural pheromones.

"Before or after," Ronin said. He looked into the boy's emotion-dilated green eyes. "It's up to you."

The youth stopped struggling. He went still once again, kneeling on the cot. His gaze turned inward. For a moment, Ronin couldn't hear him. Not a whisper of thought, not a word or image. A barrier had dropped between them, and the only sound disturbing the silence was the pulsing of their hearts.

With a shudder, the boy met Ronin's gaze. "Before," he said.

"Wise choice."

Grasping a handful of blond hair, Ronin tugged the boy's head back and sank his fangs into his throat.

E STEPPED INTO THE darkened house, closing and locking the door behind him. He glanced around the room. A bottle of Wild Turkey bourbon stood on the side table beside the La-Z-Boy, a tumbler beside it. The ashtray held a single cigarette butt. E sniffed. Grimaced. The air reeked of that towelhead crap Ronin liked to smoke.

The Camaro was gone. And so was Tommy-boy.

Just as well. He was in no mood to put up with the bloodsucker's anal-retentive bullshit. He touched the knot on his forehead. Pain radiated out from beneath his finger and E jerked his hand away. His grin faded. If the Big Guy wasn't made of stone, he might as well be. Kee-rist!

E crossed the room, then shuffled down the hall to his bedroom. Maybe some Vicodin and a little whiskey would ease the pain. Pushing open the door, he stepped into his room. He plunked down on the edge of the unmade bed. His head throbbed. His stomach clenched in uneasy sympathy.

E pulled open the nightstand drawer and rummaged through the contents—several red and white packages of Marlboros, a

lighter, a nudie pen—tip her upside down and watch her strip!—
until his fingers latched around the Baggie of pills.

E unzipped it, his hands shaking a little, and poured the pills
onto the nightstand. Peach, old-lady blue, and yellow, the pills
bounced and tumbled across the wood.

E tossed five or six of them down his throat. He picked up the
whiskey bottle from the nightstand and chased the pills down
with a long swallow of gut-burning Canadian Hunter. Nausea
rolled through him. Shaking again, E set the bottle on the floor
beside the bed, then stretched out on the mattress. He stared
into the darkness, waiting for the pills to kick in.

Closing his eyes, E snuggled his face into the pillow. He
smelled Gina, dark cherries and sweet sex. He'd hidden her
stocking inside the pillowcase. He loved keepsakes, little things
that said, *Remember when?* He touched his right front jeans
pocket, his fingers tracing the smooth rectangular shape of his
newest keepsake.

*He wakes in a vampire's house, sprawled on a vampire's sofa. He
slits his eyes open. Candlelight flickers, etching wavering shadows on the
wall. Only the steady tick-tock of a pendulum clock disturbs the silence.*

*Head aching, he rolls onto his side. His gaze falls on the figure curled
into an easy chair across from him.*

*He wonders if she's faking, playing with him, watching him from
beneath long, black lashes. But her deep, even breathing convinces him
that she's asleep. He's never been this close to her—not even when peeking
through windows.*

If he touches her, what'll happen?

*His lovely Heather, his very own stalker, sleeps in his presence. Allow-
ing herself to be vulnerable before a god.*

*He watches her for several minutes, drinking in the color of her hair,
the curve of her cheek, the parted lips.*

*Above him, the ceiling creaks once. He suddenly remembers where
he is—in a house full of bloodsuckers. The warm, golden godlike feeling
evaporates.*

Rolling to his feet, he crosses the short distance to the easy chair, practically on tiptoe, his gaze locked on Heather—his beacon. He tries not to think of what else walks soundlessly through the house.

He bends over Heather until his breath ruffles her hair. He touches a strand and it slides like silk between his fingers. He picks up his cell phone from the arm of the chair. Tilting his head, he regards Heather for a moment. What message is she trying to send him by setting his phone out?

The ceiling creaks again. He backs away from the chair, from the woman nestled between its arms. Reluctant, he turns away. Piled on the floor beside the sofa are his wallet and shivs and every little thing he kept in his pockets.

He squats and gathers up his belongings. When he stands again, he finds himself walking into the kitchen. A voice in his mind tells him he's a fucking idiot, get out, get out, get out!, but it's too late, really, he's already claiming keepsakes.

Heather's purse and trenchcoat are draped over the back of a chair. He searches both until he finds what he wants, then he takes it. His gaze skips around the kitchen, looking for some trace of Dante—some reminder of the hot, hot, hot little vampire who'd earned looks of lust from his Heather. A token from his Bad Seed bro.

Finally, he seizes the black coffee mug and slips out of the kitchen.

He pauses beside the easy chair, a shiv sliding without thought into his hand. Heart pounding, he forces himself away from her. Forces himself to the door. Forces himself to open it. Outside. Ease the door shut. Run like a motherfucker.

E smiled and opened his eyes. He pulled his keepsake out of his pocket. The magazine for a Colt .38 gleamed in his palm.

DANTE KNELT BESIDE TREY'S recliner. Computer light and images flickered across the web-head's composed face, danced across the cables connected to his neck and to the tips of his fingers.

"Can you get into the morgue's system?" Dante asked.

Images and pages winked across the monitor's screen. Trey's fingers blurred in the air. Dante listened to the electronic crackle and hum. He wondered if data burned like fire through Trey's veins, ever-changing and molten.

A page locked onto the monitor. MORGUE–INTAKE.

Dante squeezed Trey's biceps. *"Très bien, mon ami."*

A smile flickered at the corners of Trey's mouth, then vanished. Dante tugged affectionately on one of his dreads.

Scanning through the intake photos, Trey stopped on the most recent—a young man, throat slit. Dante leaned forward, studying the photo. The hair might've been blond, but wet, it was hard to tell. Eyes closed. Face and lips drained of all color. A gaping bloodless wound stretched across the throat.

Dante sat back on his heels, relief flooding through him like hot, fresh blood. Whoever the cops had pulled from the Mississippi, it wasn't Jay.

That meant whoever murdered Gina still had him.

"Who IDed this body as Jay's?"

<*Detective LaRousse,*> Trey sent. His eyelids shuttered to half mast.

Dante felt it, too, spiraling through his veins. Sleep.

"Ferret out his evidence, his connections, *mon ami*," Dante said. Reaching into his back pocket, he pulled out Elroy the Perv's driver's license. He flipped it onto the desk, in front of the monitor.

Trey glanced at it, then nodded.

<*Check him, too. And Thomas Ronin.*>

<*After Sleep.*> Trey yanked the cables from his body, unplugged from the web.

Simone walked into the room, half-asleep, to guide her brother to his bed. Bending over, she kissed Dante's cheek, her soft lips cool against his skin.

"Sweet dreams," she whispered.

"Et toi." He trailed a finger along one fragrant lock of hair.

Simone straightened, and her hair slipped from his grasp. She eased Trey to his feet. Arms around each other, they half walked, half staggered out of the room.

Sleep swept through Dante, slowing his heart. Gripping the arm of Trey's recliner, he fought the drowsiness claiming him.

Jay was still out there, waiting for rescue. Dante hoped with all his heart that Jay wasn't waiting in pain, cut and sliced like Gina. Fury blasted through him and, for a second, Sleep receded. Dante rose to his feet.

Gina's voice whispered, her words reverberating through him, mind and heart: *Tomorrow night?*

Pain prickled behind Dante's eyes. Stabbed his temples. But Sleep crept back in, leaving him as drugged and drowsy as a hype of morphine. He swayed.

Hands touched his temples, cooling the pain in his head. He stumbled back against Lucien. Lucien seemed to fold himself around Dante, solid and protective. A voiceless, wordless song vibrated up from the core of Lucien into Dante. And something within him sang in wordless response.

Dante half dreamed of wings. Of flying.

<*Stop struggling, child, and Sleep. Stop stirring up the pain.*>

Shaking himself, Dante wrapped a hand around Lucien's muscled wrist. <*I appreciate what you're doing,* mon ami. *But, please—*> Something Dante couldn't name clenched around his heart. His breath caught in his throat at its intensity; an inner hurt that felt strangely familiar. <*I want this.*>

Pushing at Lucien's hands, Dante stepped away from him. But all the rage and hurt in the world couldn't keep him awake.

He felt Lucien's arms wrap around him as he fell.

THE CAB DROVE AWAY, exhaust puffing up white smoke into the gray predawn sky. Stearns stepped carefully onto the snow-shoveled sidewalk. Overnight ice glimmered on its concrete surface. He shifted his briefcase from one hand to the other.

From Seattle rain to D.C. snow and ice. How come a black bag job never led to Hawaii or Florida?

Stearns moved around to the back of the elegant and, no doubt, expensive townhouse. Each step onto the ice-encrusted snow crunched, the sound sharp in the dying night. Stearns gritted his teeth and hoped the neighbors were either heavy sleepers or thought it was only the paperboy making his rounds.

Stearns paused, glanced around the small yard, his gaze skipping from the townhouse behind and the ones to either side. Yellow light glowed from a few windows as people began to waken. He listened, his breath pluming white, his fingers tingling within his gloves.

He'd called the Bureau to check on Johanna's whereabouts. In the past, she'd taken specially designed pills that kept her awake during the day, effectively neutralizing the narcotic effect of Sleep. Of course, she could only do that for so long before she paid a price. Stearns had gambled that she was downing the pills so she could keep on top of things in New Orleans. He'd learned that Johanna had pulled an all-nighter—not uncommon for her—and had yet shown no inclination of calling it a day.

Crunching across the yard to the steps leading to the back door, Stearns could only hope that Johanna hadn't yet reached her limit for the pills. Even so, she might get caught in traffic, buying him a little more time.

Setting his briefcase down on the top step, Stearns studied the door's lock. A red telltale gleamed in the fading darkness. It scrolled sideways, reading LOCKED. Stearns nodded. Pretty much what he'd expected. The tricky part would be any security or secondary systems.

Stearns knelt and flipped open the briefcase latches. Picking up the goggles, he slid them on. He palmed the em-pulse mini-bomb from the papers lining the briefcase. Using wire cutters, he stripped the insulation from the mini's wires. He pried the case from the lock's keypad and scanned the wires looped within the box. The goggles revealed blue lines criss-crossing the wires. Secondary system.

A sniper is climbing to the roof behind you and as soon as he scopes you in, you're dead. Get busy and get inside. Move! Move! Move!

No longer feeling the cold, no longer pondering the best move, Stearns let his adrenaline-fueled instincts kick in. His hands, steady and quick, picked the wires to nick with the cutters. He twisted the mini's exposed wires to the lock system's. That was for the secondary system.

He imagined the sniper going belly down on the roof. He snipped the primary system's lead wire and, turning his face away, set off the mini at the same time.

When Stearns looked again a heartbeat later—*sniper's lining you up*—the LOCKED readout was gone, the screen black and blank. No frantic electronic bleating from the secondary system. Stearns turned the knob. The door opened. Scooping up his briefcase, Stearns dove in through the door.

He imagined the high-velocity bullet whinging into the brick where his head had been a split second before.

Stearns closed the door. Locked it the old-fashioned way, pushing down the button in the center of the knob.

He was in.

14

LOST IN THE SYSTEM

Heather glanced at the clock. One fifteen p.m. Sucking in an irritated breath, she walked to the glassed-in records area where two busy clerks ignored her. She rapped on the glass shield with one knuckle.

The rapid clacking of fingers across a keyboard stopped. The male clerk looked at Heather, one eyebrow raised, expression unhappy.

"You *positive* Doctor Anzalone knows I'm here?" Heather asked. "I've been waiting nearly two hours."

Heather noted the clerk's bedhead-gelled hair and the uber-geek short-sleeved white shirt he wore paired with a skinny black tie. Retro. *And wishing I'd give up or vanish or wither and die.*

"Yes, ma'am, she knows," he said, his voice muffled by the thick shield. "But she's very busy."

"So am I. Check with her again."

Heather returned to the ass-numbing bench she'd been sitting on and perched on the edge. *Let's see if Collins is faring any better.* Pulling her cell from her purse, she punched in the detective's number. He answered on the second ring.

"Hey, Wallace," he said, his voice tight.

"Hey, Collins. Is that police report ready yet?"

"Get this. It's *lost* in the system. They can't fucking find it."

Warning prickled along Heather's spine. She lowered her voice. "Lost . . . I see. And the officer's handwritten report?"

"Funny you should ask. Misplaced. They're looking, but . . ."

"Ah. And the officer himself?"

"Left this morning on vacation. Accrual. Had to use it up—"

"Or lose it," Heather finished. The warning prickles intensified. "Things aren't much better here. I've been on physical hold ever since I arrived."

"I'll keep poking around with a sharp stick. See what turns up."

"Ditto." Heather thumbed the off button, then slid the cell back into her purse.

What the hell is going on? Heather rubbed her forehead. She scrolled her thoughts back, trying to pick out other off-kilter details, to discern a pattern.

Denial of access to the CCK files; ViCAP *and* NCAVC.

Blood messages left at two crime scenes. The anarchy symbol.

A dead perp—supposedly the CCK himself, and caught in the act.

Missing reports, misplaced evidence, a vacationing cop.

Her inability to connect with her SAC. Her calls unreturned.

But the puzzle kept shifting every time she tried to put a piece in place. Face in hands, Heather closed her eyes. She needed sleep. The few hours caught in a chair at Dante's house hadn't been enough. Her thoughts lagged and her reflexes were sluggish.

"Agent Wallace?"

Heather dropped her hands and straightened. The uber-geek clerk stood before her. A nervous smile twitched across his lips.

"Doctor Anzalone asked that you wait in her office," he said.

Heather stood. "Great."

The clerk led her down a hall, past the metal double doors leading to the autopsy theater, to an office marked CORONER. Opening the door, the clerk stepped aside as Heather walked into the office.

"Thanks," Heather said smiling. With a quick nod, the clerk hurried away.

Ignoring the chairs positioned in front of the desk, Heather returned to the doorway. Looked down the quiet hall to the autopsy theater.

Given that Anzalone doesn't seem to be real big on courtesy or protocol . . . Heather walked out of the office and down the hall, her stride brisk and, she hoped, silent. *I'll return the favor.*

She shoved through the autopsy theater's doors. A startled, lab-coated assistant looked up from the body he was suturing.

"Hey!" he exclaimed, disbelief on his face. "You can't be in here!"

Heather smiled. "I'm the lead investigator in the Cross-Country Killer case," she said, pulling her badge from her purse and flipping it open. "Doctor Anzalone expects me."

"She didn't say anything to me," the assistant said. "Really, you can't be in here." Placing the suture needle on the corpse's belly, he hurried across the room. He stopped in front of Heather, his gaze on her badge. He frowned. "I don't think—"

"That the vic? Rosa Baker?" Heather nodded at the body.

"Yeah, it is. But seriously—"

"Where's the perp's body?" Heather stepped past the assistant, walking to the body-laden table. She paused beside a tray of bloody instruments positioned near the head of the table.

"The perp's body?" the assistant repeated, voice unsure.

"Uh . . . you'd have to ask Doctor Anzalone for sure, but I think it was sent to the funeral home."

Heather froze. No way she'd heard right. *No way*. She whirled around to face the assistant. She met his gaze, took in his tight-muscled stance, the anxious way he rubbed his hands together.

"Did you say funeral home?"

"Uh . . . yeah. The body might've been sent there. Accidentally."

Lost. Misplaced. Missing. The assistant shifted his weight from one hip to the other. Glanced away. Heather felt a tight smile curve her lips. *Holy hell, there's more.*

"Don't tell me," Heather said, voice flat. "He was cremated. Accidentally."

Without looking at her, the assistant nodded. "Might've been."

"You'd better fetch Doctor Anzalone."

Swallowing hard, the assistant turned, the soles of his sneakers squeaking against the tile floor. He pushed through the double doors.

Heather breathed in deep and slow. Rage knotted her muscles, but blurred her thoughts. Deep and slow. After a few moments, she looked the body over: middle-aged woman, a little heavy, ash-blonde hair, her eyes half-open and reflecting nothing. Stab wounds, bruises at throat and thighs.

Heather's gaze dropped to the threaded suture needle. Given the Y-incision the assistant was closing, the autopsy had already been performed. The interrupted sutures stopped just below the belly button.

A day ago, Rosa Baker had been a living, breathing woman: washing her face, folding her laundry, planning lunch. Now . . . Heather shifted her attention back to Rosa's lax, pale face and empty eyes. Now nothing remained of Rosa Baker. And nothing remained *to* her but the grave or the fire.

Could I have prevented this death?

One killer would always replace another and she'd always stand beside a metal table bearing the slashed/shot/bludgeoned/strangled remains of yet another victim.

For some, their brutal death would be the most attention they'd ever receive. In dying, in being murdered, they were noticed for the first time, then just as quickly forgotten.

But *she* remembered. Each and every one. Carried their images in her mind: a mental photo album of the dead, a yearbook of ended lives.

Empty promises. Silent victims.

She yearned to be a finger pointed at a murderer; to be the mouth through which they could speak one last time: *It was him. He killed me.*

Heather looked up at the ceiling, at the bright overheads, the microphone dangling down. One victim wasn't dead yet. He still breathed in New Orleans and—she glanced at her watch—slept. She could keep her promise to Dante. But first she needed to find out why the situation here reeked of cover-up.

Rolling back her shoulders and swiping stray wisps of hair from her forehead, Heather walked the room until she found the transcribing station that the microphone connected to, recording the M.E.'s comments and observations. Heather clicked it on, typed in MOST RECENT, then walked back to the table.

The medical examiner's impassionate voice ended the silence.

"The victim is a well-nourished female Caucasian in her mid-to-late forties. . . ."

Heather kept her gaze on Rosa's face as Anzalone spelled out what Heather already suspected: wrong victim type, wrong M.O., wrong killing site. She grew colder with each word.

JOHANNA KEYED IN HER code and opened the door. Closing it, she reset the lock. The keypad beeped. UNAVAILABLE scrolled in red across its tiny window. She stared at the word, trying to make sense of it. She must've punched in the wrong numbers. Frowning, she carefully punched the code in again.

The keypad beeped. UNAVAILABLE.

Johanna went still. *Listened.* The refrigerator hummed in the kitchen. Water dripped from the bathroom faucet. Outside, car tires crunched on the snow and ice-layered street.

Nothing breathed in the house but her. No heart beat but her own.

Still . . . delayed Sleep had stolen her edge, numbed her senses.

Johanna turned away from the door. She scanned the empty room: plush sofa, leather easy chairs, dark fireplace, photos and small treasures on the polished wood mantel; lamps on low. No footprints on the carpet.

Johanna set her purse down on the side table and withdrew her Glock 36. She kicked off her shoes and moved silently across the carpet, gun in a two-handed grip. Ghosting down the hall, she paused when she noticed footprints in the carpet. Too large to be her own.

A burglar? Expensive neighborhood. Fancy toys. Possible.

She swung into the bathroom, flicking on the light, and clearing right, then left. Empty. No shadows behind the beveled-glass shower door. The medicine cabinet was closed. No smudges. Untouched.

Not looking for drugs, then.

Leaving the light on, Johanna stepped back out into the hall and pressed her back up against the wall. The footprints trailed on down the hall.

What if E had come home? What if he'd brought S with him?

Johanna froze, heart hammering against her ribs. Blood rushed in a frenzy through her veins, yet she was cold, colder than the layers of ice outside on the concrete.

She stepped into the spare bedroom, flicking on the light. Nothing.

If E or S *were* here, bullets would help only where E was concerned. It would take more than bullets to keep her True Blood child down.

Whoever had broken into her home, violated it with their uninvited presence, was long gone. She felt nothing but her own panic.

Johanna strode out of the guest bedroom and into the hall, gun held at her side. She stepped into her office and flicked on the light. She crouched in front of the black file cabinet, pulled on the handle. The drawer slid open.

It had been locked when she'd left the house.

Rising to her feet, calmer despite the knot in her stomach, she circled around to her desk and opened the drawers. All *had* been locked—just like the file cabinet. She searched the contents of the deep bottom drawer—all files seemed to be in place, all disks and CDs accounted for. But that didn't mean files hadn't been photographed. Or disks copied.

Nothing jimmied. Nothing damaged. She'd been black-bagged by a pro.

Which meant FBI or CIA or DOD.

She ran a hand through her hair. Who and why? Who'd have the balls? And for what? Whirling, she walked back to the living room and fished her cell phone from her purse. She speed-dialed Gifford's cell, her adrenaline rush already fading. He answered on the first ring, but said nothing, waiting for her to speak first.

"I've been black-bagged," she said, voice thick with Sleep. "Call security. Have them check the office. Then go there yourself."

"Consider it done." His voice was steady, unruffled.

She thumbed the off button. The Glock slipped from her fingers and thudded onto the carpet. Sleep. She'd waited too long.

Johanna staggered from the room and into the hall. She pulled herself along the wall, her gaze locked on her bedroom doorway. It seemed she never got any closer. Her head thumped against the wall and her eyes flew open. She was on the floor.

She curled up in the hallway, lips parting, drinking in Sleep like blood. Just before conscious thought winked out, she realized what had been missing. What she'd been reviewing—for pleasure—at home. The file on S and the CD documenting his experiences as a member of Bad Seed.

DR. ANZALONE SLAMMED THROUGH the double doors into the autopsy theater. Heather spared her a quick glance, then pulled the sheet over Rosa Baker. The playback ended abruptly as the M.E. hit the stop button on the transcriber.

"You have *no* right to barge in here," Anzalone said. "I don't care if you're FBI—"

"Who requested that the forensics be altered in this case?" Turning from the table, Heather locked gazes with the medical examiner. "Altered to match the Cross-Country Killer's M.O.?"

Hazel eyes, curly brunette hair, a little on the heavy side—like Rosa—Anzalone's brows knitted together, her hands jammed into her lab coat pockets. Defensive.

"How *dare* you imply—"

"My perp is left-handed," Heather said, crossing the floor. "These stab wounds were inflicted by a right-hander." She stopped in front of the tight-jawed medical examiner. "But the transcription I just listened to indicated that the killer was left-handed."

Anzalone stiffened. "Before you make any accusations, you'd better check with your superiors." She spun around and strode from the autopsy theater.

Heather stared after her as the doors swung closed. *Check with your superiors.*

Dante was still being stalked.

And she'd been lured away.

Was Stearns part of it?

Half walking, half running out of the theater, Heather yanked her cell from her purse and called Collins. "We need to get back to New Orleans right away. Stay there. I'll pick you up."

Shoving through the front entrance, Heather raced for the rental, punching Dante's home number on her cell. The phone rang and rang. She unlocked the Stratus and slid inside. *C'mon! Answer!* She glanced at her watch. Almost four, Pensacola time, which made it almost three in New Orleans. Maybe Dante was still sleeping.

Starting the car, Heather threw it into reverse and hit the gas pedal. The tires screeched as she whipped the car out of the slot, spinning the wheel one-handed into a quick reverse-to-drive L. She wished she had her Trans Am with its get-up-and-go.

The ringing stopped. De Noir's deep voice said, "Agent Wallace."

"I need to speak to Dante." Heather stepped on the gas. The Stratus arrowed out into traffic. "It's urgent."

"He's sleeping."

"Dammit, De Noir! Wake him!"

"Not possible. But I will take a message for him."

"I don't fucking believe you." Throat tight, lightheaded with anger, Heather pressed harder on the gas pedal.

She glanced over her shoulder as she switched lanes, smoothly merging with the heavy traffic. "He's still in danger. The killer isn't dead. Don't let Dante leave the house and don't leave him alone."

"Dante does as he wishes," De Noir said, voice amused. "But I will tell him your concerns. When he awakens."

"Great," Heather snarled. She threw the phone down onto the passenger seat.

Either De Noir didn't get it or he didn't believe her or he

thought he could keep Dante safe. Any of those reasons would be enough to get Dante killed.

Keeping her gaze on the traffic, Heather fumbled for the cell phone, then tapped in Stearns's number.

"Wallace," he said, answering on the first ring.

Heather didn't know whether to feel relief or concern. "Sir. I'm leaving Pensacola right now. We've been deliberately misled. The M.E. falsified—"

"The case is closed," Stearns said. "The investigation's over."

Someone honked and Heather realized the light had turned green. She stepped on the gas. Her heart thudded against her chest. "Who closed the case, sir?" she finally managed to say.

"That's not the issue, Wallace."

Stearns's voice was flat. Stoic. Was her mentor repeating words he had no wish to say? Or was he a willing party? Heather felt sick.

"I think it is. The CCK is *not* dead, sir. Who'd want to protect him?"

"The investigation's over." Stearns's voice sounded weary, drained. "Get back to Seattle ASAP."

"He has another victim targeted."

"Forget Dante Prejean, Wallace. He's not what he appears to be."

At Dante's name, Heather's blood ran cold. "What do you mean?"

"He's no longer your concern."

"With all due respect, sir, are you a part of the cover-up?"

"Heather, listen carefully." Desperation weighted Stearns's voice. "Stay out of New Orleans. Your safety depends upon it. You are not among friends."

"Apparently that's nothing new, is it, Craig?" She hung up.

What had happened? Was the CCK the son of a government star? The brother of a diplomat? And why was the investigation being halted *now*?

Something to do with Dante. Think. Someone wanted him dead. Why not just shoot him in his sleep? Could it be something to do with the past he didn't remember?

A bloodred anarchy symbol caught Heather's attention. She stared, breath caught in her throat, heart pounding. A sign in the window of a music store.

Above the anarchy symbol: Just in! The latest release from New Orleans's INFERNO! *Deliberately Set.* And below it: Wake up and smell the fire!

WAKE UP written in blood at two different crime scenes. A past Dante doesn't remember. Heather hung a right, then pulled to a stop in front of the precinct house. Collins waited on the steps.

Dante didn't remember, no. But someone *wanted* him to remember.

"We've got trouble," Heather said as Collins scrunched into the car. She hit the gas before he'd closed the door.

Unruffled, the detective strapped on his seat belt. He glanced at Heather. "The bastard's not dead, is he?"

"They made you detective for a reason," Heather murmured, goosing the Stratus through two high-speed lane changes. "It gets worse. It's a deliberate cover-up."

"Shit." Collins stared straight ahead, jaw tight, face grim.

15

WHIRLING INTO MOTION

E CREPT DOWN THE hall to Tom-Tom's room. He pressed himself against the closed door. Was Tommy-boy still asleep? The sun hadn't set yet, the gray afternoon lingered, sullen sky pissing rain.

E listened. Nuthin'. Not even snoring. *Did* vampires snore? Was he even in there? What if he stood behind E? Watching? Grinning? E whirled, heart hurdling into his throat, shivs in hand.

Nuthin'.

E stood motionless, staring down the empty hall to the dirty light streaming in through the front window. His heart gradually slowed. With a flick of both wrists, he slid his shivs back into their wrist sheaths.

E swiveled around to face the closed door once again. Still no snoring. If he was in there, he'd be sound asleep. If not, then E didn't have to worry about noise. His fingers closed around the cool brass doorknob, and turned.

Ronin lay on the bed like a dead man. Fully dressed. Not breathing. Hands at his sides. His eyes were half-open, but all that showed were the whites. E twitched. His skin felt creepy-crawly, like he'd stepped into an anthill. He fought the urge to slap and brush at himself.

He narrowed his eyes. He subtracted the not-breathing assessment. Fucker was, indeed, breathing. Just barely.

E stepped into the bedroom, his gaze locked on Ronin's stretched-out form, and held his breath. Nuthin'. He stepped further into the room.

E circled the bed. Tilted his head. *Mourner viewing corpse.* Circled again. A knife across the throat would do it. Maybe not *kill* the bastard, but all that blood pouring out would *have* to be a major inconvenience.

Why hadn't Ronin locked the door? Did he think so little of E's abilities, his work, that he felt *safe*? Thought he could handle ol' E even asleep?

Muscles knotting, belly burning, E popped his shivs into his hands. He inched closer to the bed. Ronin's face looked almost as smooth as a kid's, even though he was supposedly centuries old.

How long would it take to kill him? Flat-out flesh-to-skeleton-to-ashes *kill* him?

He leaned over Ronin, angling a shiv for the soft throat when he remembered the files. E hesitated, tensed, longing to slash. The files—his and Dante's—he needed those. Needed to know where to find the Bad Seed Mama-Bitch. Needed to know her name. Needed to know why.

He needed to know more about Dante, too—Bad Seed little brother, kindred spirit—more than the shit Tom-Tom spoon-fed him. E summoned Dante's image, but saw instead Heather's hunger as her gaze slid along Dante's body. E shivered, shiv extended, aching, blood boiling, wanting them both. But willing to claim only one.

E forced himself away from Ronin. Straightened and tucked away his shivs. Daylight was burning. Circling to the other side of the bed, E searched the nightstand, carefully pulling open the drawers. Nuthin'.

Crossing to the dresser, he opened one drawer after another. Folded clothes, undies—hmmm, silk—rolled pairs of socks, but no files. Blowing air between his teeth, E leaned against the dresser. He'd seen the files briefly in New York, thick with reports, photos, and CDs. Tommy-boy'd also had a case full of special things—special things for Dante—in case he needed to be restrained.

E headed for the closet, but catching a glimpse of gold out of the corner of his eye, he halted. Crouching, he looked under the bed. Dante's pretty Goth boy was curled up on the hardwood floor, tucked in with the shadows and the dust bunnies, eyes closed, face white. Wrists handcuffed. One ankle cuffed to a leg of the bed.

E grinned. Tommy'd raided the cupboard and grabbed himself a toy. A snack *and* a toy. Did Tom-Tom intend to dangle Goth-boy like a bag of blood in front of Dante's nose? Or was he going to send E out to collect another?

E crawled to the closet, dazzled by Goth-boy's golden hair, imagining it spun like golden thread, a glimmering coil seeking the warmth of his hands.

E opened the closet. Worn-edged cardboard boxes nestled on the floor among Tom-Tom's boots and expensive loafers. A zippered black bag sat next to the boxes.

E dug through the boxes, hands trembling, mouth dry, until he found the file marked *E* and the one marked *S*. Tucking them under his arm, he scooped up the black bag, then closed the closet door. He swiveled on his knees, expecting to see gold, but all he saw was a lank strand of blond hair.

Let Tom-Tom have him, he thought, elevatoring to his feet. Less likely to notice anything's missing if he's busy playing.

E walked from the room and oh-so-carefully closed the door.

He strode down the hall and out through the front door into the dying afternoon.

He had a lot of research to do.

Wasps crawled over Dante's body, heavy abdomens curving as stingers needled venom into his flesh. Paralyzed by Sleep, caught in a nightmare-woven net, he couldn't move, couldn't leap to his feet, brushing and slapping at the thousands of busy wasps. Poison snaked beneath his skin, wormed into his veins, burrowed into his heart.

Behind the high-pitched wasp drone, a voice called, *Dante-angel? You okay?*

He burned.

A wasp wriggled into his nostril. Another jimmied open his lips, scraped down his throat. Stingers pricked his eyelids, but he kept quiet. Screaming equaled straitjacket and restraints. Screaming equaled sunlight slanting across a wooden floor.

His eyelids puffed and swelled. His heart thudded hard against his chest. His throat closed. Air thinned to a trickle. His lungs burned.

He kept silent.

Windows surrounded him. Some he could barely make out, their shape distorted, the glass warped. He looked away, heart pounding—*don'tlookdon'tlookdon'tlook*. A few of the windows rippled like water beneath the wind and he looked, even though he knew it'd be bad.

A burning house.

A laughing little girl with red hair, holding a stuffed orca.

A metal examination table loaded down with restraints.

A smiling woman, fangs revealed, reaching for him.

Dante tried to move, but venom and Sleep kept him motionless. Sweat trickled down his temples.

Dante-angel?

The voice, childish and low and familiar, lingered, the words squeezing his heart. Pain blazed through his mind, torched his thoughts. If he kept quiet, she'd live. Then kicking the ass of that thought was another: If he didn't move, she'd die.

The fresh scent of rain and sage glided across his consciousness and, for a moment, he forgot the pain, forgot his impending, irreversible loss.

For a moment, she'd never died.

For a moment, he'd never killed her.

Then truth doused him in gasoline and tossed a match.

He screamed.

RONIN WALKED DOWN THE hall to the front room. Starry night gleamed beyond the window. He picked up his cell phone and tapped in the number for his New Orleans police contact.

"LaRousse."

"Thomas Ronin. I watched an interesting exchange of words last night between a vampire named Étienne and Dante Prejean. I believe Étienne has a grudge or two against Dante."

"You could say that," LaRousse said. "His home was torched one morning. Burned down to the ground. A handful of Étienne's nearest and dearest died in the fire and he believes Prejean's the one who set it."

"Ah. Why does he believe that?"

"Couldn't say and don't care."

"Can you get in touch with Étienne?"

"I can. What's this about?"

"Let's just say an opportunity for payback. Give him my number, Detective. I appreciate your help in this matter."

Ronin touched the end button. Shaking a slim, black cigarette from the pack on the coffee table, he slipped it between his lips and lit it with a match. He inhaled the sweet-smelling smoke, savoring the rich tobacco taste on his tongue.

Cell in hand, he walked back down the hall to E's room and pushed open the door. An empty, rumpled bed, but that was no surprise. Although E's woodworm-bitter scent lingered in the air, Ronin had known upon awakening he was gone. No prickly aura. No wary tension.

Streetlight slanted in through the partially opened blinds, crosshatching the bedroom with lines of light. The room's darkness felt thick and close and stale, shut off from the untamed night outside.

The instant E had climbed out of his Jeep and walked across the street to Dante's house, he'd become a liability. Dante's phone call had made Ronin realize the truth. Peeping Tom and his assistant, Elroy the Perv. A smile flickered across Ronin's lips. Boy had a way with words—quick-witted and sardonic.

We'll see how quick-witted he is tonight.

Ronin drew on his cigarette. The gray smoke curled up and away, hazing the room's still air. E had fucked up, no two ways about it. Ronin wasn't sure how much longer he could control him and wondered if he ever really had.

A sociopath. A serial killer. A sexual sadist. How pleased Johanna must be. All her hard work coming to bloody and clever fruition. But what was she saving Dante for? Why had he been allowed to slumber? How had he survived all that she'd done to him?

Then again, he was True Blood. Johanna would have *centuries* to guide him, twist him, *trigger* him with programming subliminals and implants. Dante was a mere twenty-three years old. He was a child. His gifts, the full extent of his abilities, probably wouldn't be revealed for decades, perhaps centuries.

What would it take to awaken him? To spring Dante like a hidden trap on his *fille de sang*, the woman who'd dared to corrupt and twist a True Blood.

The medical and psychological procedures Johanna and the mortal Doctor Wells had performed on Dante's mind and brain had been conspicuously missing from the Bad Seed files an anonymous donor had sent him. So, in truth, he was experimenting. Ronin had expected Dante's subconscious to react to the messages, but so far—zip. Maybe a more direct approach—using Dante's unexpected sentimentality for mortals—would work like a crowbar upside his lovely head.

Ronin stepped inside the room. Sheets and blankets lumped the unmade bed. A book, an ashtray, and an empty glass rested on the nightstand.

Stubbing out his cigarette in the ashtray, Ronin sat on the edge of the bed. Glanced at the book—*Inside the Monster's Heart and Other Poems.* The faint scent of whiskey drifted up from the glass. From the bed, he caught a whiff of dark cherries. He followed the faint scent down to the pillow. Reaching inside the pillowcase, he pulled out a black length of nylon. Gina's stocking, a dream catcher for her killer, tucked close to the monster's heart. Ronin dropped the pillow back onto the bed.

The cell phone rang. Ronin tapped the on button. "Yes?"

"This is Étienne. I am listening."

16

BLOOD SWORN

DANTE OPENED HIS EYES. Candlelight flickered white and gold on the ceiling. Shadows shimmied. He smelled vanilla-scented wax and tasted blood at the back of his throat. His head throbbed, but the pain was distant as though numbed by morphine or eased by Lucien's cool hands.

It hurt to swallow. The blood he tasted was his own. Another headache? Another nosebleed? What *night* was it? He tried to think back, to remember what he'd been doing before Sleep, but hit a big blank wall.

Sudden vivid images swirled through his thoughts—a wasp, chains dangling from a meat hook, a bloodied baseball bat—morphing his consciousness into waking nightmare.

Barbed-wire thorns bit. Wasps droned. Dante shook his head. He felt Trey nudging gently at his shields. Sucking in a deep breath, Dante let him in.

<*A message for you on club e-mail.*>

<*Oui.*>

<*"I know where your pretty plaything's been stashed. He's alive and mostly well. Play nice and he'll stay that way. I'll leave word for you*

at the club." Traced the message back to a net café. Blind credit. Dead end.>

Pulse racing, Dante sat up. Blood pounded in his temples.

"Agent Wallace phoned while you were Sleeping," Lucien said, stepping into the room. "The killer is *not* dead and she advised you to stay home."

"So, she was right," Dante said. "But I ain't staying. I got a promise to keep."

<You trust this information?>

"Fuck, no. But it's all I got right now." Dante threw aside the sheets and stood.

I'm coming for you, Jay. Keep breathing. Keep fighting.

HEATHER SUCKED IN A deep breath of Hell's patchouli-, clove-, and sweat-reeking air and plunged into the crowd. As she weaved and pushed between hot and sweaty bodies, she kept her gaze on Dante.

He sat on the edge of his bat-winged throne, muscles tensed, body coiled. He wore leather pants and a metal-strapped latex shirt. Light flashed from the rings on his fingers and from the ring on his bondage collar. A black-haired Goth princess nestled against his leg, her fishnet-covered arms wrapped around his calf, a smile on her bloodred lips.

Dante's fingers stroked the Goth chick's hair, the gesture absentminded but gentle, his dark gaze on Heather. His pale face revealed nothing. No hint of welcome. Just watchful.

Music battered and rib-kicked the moshing crowd. The heavy bass beat vibrated the walls and mist-shrouded floor, the sound like a defibrillator to the heart.

Not bad. Heather thought, raising a forearm to fend off a crowd surfer. *Reminds me of Annie's old band.* Hands shoved and bounced the surfer off to Heather's left. She lowered her arm. She'd half turned to shoulder in when she realized someone had stepped directly in front of her, blocking her path. Frowning, hands knotting into fists, Heather looked up—and her heart skipped a beat.

"You know how to handle yourself," Dante said. A half smile tilted his lips.

"Yeah, well, my sister used to front a band," Heather shouted. Looking at him now, she saw welcome in his dark eyes, and some of her tension unraveled.

"Which band?"

"WMD."

A circle cleared around them as the crowd suddenly realized who stood among them. Hunger of all kinds dilated their eyes. Voices whispered. Trembling fingers reached. Heather's gaze jumped from one person to the next, wondering if a killer moshed among them. She jerked when a hand gripped her shoulder. Dante leaned in, his lips beside her ear.

"You don't need to shout," he whispered. "I can hear you fine. And WMD were among the fucking best." He straightened, his fingers lingering on her shoulder for a moment.

"They were." Heather held Dante's gaze, only half-aware of the whispers buzzing and droning around them like flies.

A thin young man in dreads and camo shoved an Inferno CD—the new one, *Deliberately Set*—and a Sharpie at Dante.

"Dudeifyoucouldit'dbetotallyawesome," he blurted, eyes wide.

Dante handed the signed CD and the Sharpie back to Camo-boy.

He blinked. "Uh . . . thanks."

Heather hadn't seen Dante take the CD and sign it either. She'd caught a blur of movement, his hands, maybe, but nothing else. Dante glanced at her. Held out his hand. She took it, wrapping her fingers around his warm palm.

Dante led her through the crowd. A path opened before them and Dante's name rippled through the moshers, every murmur another tossed stone. Yearning glances followed him. Fingers brushed against him. Pleading. One honey-haired young man in an old-fashioned frock coat was bold enough to step in front of Dante. He closed his kohl-lined eyes, spread his arms wide, and offered up his lips.

Dante stopped, surprising Heather. Still holding her hand, he stepped forward until he was face-to-face with the young man, until just a breath of air separated their bodies, and kissed the offered lips.

A pining sigh gusted through the watchers. Heather stepped beside Dante, scanning each sweating, painted face near him. A few wept, tears black with eyeliner and mascara streaking their faces.

They adore him. Utterly. Is it his looks? Who he is?

Or what he's supposed *to be?*

The kiss ended. The honey-haired young man staggered back, then bowed, sweeping one arm across his waist while extending one leg. An elegant gesture unmarred by his trembling hands.

"*Merci beaucoup, mon ange de sang.*" He glanced up, face flushed, dazed. "You honor me."

"*Pour quoi? Sa fini pas.*"

Heather heard strain in Dante's voice. *He hasn't had time to grieve*, she thought. *So much has happened in the last couple of days.*

Still bowing, the young man stepped out of Dante's path. The sighs and murmurs intensified. Dante resumed walking, his fingers locked around Heather's hand. The path merged behind him and disappeared. When they reached the steps to the dais, Dante squeezed Heather's hand, then released it.

She followed him up the steps, past the Goth lords and Goth princesses curled on the steps like contented cats. The black-haired lap kitty who'd been snugged against Dante's leg earlier perched on the edge of the dais, her hungry gaze fixed on his face. Behind the throne, De Noir stood in a crimson shirt, the X-rune pendant glittering at his throat, his face impassive.

Dante knelt on one knee beside the waiting Goth chick. Skimming his fingers along her jaw, he bent and spoke into her ear.

Heather noticed how black Dante's hair was in the club's low lights, black as the deepest part of night; natural and glossy—not flat like the dyed hair of the girl listening to his whispered words.

The Goth princess lowered her eyes; her lower lip quivered. Dante tipped her face up and kissed her. She laced her arms around his waist.

Most people shake hands. Dante kisses. Could get real *interesting at a company picnic.* Heather folded her arms over her chest.

When the kiss ended, the fishnet queen reluctantly released Dante, her hands sliding over his hips as she did. Smiling, she smoothed her thumbs over his lips, wiping away the lipstick. She glared at Heather as she scooted down a step, her disdainful gaze sweeping her from head to toe.

Heather smiled and stepped past her.

Dante sat cross-legged on the dais in front of the throne, motioning for Heather to do the same. She did, slipping her purse strap over her head and around her opposite shoulder so she didn't have to worry about it disappearing.

Music pounded and throbbed. It pulsed up Heather's spine and into the back of her skull. Someone in the Cage howled in pain. Feedback squealed through the amps. Heather winced. Her gaze flicked to the fetish-hung Cage. The band kicked and pried at the hands clutching the downed front man. Fingers waved in the air, blood-streaked, holding aloft torn pieces of material and long strands of red hair.

Finally the band freed their front man, who scooped up the mike, rolled to his feet, and resumed singing, blood trickling down his face.

"Dark Cloud 9 from Portland," Dante said, leaning forward to speak into her ear.

"He isn't dead," she said.

"Lucien told me. You were right. Whatcha gonna do now?"

"Guard you."

An amused smile quirked up the corners of Dante's mouth.

"Oh, you don't think you need it? Mister Indestructible Vampire?"

"I never said I was indestructible."

"You must believe it, though," Heather said, locking gazes with him. "You didn't stay home. What the hell are you doing here?"

Dante's smile faded. "I have a promise to keep."

"A promise? How about promising to play it safe?"

"Fuck, Heather," Dante muttered. "I never promised you anything. But I *did* promise Jay I'd protect him and I mean to do it."

"Jay's dead, Dante, it's too late," Heather said, touching his knee.

"No, he's not. The body they fished outta the river wasn't his. I checked." Fire gleamed in Dante's dark eyes. "I got a message tonight. Someone knows where Jay's stashed. Said they'd leave word for me here. I'm waiting."

Heather stared at him, speechless. What had Dante said last night? Bait the hook? But there was a difference between that and tossing the bait into the shark's jaws. And wasn't it interesting that the message wasn't sent until *after* she'd left New Orleans?

"The only one who could *possibly* know where—"

Dante held up a hand and glanced across the bobbing crowd toward the entrance. Heather fell silent. Following Dante's gaze, she looked across the room.

"Peeping Tom's here," Dante said. He uncoiled and stood, the sudden movement graceful and fluid. "And he wants a moment of my time."

Heather eased to her feet, apprehension curling in her belly.

The moshing crowd parted like an amoeba as two figures strode from the entryway onto the dance floor. Von led the way in loose, long-legged strides, fight-scarred hands at his sides. His leather jacket bulged slightly, and she realized he wore a double shoulder holster underneath.

Her gaze skipped behind Von to the man following in his wake. Thomas Ronin. She'd seen pictures of him online and on book jackets, but this was the first time she'd seen him in the flesh. She'd expected a striking man—tall, athletic stride, skin just a shade lighter than night under the house lights, short-cropped hair, trimmed beard—but she hadn't expected his *presence*. Even from across the room, he commanded attention, drew the eye.

The journalist's gaze flickered over Heather. Surprise flashed across his face. Surprise and recognition. *He knows who I am*, she thought. *And he didn't expect me to be here.* She nodded. A tight smile skimmed Ronin's lips, then vanished.

Von climbed the steps to the dais. He paused in front of Dante. The crescent moon tattoo under the nomad's eye seemed to vibrate beneath the dim lights.

"*C'est bon*," Dante said. "*Gètte le.*"

With a quick nod, Von stepped past Dante, then stood at his right hand, but at a slight angle as though he needed to watch everyone.

Ronin stepped onto the dais. Turning, he half bowed to Von. "An honor to be escorted by you, *llygad*."

Von didn't react to the journalist's words. He stood motionless, legs apart, hands at his sides.

Apparently, Ronin hadn't expected a reply, because he turned to face Dante without waiting for one. His gaze slid past Dante to De Noir standing behind the throne, then back.

"I'm surprised to see you still here, Agent Wallace," Ronin said, voice smooth.

"And why is that?"

Ronin shrugged. "I read in the paper that the CCK had been

nailed in Pensacola. The Bureau and local authorities say the case is closed."

"So why aren't *you* in Pensacola following up like a good journalist?" Heather thumped her hand against her temple. "Oh. I forgot. You're *not* a good journalist."

Ronin smiled, arched an eyebrow, and said, "Ouch."

"You got your moment, Peeping Tom," Dante said.

"Tell me if this means anything or if it's just bullshit." Ronin reached a hand into the inside pocket of his denim jacket.

The hair prickled on the back of Heather's neck. Glancing over her shoulder, she saw De Noir now standing just behind Dante, his gaze locked on Ronin.

Dark Cloud 9's wall of industrial sound revved down to drums and bass, the beat tribal and hypnotic, punctuated by the front man's growled refrain, repeated over and over: *One step closer to the end / one step closer / one step closer to the end . . .*

Ronin tugged a folded piece of paper out of his pocket. He extended it to Dante. "I found this in my newspaper this evening."

Dante tugged the paper free of Ronin's fingers, then flipped it open and scanned it. Heather leaned in and read over his shoulder.

> jay mcgregor sends his regards, ask dante why. ask dante how much blood will it take to wake him up. how many? write the truth. tell dante to look in his car.

DRUMS POUNDED, BASS THROBBED, pulsing beat. *One step closer to the end / one step closer / one / step / closer / to the end . . .*

Dante tucked the slip of paper into his back pocket. *"Merci,"* he said, voice low. "But this doesn't change anything."

Ronin shook his head, stepped closer. "What are you afraid of . . . True Blood?"

Heather's hair fluttered in a rush of air at the same moment she caught a peripheral glimpse of Dante *moving*. He'd reacted to Ronin's invasion of his personal space by moving in even closer; a handspan separated the two. The journalist's dark skin contrasted so sharply with Dante's pale complexion—midnight and winter white—that the image of the yin-yang symbol burned within her mind.

"Not you, Peeping Tom." Dante's hands curled into fists. "What the fuck do you mean by 'True Blood'?"

"Nothing," De Noir said. He stepped past Heather and beside Dante. "Absolutely nothing." His gaze locked on Ronin. "He's playing games."

Heather glanced at Von. An eyebrow arched above his shades at De Noir's remark. *Looks like the nomad isn't so sure about that. Interesting.*

Dante suddenly shuddered and closed his eyes. *"T'es sûr de sa?"* he whispered.

Concern flickered across De Noir's face, his brows knitted. "Time for you to leave, *M'sieu* Ronin."

"Not yet." Ronin's hands swung up, reaching for Dante's shoulders.

Eyes still closed, Dante parried the journalist's grab, his own hands flashing up and out with heart-stopping speed. His fingers curled around Ronin's wrists. His eyes opened. Ronin stared at him, lips parted, unmoving.

Not surprised by Dante's speed, Heather realized, but caught off guard by his actions. How long had Ronin and his creepy assistant been watching Dante?

Shoving Ronin's wrists away, Dante reached up, cupped the journalist's bearded face, and brushed his lips against his mouth.

Shock blanked Ronin's face as Dante stepped back, hands at his sides. Ronin's head turned to the side, gaze down. A muscle jumped in his jaw. His hands fisted, then relaxed.

Dante stopped beside Heather, glanced at her. A half smile tilted his lips, but red streaked his dark irises.

"Be careful," she said. "You're playing with fire here."

"I like fire." His gaze shifted back to Ronin.

"Why didn't you turn the note over to the cops, Ronin?" Heather asked. "What do *you* want?"

Lifting his gaze, Ronin swung his head around to face Heather. He smiled, but something dark and sardonic wriggled in his eyes just long enough for her to see. "All I want is the story," he said.

"Liar," Dante said.

Amusement danced in Ronin's eyes. "I hang out. I chronicle everything that's going down."

"Why wouldn't we give your note to the cops?"

Lifting an eyebrow, Ronin glanced at Dante. "*We?*" He shook his head. "Even if you call in the cops, Agent Wallace, I still get the story."

The bass dropped down to a steady throb, the drums pulsed, the front man's growl intensified, accelerated into a scream:

One step closer to the end / One fucking step closer . . .

"I'll tell you what I meant by 'True Blood,'" Ronin said.

Dante shrugged. "Who says I want to know?"

Ronin grinned. "I do."

Heather stared at the journalist's fangs. Cold snaked into her, icing her blood. *Am I the* only *fucking person in the world who doesn't have fangs or imagines she's a vampire?*

She glanced at Dante. Breathtaking. Creative. Inhuman speed. *Was* he?

De Noir reached for Ronin's elbow, apparently preparing to escort the journalist off the dais, when he stopped, hand still in midair, gaze turned inward.

The music stopped. The house lights dimmed, then went out.

"Do you hear that?" Dante said, his voice full of wonder. "I feel a rhythm . . . like fire, like *your* song, Lucien, like–"

Heather stepped toward the sound of Dante's voice. In the darkness, anything could happen. A killer could close in. One quick slice across the throat . . . Small comfort that the killer would prefer Dante alive . . . for a while. Reaching out a hand, she fumbled for his arm. Her fingers slid across latex and squeezed around Dante's forearm.

"Listen to me very carefully," De Noir said, his voice tight and urgent.

Dante hissed in pain.

"What?" Heather said, body tensing. "What's wrong?"

The lights switched back on.

Ronin stood motionless at the edge of the dais, his brows drawn down, his gaze intense as he watched Dante and De Noir. De Noir's hand was locked around Dante's shoulder and, it seemed to Heather, his fingernails pierced Dante's shirt. Dante met De Noir's gaze, his expression dazed.

Heather released her grip on Dante's arm. "What's wrong?" she repeated.

"Listen to me," De Noir said. "Shield yourself. Shut it out." He tipped Dante's chin up with a *taloned* finger. "I must leave. Promise me you won't follow."

Dante held De Noir's now glowing golden gaze and even though he didn't say a word, Heather had the feeling much was passing between the two.

"Let me help," Dante whispered, frustration shadowing his face.

"Promise me."

Jerking free of the finger beneath his chin, Dante looked away, jaw clenched. Then he reached up and slid two fingers in under the neck of his shirt beside the thumb talon piercing him. He pulled his fingers out, blood-slicked, and pressed them against De Noir's lips.

"I promise."

"Blood sworn," Ronin breathed. His dark eyes gleamed.

With Dante's blood still on his lips, De Noir strode down the steps and into the watching crowd.

Dante watched him go, arms wrapped around himself, pale face troubled.

"What was that about?" Heather asked.

"I don't know," Dante said, voice husky. "He wouldn't tell me." His gaze shifted above the crowd, and Heather followed it.

De Noir was already climbing the stairs to the third-floor landing. He peeled off his crimson shirt. Powerful muscles flexed. The shirt fluttered down the stairs like a rose petal dropped from a lover's bouquet.

A silhouetted figure scurried up the stairs after De Noir had rounded the corner and vanished from view. A red-haired Goth princess in black crinoline and fishnet scooped up the abandoned shirt. She pressed it against her cheek as she trotted back down the stairs.

"Is De Noir a vampire . . . *nightkind* . . . too?" Heather turned to look at Dante.

Dropping his arms to his sides, Dante shook his head. "No. He's Fallen."

Talons. Golden eyes. Blue fire. "As in angels?"

This doesn't concern the Fallen.

Dante shrugged. "That's one of the stories."

"So *that's* it," Ronin murmured.

"Time for you to go, Peeping Tom," Dante said. "We're done here."

"Okay." Ronin held up his hands. "I didn't come here to make enemies."

A smile quirked up one corner of Dante's mouth. "Liar."

A flicker of movement out of the corner of Heather's eye, the sudden scent of smoke and frost on a gust of air, and then Von stood beside Ronin. The two men—*vampires*?—were the same height, and looked eye to eye.

"I walked you in," Von drawled. "I'll walk you out."

"Again, *llygad*, I'm honored."

The nomad walked past Ronin and down the steps. Ronin met Dante's dark gaze. "True Blood," he said. "Let me know if you change your mind."

Turning, he followed Von down the steps. Heather watched until she saw him stride into the entrance hall, the nomad in his wake.

"True Blood?"

Dante shook his head. "He's full of shit."

"But what does it mean?"

"It doesn't matter," Dante said. "The note mentions my car. I'm gonna look."

Heather stepped in close, inhaling his warm, earthy scent. "Not alone. Too dangerous."

"I ain't asking permission," Dante said. "I'm not gonna sit on my ass and let someone else I care about die."

"Of course not. But I'm coming with you."

Surprise flashed in Dante's eyes. "As a friend or as a cop?"

"Both," Heather said, voice low. "I'm both."

"Yeah?" A smile curved Dante's lips.

"Yeah. You're gonna need a friend and some luck—"

Dante cupped Heather's face, his hands warm against her skin. "For luck," he murmured against her lips, then he kissed her.

Her eyes closed. His lips, soft and firm against hers, stoked the fire simmering in her veins, stirred the embers glowing in her belly.

Too soon the kiss ended and Dante's hands slid from Heather's face. She opened her eyes. She didn't see amusement in his expression, or a smirk on his lips. He just looked at her, completely open.

Her spinning thoughts slowed. Heat flushed her cheeks when she realized she'd been so stunned by the kiss that she hadn't touched him, had stood there with her hands hanging at her sides. Like she'd never kissed before.

Sure beats a handshake, though.

"Let's go," Dante said. He held out his hand.

Heather grabbed it and followed him down the steps. Faces and scents blurred past her—dreads, mohawks, golden Claudia curls, acrid tobacco, clove, patchouli. She flew, weightless, Dante's warm hand in hers.

Suddenly outside, Heather's weight returned and Dante released her hand. She followed him through the narrow alley between the pizza parlor and Club Hell to the back street behind the club.

Dante stopped beside the MG parked at the curb. Heather paused on the passenger side. "You don't have a driver's license," she said.

"True." He opened the door and slid into the driver's seat. "That a problem?"

Heather pulled the passenger door open, then bent down and peered inside. "You don't lock your car?"

Dante didn't answer. He stared at something tied to the steering wheel, face stricken. He untied it with trembling fingers. It unfurled from the steering wheel. A sheer black stocking.

Just like the one left knotted around Gina's throat.

17

BORN SOCIOPATH

B LOOD SLICKED E'S FINGERS. He gritted his teeth and dug his shiv in a little deeper. The tip scraped across something, stuck. He paused, waiting for the pain. Nuthin'. Reaching back with his other hand, he slid his fingers across the wound at the base of his skull. Gingerly touched the thing his shiv had nicked. Soft edges. No sensation.

Laughter poured from E's throat, the sound low and strained and pissed.

So that's *how he found me in New York. How long had the fucker been tracking me? Interesting that he never mentioned the bugs.*

E tugged. His fingers slipped and he lost his grip on the implant. Blood trickled inside the back of his collar, warm against his icy skin. Shifting the bloodied shiv to his other hand, E wiped his sweaty palm off on his jeans. Switched hands again. Tightened his grip and went back to work.

E gripped the implant's edge. Pried with his shiv. Wormed with his fingers. Here he was, at one of the cheap motels he despised, straddling a wobbly kitchenette chair, digging a satellite chip out of his fucking flesh with one of his own fucking shivs.

Thanks, Tom-Tom.

Blinking sweat out of his eyes, E levered the tip of his shiv under the implant. Flipped it. A sudden sharp pain, poking fire all the way down his spine, then the bug popped free.

Cold and shaking despite the fire raging at the base of his skull, E lowered his hands to the table. The bloody shiv *tunk*ed onto its cheap, laminated surface. His other hand cupped the tiny, blood-smeared transmitter. He poked it with his index finger. Nuthin'.

E's fist closed around the implant. He swiveled in the chair and looked at the file contents strewn across the stained bedspread, at the image on the cheap laptop monitor: Dante, thirteen or fourteen years old, tearing open his foster father's throat with his fingertips, blood spraying his pale, gorgeous face. Mrs. Prejean was already dead, crumpled on the dining room floor, her head little more than bits of white bone, hanks of hair, and oozing brains.

Fuckin' beautiful! Go, little bro, go!

Foster parents, E snorted. Yeah, right. If you consider *pimps* parental figures.

Of course, Bad Seed Mommy and Daddy knew all about the Prejeans, knew how they used the kids the state handed over to them. Knew how they'd piss themselves with delight when Dante was placed in their home.

The Prejeans had made a *lot* of moolah off Dante. Course, even with their ward properly restrained, a few of their clients had taken serious injuries. Something about a dick bitten off, or nearly, anyway.

E grinned. He stood, then walked into the john. Standing over the toilet, he opened his hand and dropped the implant into the bowl. Thin swirls of blood tinted the water red. He flushed.

Let Tom-Tom track him now.

Let Johanna Moore sweat.

Mommy, I'm coming home and I ain't coming alone.

Walking back into the other room, E knelt beside the bed. He popped the CD out of the laptop. Folded the monitor down. He shuffled the documents, reports, and photos back into the manila folders.

One photo caught his eye and he pulled it free from the pile. A small boy, two or three years old, a tuft of sandy hair sticking up at the back of his head, grinned at the camera. Behind him, a man and woman slumped on a vine-patterned sofa, blood smearing the cushions. A dark hole gaped in the man's—*Daddy's*—temple, and in the woman's—*Momma's*—forehead. A gun was on the floor just beneath the man's dangling hand.

E couldn't remember if he'd seen his father ice his mom, then himself in the standard murder-suicide thing. If he had, it must not've bothered him much. He couldn't remember the incident and he'd never been troubled by nightmares.

Well, not about his parents, anyway.

E tucked the photo back in with the papers and shoved them all into the folder. So, his parents had died when he was almost three, and Bad Seed had directed his life from that moment on. Dante's mother had been taken by Bad Seed while pregnant, then slaughtered once she'd given birth.

E shook his head. Born a bloodsucker. Who woulda thought?

Back at the kitchen table, E mixed himself another gin and tonic. He took a long, cool swallow and washed the day's flat taste out of his mouth.

Created sociopath. So Bad Seed named him.

Born sociopath. So Bad Seed named Dante.

But they were wrong. He tossed back the rest of his drink, the gin's clean taste clearing his head. Very wrong. He set the glass down and walked into the bathroom. The fluorescent light buzzed. The mirror reflected his shaded gaze, his blood-streaked neck. He grinned. Switched off the light. Switched it back on. Grinned again.

Wetting a hand towel at the tap, E wiped at the blood on his neck. Dante wasn't the only true blood. Bad Seed hadn't created E from little grinning Elroy. E had already existed and had been busy nudging little grinning Elroy outta the picture.

E rinsed the towel in the sink. Bloody water swirled down the drain. He patted the towel against the implant site and sucked in a breath through his teeth. Damn if it didn't sting like a *mother*fucker.

E's little sister hadn't died of SIDS. He'd suffocated her. Had pushed her blankie against her face until she'd quit squirming and gone still. He remembered that as one of his earliest memories. Odd he didn't remember his folks, but, hey, that's the way it goes. Maybe if he'd been the one to snuff 'em, he'd've remembered.

Draping the bloodstained towel over the edge of the sink, E turned off the faucet. He'd have to buy some Band-Aids. He wondered if Dante'd need bandaging after he dug the implant out of him. Vampires were supposed to heal fast and shit, so maybe not.

Bad Seed had fucked up. They didn't have just one born sociopath, they had two, true bloods—vampire *and* human—and they'd just lost all control of their little project.

E gathered up the file box and the black bag he'd borrowed from Tom-Tom's closet, opening the motel room door with one cramped hand and a kick from his Nikes. He strode across the semideserted parking lot, gravel gritting beneath his sneakers. Balancing the box and bag on his uplifted thigh, E managed to unlock the Jeep and wrestle the door open. He shoved the box onto the backseat, then tossed the bag in beside it.

The black bag was full of all kinds of goodies to subdue a bloodsucker. Drugs—only drugs derived from natural shit or designed for bloodsucker systems worked on 'em; handcuffs—oh, not your ordinary, for-humans kinda cuffs, oh no; and a strait-jacket, a *special* straitjacket.

At first, E had thought he'd pay Ronin a surprise visit during daylight hours and try some of the goodies out on his black bloodsucker ass. But then he'd gotten another idea.

A *better* idea.

He was gonna play possum. Go back to the rental. Put all the goodies away. Pretend he still didn't know shit. Until the right moment . . . the moment Tom-Tom managed to bring Dante home or the moment Dante decided to crawl in through Ronin's window to take care of business.

In either case, E would be ready.

E slid into the driver's seat and keyed on the ignition. The Jeep started up right away, the pungent smell of gasoline and exhaust puffing white into the chilly air. He glanced at the newspaper lying beside him on the seat, and reread the headline.

CROSS-COUNTRY KILLER DEAD IN FLORIDA.

Really?

A scraping, steam-roller-over-rocks sound filled the Jeep's interior. E forced his jaw open. The sound stopped. Pissed enough to grind his teeth. Either some idiot had dared to copy his work and had been fucking nailed in the act . . .

Or someone wanted to lure the Bureau away . . . lure *Heather* away from him. That someone would have to be Bad Seed momma, Johanna.

If he continued to cull, it'd be obvious he wasn't dead, unless Bad Seed planned to make sure he never killed again.

Sweat popped up along E's hairline. Did they think they were smarter than he was? Did they think they knew more about death than a true-blue sociopath, one born, not created?

E fetched his satchel of tricks from the Jeep's floorboards and took inventory: a length of rope, coiled wire, pliers, latex gloves, duct tape, a small cutting torch. The only thing missing was his book of Navarro's poetry. He'd pick that up when he dropped Ronin's goodies off.

Tonight he'd assert his independence. Tonight he'd look for

that special someone. Someone who'd appreciate both his skills and his poetry . . .

With a little coaxing.

SLEEP RELEASED JOHANNA AND her dreams dissipated like night mist caught in sunlight. Fat bumblebees buzzed, the sound vibrating in through her fingertips. She opened her eyes. No bumblebees. No sunlight. Just carpet under her cheek and a buzzing phone.

She pushed herself up to her knees. How long had she been Sleeping? Hours? Days? The pills threw her natural rhythms out of sync. With each use, it took longer and longer to regain the flow.

Scooping her cell phone up from the floor, she flipped it open. "Yes?"

"I checked all incoming flights for the last twenty-four hours," Gifford said. "Craig Stearns arrived at Dulles at five-thirty this morning."

"When did he leave?"

"Seven p.m. For New Orleans."

Johanna raked her fingers through her hair. She'd underestimated Stearns or, more accurately, his attachment to Wallace. "Call your people in New Orleans," she said. "Give them Stearns and Wallace. Extreme prejudice."

"Understood."

Johanna folded the cell phone shut. In truth, she'd made more than one mistake with Stearns. She should've killed him the day he discovered Bad Seed. But she'd thought his own black past and her knowledge of it would keep him silent.

She'd been right about that—his silence.

She'd simply forgotten Stearns was a man of action, not words.

18

ALL OF THIS FOR YOU

Pulse roaring in his ears, Dante held the sheer black stocking in both hands. A yellow sticky note clung to the delicate fabric. He plucked it off.

1616 St Charles

Dante lifted the stocking to his nose. Sniffed. Nothing of Gina remained. No trace of her black-cherries scent. Instead he caught the clean odor of soap and the rubber tang of latex gloves. He lowered the stocking, throat tight. Every bit of her was gone.

His fingers clenched around the stocking. His eyes squeezed shut. Fire burned through his veins; rage ignited his thoughts, his heart. In the distance, wasps droned.

Was Jay still alive?

Wasps burrowed beneath Dante's skin. Crawled into his mind. His body reverberated with their deep droning. His head ached with it.

Dante-angel? Did she trust you? Did she believe in you?

'Fraid so, princess.

She knows better now, huh, Dante-angel?

A hand seized his chin, forced his head around. Dante opened his eyes. Heather stared at him, *into* him, held his gaze. He heard her heart pounding hard and fast.

"Breathe, Dante," she urged, releasing him. "Are you all right?"

Dante held up the stocking. "How the *fuck* am I supposed to wake up?"

Understanding lit Heather's blue eyes, but something else shadowed her face. She tugged the stocking from his grasp, the fabric whispering against his palm. He sucked in his breath when he saw the runs and tears. He glanced down at his hands, his nails. Closed his hands into fists. A wasp's swollen abdomen disappeared beneath his knuckles—glistening and wet and Giger-esque. He shuddered.

"—and he's not only hooked you, he's reeling you in."

Dante glanced at Heather. He realized she'd been talking for a while before he'd heard her. The droning faded.

"Let him have me."

Heather's brows knitted. "That again," she muttered. "He knows what you don't—your past. He knows how to play you. I wish I knew why."

"I don't give a fuck." Dante keyed on the MG's ignition and stepped on the gas. The car roared to life. He grabbed the gear-shift.

Heather's hand wrapped around his, warm and strong. He looked at her. "He's got the advantage," she said.

"Yeah, maybe so," Dante said. "But he's the one you've been tracking for three years. Gonna let him walk?"

Dante held her gaze, listening to the steady beat of her heart. She smelled clean and sweet, like the air after a storm, and, for a moment, the droning stopped as he looked into her eyes.

Heather released his hand and pushed her hair back from her

face. She drew in a long, deep breath. "We're on our own," she said, strapping her seat belt shut. "The case has been closed. I can't call for backup."

"Me neither."

Dante touched his link to Lucien. It was closed. A burr of dread hooked into his stomach. The sudden alarm in Lucien's dark eyes had rattled Dante; had shaken him free of the unknown song lacing through the night and pulsing in time with his blood.

What could frighten Lucien? That question left Dante cold.

Shifting the car into first gear, Dante nosed the MG out into traffic. Partiers crowded the street, unknotting reluctantly when the MG nudged against them.

"Can knives hurt you?" Heather asked. "Bullets?"

Dante glanced at Heather, surprised. "Sure, anything can *hurt*. A bullet to the head or the heart would put me down for a while . . . so I've been told." He shifted his attention back to the street. "Never taken a bullet before."

"You're fast. Can you take him?"

"Yeah, if he's mortal. If he ain't, maybe," he said, swinging the steering wheel to the right and tapping the horn. A partier staggered backward, a drunken smile plastered across his face, and extended his middle finger.

"All DNA has been human."

"Should be no problem then."

Dante maneuvered the MG through the people-clotted street, his reflexes steering the car around pedestrians and cops on horses, goosing the gas every time a gap opened.

"What did Ronin mean by True Blood?"

Dante glanced at her. "Is my friend asking or is a cop asking?" He shifted the MG into second as he pulled out onto Canal.

"I'm both, Dante. That hasn't changed."

Dante nodded. Picking up speed, he shifted into third. Neon light danced along the windshield. Headlights hit his eyes like runway spotlights. Pain prickled like thorns within his aching head. He winced. Spots of color floated in front of his eyes.

He unhooked his shades from his belt, then slid them on. Oncoming headlights muted, the pain faded. Dante drew in a deep breath, tried to ease the tension from his shoulders, but his muscles refused to relax.

Heather still waited for an answer. She said nothing, but he felt her anticipation.

Fourth gear. Still picking up speed. Lights blurred.

"A True Blood is a born vampire."

"*Born*? That's possible?"

"So I've been told."

"Why would he call you that?" Heather's tone was soft, perplexed. "If you're a vampire—and I'm willing to admit to the possibility—then someone made you, right? Who made you? And when?"

Pain shafted Dante's temple. And, below, behind his thoughts, something shattered like glass. His hand locked onto the steering wheel. White light squiggled at the edges of his vision. He clenched his jaw, willing the pain away. *Not now. Not fucking now!*

Horns blared and tired screeched as Dante missiled the MG through a red light. Streetlights, shadow-darkened old oaks, and gleaming streetcar rails merged into one continuous image.

"Jesus Christ!"

Dante heard vinyl creak as Heather latched her hands onto the dashboard. "Slow down," she said, her voice even. Coaxing. "Maybe you'll survive an accident at this speed, but I won't."

Wasps droned. Venom burned through Dante's veins. Warm fingers wrapped around his on the gearshift.

"Please, Dante. Slow down."

Heather's calm voice was like a waterfall dousing the fire consuming him, tumbling wasps back into the shattered depths within. He drew in a shuddering breath and eased his foot up off the gas pedal. Downshifted to third. Lights and colors shifted from streamers to distinct images: houses, trees, cars. Sweat trickled along his temple.

"Listen," Heather said, her hand still grasping his. "A trap's been set for you. You know this. I know this. You plan to walk right into it. Then what?"

Dante glanced at her. Shadow and light flickered across her face. Streetlight burnished her hair. He shrugged. "No plan. I'll play it as it comes. But I'll walk out with Jay."

Heather sighed, rubbing the bridge of her nose. "Uh huh."

Shifting his attention back to the road, Dante scanned for building addresses.

"I think he believes you're nightkind," Heather said. "So he'll be planning for that. But he isn't planning for me. Even Ronin thought I'd be in Pensacola."

1500. They were close. Dante reduced speed. His gaze swept from one dimly lit warehouse to the next. Another block. A stone building on the right with a weather-faded sign reading CUSTOM MEATS. Boarded-up windows. Vacant. His gaze flicked back to the sign. CUSTOM MEATS. Unease twisted through him.

"Go past," Heather murmured.

Dante drove several blocks farther, then hooked a left, swinging the MG to the next parallel street. Arrowing in against the curb, he downshifted to a stop and switched off the engine. Pocketing the keys, he yanked open the door. A hand grabbed his arm, fingers latched around his forearm.

One twitch and he'd walk away.

Would he be leaving behind his friend or the cop?

He eased back against the seat. Looked at Heather. He'd be leaving both.

"I'll follow," she said. Adrenaline sharpened her scent, warmed her blood. "I'm your backup." Sudden intensity lit her blue eyes. She radiated a dark, desperate, almost violent emotion—one Dante couldn't name. "Promise me you'll play it safe."

He held her gaze, breathing in her adrenalized odor, listened to the steady beat of her heart. He brushed the backs of his fingers against her cheek. Her skin felt feverish.

"No."

Heather nodded, jaw tight. She released him.

He slid out of the car.

Does she trust you too, Dante-angel?

'Fraid so, princess.

He ran.

RONIN EASED THE CAMARO along the curb, then switched off the engine and glanced at the GPS receiver. Dante was on the move, running, judging by his speed; aimed for CUSTOM MEATS like a wrecking ball.

Hope Étienne is ready.

Ronin opened the driver's side door, uncurled from the seat, and walked across the street. Of course, Étienne really had no clue. He was so blinded by his rage and his grief, by his desire to make Dante feel a little of the same, that he hadn't recognized True Blood. Hadn't recognized death coiled into a slender five-nine form, hadn't recognized danger in a beautiful, pale face.

Had Dante put the torch to Étienne's household? If so, it wouldn't be the first time he'd played arsonist. Or had someone else done the dirty work and left Dante to take the blame? Who knew? All that mattered was that Étienne believed Dante responsible and would do anything to punish him.

GPS receiver in hand, Ronin *moved*, gusting like a night breeze along the empty street. He watched for Agent Wallace. Her presence at the club had caught him completely off guard.

Blue eyes watchful, she'd stood beside Dante on that dais like she belonged there.

Like an equal. A *mortal*.

He'd underestimated her. She'd understood the messages when Dante hadn't; she hadn't bought Johanna's desperate cover-up—which begged the question, How much longer *did* Wallace have to live?

Ronin knew his *fille de sang*—Wallace's return to New Orleans was a death sentence. E would miss her, but then, he didn't have much longer to live, either.

It bothered Ronin that he hadn't seen E recently. Was he out proving the papers wrong? Pouting? The fact that he hadn't been able to track the jittery psycho on the GPS had left Ronin cold. Had Johanna already switched him off, so to speak? Or had E discovered a truth Ronin had hidden from him?

Ronin slipped into the shadows between buildings, shades on to keep his lambent eyes from giving him away. A movement above caught his peripheral vision. He froze. Looked up.

Dante climbed onto the roof of CUSTOM MEATS, moonlight gleaming on leather and metal. He prowled along the roof's edge, lithe and quick, his shaded attention focused on the concrete beneath his feet.

Ronin drew his shields in tight. Stilled his questing mind. Dante seemed like a slice of the night itself, black hair and moonlit face stalking the edge of dreams, an elemental of old.

He remembered the feel of Dante's lips against his, the unexpected warmth of his hands against his face. Remembered the smell of him, smoke and musk and frost.

Remembered what Dante had murmured against his lips.

You'll never taste my blood.

Ronin's hands pressed against the wall behind him, his palms scraping across brick and rough mortar. *We'll see, child, we'll see.*

Dante stopped. Tilted his head, listening. He crossed to the roof's center, paused, then took one more step. He vanished. The sound of shattering glass echoed throughout the sleeping street.

A smile touched Ronin's lips. Hard boy to predict.

Dante'd just dropped through the skylight.

WITH THE TOUCH OF his fingers still lingering on her face, Heather watched Dante run across the street, blurring, moving too fast for sight. He vanished into the night. Or merged with it.

She stared at the empty sidewalk. The MG's engine ticked and clinked as it cooled. Apprehension lodged in her belly, twisted tendrils of doubt around her spine. She opened the passenger door.

She thought about calling Collins, but realized she'd be asking him to risk his career. He'd probably do it, too.

Heather got out of the car and quietly closed the door. Nothing moved across the street. Shadows stretched away from buzzing streetlights. Most houses were dark, as were the little neighborhood businesses. Mom and Pop market. Used-book store. Antiques.

She trotted across the street, her rubber-soled Skechers nearly silent against the pavement. Her purse bumped against her hip, and she paused; but it was too late to run it back to the MG. Swinging the body of it behind her, she loped down the gravel alley between the antiques store and the used-book place.

Where was Dante? Inside, already?

Promise me you'll play it safe.

No.

His voice, low and firm, had brushed against her heart just like his fingers had against her face. Anger surged through her, stoked a fire in her belly. Gorgeous, sexy, but pigheaded. Loyal to a fault.

Simone's voice whispered into her thoughts: *What you need to remember,* m'selle, *is that Dante never tells a lie.*

So how could he promise when playing it safe might cost Jay his life? And if Jay was already dead? She pushed away the thought.

Heather stepped out of the alley and into the shadows clustered along the sidewalk. Across the street was the front of CUSTOM MEATS, windows boarded, red paint weathered to a faded-out rust color.

The sharp sound of breaking glass shattered the silence. Heather yanked her .38 from the trench's inside pocket. Even as she raced across the street, she realized the gun's weight was all wrong. It wasn't loaded. As she glanced down at the .38, sudden motion in front of her yanked her gaze back up.

She dropped to the damp pavement, then rolled to her left. She swung the empty .38 up in both hands, aiming between her upraised knees at the darkness rushing toward her with heart-stopping speed. She squeezed the trigger. The .38 fired, fracturing the night, the bullet *twipp*ing into flesh. Heather released the breath she held. No magazine, but a round had still been in the chamber.

Thomas Ronin stood about a foot from her, a hand pressed to his side. Blood leaked between his fingers. He frowned, his gaze on the wound.

"Fuck."

Heather rolled to her feet, swinging the .38 up again. She had another magazine in her pocket, but no time to grab it and slam it home.

"Don't move." She aimed the empty .38 at the journalist's forehead, hoping he'd buy her bluff. "A bullet to the brain will put you down for a little bit."

Ronin glanced at her. A smile curved his lips. "Naughty Dante. Telling trade secrets. Even more amazing, you believe him." He shook his head. His hand dropped from his wound.

Something slipped from his fingers and *tink*ed against the concrete.

"Did he tell you that it hurts? A lot?"

Sweat slicked Heather's palms. "If you don't want it to hurt *a lot* again, stay right there."

Wiping his bloodied fingers against his jeans, Ronin chuckled. "You've got brass."

"You here for the story?" Heather asked, keeping careful aim on the journalist's forehead and hoping he couldn't hear her thundering pulse. "Or did you set us up?"

Ronin tilted his head. "There it is again . . . *us*. I set *Dante* up. I can't help it if you're along for the ride." He *moved*.

Something slammed against Heather's temple. Blue light flickered through her vision. She staggered. The .38 was ripped from her grasp, tearing the fingernail on her trigger finger down to the quick. Pain arced up to her elbow. A gleaming pinwheel spun through the air. The .38 clattered onto the roof of CUSTOM MEATS. Rough hands spun her around, an arm slid around her throat. Squeezed.

"Time for Dante to wake up," Ronin said, his voice smooth, affable. "And time to bid you good night."

Heather's vision darkened. She drove an elbow back, hoping to connect with Ronin's wounded side, and slammed her foot down on his at the same time.

He squeezed harder.

She gasped for air. Her fingernails tore into his arm.

Darkness swallowed her whole.

IN A JAGGED SHOWER of glass, Dante landed in a half crouch on the concrete below. An old stench of spilled blood and terror permeated the building, clung to it like a starving leech. He straightened, bits of glass dropping from his shoulders and hair and scattering across the stained and dusty floor. Thick curved hooks and dangling chains gleamed in the darkness. No power. No lights. Only a little bit of moonlight leaked in from the broken skylight. But that was all the light he needed, and more.

An image flickered: blood spraying across white walls, blank faces, a window. A voice, asking, *What's he saying?*

The image vanished, but Dante's unease deepened. Pushing his shades to the top of his head, he listened. Two hearts. One slow, a little erratic; the other deep and steady. One mortal. One nightkind. Adrenaline burned through Dante's muscles. Drawing in a deep breath of tainted air, he *ran*.

Chains clinked in Dante's wake, and memory clawed at him with cold fingers. Pain prickled behind his eyes. He ignored it. Just as he reached the cavernous building's far end, a door scraped open, metal shrieking against concrete. Nightkind scent. Clean and spicy, blood-fed and warm. Familiar.

Flickering light spilled from the opened freezer door—candlelight—and a form hurtled out with nightkind speed. Black braids, café au lait skin, eyes black as burned coffee and just as bitter.

Étienne.

Dante headed straight for him, going low and fast. Étienne swerved at the last moment before impact, but Dante spun with him, slamming a forearm across his face.

Blood spurted from Étienne's broken nose. He hit the floor hard with Dante on top of him. Air exploded from his lungs. Grabbing a handful of blue-beaded braids, Dante slammed Étienne's head against the concrete over and over. Something cracked—floor, skull, Dante wasn't sure. A deep ache radiated through his right side. Glancing down, he realized Étienne was hammering a fist against his ribs.

Dante smashed his fist against Étienne's swollen nose. The vampire's eyes rolled up white and he went limp. Dante paused, blood-smeared fist still lifted, braids still clutched in his other hand. He listened. The hair on the back of his neck prickled.

Too easy. Too fucking easy.

Heather was wrong. Either someone—Étienne?—was copycatting her killer or her killer wasn't working alone. Mortal DNA, she'd said.

Glass crunched beneath boots. Dante let go of Étienne's braids and lowered his fist. Another heartbeat. Another familiar scent. Nightkind. His muscles coiled. He slid off Étienne's motionless body and straightened. His hair fluttered as the newcomer rushed past him. Dante breathed in the smells of dark tobacco, ink, and desert sand. His hands knotted into fists.

How about a nightkind journalist with a pervy mortal assistant who liked to sneak peeks?

Dante swiveled around to face the open freezer door. Ronin leaned against the wall beside it, one leg braced behind him, a cold smile stretching his lips. His eyes gleamed. Shades dangled from his hand.

"Lying motherfucker," Dante spat.

Ronin spread his hands. "You should know. You've been *living* a lie." He tapped a finger against his temple. "Wake up, S. Time to wake up. All of this is for you." He stepped into the freezer, stepped toward the source of the irregular mortal pulse.

Jay.

Dante launched himself, diving across the threshold and into quivering orange light. Rolling to his feet, he looked up. And froze.

A figure hung by the ankles from a metal hook, wrapped and hoisted in dull chains, strapped into the white cocoon of a straitjacket. Blond hair swept against the floor. Pale face. Nearly white lips. Closed eyes.

Images flashed and whirled through Dante's mind. A glimpse of red hair. The reek of clotting blood. The cold gleam of chains. Pain blasted through his mind, dropping him to his knees like a sucker punch to the temple. His vision whited out.

Dante-angel?

What's the little psycho saying?

"You can still save him, True Blood. All you have to do is wake up."

Wasps droned, crawled angrily beneath Dante's skin. Staggering to his feet, dizzy with pain, he threw himself at Ronin.

The journalist sidestepped Dante's rush, shoving as he passed. Off-balanced by Ronin's push and his own momentum, Dante slammed shoulder first into the wall. As he twisted around, a hand latched onto his throat and bulldozed him into the wall. Dante's head snapped back against the concrete. Color fractured his vision.

The fingers around his throat squeezed. Struggling to breathe, Dante locked one hand around Ronin's steel-corded wrist. Energy pushed at Dante's shields. Sweat trickled down his temples, stinging his eyes. His shields rippled, faltered. Gasping for air, he hammered his other fist into Ronin's gut again and again.

Ronin doubled over, his fingers sliding away from Dante's throat. Sucking in a throat-burning gulp of air, Dante hooked his hands on either side of the journalist's head and rammed Peeping Tom's smug, lying face into his upraised knee.

Bone crunched. Blood sprayed.

Dante shoved Ronin away from him, tossing him completely across the freezer. The journalist stumbled, struggling to retain his balance.

Blood slid down Dante's throat. He wiped a hand under his nose. Blood, gleaming almost black in the candlelight, smeared the back of his hand. Wincing in the light, he reached for his shades and realized he'd lost them in his fight with Étienne.

Nausea twisted through Dante's gut. The migraine pierced his mind with blinding shards of white light, hacked at his thoughts. But one thought persevered—Jay.

Dante shoved the pain below. Pushing himself away from the wall, he went to the center of the freezer. Jay's eyes opened. Relief flickered in their green depths. A smile ghosted across his lips.

"Mon ami," he breathed. "I'm so sorry—"

"Shhh. *Je suis ici.*"

Dante circled Jay's bound and dangling body, his eyes on Ronin. The journalist straightened, his dark eyes calm above his blood-smeared face. Gaze never leaving Ronin, Dante slipped his arms around Jay, lifting him up and off the hook. As he crouched, easing Jay onto the concrete floor, Ronin grinned. Then he *moved.*

Uncoiling upward, Dante placed his feet on either side of Jay's body and braced himself for Ronin's attack. Denim slid across latex. As Dante ducked and swiveled, something caught his hair and yanked his head back. Pain rippled through his scalp.

"Caught you, *marmot.*" Étienne, up from concrete floor and joining the fight.

A flurry of fingertip jabs hit Dante in quick succession, stone-edged and quick; then Ronin whirled away. Minefields of pain exploded with each jab. Base of throat. Sternum. Gut. Crotch. Dante gasped for air, but gagged instead as his burning insides tried to turn themselves inside out. He spat blood onto the floor. His vision blurred.

Ronin wheeled around for another pass. Dante swung his arms up, blocking the first two blows. The last two knifed into his ribs on either side. Pain stole his breath.

Send it below or fucking use it.

"Your pretty little FBI agent won't be joining you," Ronin said. He knelt beside Jay. "A shame, really. Might've been amusing."

Heather. The thought hurt, a jagged splinter of glass. Light pinwheeled through Dante's vision. His head ached. Pain pounded at his temples. *Jay.*

Send it below or fucking use it.

Dante leaned back into Étienne's warm body, then stepped forward and kept moving. Pain tore through his scalp as tendrils of hair ripped loose, still wrapped around Étienne's fingers. Blood trickled down his neck, sticky and warm.

"Wake up, S," Ronin murmured. His forefinger slipped across Jay's throat.

Blood sprayed across the grimy floor and spattered Ronin's face, the white straitjacket. Jay choked.

"No!" Dante dropped to his knees beside Jay and bit into his own wrist. Blood welled up, dark and rich and full of life.

Jay looked at him, eyes dilated, scared. And dying.

Arms locked like steel bands around Dante. Yanked him onto his ass. He struggled to break free, twisting, and driving an elbow back into Étienne's ribs. The vampire's breath exploded from him in a pained *whoof*. Dante scrambled to get his feet under him. Etienne dug in his fingernails, piercing latex and skin. Dante hissed.

The blood flowing from Jay's slit throat had already slowed. It spread in an ever-widening pool around Jay, staining his hair red. Jay's half-lidded gaze fixed on Dante.

"Hang on," Dante said. "Hang on."

A smile flickered across Jay's pale lips.

Throwing himself forward with every bit of adrenaline-fueled strength he had, Dante dragged Étienne with him across the floor as he crawled to Jay. Sweat trickled into his eyes. Pain needled his temples. He sank his teeth into his healing wrist. Blood welled up again.

I knew you'd come for me.

Jay's thought penetrated the pain snaking through Dante's mind, silenced the voices whispering from below.

I knew you'd come.

More weight dropped on Dante, flattened him against the concrete floor. Another set of hands pulled at him, yanking him back up onto his knees. Straitjacketed him with steel arms. Thighs pinned him. A hand closed on his throat, around the collar.

I knew.

Dante strained to pull free of the limbs holding him, strained to lower his mouth to his wrist. Strained to haul all three of them across the floor. He slid maybe a foot forward before his strength gave out.

A sigh escaped Jay's lips. His heart stopped. The light winked out of his eyes.

A hand brushed Dante's hair aside. Warm lips touched his ear.

"How does it feel, *marmot*?"

Dante screamed.

19

ELOHIM

WINGS SLASHING THROUGH THE night air, Lucien flew, eyes closed, listening to the complicated aria vibrating through his heart and mind and weaving a dark refrain of information into his consciousness. He now knew the singer, how far he had traveled. And why.

So Lucien kept silent, his own *wybrcathl* unvoiced. He refused to share anything with the one warbling into the lush New Orleans night.

Cool, moist air rushed past him, beading his face with moonlit drops of dew. Lucien still tasted Dante's blood, dark and sweet, on his lips. Still felt his reluctance and frustration. Smelled his hurt, sharp and bitter.

You've always been there for me. Whatever's wrong, let me be there for you.

No. Close your mind. Shield it. Promise me.

Fuck you.

Promise me.

Opening his eyes, Lucien pushed all thought of Dante out of his mind. His song wasn't the only thing he refused to share.

His wings swept through the night, kiting him to the ground as he descended into St. Louis No. 3. Dead leaves swirled along the cemetery path, caught in his wing gust. Lucien touched bare feet to the cold stone walk.

An *aingeal* was perched on a mist-shrouded tomb marked BARONNE, his black, leathery wings encircling his body and sheltering him from view—except for his taloned feet. Silver markings, visible only in starlight, etched his wings. His scent, ozone and fallow earth and night-chilled dew, perfumed the city of the dead.

Sudden, unexpected longing burned through Lucien's veins and tightened his throat. His pulse pounded in time with the *wybrcathl*'s haunting rhythm. Loneliness snaked around his heart. It had been *so* long. Ah, but by his own choice.

"Hail, Loki. Well sung," Lucien said. "Your invitation has been received."

The *wybrcathl* ended abruptly and thick silence, absent even of insect song, wound through the cemetery.

"But not answered in kind. Most intriguing, brother." The *aingeal*'s wings curved back to reveal his bowed head.

Silver markings looped and whorled along the entire right side of Loki's nude body, across his throat, torso, and taloned hand. Gold-lace bracers encircled both corded wrists and his right biceps. A thick gold torc twisted around his throat. Long red hair veiled his face. Several strands fluttered in the breeze.

Loki lifted his head. Golden eyes glowed in the darkness. "Expecting to be challenged for your aerie?"

"A challenge?" Lucien snorted, folding his arms across his chest. "From *you*?" His wings arched up behind him. "Are you trying to kill me with laughter, brother?"

Folding his wings behind him, Loki glanced up at the moon, a long-suffering expression on his face. "Phaaugh! Same old Samael. No sense of humor."

"At least I have more than Lilith." Even after a thousand years or more, he still felt a twinge when speaking her name.

"Spoken like a true former lover."

Stepping forward, Lucien reached up and seized Loki's ankle. Yanked. Expression startled, wings fluttering, Loki tumbled from his perch.

"Has she forgiven you that 'Angel Moroni' stunt yet?" Lucien asked.

"Well, more or less," Loki muttered. Kneeling on the mist-shrouded ground, he glared at Lucien. "Was that necessary?"

"Absolutely. Tell me, does she still rule Gehenna?" An image of flowing black hair, dark eyes, and creamy skin flashed into Lucien's mind. He went cold as he realized how much Genevieve had looked like her. *Had?*

Still kneeling, Loki plucked several yellow carnations from the vase in front of the tomb's padlocked iron fence. "I'm surprised you care after all these centuries tucked away in the mortal world," he murmured. "But, yes. And Gabriel has joined forces with the Morningstar to mount yet another campaign against her."

Lucien crouched in front of Loki. "And you, naturally, are playing both sides."

Loki breathed in the carnations' sweet scent, his eyes closing in pleasure. Mist snaked around his nude form. Clung to his wings in wisps. "Mmmm. Naturally. But that's not why I'm here."

Lucien touched a talon to the X-rune pendant at his throat. The breeze whipped strands of hair across his face. "No, it's not. You seek a branch of the Elohim that no longer exists, a branch that died with Yahweh."

Opening his eyes, Loki regarded him speculatively. "No longer exists? Please. We *both* know there's a Maker here." He nibbled at the yellow petals with sharp teeth. "I've heard his *anhrefncathl*, brother—wild, *young*, masculine. He's powerful. But you must've heard his chaos song, too."

Lucien held the *aingeal*'s gaze and said nothing. He'd believed—he'd *hoped*—that since the Elohim had withdrawn from the mortal world so long ago, that Dante's song would remain unheard; that the first *creawdwr* born since Yahweh—and the first mixed-blood Maker ever—would remain undiscovered.

A foolish hope. A desperate belief.

Loki lowered the carnations and looked at Lucien for a long moment. "I never expected to find you, though. You're still spoken of in whispers."

Lucien shook his head, disgust knotting his muscles. *Spoken of in whispers.* Because he'd tried to defend a tormented *creawdwr*. The sound of Yahweh's anguished words still echoed through his mind after all this time.

Let them have me.

His thoughts strobed back to Dante. A fist clenched around his heart. He met Loki's careful gaze. The *aingeal* plucked a petal from a carnation and slipped it into his mouth. Starlight glimmered along his tribal markings.

"Together we could bind this *creawdwr*," Loki said. "Keep him safe from insanity. Bind him and *train* him. We could unite the Elohim and you could rule Gehenna once again."

"Rule," Lucien spat. "Think twice before you insult me again." He stood, hands knotted at his sides. "I'll never allow this *creawdwr* to be chained to Elohim will. Mark me well, I will kill him first."

All expression vanished from Loki's face. He shifted his attention to the graveyard bouquet in his hand. "You can't keep him from going mad, brother. Not alone," he said, his voice thoughtful. "If you won't bind him, perhaps death *would* be best."

"I can't bind him alone." Bitterness edged Lucien's voice, a bitterness that surprised him. He glanced away.

"You *need* me."

Lucien laughed. "I've gotten along just fine until now." He

looked at Loki, met his golden gaze. "Leave it to you to throw the truth in my face."

Loki brushed pollen from his lips, trying to hide his smile. "Our secret," he said. "Lilith and the Morningstar will *never* know. None of them will. You can trust me in this." False sincerity lit his eyes. "I swear, Samael. Upon my name."

"Ah." Lucien lifted his palms and examined the blood welling in the wounds left by his talons.

"I'm intrigued by your pendant," Loki said through a another mouthful of carnation. "The rune for partnership. A gift?"

"Yes. From my son. A very special child."

Loki choked, coughed, then smiled. "A *son*? Congratulations—"

Lucien lowered his bleeding hands over Loki's head. Pale, ethereal light curled away from his palms, mingling with the mist. Blood dripped onto the *aingeal*'s red mane, then onto the shrouded earth. Bound.

Loki's eyes widened in horrified realization. "Special . . . ? The *creawdwr*!" Unable to move from where he squatted, he curved his wings forward protectively. The pale mist roped around the hunched *aingeal*, weaving a solid web.

"By earth, blood, air, and the power of your true name, Drwg of the Elohim, I hold you to your vow and seal you to stone," Lucien said, his deep voice carrying into the night. "No voice, no sight, no breath until I break the seal and restore you to flesh. Upon my name, it is done."

Weariness burning behind his eyes, Lucien dropped to one knee and painted a blood glyph on Loki's stone forehead. He gazed at the crouched statue. Wings curved forward, mouth open in an endless scream, partially devoured flowers clutched in one taloned hand, Loki guarded the iron-gated tomb behind him—an unwilling gargoyle.

"*Now* I trust you, brother."

Lucien's wings lifted him into the night. He spiraled up

above the glittering city and the wide, light-slicked river stretching into the distance. He drew in a deep breath of icy air. But dread, black and hard as a stone, lodged in his belly.

Dante's *anhrefncathl*—a *creawdwr's* unique song—had breached the thin wall between Gehenna and the mortal world.

Had only Loki heard Dante's song? Had he come on his own? Or been sent?

Far above Lucien, a plane soared through the night, lights strobing through the darkness. The dragon roar of its passage gradually faded.

How much longer could he hide his child from the Elohim? How could he keep Dante from using his *creawdwr* gifts? Gifts? Since when was madness a gift? The last *creawdwr* had remade his face into a searing pillar of light. Had torched bushes with a single glance.

I am.

Old sorrow tightened Lucien's throat. He'd been unable to protect Yahweh from Elohim court intrigue. Or from his own disintegrating mind.

Yahweh had called him friend, too.

Lucien's fingers closed around the wind-chilled pendant at his throat. Time to tell Dante the truth; time to give Dante his name. His thoughts slipped back to Genevieve, to the beautiful young mortal he'd loved for a brief time. Dante was True Blood, born vampire. Which meant Genevieve had been turned during her pregnancy.

Lucien released the pendant. Where was Genevieve now? Nightkind or mortal, she never would have abandoned their son. Not while she still breathed.

A dark certainty roosted in Lucien's heart. Genevieve, the laughing, questioning little Ursuline Academy graduate, no longer drew breath. He remembered the honeysuckle fragrance of her black hair, the warmth of her embrace, the questions in her dark eyes.

If you exist, then God must, also.

Yahweh died, little one. Mortals must become their own gods.

The Church wants to be God. But it's empty. I felt that the first time I knelt at a pew. Love is real, though. Love and faith.

Faith in a dead god?

No, mon chéri. *In each other.*

Cold wind stung Lucien's eyes and iced the moisture on his face. Dante would never forgive him. For not speaking. For lying. For not knowing he existed. *Would that be penance enough, my Genevieve? If I gain our son's hatred, but keep him alive and sane, would that be enough?*

I always intended to return to you. . . .

Lucien unblocked his link with Dante and opened it with a flick of energy. Sharp-edged, crystalline pain blasted through his mind. Rage, heartbroken and primal, howled through his very essence. Dante's inner shields had shattered and fallen.

Stunned, overwhelmed by the cacaphony, Lucien tumbled and plummeted toward the glittering city.

20

THE DARKEST HEART

"*Beneath still waters I lie / my mother's fingers anchoring my hair / to the porcelain bottom / she ripples above me / a goddess / not a woman / seeking to wash taint from blood / beneath still waters I lie / my mother, my anchor / I close my eyes / and breathe / beneath still waters . . .*"

E read the poem aloud, speaking over the gurgling, wheezing sounds issuing up from the sofa. He closed the book and slipped it back into his satchel.

"I fucking *love* Navarro's work," he said to the gasping thing on the blood-soaked sofa. "He speaks to the darkest heart."

Leaning back in the easy chair, E tilted his head and regarded his latest creation. *Thing* was apt. He'd removed everything that made Keith male and placed them artistically around the room. On the coffee table beside a candle. On the bookshelf nestled next to a framed photo of Keith and someone . . . lover . . . sibling . . . who gave a rat's ass?

He grinned. Well, *Keith* probably gave a rat's ass.

The gurgling, wheezing sounds continued. E smoothed his latex-gloved hands down the front of the blood-spattered butcher's apron he wore. Buck-ass naked underneath. Kept his clothes clean and was, frankly, liberating. He leaned forward and dug in his satchel until his fingers found the shape he sought. He pulled out a cordless drill. Tapped the on button. It whirred to high-speed life. He pulled down the welding goggles parked on top of his head and walked to the sofa.

Dead, was he?

Case closed, was it?

The wet gasping sounds became faster and more frantic.

"Time to recite a poem for me," E murmured, lowering the drill.

21

DESCENT FROM GRACE

LUCIEN FELL. THE WORLD spun beneath him. The city blurred into a single point of dazzling light. Cold air whistled past, frosting his cheeks and icing his hair, his wings.

Dante's barriers had been smashed. Fragmented memories crept out of the depths and slithered across his consciousness. Pain devoured Dante from the inside out, pain strong enough to knock Lucien from the sky.

Chaos song, dark and twisted and pulsing, flowed into Lucien's scorched mind. Maker. Unmaker. Unguided and abandoned.

He knew in that moment he'd failed his son. Just as he'd failed Genevieve. Just as he'd failed Yahweh.

The tall spires of a church loomed up beneath him; weathered black steeples filled his vision. He crashed through the ancient wood, plummeting through attic and ceiling and thick wood beams, body spinning with each blow. His bones broke. Fractured wood punctured his wings. Pain enveloped him in a red-hot web.

Like a star, Lucien fell into a gleaming chamber. Above him

the words SANCTUS SANCTUS SANCTUS DOMINUS DEUS SABAOTH curved across the high arched ceiling.

His pain backwashed into the link. Dante's song faltered, and then stopped.

<Lucien?>

Using the last of his strength, Lucien closed the link between them. Then he smashed into the thick wood pews. Pain wracked his body as splintered slabs of polished wood flew up into the candle-perfumed air of St. Louis Cathedral. He hit the floor.

The golden ceiling whirled. SANCTUSSANCTUSSANCTUS blurred into a streak of amber paint.

Lucien fell into darkness.

HEATHER DRIFTED UP FROM the dreamless dark. Her head ached. She opened her eyes and stared into a cloud-smudged night sky. She was on the ground—hard, damp gravel judging by the way her back felt. Her thoughts spun backward.

A rush of wind. Exploding glass.

Time for Dante to wake up.

Ronin's voice echoed through Heather's throbbing head. She sat up, or tried to. Something jerked hard on her right wrist, clunking, and she slid onto her side. She sucked in the smell of wet dirt, oil, and moldering trash. She glanced at her right wrist. Metal gleamed. She was handcuffed to a drainpipe in the alley.

How long had she been out? Was Dante still inside? And Ronin?

Heather scooted toward the drainpipe. Putting her back to the building, she sat up. She examined the cuffs. Probably her own. She reached for her purse, but it was gone. She finally spotted it at the other end of the alley, the contents strewn like confetti all along the packed-gravel lane. She thumped her head against the building.

And her .38?

A quick look around confirmed it was nowhere in sight.

"Shit. Shit. Shit!"

Memory sparked. A pinwheel of metal whirling through the night. She looked up at the roof of CUSTOM MEATS. All right. Had to be a way up. A full clip in her pocket . . . Heather grabbed at the trench, feeling for the magazine beneath the fabric. Her hand closed over a rectangular shape.

Exhaling in relief, she looked at the building's side entrance. The door stood partially open, spilling shadows into the narrow alley. She listened, but heard nothing. Her gaze skipped across the debris from her emptied purse: Makeup bag, badge, wallet, keys, spearmint gum, fingernail clippers, cell phone, nail file, mini-flashlight.

Heather's gaze whipped back to the nail file. If she could reach it, maybe she could *dig* the bracket loose; dig and chip and pry.

Leaning over as far as her cuffed wrist would allow, she reached for the file, her fingers wriggling through the gravel. She stretched, cuff scraping her wrist, bruising the bone. Her fingers scrabbled, dirt working up under her nails.

Breath rasping in a throat gone tight, wrist throbbing, Heather pushed herself back against the building. Too far. If she had something she could snag it with, pull it in . . .

Easing down on her side, cuffed arm extended behind her, she felt around in the gravel with her feet, scooping with her shoes, kicking pebbles, little bits of shells and glass, cigarette butts, and petrified wads of chewing gum up toward her hand.

Her fingertips glided over metal. She looked down into the gravel. The dirt-stained file rested next to her hand. She curled her fingers around it, clutched it tight against her palm.

Scooting back into a sitting position, Heather twisted the file around and, grasping it like a knife, worked it under one edge of the bracket and pried. The file chipped paint from the drainpipe and its bracket. Gritting her teeth, she twisted the file under the bracket. *Give, damn you!*

One edge of the bracket abruptly pulled away from the building. The file sliced through the air and Heather fell back onto her elbow. Dropping the file, she worked the cuff down and off the drainpipe.

She scrambled to her feet and ran to the back of the building. She jumped up, caught the bottom rung of the fire escape ladder, and pulled. The ladder slid down, the clanging metal loud as a falling Dumpster lid at four in the morning. She grabbed the cold rungs with both hands and climbed, dangling handcuff tinking against the rail.

As she stepped from the ladder onto the roof, shards of starlit glass caught Heather's attention. She saw a broken skylight at the roof's midpoint.

Exploding glass. Dante.

Heather paused every few steps to break up the rhythm. Didn't want Ronin to know she'd escaped. *If* he was still here. She crouched down and scanned for a gleam of metal, for the .38 Colt's familiar shape. Then she saw it among the broken glass near the skylight.

She stood, forcing herself to continue the step-step-pause step-pause unrhythm. Slipping her hand into the trench's pocket, she pulled out the magazine. She knelt, careful not to crunch any of the spilled glass, and picked up the .38. Slammed the cartridge-filled clip into it.

A scream sliced through the silence, desperate and raw with denial. She froze, pulse pounding. The sound died away after several time-stretching seconds, fading into a low growl of long-simmering rage.

Dante.

Heart pounding, Heather jumped to her feet and ran for the ladder. She flung herself onto it and half climbed, half jumped to the ground. She rounded the back corner and pelted up the alley to the side door, then slipped inside CUSTOM MEATS.

DANTE'S ANGUISHED HOWL LIFTED the hair on the back of Ronin's neck, iced his blood. He almost released the boy. *Almost*. More than a little madness and blood rage edged that echoing cry. Even Étienne's mouth snapped shut—gloating whispers silenced.

Ronin tumbled into Dante's mind as the shields he pushed against crumpled inward, pain swarming against his intrusion like a disturbed hive of wasps. Images whirled, broken and fragmented, through Dante's mind—images Ronin had difficulty deciphering.

An anarchy symbol cut into a pale torso . . .

A falling drop of blood forms into a metallic-looking wasp and flies away . . .

A shattered window, but one that stretches across the horizon . . .

Dizzied, Ronin withdrew from Dante's mind. Johanna had done her job well. The boy was more fucked up than he'd imagined. Disappointment curled through him. Dante's shields had fallen, but memory still hid, disguising itself with symbols. He'd awakened, but saw only in tarot card pictures—powerful, but confusing. True memory lurked within his subconscious.

Maybe a little more incentive?

Hooking his fingers in Dante's silken hair, he yanked his head back, pulled his throat taut. The boy struggled against Ronin's and Étienne's tight hold, muscles straining.

You'll never taste my blood.

Ronin sank his fangs into Dante's throat, just above the bondage collar. Hot blood tasting of dark, sun-warmed grapes and spiced with adrenaline and rage spurted into his mouth. Ronin swallowed mouthful after heady mouthful. True Blood, oh yes. And more. Electric energy surged through Ronin's veins.

He wrapped his arms ever tighter around the struggling young vampire, pressed his lips ever closer against his fevered flesh. Dante's strong heartbeat pulsed through his consciousness.

Ronin hears a rush of wings.

No longer able to separate his heartbeat from Dante's, Ronin wrenched his mouth from the boy's throat. The taste of Dante's blood lingered on his tongue, simmered in his veins, blazed like holy fire in his mind.

"You were wrong, boy," Ronin said. "I've had more than a taste."

"Let me up, *chien*, and we'll see how long you keep it," Dante said, voice low and strained.

True Blood *and . . .* ? The memory of Lucien De Noir's dark and earthy scent quickened Ronin's thoughts. And *Fallen?* Intriguing possibility. If so, it was information Johanna'd lacked. She'd never known or cared who had fathered Dante. Careless and a mistake.

Heart slowing, Ronin unwrapped his fingers from Dante's hair. Slid his hand once again across the leather collar circling the child's throat. His fingers tightened.

"All of this for you. See?" Grasping Dante's chin with his other hand, Ronin aimed the boy's face at the mortal's straitjacketed body. "For you."

Dante's fury battered against his shields like a jackhammer. Ronin's fingers squeezed until the boy, gasping for air, slumped against him. Étienne slammed a fist into Dante's damaged ribs. A rib cracked. The boy hissed in pain.

"I'm gonna burn your household and make you watch, *marmot*," Étienne said. "I'm gonna drink dry . . ." His words trailed off. He glanced at Ronin, face puzzled. "What's *that*?"

A faint bluish light glowed from Dante's palms. Ronin tensed. Inner alarms sounded, flooding his system with adrenaline. What, indeed? Power surged from the youth, chaotic and uncontrolled.

And definitely *not* vampiric.

Dante twisted in his embrace, struggled to bring those glowing hands up. As Ronin released the boy, flinging his arms wide, three things happened simultaneously:

Étienne said, "You're not going anywhere, *marmot*."

Dante's skin brushed against the last two fingers of Ronin's left hand.

Étienne's head snapped forward, then back, braids flying, as a gunshot cracked through the building.

Ronin leapt to his feet. Chaotic energy scrabbled through his hand. Plucking. Unraveling. *Unmaking*. Sweat beaded his forehead. Grasping his wrist, he glanced down. The last two fingers of his left hand were *gone*. As in, no longer existed. His hand had reshaped itself as though it'd always possessed only two fingers and a thumb.

He stared, heart thudding hard against his chest. The pain ebbed. His mind refused to accept what it was seeing. A flash of motion caught his attention and he looked up.

Dante stood and swiveled with mind-numbing speed to face Ronin. Even blood-spattered and bruised, Dante's beauty mesmerized. Rage smoldered in the boy's suddenly *gold*-streaked eyes, a sharp-edged rage honed for twenty-three years. But beneath that—old grief, renewed.

Gold-streaked eyes. A Fallen attribute? Or was S awakening?

"Her name was Chloe," Ronin said. "And you killed her."

Dante froze. Pain flickered in his eyes.

Ronin *moved*.

Heather squeezed the .38's trigger again. The shot tore through empty space, the sound exploding in the room. She whirled, trying to track Ronin, and caught him hitting Dante with a flurry of blows, pummeling him down to all fours on the concrete floor. Before she could even blink, Ronin landed a vicious kick into Dante's ribs, knocking him halfway across the room.

Heather fired two more rounds. A pained grunt told her that at least one bullet hit the mark. She circled the room, .38 clasped in her white-knuckled hands. Edged ever closer to Dante.

Dante coughed, then spat.

Silence.

Heather lowered the .38. Ronin was gone. Drawing in a deep breath of blood- and candle-wax-scented air, she stepped over to Étienne's Raggedy Andy–sprawled body.

"Dante," she called over her shoulder. "You okay?" She realized how inane that sounded—of *course* he wasn't okay; his friend was dead and he'd had the crap beaten out of him—but she needed to hear his voice, to gauge how *much* he'd been hurt.

"Lucien . . . no!" he said, voice husky, alarmed.

Lucien? De Noir was nowhere in sight. But Dante had told her what she needed to know. He was hurt. Maybe bad. Heather crouched beside Étienne. She risked a quick glance over her shoulder at Dante. He knelt on the floor, head bowed, black hair hiding his face. His fingers touched the floor on either side of him as though for balance.

"Sanctus, sanctus, sanctus." He swayed.

"Hold on," she said. "Hear me? We're walking out of here together."

A *healing* hole marred Étienne's pale forehead. Blood streaked his face, trickled from one nostril. His eyes were half-lidded. Heather touched a hand to the vampire's throat. Blood pulsed beneath her fingers. *Guess he has a heart after all.*

She shoved the .38's muzzle against Étienne's chest, right above that theoretical heart. *This is an execution. You do this, you might as well leave that badge and all it stands for in the dirt outside.*

Sweat trickled along her temples, between her breasts. Her muscles trembled. *And how would I bring this bastard before a court? He's a vampire,* she thought, realizing she finally believed it. *He's a killer.*

So is Dante.

That's the way of it, Pumpkin. Some you bring to justice. Some you silence. Some you let walk away.

No and no and no. Her finger tightened on the trigger. Her breath rasped in her throat.

"Mine."

Startled, Heather yanked the .38 away from Étienne's chest, her finger easing off the trigger. She looked up into Dante's dark, pain-dilated eyes. No glimmer of recognition lit his face.

He doesn't know who I am. That the realization stung so sharply surprised her. Like Annie, when she was lost to migraine pain, booze, and madness: *Who the* fuck *are you?* Like Annie—pissed. Hurting. *Feeling.*

Heather rose to her feet, her gaze on Dante. He was definitely feeling. It burned in his eyes, fevered his pale face, coiled through his taut-muscled body. He straddled the head-shot vampire, twisted a handful of Étienne's blood-spattered shirt around his fingers, and jerked his torso up.

"Let this go," she said. "Dante, you're hurt. Let me help you."

But Dante didn't reply and Heather wasn't sure he'd even heard her.

Étienne's head hung limp, his braids sweeping the floor, beads clicking against the concrete. She caught a glimpse of Dante's fangs as he bit into Étienne's arched throat. Saw the vampire's body convulse and his eyes fly open. Heard him hiss. Dante ripped into Étienne's throat. Blood sprayed.

Heather stared, pulse pounding hard through her veins. Her fingers tightened around the .38's grip. Dante wasn't feeding, no, this was something else. Primal. Pissed and hurting. Every instinct she'd honed during her years with the Bureau screamed at her to swing up the .38 and stop the slaughter happening right in front of her.

But—*did* she have a right to interfere? Dante wasn't human, she knew that now; neither was Étienne. Did human laws apply here? Was there nightkind law? Nightkind courts?

Or was nightkind justice dispensed like this—one to one, savage and bloody and personal? Was Dante within his rights? Was Étienne?

Heather's shoes squelched in something. She looked down. She stood in the pool of blood circling the straitjacketed body—*no, Jay, his name is Jay*—circling Jay. She had backed up unaware.

She swiveled around and gazed into Jay's empty green eyes. Crouching, she brushed her fingers against his still warm cheek. Had he been killed as Dante watched? She remembered the heartbroken sound of Dante's scream and her throat tightened. She should've never let him go in alone.

We're on our own. The case has been closed. I can't call for backup.
Me neither.
I'm your backup.

She slid her hand from Jay's face, clenching her fingers into a fist. Some backup. When Dante'd needed her, she wasn't there. Didn't matter that she hadn't counted on being sidelined by a vampire. What mattered was she'd failed Dante and the friend he'd tried to save.

Ronin and Étienne had kidnapped and murdered Jay. And Gina too? Could she have been wrong about the CCK's involvement? The perp she'd followed for three years was human. Human DNA.

Then it all clicked into place.

Ronin's assistant—Elroy Jordan.

A pair of killers. A tag team? It was a possibility she'd never seriously entertained. The Hillside Strangler had been two men, cousins. Were Ronin and Elroy Jordan together the CCK? Or just playing at it? She wasn't sure how Étienne fit into the picture; maybe he'd just tagged along, lugging his hatred for Dante.

So . . . where was Elroy Jordan?

Something thudded against the concrete. Heather swiveled around on the balls of her feet.

Wiping blood from his mouth with the back of his wrist, Dante stood. Étienne's head dangled from his other hand, braids wrapped around his fingers. He dropped the head onto Étienne's chest. The braids jittered with each beat of the heart. The eyes blinked.

Stepping over the still living body, Dante picked up a candle from the crate beside the door, and carried it back to Étienne. The head's eyes rolled, wild, white. Dante touched flame to the black braids and to the expensive shirt and designer slacks. Smoke curled into the air. Hair and clothing burst into flame.

Dante stood, the movement swift and smooth. The stench of burning hair and roasting flesh closed Heather's throat. With a last glance at Jay, she rose and stepped out of the sticky pool of blood.

Dante watched Étienne burn.

"Hey," Heather said, voice low. She reached for him, but he spun abruptly, knocking her hand away and grabbing her, his fingers clamping around her upper arms. He yanked her in close. Lowered his head.

Heather shoved the .38 against his ribs, heart hammering. In his eyes she'd seen loneliness and loss. Yearning. He burned against her, his body raging with an inner fire to rival the one consuming Étienne's body.

Dante nuzzled her throat, his lips brushing against her skin and she stiffened, even though fire flared within her at his touch. She wrapped her finger tighter around the .38's trigger. Dante lifted his head. Sweat-damp tendrils of hair clung to his face and blood trickled from his nose. He closed his eyes. The muscle in his jaw twitched. His wire-taut muscles trembled as he struggled for control.

Heather's arms tingled, her fingers cold, as Dante's tight grip cut off the circulation. She wondered if he was aware of the gun against his ribs. She wondered if he cared. Desperation knotted around her heart.

"Dante, don't do this."

His eyes opened. Pupils dilated and rimmed with red-flecked brown, he looked into her. He released her, then touched her face with shaking fingers, brushing stray strands of hair back from her face.

"Heather," he breathed.

Pain prickled through Heather's arms as the blood resumed flowing. She lowered the .38 to her side. The relief, the wonder, in Dante's voice told her that he'd believed her dead. She could just imagine what Ronin had told him: *Caught the fed outside. Her neck snapped real easy.*

The question was, why *hadn't* he killed her?

Heather touched cold fingers to Dante's face. "You're hurt," she said. "Let's—" She felt smooth, fevered skin beneath her fingertips, then air.

"Run as far from me as you can." His voice was strained, edged with pain.

She spun toward the sound. Dante stood in the doorway, hands braced on either side. She opened her mouth to argue, but it was pointless.

Dante was gone.

22

ANGE DE SANG

LUCIEN'S SONG SMOLDERED WITHIN Dante, its rhythm faint and faltering, dying embers of a fire that had burned hot and steady for hundreds—no, *thousands*—of years. He rushed up the cathedral's steps to the locked double doors. He looked up. Shutters blinded the windows.

The image of an arched chamber—*SANCTUSSANCTUS-SANCTUS*—strobed within Dante's mind, then flared into a golden burst of color. He touched his link to Lucien, but it was closed. He pushed. The seal held.

Voices whispered and droned. Wasps crawled.

Lucien, mon cher ami—

Jay's green eyes, steady and full of trust, even as the light went out of them, filled Dante's mind.

I knew you'd come for me.

Would he fail Lucien, too? Would he watch the life ebb from his eyes?

White light etched mysterious glyphs at the edges of Dante's vision. Blood dripped onto the concrete beneath his feet. Voices shouted and shrieked and murmured behind him, none of them making any sense. He grasped the door handles and *pushed*.

Dante didn't have to look behind him to know that mortals circled the MG parked at the foot of the cathedral's steps; he smelled them, blood and sweat, booze and desperation. He heard their hearts, pounding and hammering and pulsing; a disjointed rhythm threading through the night beneath the buzz of their voices.

With an echoing snap, the locks broke. Dante swung the heavy doors open and stepped into the golden chamber he'd seen in his mind before pain, white hot and not his own, had stolen his breath and his song.

A gold cherub stood in the aisle near the dark, gleaming pews. The smell of incense and candle wax, sharp and fragrant—sandalwood, rose oil, and sorrow—drifted through the cathedral. Silence as thick as cotton muffled the sounds from outside, but amplified the beat of Dante's heart.

Dante glanced up. Painted in amber across an arched ceiling beam were the words SANCTUS SANCTUS SANCTUS. A jagged hole marred the gold ceiling, destroying one of the painted oval images of Christ or Mary or some fucking saint. He dropped his gaze to the shattered pews on the left side of the aisle. The tip of one black wing poked up beyond them like a distant sail.

Dante ran up the black-and-white-tiled aisle to the cathedral's center, then slid to a stop beside the ruined pews. Sprawled on his side across part of a broken pew, one tattered wing against the floor, long black hair veiling his face, Lucien lay motionless.

Dante's breath caught in his throat. A splintered shaft of wood impaled Lucien—in through his lower back and out through his sternum. Blood stained the shaft's tip. It quivered with each slow beat of Lucien's heart. Light gleamed on the X-rune pendant at Lucien's throat.

Dante dashed up the wood-and-plaster-littered aisle and knelt beside Lucien's unmoving form. He stretched out his hand to brush his friend's hair aside. His fingers trembled. His hand shook. Jaw clenched, he reached—and images exploded in his mind, vivid and searing—

Gina, black stocking knotted around her slender throat, her glazing eyes fixed on the empty doorway: *Tomorrow night?*

Jay, blood spreading like dark wings beside him: *I knew you'd come for me.*

Chloe, choking on her own blood, hand reaching for Orem, her plushie orca: *My Dante-angel.* Pain shafted through his mind and that brief image-memory shattered and vanished.

Dante's vision cleared. He sat on the debris-littered floor, his hand frozen over Lucien's hidden face, heart hammering, head aching.

Promise me you won't follow.

"Fuck you," Dante whispered, and brushed Lucien's hair aside.

Blood trickled from several small cuts on Lucien's face and from a gash along his throat. Dante touched fingers to his cheek, surprised his hand held steady. The skin felt hot beneath his fingers.

Leaning over, Dante pressed his lips against Lucien's, tasted tears and blood.

<*I won't lose you.*> The thought bounced back, unheard. "I won't."

Dante rose to his knees. Seizing the bloodstained spear of wood, he yanked. The broken length of wood slid free and blood gushed from the wound, so dark it looked black. Dante tossed the wood shaft aside. It clunked against a pew, the sound echoing through the cathedral.

Dante wrapped his arms around Lucien, gathered him close. He'd expected his friend to be heavier and he nearly tipped them both over onto the debris-strewn floor. Then he remembered how effortlessly the angel would launch himself from the balcony into the night sky, black wings unfurling.

Lucien cradled in his lap, Dante pressed his hands against the chest wound. Blood seeped hot and sticky between his fingers. Lucien's heartbeat slowed. The dying embers of his song cooled, the fire of its rhythm dimming.

Dante brought his arm to his mouth, bit into his wrist, then lowered it over Lucien. Blood spattered against Lucien's lips, spilled untasted and unswallowed from the corners of his mouth.

"Drink, damn you. Don't you dare—" The words withered in Dante's throat. Pain jabbed his temples. He squeezed his eyes shut. His chest hurt, like he'd taken a brass-knuckled punch to the sternum. Pain hooked around his heart.

I'm not gonna sit on my ass and watch someone else I care about die.
But he had.
I knew you'd come for me.

Dante opened his eyes, raised his healing wrist to his mouth again, slashed it with his fangs. Drank in his own blood until it filled his mouth. Bending over Lucien, he kissed him, parting the angel's cool lips with his tongue. His blood poured like mulled winter wine into Lucien's mouth.

Dante breathed into Lucien, fanning the embers of his song into red-hot life again. His own song flowed into Lucien, dark and wild and pissed, twisting through the angel's veins, his nervous system, flooding him with pale blue light.

He remembered Lucien's wings, black and velvet smooth, a hint of dark purple underneath. Remembered the strength of his bones. The thickness of his talons. He remade Lucien as he remembered him; wove blue light into the fabric of his being, pulled loose threads and braided them together.

Remembered that first night on the wharf—sinking his fangs into the winged stranger's throat, his pain fading—then waking up in Lucien's arms as he flew through the night.

You will never be alone again, child.

Pain twisted like a screwdriver behind Dante's left eye. His song blazed and he burned with it. Flesh knitted itself whole. Bones snapped back into place, unmarred; holes vanished in wing membranes.

Healed? Remade? Dante didn't know.

He ended the kiss, drained and shaking. As he lifted his head, Lucien opened his eyes. Wonder lit his black eyes.

"Genevieve."

A name Dante had never heard before, but it didn't matter; Lucien's heart beat strong and slow, life sparked golden in his dark eyes.

"Mon ami," Dante whispered.

"You look so much like her," Lucien murmured dreamily, trailing a finger along a strand of Dante's hair.

"Like who?" Dante stared at Lucien, suddenly cold, his joy clotting up like old blood.

"Your mother."

HEATHER GOT OUT OF the cab on the corner of Royal and St. Peter. She pushed through the crowd jam-packed in the street, breathing in the odors of sweat, beer, and Dentyne as she forced her way through the revelers.

The door to the club swung open. The faint bass beat exploded into full-on screaming sound. Von strode out, Simone beside him, her face tight with concern. Von stopped, his shaded gaze seeming to lock onto Heather. He lifted his hand. No wolfish grin this time, just a crooked c'mere finger.

Heather angled across the street to the sidewalk, her hope that Dante had returned fading with each step. It scared the shit out of her to think of him cruising the streets alone looking for Ronin, pissed and hurting and out of his head. She'd promised to stick with him, to be his backup, and she'd failed him.

Dante hadn't walked out of CUSTOM MEATS with Jay and she hadn't walked out with Dante.

Run as far from me as you can.

She had a feeling Dante had been running all his life.

Heather stepped onto the sidewalk beside the tall nomad. Light flickered and flashed across his shades, his leather jacket. It glimmered on the crescent moon tattoo below his eye. Simone nodded in greeting, but Heather noticed her tension, her half-clenched fists.

"Dante's not here, is he," Heather said.

Von's eyebrows drew down together. "Fuck. I was afraid you were gonna say that. Me and the others, we've been feeling some bad shit." He tapped a finger against his temple. "Then . . . nothing. What happened?"

Disappointment sliced into Heather and her remaining strength bled out. She bit her lip, looked away. "Ronin set him up," she said finally. "Jay's dead. Dante—"

"*Mon Dieu,*" Simone whispered.

"That sonuvabitch!" Von spat. "He fucking lied in *front* of me." His muscles flexed, then coiled, snake tight. Fury and contempt radiated from him.

Von was much more than a bouncer, more than a strapped nomad vampire—and that alone was enough to spin Heather's thoughts. What had the others called him? Lew god? What was his role in nightkind society?

An honor to be escorted by you, llygad.

"Where'd Dante go?"

Heather shook her head. "He killed Étienne." The nomad and Simone exchanged glances at that name. "Then he took off. I don't know where. He was half out of his mind . . . Jay . . ." Her words trailed away as a pang of regret pierced her.

She'd walked out of CUSTOM MEATS and left Jay lying on the concrete floor in a pool of his own congealing blood, still locked inside the blood-spattered straitjacket. She'd walked into the alley and searched it until she'd found her cell phone.

She stares at the cell. She needs to call the bodies in. But she can't wait for the cops. Can't wait around to make a report. She needs to find Dante. Nightkind or not, he was in no shape to take on Ronin.

The air reeks of Étienne's torched body, his burned dreads. The stench clings to her like rank incense, settling into her trench, her hair.

Caught in the moonlight, her badge sparkles like mica in the dirt. Fidelity. Bravery. Integrity. Her throat tightens. She punches in Collins's number. When he answers, she reminds herself he doesn't deserve to be dragged through the shit. Her finger hovers over the end button.

"Wallace?"

"There's been a murder at 1616 St. Charles, inside the Custom Meats building. Two bodies."

"Okay, hang on. I'll get some units there—"

"I can't wait. I can't prove it . . . yet, but one vic was killed by Thomas Ronin."

"Whoa! Ronin . . . the journalist? That Ronin? Evidence? Witnesses?"

"Yes. A witness, but I've got to go find him before Ronin does."

"Don't tell me. Prejean."

"I think the CCK is a tag team—Ronin and Elroy Jordan."

"Wallace, hold on. You said two bodies."

"Right."

"Is Ronin good for that one, too?"

"No . . . parties unknown. I'll catch up with you later." Her finger touches the end button, then switches off the ringer. She slides the cell into her purse.

She's surprised that it was so easy. Her heart isn't pounding. Her palms aren't sweaty. Her head is clear.

She walks down the alley to her badge, bends over and picks it up. She brushes the dirt from it, shakes the gravel from the holder. Fidelity. Bravery. Integrity. She wraps her fingers around her badge.

She remembers the raw sound of Dante's scream.

Something stings Heather's eyes. She blinks until the sensation is gone. Dropping her badge into her pocket, she walks from the alley. She has a promise to keep.

A hand squeezed Heather's shoulder. She tensed, startled, and looked up into summer green eyes. Von peered at her from over the tops of his shades.

"Did you hear me?"

She shook her head. "Sorry. No."

The nomad released her. "Did Dante say anything?" he asked.

Yes. Run from me as far as you can.

"He mentioned De Noir, but I don't know why."

Simone sucked in her breath. A muscle flexed in Von's jaw. "We've lost contact with Lucien," he said, face grim.

"He also said *sanctus* several times," Heather said. "I think it's Latin for holy, but I don't know why he said it. He was dazed, hurt."

Von glanced down the street, a finger stroking his mustache. He tilted his head as though listening. After a long moment, he said, "Dante asked Trey to do a search on lying Mister Ronin and his creepy friend." He fixed his attention on Simone. She met his shaded gaze, her pale face still, listening.

They're communicating somehow. Heather looked from one to the other, feeling cut off, out of the loop. And alone.

Simone nodded. She shifted her gaze to Heather, and smiled. "We should go to the house and speak to *mon frère*. He'll know where Dante went."

"Can't you call him?" Heather said. "Or *speak* to him?" She tapped her temple.

Simone laughed. "You've changed since we last spoke. No. He doesn't listen when he's online. Come."

"Shit." Heather rubbed her face, weariness blurring her concentration. "Okay. But we're gonna get Ronin's address, right? And go after the bastard?"

Fire flickered in Simone's dark eyes. Her lips parted, revealing the tips of her fangs. "Oh, yes," she said.

"YOU *KNEW* MY MOTHER?"

Dazed by the *creawdwr* energy still prickling through his body, Lucien looked into Dante's disbelieving, gold-flecked eyes and realized he'd spoken aloud, that he hadn't been dreaming when he'd opened his eyes and seen his son's beautiful face.

Dante shook free of his hand and, sliding out from under him, rose to his feet. Blood trickled from his nose. His muscles trembled. Fury spiked his aura; exhaustion smudged it nearly black.

"Child, listen, I was—"

"You knew her all this time? And you never said anything?"

Lucien struggled to his knees, his wings fluttering behind him. His healed—or remade—flesh was tender. He tasted Dante's blood in his mouth, sweet and dark, intoxicating.

Child, how much of yourself have you poured into me?

"I was waiting for the right time," Lucien said.

"How 'bout the night we met?" Dante said, voice husky, edged with rage. "Huh? Why not then?" His gaze dropped to the pendant hanging at Lucien's throat. "Fuck!" He looked away, his jaw muscle jumping. He wiped absently at his nose, smearing blood across his face and the back of his hand.

Wings flapping, Lucien stood. Cool night air, caught by his wings, breezed through the chamber. The thick smells of incense and beeswax faded for a moment.

Lucien remembered the pain that had blasted through his mind and dropped him from the skies; remembered the rage and grief that had poured in through the link. And remembered with heart-stopping clarity: Dante's shields had been breached.

But how? Had it been some*one* or some*thing*?

"Why the fuck didn't you tell me?"

"You were dealing with so much at the time," Lucien said, voice low, soothing. "I didn't want to add to your concerns."

Dante squeezed his eyes shut, shuddered.

"Let me take you home," Lucien said, stepping toward him. Wood snapped beneath his feet. "You're hurting, exhausted. Dante, *s'il te plaît.*"

Dante looked at him then, his eyes blazing, pale face cold. He backed up the aisle. "What was her name? Genevieve . . . what?"

"Later, after you've Slept. I don't think you know how much you've been hurt."

"No!" Dante shouted. "Tell me, damn you! What's my name?"

Lucien sighed. "Baptiste."

"Baptiste," Dante repeated. The fire ebbed from his eyes. He swayed, then grabbed the back of a pew. "Genevieve Baptiste."

"Let me take you home." Taking another step forward, Lucien held out his hand.

Dante looked at him, and Lucien's heart constricted. He saw the hungry, hurting stranger from the wharf; the beautiful and deadly boy, ready to drain him of every drop of blood without a second thought.

His friend, his child, his companion was gone. The X-rune pendant burned against his skin like ice.

"Did you know my father, too?"

"Dante . . . enough. Not now."

A rush of rain-damp air, smelling of clove and old leather, whirled into the cathedral. Von suddenly stood next to Dante. The nomad looked up at the hole in the cathedral's ceiling and whistled.

"Holy shit! Someone sure ain't gonna be happy about the new ventilation."

Von's gaze skipped from the shattered ceiling to the blood-speckled pews, then to Lucien. He stroked the sides of his mustache thoughtfully. He held Lucien's gaze for a long moment, and Lucien had no doubt that the *llygad* sensed and smelled the tension between him and Dante. Questions glimmered in the nomad's eyes, questions he didn't voice.

Von glanced at Dante. "You okay?"

Dante shook his head. *"Je sais pas."*

"I heard about that lying bastard Ronin," Von said. "And Jay. I'm sorry, man."

Dante glanced away, jaw tight, body coiled, practically vibrating with checked rage. Blood trickled from his nose.

Lucien straightened, startled by the nomad's words. What had happened since he'd winged down into St. Louis No. 3 and dealt with Loki? Had *Ronin* breached Dante's shields? Awakened Dante's memories?

Brow furrowed, Von touched a hand to Dante's forehead. "You're burning up."

"I could burn forever, *llygad*, and it wouldn't be enough."

Lucien felt Von reach for Dante's unshielded mind. "No!" he cried.

Von jerked his hand from Dante's face and stumbled back a step. Sweat beaded his forehead. He touched a trembling hand to his temple. He stared at Dante, face stricken.

Dante met his gaze. Mingled streaks of gold and red slashed his dark irises. Stepping forward, he squeezed the *llygad*'s shoulder with a blood-smeared hand.

"Later, *mon ami*."

To Lucien, he said nothing.

Dropping his hand, Dante turned and walked down the aisle. As he strode toward the wide-open double doors, he stretched his arms out to either side and trailed his fingers over the tops of the pews.

Lucien watched, throat tight. Dante's wintry, unrecognizable gaze had iced his heart. Unforgiven, he wouldn't be able to teach Dante how to use his *creawdwr* gifts. Unforgiven, he wouldn't even be able to teach his son to *hide* those gifts. He'd hoped for more time. Or, more exactly, the *right* time. But Loki's appearance meant that time had run out. But even forsaken and unforgiven, he'd still do everything possible to protect and hide Dante from Elohim eyes.

Von whirled and started after Dante.

"Wait," Lucien said. "Let him go. He needs to be alone."

"Are you kidding? He's all fucked up."

Lucien clamped a hand onto the nomad's shoulder. Pressed with his talons. And stared. His talons seemed thicker, and shot through with deep blue. He looked up as Dante reached the doors and the crowd gathered at the threshold.

Fervent mortal voices whispered, *"L'ange de sang. L'ange de sang."*

"Let him release his rage," Lucien murmured. "Then go after him. Take him home and to Sleep."

Dante slipped through the mortals crowding the doorway as though they were insubstantial, the last tattered dream before waking. The mortals watched him as he descended the steps and climbed into his MG. They watched, perplexed, but awed. He'd walked through them like a true immortal. Like True Blood.

And they loved him for it.

Von twisted free of Lucien's hand, leaving strips of leather clinging to his talons. He looked at Lucien, green eyes wondering. Candlelight and shadows flickered across his face. He glanced at the yawning hole in the vaulted ceiling again.

"Musta been a hell of a fall," he said.

Lucien's fingers curled around the X-rune pendant. He nodded. "It was."

The nomad nodded as well, then turned and strode down the aisle to the doors. He breezed through the crowd—who stared in wide-eyed wonder at the black-winged creature standing beneath the cathedral's shattered ceiling—then disappeared from view.

Lucien's fingers gripped the smooth curving back of a pew. He could find Dante through the link, whether the boy responded to him or not. He'd told Von the truth: Dante needed to be alone. He needed to unleash his rage. But now was also the time when he needed someone most—to guide him through his rage, to help him survive it.

But it wouldn't be Lucien. Maybe never again.

With a sharp echoing crack, the pew splintered beneath Lucien's hand.

23

FIRESTORM

She stands beside him, little fingers clasped around his hand, stuffed orca tucked under her other arm. Her blue eyes are too direct for an eight-year-old. Red hair tumbles beside her freckled face.

I'll send them to hell, Chloe. Promise.

And you? What about you?

I'm already burning.

Chloe's body wavers, her image fades. Her warm fingers slip from his grasp.

That's not enough, Dante-angel.

"I know," Dante whispered, shifting the MG into fourth gear. His foot smashed the gas pedal to the floorboards. The engine whined. Headlights blurred, blue-white streamers streaking the night.

He didn't remember getting in the car. Didn't remember keying it on. Didn't know where he was going. Didn't recognize the road. But he knew one thing:

The voices no longer whispered.

You can still save him, True Blood.

Mon ami, *I'm so sorry . . .*

How does it feel, marmot?

He wondered if he could travel faster than sound.

A horn blared, a long, angry wail. Beyond the windshield, a double yellow line disappeared beneath the MG. Light circled ahead, expanding, brighter than a UFO. Another horn bleated. Dante yanked the steering wheel to the right, swerving back into his own lane.

Sweat trickled down his temples. The night blurred past the MG. The gearshift vibrated against Dante's palm. He tasted blood.

You look so much like her.

A fist clenched around Dante's heart. His breath rasped in a throat suddenly too tight. He pushed away the image of Lucien's face. Tried to forget the sight of him sprawled and broken on the cathedral floor.

Good thing he's restrained ... fuck! What's he screamin'?

The yellow lines dividing the highway blurred then doubled. Eyes burning, Dante blinked. A blue neon rectangle shimmered against the windshield. Fractured. Twinned. Letters and characters squiggled within the rectangles, but Dante couldn't make any sense out of them.

He's making a very loud, very clear, demand.

"Kill me."

Dante squinted, trying to make out the wriggling letters inside the expanding blue rectangle. Words. A sign.

So do it. He's too dangerous. Little fucking psycho.

The blue rectangle morphed into a neon roadside sign proclaiming: TAVERN.

Say that again and I'll give you to that little fucking psycho.

Swinging the steering wheel to the right, Dante downshifted the screaming MG into the tavern's parking lot. Gravel and dust sprayed out from beneath the tires. A couple of pickups, gearladen nomad bikes, and an old flame-painted Chevy huddled in front of the weathered building.

AS THE CROW FLIES flickered in red over a flapping neon crow.

Dante parked the MG across from the other cars, skidding in sideways. He switched off the engine. Pocketed the keys. For a moment, all he heard was his pounding heart. For a moment, he thought he could board up the broken window, nail it shut with rage and blood. For a moment, he thought his heart was caged and guarded with fetishes.

I knew you'd come for me.

You look so much like her.

For a moment.

Then the boards rotted and the nails shifted into wasps. The cage crumpled, the fetishes false.

Shhh. Je suis ici.

Blood dripped on his hand, trickled down his throat. His head ached. Squiggles of white light bordered his vision.

The pain needed to be *more.*

I'm already burning.

That's not enough, Dante-angel.

Scooping a pair of shades out of the glove box, Dante slipped them on, then stepped out of the MG. *A drink. Need a drink.* Gravel crunched beneath his boots. As he walked toward the tavern's front door, it opened, spilling light into the parking lot.

Two nomads stepped out wearing dusty road leathers and disgusted expressions. Laughter and bouncing zydeco music followed them out into the night.

"Motherfucking squatters," the horse-maned male muttered, then spat into the dirt. Silver gleamed at his eyebrow, his ears, his throat. A black bird-shaped V was tattooed on his right cheek.

Clan Raven, Dante thought, remembering what Von had taught him. Ravens and Nightwolves often traveled together, guarding each other's flanks.

The dreadlocked female, bird V inked on her right cheek,

glanced at him. She looked him over, head to toe, then back again. A smile curved her lips. Light sparked in her eyes.

"Not your kind of place, nightwalker," she said, stepping off the porch. Her smile vanished as she got a closer look at him. "You hurt?"

Dante caught the door before it closed. Warmth and booze and tobacco and sweat-laden air curled against him. His head throbbed.

"Maybe," Dante said. Then he stepped inside. The door swung shut behind him. A moment later, he heard the deep, throaty roar of the bikes as the nomads tore out of the parking lot, flinging gravel behind them.

"Terry, look at that, wouldcha! Do ya think he's lost?"

"Kee-rist! First nomads, now Bourbon Street gutter trash. What the hell's this place comin' to?"

Dante glanced at the speakers, two mortals in baseball caps and work-stained T-shirts hunkered at a table toward the rear of the bar. A haze of cigarette smoke hung motionless over the table. One of the mortals leaned back in his chair and met Dante's eyes, his tight smile daring him to say anything.

Two other mortals stood at a pool table, cue sticks in hand as they stared at Dante, game interrupted. One had a beer gut and the other was muscled like an athlete. Brutal energy spiked with an overdose of testosterone rippled around the athlete.

"Look at the collar, will ya?" Athlete said to Beer Gut. "Don't see no leash. Musta gotten away. Better call the pound." He laughed, pleased with his wittiness, and nudged Beer Gut. "Call the pound. Get it?"

Dante looked away and weaved past empty tables to the bar. The bartender looked up as he approached, a mixture of concern and wariness on her face. She was pure New Orleans with her brown skin, green almond-shaped eyes, and curly black hair. Haitian, Spanish, French, Chinese, whatever. The true heart of Louisiana.

The bartender touched a hand to the bar rag slung over her shoulder. Bottles of booze lined the shelves behind her, fancy labels and fascinating colors.

Dante stopped at the counter, gaze flicking over the bottles.

"Can I help you?" the bartender said. The badge on her black AS THE CROW FLIES t-shirt read: Maria.

"Tequila. Bourbon. Whatever's closest." Dante reached into his jacket pocket and pulled out a wad of crumpled-up old bills, tossed them onto the bar.

"You all right? Your nose is bleeding."

"Got a place to wash up?"

"Sure." Maria pointed to a short hall on the right.

Pushing himself away from the bar, Dante followed the arrow sign reading RESTROOMS to a grungy men's room featuring stained porcelain, graffiti-etched walls, and the reek of old piss.

A small window sat high above the urinals, too small to squeeze out on your tab or your bad-ass date. Dante stepped over to the chipped sink and turned on the faucet. He slipped off his shades, tucked them into the front of his shirt. He rubbed his hands together under the stream of water, then bent over the sink and splashed water on his face.

He burned. He half expected the water to hiss and turn to steam when it touched him. Instead, it was so cold it stole his breath. Dante gripped the sides of the sink, as bloodstained water swirled down the rusty drain.

Dante? I'm cold. Can I get in bed with you?

C'mere, princess. Snuggle close. I'd hold you, but . . .

How come Papa Prejean handcuffs you at bedtime?

Cuz I don't sleep at night. The prick thinks I'll murder everyone in their beds.

Wouldcha?

Yeah. Probably.

Dante-angel, if I found the key and let you go, wouldcha take me with you?

A spreading pool of blood surrounds Chloe's pale face like a halo. Her half-open eyes stare sightlessly at the orca just beyond her reach.

I'd never leave without you, princess. Just you and me—

Meat hook, chain-wrapped ankles, bare feet. Light flashes from the hook.

Forever and ever.

Water splashed into the sink, spattering against Dante's knuckles. His muscles coiled. He stared into the sink.

She trusted you, kid. I'd say she got what she deserved.

Pain torched him. He lifted his head and looked in the mirror. He didn't recognize his reflection; the pale face and smeared eyeliner and damp, tousled hair were his, sure, but the expression was cold and distant and unforgiving, eyes red-streaked with fury.

Is this what Lucien just saw?

He dropped his head, shaken. No, the pain stabbing his temples wasn't nearly enough. Not by a long shot. But like he'd promised, he wouldn't burn alone. Peeping Tom, among others, would join him in the flames. Étienne was already ash.

He wiped his face dry with a brown paper towel, then slid on his shades and walked out of the men's room. As he approached the bar, he caught a familiar scent, Brut and soap, and yet another—smelling of dry cleaner's chemicals and deep, dark secrets. He slowed. Remembered a lazy smile and a wink.

Take him in. Lock him up. He'll be asleep in no time. I guarantee.

What the hell are they *doing here? No coincidence. No fucking way.*

Dante walked past without glancing at either detective. He stopped at the counter. Maria poured something golden into a shot glass.

"Y'all left nearly eighty bucks on the bar."

"Keep twenty for yourself," Dante said, picking up the shot glass. "Let me know when I've drunk up the rest."

"Sure thing, sugar." Maria tapped a finger under her nose, looked meaningfully at Dante, then handed him a napkin.

He took the napkin from her, pressed it against his nose. It came away red.

"Fuck." He tossed back the shot. Tequila. It burned down his throat, cleared out the lingering blood. He felt sweat trickle along his temple.

Dante-angel?

Forever and ever, princess. Forever and ever and ever—

A smooth voice drawled, "Abita for me and Davis, darlin'. And lookee here! If it ain't a *small* fuckin' world."

Dante set the empty shot glass on the bar.

"How's it hangin', rock god? *Comment ça va,* eh?"

As Maria poured Dante another shot, he glanced to his right. Perched on a stool, Dickhead LaRousse leaned against the bar, a smirk tilting his lips. He held what looked suspiciously like an arrest warrant in one hand.

"Talk about luck," Dickhead said. "We were on our way back from your place. Seems you weren't there. Then we saw your car in the parking lot." He slapped the warrant down on the counter. "You here all by your lonesome?"

Dante lifted his hand and flipped him off. Shifting his attention to the refilled shot glass, he picked it up, tossed it back.

"Dirtier than original sin, this boy, believe you me," Dickhead said to his partner, loud enough for everyone in the bar to hear. "The shit I found in his juvie records. No wonder they sealed 'em."

Dante carefully set down the empty shot glass. He grasped the edge of the bar to keep his hands from trembling. Even *he* didn't know what was in those records. His memory only tracked back a handful of years and even then there were gaps. Hell, he didn't even know how old he was.

"Christ," Maria said, a hint of anger in her voice. "If y'all are going to arrest him, do it outside."

"A word to the wise, sugar," Dickhead said, his voice all Southern charm. "Mind your own fuckin' business."

Maria glanced at Dante from beneath her lashes as she filled a stein at the tap. He met her gaze and shook his head.

"Sixty foster homes, two stints in the loony bin," LaRousse said, his tone conversational, his voice on the verge of a chuckle. "Words like *schizophrenia* and *homicidal* tossed around. A missing little girl and . . . oh, yeah! . . . the last foster home burns to the ground with the foster parents still inside. That'd be the Prejeans."

Turning his head, Dante met LaRousse's gaze. The detective stared at him, handsome face hard, cold light glinting in his eyes.

"You're a fucking liar," Dante said. His hammering heart said *maybe not*.

"That right?" Dickhead leaned in closer. "So tell me, does that good-looking FBI bitch know she's balling a stone-cold psycho?"

Dante slammed his fist into LaRousse's nose.

"WHO MADE YOU?"

Simone glanced at Heather, her pale face tinted green by the van's dashboard lights, then returned her attention to the road in front of them.

"Nightkind, *oui*? That's what you're asking?"

"Yeah, that's what I'm asking."

Heather had never imagined having this conversation, never imagined vampires existed outside of horror movies or outside of Goth clubs. Never imagined the undead lived, worked, and fed alongside those who weren't.

But after watching Dante, after shooting Ronin, after witnessing parts of Étienne's body try to escape the flames consuming him, her skepticism, her doubts, had ended and her understanding of the world altered. She didn't want to look out the passenger window into the night. Didn't want to know what might look back from deep within the shadows alongside the road, eyes full of moonlight, mouth full of sharp teeth.

Simone sighed. "A friend of the family turned me, just after Papa's funeral."

"Was it something you wanted?"

The blonde shook her head. "No. But she didn't offer me a choice."

Shadows flickered across Simone's face. Her hands were relaxed on the steering wheel. No bitterness edged her voice. If a family friend had done the same to her, Heather would've tracked her down and . . . what? Killed her? Forced her to take it back? Maybe Simone had had time to come to terms with the situation.

How did one come to terms with being made into a vampire? How did a mortal adjust to immortality?

"And your brother?"

"He was all the family left to me," Simone said, her voice low, taut. "I gave him a choice. If he'd a said no, I probably woulda set myself on fire."

"You turned your own brother?" Heather asked, surprised.

"I couldn't bear the thought of watching him grow old and die."

Heather thought of Kevin, of Annie. Could she have done the same to them? Siphoned off their humanity? Or let them age? Bury them one after the other next to Mom? Her throat constricted.

"So, how does this undead stuff work? Dante's skin is warm. He has a pulse. He's intensely alive."

The corners of Simone's mouth quirked up in a smile. "*Oui*, Dante's intensely *everything*."

Heather stared at her, shoulders tight. Remembered Dante

leaning over Simone on the dais steps, whispering in her ear, and touching her hair. She had a strong suspicion they'd been more than just friends once. Were they still?

"We're *not* undead," Simone said. "We're a separate species. We've always lived alongside mortals." She looked at Heather and smiled.

"And Dante? Do you know who made him?"

Simone's fingers tightened on the steering wheel. "No. He's never said." She glanced at Heather. "I don't think he knows. Maybe it's lost to him." Sorrow sharpened the planes of her face.

"Like so much else," Heather said. "Hidden behind his headaches." Or was he what Ronin had called him—True Blood? Born vampire?

Her name was Chloe and you killed her.

Ronin's smooth, commanding voice wormed through Heather's thoughts. What if Dante didn't remember his past because he'd done terrible things? Things he couldn't bear to remember?

Were Ronin's attempts to awaken Dante a desire to trigger him, to wind him up and turn him loose? But if Dante could be *triggered*, wouldn't that mean he'd been *programmed*? And wouldn't that mean his memory had been *deliberately* crippled? Would certain questions trigger protective subliminals like migraines? Unconsciousness? Madness?

Heather's heart pounded in her ears, drowning out the sound of the road rushing beneath the van's wheels, beating cadence for the thoughts pulsing through her mind—black ops ran mind experiments, had for decades. Government funded and Bureau protected.

She heard Stearns's voice: *He's no longer your concern.* But that meant he was *someone*'s concern. Whose? And which agency? How deep did this go?

Heather looked out the passenger window. Her reflection,

pale, pensive, and weary, hid the night beyond. The shadows and what they *might* contain no longer seemed so scary. Not compared to the place her suspicions had brought her—a place both very dark and very real.

And Dante was caught in the middle—lost, maybe. Heather's hands knotted in her lap. Not if she could help it.

And her investigation? If Ronin and Jordan together were the Cross-Country Killer, the evidence would nail them, give a clear voice to their victims. The dead would finally speak.

Link the DNA evidence. Nail Jordan. Prove the CCK hadn't died in Pensacola. But what about Ronin? Could a human court even touch him? If she suggested he was vampire, the case would be thrown out of court and her career'd be over.

Would nightkind care if one of their own butchered mortals? Dante cared, but was he an exception?

Maybe she'd have to settle for Elroy Jordan.

The van slowed and Heather opened her eyes. Simone parked in the gravel drive curving in front of the house. Heather glanced at the dark windows. "Is your brother home?" she asked, pulling the door latch.

"*Oui.*" Simone opened the driver's door and slipped out of the van. "He just doesn't need light."

Heather climbed out of the van and into the chilly, humid night. The air was sweet with the scent of wild roses and cherry blossoms and moss.

"Wallace."

Heather froze. She recognized the voice. She'd listened to it for years. Been guided by it. The fact that he was in New Orleans was enough to ice her blood. The fact that he was at Dante's house scared the shit out of her. She slid her right hand into her trench. Reached for her .38.

"I wouldn't."

Heather turned around, pebbles from the path crunching beneath her shoes. Stearns stood beside the van's driver's side door, a silencer-equipped pistol pressed to Simone's left temple. He held the vampire's arm in a tight-fingered grip.

"We need to talk," he said.

DICKHEAD'S NOSE FLATTENED. HE fell off the stool, mingled pain and surprise flickering in his eyes. He hit the floor, blood spurting from his nostrils.

His sidekick, Davis, blinked, his mouth half-open. He reached inside his jacket, but Dante stepped forward and back-fisted him with his blood-smeared left hand. Seizing the stunned detective by the back of the neck, he pounded Davis's face against the bar's polished surface. The detective crumpled to the floor.

Standing between the two downed mortals, Dante glanced up to see Maria pressed up against the bottle-lined shelves, eyes wide, a hand to her mouth. Movement on the floor caught Dante's attention.

LaRousse struggled to his knees, eyes watering, nose swelling. He reached inside his jacket and pulled out a gun—looked like a nine mil.

"You ain't walkin' from this—" LaRousse's words, blood-thick and harsh, ended abruptly when Dante kicked the nine mil out of his hand. The detective's wrist snapped, bent at an unnatural angle. He screamed through gritted teeth.

Dante crouched in front of LaRousse. Pain prickled along his temples, behind his eyes. His vision blurred. Latching onto the detective's shoulder, he forced LaRousse's head up and to the side with a hand to his chin. Blood pulsed fast and frantic within the mortal's arched throat.

Baring his fangs, Dante lowered his face to LaRousse's warm, reeking flesh.

"I work for Guy Mauvais. I have his protection," Dickhead said, his voice a strained whisper.

Dante let go of LaRousse's shoulder and tore at his tie and shirt buttons. A button flew through the air. The shirt ripped. There, glimmering in the hollow of the detective's throat, iridescent, was a rose; visible only to the eyes of nightkind.

"Hey! Asshole! What the *fuck* you think you're doin'?"

Dante glanced at the speaker. The athlete from the pool table charged toward him, face tight and glowering, pool cue reversed and brandished like a baseball bat. Dante shoved LaRousse away hard. The detective slid across the hardwood floor and slammed against the wall.

Dante straightened from his crouch, hands intercepting and seizing the pool cue as Athlete swung it down. Dante stepped past Athlete in a rush of air and wrenched the pool cue from his grasp. Athlete's expression shifted from righteous rage to confusion. He stared at his empty hands.

How does it feel, marmot?

Whirling, jaw clenched, Dante whacked the pool cue across Athlete's back. Athlete stumbled forward, body arched. A quick stride stood Dante in front of the off-balance pool player. He smashed the pool cue against Athlete's temple, canting his head to one side. The cue snapped in half. One splintered end pinwheeled through the air and crashed against the wall phone behind the bar, knocking it from the wall. It exploded against the floor, dinging once.

As Athlete slumped to the floor, Dante swiveled and looked at Maria. She'd turned her face away from the flying spear of wood, shielding herself with one hand, the other still outstretched toward the now useless phone.

A raw-throated scream of rage spun Dante around again, the other half of the pool cue still clenched in his hand. Good Ol' Boy Terry lunged at him, fingers wrapped around the hilt of a hunting knife. Beer Gut followed, red-faced and sweating, hot on Terry's heels, cue stick clutched in both hands.

"C'mon, Ernie! Let's take out the motherfuckin' trash!"

But Terry rushed forward alone. Dante noticed Good Ol' Boy Ernie had stopped to scoop something up from the floor.

Dante swung one arm up to grab Terry's knife hand as he slammed the broken pool cue across Beer Gut's belly. Beer Gut's breath *whoof*ed out from his lungs and he fell to his knees. His cue stick dropped from his hands, clattering against the floor.

An image of Lucien slumped on his side across broken pews, plaster and gold flecks of paint dusting his hair, a length of splintered wood impaling him, flickered through Dante's mind.

Mon ami—

You look so much like her.

Sudden searing pain fractured Dante's thoughts, scattering the fragmented images and half memories. Terry's hunting knife plunged through his palm and out the back of his hand. Wasps droned. Stung. Venom poured through Dante's veins. Snarling, he yanked his arm back, jerking the knife hilt from Terry's grasp.

"Yeah!" Terry crowed. "Take *that*, mother—"

Dante swiped the back of his impaled hand across Terry's work-grimed throat. Blood sprayed Dante's face and shades, hot and fragrant. He licked it from his lips. He tugged the knife from his hand and dropped it on the floor.

The frenzied drumming of Terry's dying heart sucked Dante in and, unable to resist the pungent blood scent, he wrapped his arms around the man, pressed his parted lips against the gashed throat. Blood poured into his mouth. Together, Terry and Dante dropped to their knees.

You were wrong, boy. I've had more than a taste.

You can still save him, True Blood.

As Dante drank the diminishing flow, he heard whispers, whispers *not* from within. "Aim for the head and don't . . . fuck in' . . . miss."

Dante *moved*—diving to the floor and then rolling to his

feet—as fire flashed from a gun's muzzle. The bullets slammed into Terry's still crumpling body—one, two, three.

"Shit!" Davis cried.

Dante scooped up the broken pool cue half and hurled it at Davis, hitting him in the temple as he pulled the trigger again. The shot went wild, hitting—

"Wayne!" Ernie screamed.

Dante slammed his fist into Davis's chin, snapping his head back. At the same moment, he seized the cop's gun hand and wrenched the pistol from it, tossed it away. He punched the cop again. Stumbling, spitting blood and teeth, Davis grabbed at a table for balance, but missed. As he went down, the back of his skull connected with the edge of a chair with a loud crunch. He slumped onto the floor, eyes half-closed. The smell of blood and shit curled into the air like smoke.

Dante winced as a hoarse scream behind him pierced his ears, his aching head. It was followed by *klik-klik-klik-klik*. He turned.

Ernie held Dickhead's nine mil in a white-knuckled, two-handed grip, his eyes squeezed shut. On the floor at his feet, Beer Gut—Wayne—had toppled, a bullet hole in his temple.

Dante jerked the gun out of Ernie's trembling grasp and saw that the safety was on. He looked up from the nine mil, caught a glimpse of his reflection in Ernie's ever-widening eyes. Then both eyes rolled up to the back of Ernie's head as he crumpled to the floor in a dead faint.

Tucking LaRousse's gun into the back of his pants, Dante swiveled in time to see the detective scuttling along behind the bar, headed for the restroom hallway. Dante started after the detective, but a low, harsh sob stopped him at the bar's edge.

He vaulted over the bar, landing in a crouch in front of the black-haired bartender. She'd huddled down against the counter. Terror rippled across her face when she saw Dante and she clapped a hand over her mouth. Gaze locked on him, she groped for the baseball bat propped against the counter. Dante swatted it out of her reach. It *tunk*ed to the floor, then rolled away.

"Mother Mary, Papa Legba, protect me from this angry *loa*," she whispered.

She smelled of jasmine and deep water, but fear edged her scent, stealing the sweetness from it. Dante lifted his shades to the top of his head. Tears spilled over her dark lashes. He leaned in and brushed his lips against hers. He wiped away one of her tears with his thumb, smearing blood across her dark cheek.

He thought of red hair and cornflower-blue eyes and creamy skin. Remembered a friend saying, *I'm your backup*.

Dante pulled back. Stood. Lowered the shades over his eyes again.

Dante walked past the counter and down the hall. He paused at the men's room door and listened. Dripping water. Crossing the hall, he walked into the women's room. No urinals, but just as graffiti-etched and grungy as the men's room. Dante strode across the stained floor.

Dickhead stood beneath the no-escape window, smoothing his sweat-damp hair back with his hands. Bruises darkened the skin around the detective's eyes and across the bridge of his smashed nose. He watched Dante warily, but made no move to run.

"Wallace's boss is looking for her. He called."

Dante seized LaRousse by the lapels of his jacket and jerked him close. Only an inch separated their faces. Reeking of blood and beer, LaRousse stared at him, fresh sweat beading his forehead.

"Whatcha tell him?"

"To look for you." A sardonic gleam lit LaRousse's eyes. "That you had her all hot and bothered. That's what you do, right? Stir people up. Suck them dry."

The detective stank of envy and frustration.

Prick thinks I'll murder everyone in their beds.

"Who you working for?" Dante asked, voice low. "Besides fucking Mauvais?"

"Look, I can spy for *you*, if you want. I—"

Fingers still latched onto the detective's lapels, Dante shook him. "Who else?"

Wouldcha?

Yeah. Probably.

All color drained from Dickhead's face. "The writer, Ronin."

"Whatcha do for him?"

"I helped him contact Étienne—"

Vision blurring, Dante flung LaRousse into one of the stalls. The door *whang*ed against the metal side. The detective landed on the toilet, his head and shoulders thumping against the tiled wall. Pain contorted his face.

Is the rock god over there good for it?

We gotta go, sexy. Tomorrow night?

Shhhh. Je suis ici.

You can still save him, True Blood. All you have to do is—

"Wake up," Dante whispered. The drone of the wasps died.

Walking into the stall, Dante pinned LaRousse with a hand to one shoulder and a knee snugged against his crotch. He forced the detective's head to one side, baring his throat. The rose tattoo sparkled under the fluorescents.

"You never cared who killed Gina," Dante said, lowering his head, listening to LaRousse's galloping heart. "You only wanted to nail me."

"I have Mauvais's protection—"

"Not from me, you fuck. Not. From. Me."

Dante tore into the detective's throat. LaRousse screamed.

HEATHER WRAPPED HER FINGERS around the .38 in her pocket. Stearns's tousled hair and shadowed eyes told her he hadn't slept in a while and his steady hand told her he'd pull the Glock's trigger without hesitation.

"Let go of her," Heather said. "If you want to talk to me, fine. Since when do you need hostages?"

"I don't think you understand the situation," Stearns said. His gaze flicked to Simone. "Or what you've allied—"

Simone twisted and ducked with mind-boggling speed. The silenced Glock went off with a hushed *thffft* at the same moment she seized Stearns's gun hand and wrenched it back. The Glock dropped into the dew-glistening grass.

"Down. Or I snap it," Simone said.

Eyes squeezed shut, hissing in pain, Stearns dropped to his knees. The blonde eased up on his wrist, but kept it in a firm grip.

Heather scooped the Glock up from the grass and pocketed it. She pulled her .38 free of the trench and aimed it at Stearns. "What are you doing here?"

He opened his eyes. A wry smile stretched his lips. "Rescuing you."

"Are you involved in the cover-up?" Heather asked. Her aim didn't waver. "The Pensacola murders?"

"No. But I know who is. And I know what they're protecting."

She stared hard at the man who'd guided her career, who'd attended her Academy graduation, and who'd helped her with Annie when her father refused. Stearns held her gaze, hazel eyes steady. Stubble darkened his face. Unshaved. Sleep-smudged. Wired. A man on the run?

All through my career, he's had my back.

Would that change if the Bureau asked it of him?

Heather lowered her .38. *If so, I'd already be dead.* She nodded at Simone. With a dry tsk and a toss of her head, Simone released him. He stood, wiping at the wet, grass-stained knees of his trousers.

"Where's Dante Prejean?" he asked.

Heather stared at him. "Why? What does he have to do with this?"

Stearns looked at her for a long moment, a muscle jumping in his jaw, then he glanced away. "He's not what you think he is."

"And what do I think he is . . . sir?"

"Human."

"I know what he is," Heather said quietly. She lifted the .38 again. "Nightkind. Maybe True Blood."

"True Blood . . . ?" Simone whispered.

Stearns stared at Heather, his hands motionless at his side. She thought she saw a sudden spark of fear in his eyes, then it was gone, swallowed by the shadows.

"He's also an experiment," Stearns said finally. "I have a file in the car and a CD that you need to see. Then you'll know *exactly* what Dante Prejean is."

"His name's not Prejean," Heather murmured.

Simone circled Stearns. "I'll never let you near him," she said. Moonlight gleamed in her narrowed eyes and from her revealed fangs.

The whoosh of massive wings drew Heather's attention to the house.

Moonlight shimmered along De Noir's huge black wings as he landed on the roof above Dante's bedroom. His long black hair spilled unbound to his waist. Pale blue light flickered around his shirtless form and glimmered from the pendant at his throat.

He dropped into a crouch, wings folding behind him. A breeze stirred his hair, but otherwise he was motionless. Twin points of golden light starred the night as he stared into the darkness.

Heather's breath caught in her throat. Fallen. Étienne's voice slid through her thoughts: *Nightbringer.*

"Good God," Stearns whispered.

"You see, sir," Heather said. "I know *exactly* who I've allied myself with." She turned. Looking into Stearns's stunned eyes, she added, "Right now, I trust them more than I trust you."

RONIN WATCHED AS A female face, pale and stark with fear, bolted from the tavern. She ran full-out for the flame-painted Chevy, fumbling keys out of her pocket. Unlike terrorized females in movies, she didn't trip, didn't fall down, and her Chevy roared to life the first time she turned the key. Throwing it into reverse, she nearly backed into the black MG parked at a slant across from her. She stomped on the brakes, slammed the gearshift into first and peeled out of the parking lot.

Interesting. What mischief is my little True Blood up to? Although True Blood is no longer accurate, is it? Born vampire, fathered by one of the Fallen.

Excitement curled through Ronin. To pit himself against a True Blood/Fallen hybrid . . . what greater test of his abilities existed? Especially after he *trained* the child?

Leaving the engine running, Ronin slid out of the Camaro. He kept his shields tight and his own energy tamped down. The last thing he wanted was for Dante to sense him—to come for him before he was ready.

Ronin glanced at his reshaped left hand. Definitely not in the boy's file. After he'd split from CUSTOM MEATS, he'd sat down and followed the fading wormhole created by Dante's touch. His fingers weren't merely gone, they'd been plucked from his genetic code.

The best part? Johanna had no idea that Dante had managed to keep a secret from her. A world-altering secret.

The tavern door flew open and a mortal in a baseball hat, grubby T-shirt, and jeans rushed into the parking lot. Nearly tripping over his own two feet, he skidded across the gravel to one of the pickups. He yanked the door open, then spotted Ronin.

"Mister!" he cried. "Don't go in there! There's a vampire inside! An honest-to-God fucking vampire."

Ronin smiled.

The mortal shrieked, eyes wider than a cat's, and practically threw himself into the pickup. He started the engine, but it died. The pungent smell of gasoline wafted through the air. Flooded. Throwing anxious glances over his shoulder, the mortal tried to start the pickup again. The engine caught, sputtered, then evened out into a low *chug-chug*.

Ronin stood in the parking lot, arms crossed over his chest, wondering if the mortal would give it too much gas again when he backed up.

Grinding gears as he shifted into reverse, the mortal slammed the gas pedal. The pickup lurched backward a couple of yards, then sputtered and died.

Ronin was considering putting the mortal out of his misery when the driver's side door flew open and the mortal jumped out. He ran across the parking lot, through the bushes and weeds at the edge of the road and onto the highway. He pelted away into the night, his work boots clumping against the pavement.

Shaking his head, Ronin walked to the tavern's front door. He curled his fingers around the handle, then listened. Silence. He eased the door open. Peeked inside. Bodies littered the blood-smeared floor. He counted four.

Dante's been a busy boy. Or maybe I should say S.

A throat-scraping scream sliced through the silence, then stopped abruptly. Ronin adjusted the body count to five. He wondered how many bodies Dante had left on the floor of CUSTOM MEATS. Wondered if Agent Wallace still breathed.

Ronin closed the door. He'd seen enough. He returned to the Camaro. Time to get things ready for Dante's homecoming.

Flipping open his cell, he speed-dialed E's number. Instead of the voice mail message he'd been receiving all night, Ronin heard the sullen mortal's voice.

"Yeah?"

"Where have you been?"

"Out. What are you? My daddy?"

"It's time. Trade the Jeep in for a van. Remember the speci-
fications?"

"Duh. Got Dante, huh?"

Ronin remembered the scream he'd heard inside the tavern.
"Oh, yes."

DANTE'S BLOOD-GRIMED HAND LOCKED around the handle
of the gas can sitting in the back of the pickup. Voices clamored and screeched. Renewed pain burned through his mind.
He walked back into the silent tavern. Splashed gasoline on the
tables, pool table, and bar. The heady smell went straight to his
head, dizzied him. He poured a trail of gasoline down the hall
and to the women's room.

He's quiet now. The drugs must be working. I'll take him down.

He saw a quick glimpse of a pale face framed by short blonde
hair, then pain shattered the image. Dante staggered against
the restroom door, hand to his temple. He struggled to remain
upright. This pain he couldn't transcend or use. This pain devoured.

Sucking in a deep breath of gasoline-laden air, Dante and his
gas can strolled back through the tavern. He pulled a bottle of
tequila from the booze-lined shelves behind the bar. He paused
at the table where the Good Ol' Boys had parked their dusty
butts and picked up a pack of smokes and a book of matches.

Still sloshing gasoline behind him, he stepped out through
the door and onto the porch. He tossed the empty can into the
tavern. It hit the floor with an echoing clang.

Shaking out a cigarette from the pack, Dante stuck it between
his lips, then lit it. He smoked a while, enjoying the tobacco,
trying not to listen to the voices inside.

And ... oh, yeah! ... the last foster home burns to the ground. ...
Liar.

White light dazzled Dante's vision. Pain pulsed. He flicked the half-smoked cigarette inside the gasoline-doused tavern. It lit with a *whoommf* sound that sent shivers down his spine. Flames licked up into the air.

Tell me, what does that anarchy symbol mean to you?

Heather's face filled his vision. Her hair flickered like fire. Pain needled his heart. *She's gone. Safe.*

Do you still love me, Dante-angel?

Never stopped, princess. Just forgot for a time.

Dante walked to the MG. Leaned against the trunk, tequila bottle in hand. He watched the blazing tavern, his insides all knotted up and twisted like barbed wire, but his heart, uncaged and unprotected, soared.

Tell me, what does that anarchy symbol mean to you?

Rage. Firestorm. Truth.

"Freedom," Dante whispered.

24

BROKEN TRUST

LUCIEN CLOSED HIS EYES. From his perch on the roof, he caught the smell of the Mississippi—cold water, moss, and mud. He listened, waiting for Dante's touch through their link, a touch that might never be felt again. The link was closed, but not severed. At least, not yet. The child might not realize that severing the link would harm them both.

Despite Lucien's shields, Dante's blood-frenzied rage and euphoria tugged at him through their bond. Sang to him in chaos song, like that first time on the wharf. He gripped the roof's edge, his talons puncturing the tiles. His talons—stronger and thicker. Shot through with *creawdwr* imaginings.

Lucien's muscles rippled beneath his skin. His remade flesh ached. His hair fluttered behind him in the winter breeze. What else had Dante changed, trying to save him?

Yet another strand to the bonds inextricably linking them: father and son; friend and companion; creator and created.

Was it possible to regain trust, once lost?

Sudden pain, sharp as broken glass, scraped through the

bond and sliced at his shields. Lucien flexed the pain away. His child passed out finally, freeing them both.

A lingering image haunted Lucien's mind like a retinal ghost after a brilliant flash—a concrete stall, flickering light, dripping water; an image he passed along.

<Llygad>

<*Got it.*>

Lucien fought the desire to launch himself into the sky, wrestled with the need to go to Dante, gather him into his arms and carry him home. His wings flared and flapped, but he remained perched on the roof like a night-chained gargoyle, listening.

Waiting.

HEATHER RATCHETED THE SECOND cuff shut around the chair leg. The other cuff encircled Stearns's right wrist. She straightened, brushing the hair out of her eyes.

"This isn't necessary," Stearns said. "I just want to talk to you."

"Coffee?" she asked, crossing to the kitchen counter and the coffeepot. The coffee's aroma, strong and dark, filled the kitchen.

As she poured fresh-brewed coffee into the same cup she'd used last night, her throat tightened. Twenty-four hours plus since she and Dante'd sat in the kitchen drinking coffee and brandy. Talking about the serial killer stalking him.

And who'd found him.

Her muscles knotted as she thought of Elroy Jordan stretched on the sofa in the front room, most likely the killer she'd been hunting for three years. Thought of him standing over her as she slept. Thought of him claiming his cell phone and leaving her and everyone else untouched.

"Go to my car, get the file and take a look; you'll see Dante for the monster he is."

Heather turned, hands grasping the counter behind her. Stearns scooted his chair around so he could see her. His face went blank at what he saw in her eyes.

"Monster? I saw monsters tonight," she said, voice husky, strained. "Two of them." The memory of Jay lying in a pool of his own blood burned bright in her mind. "Dante may not be human, but he's no monster." She locked gazes with Stearns. "I'd stake my life on that."

"You already have," Stearns said. "You just don't know it." He glanced away. "I came here for you, Heather."

"For me? Or for Dante?"

Stearns looked back at her, his beard-shadowed face open, weary. "For you. You've been marked for termination. Me too."

Even though she'd expected something bad, *real* bad, ever since learning about the cover-up, hearing it stated was like a slap to the face. Picking up her cup, she walked back to the table and sat across from Stearns. "Because someone wants to protect the CCK? Or because the investigation led me to Dante?" She spooned sugar into her coffee with a steady hand even though she felt like she'd been gutted.

Marked for termination.

"Both. Dante's part of the same project that produced the CCK."

Heather sucked in a sharp breath. Gut-punched again. WAKE UP S. The pieces tumbled into place and the forming picture scared the hell out of her. "His project name," she murmured. "Who heads the project?"

"Johanna Moore."

"*Doctor* Moore? Are you serious?"

"Dead serious. She's been creating sociopaths for years. To study."

Heather felt like she'd flipped into an alternate reality: everything *looked* the same, but underneath, everything and everyone were dark, tweaked opposites of their counterparts in her reality—negative images.

That or she'd fallen asleep and plunged headlong into darkest nightmare.

No such luck.

Stirring her coffee, Heather thought back to her days at the Academy and dredged up memories of Dr. Moore—tall, blonde, charismatic, and brilliant. Her courses in forensic psychology had always intrigued. Her grasp of the sociopathic personality had been uncanny. Her profiles had never missed.

But to *create* sociopaths?

"She was behind the Pensacola ruse," Stearns said. "You were getting too close."

Heather met Stearns's gaze. Cold certainty cascaded through her, an icy river that chilled her to the bone. He spoke the truth. "How high up does this go?"

"I honestly don't know," Stearns replied, shaking his head. "But I think it's best to behave as though it goes to the top."

Heather took a sip of coffee, her thoughts whirling. Elroy Jordan and Thomas Ronin—together creating the Cross-Country Killer. And Dante? Why would one part of the project be stalking another? Was Dante a *failed* experiment? One marked for termination, like herself? Like Stearns?

But what if he was exactly what he was supposed to be—a sociopathic killer?

Pushing her chair back from the table, Heather stood. Fatigue washed through her and her vision darkened. She grabbed the table's edge for balance.

"We'll discuss this later," she murmured as her vision cleared. "I've gotta find Dante."

"Take five minutes," Stearns said, voice urgent. "Get the file. Look at it." Reaching into his coat pocket with his uncuffed left hand, he tossed a set of keys onto the table. "Heather, please."

She stared at the keys, wondering if the file would contain

the secrets of Dante's hidden past. And if so, could he be freed of migraines and nosebleeds? Would the truth have saved Annie from slashed wrists, meds, and institutions?

Maybe, Heather thought, scooping up the keys. She slid them into her pants pocket. Maybe it still would. Stearns opened his mouth, but she shook her head. "Not another word, Craig."

Heather walked from the silent kitchen and into the hallway. Her overnight bag and laptop rested against the wall. Further down, a faint blue light spilled onto the autumn-etched carpet from a door near the stairway. She heard the faint murmur of Simone's voice as she spoke to her brother in rapid, musical Cajun.

Heather remembered Dante standing in the locker's doorway at CUSTOM MEATS, hands braced against the threshold, his dark eyes streaked with deep red; remembered the strain in his voice: *Run as far from me as you can.*

As she walked down the hall toward the spill of blue light, Heather also remembered Étienne's head dangling from Dante's blood-smeared hand; remembered the hot touch of Dante's lips against her throat, twisting fear and fire through her guts; remembered the wonder in his voice as he spoke her name.

Even if everything Stearns said was true, Dante struggled against whatever had been programmed into his fractured mind. He loved others, something a sociopath was incapable of. Dante's willingness to sacrifice himself for Jay was all the proof she needed.

But Ronin's voice snaked through her thoughts.

Her name was Chloe. And you killed her.

Dante struggled now, but had he always?

She shoved the doubt away, knowing she'd examine it closer at another time. For now, she was Dante's partner, his backup, and she wouldn't leave him to face Ronin alone.

Pushing open the door to the computer room, Heather

looked at Simone kneeling beside her plugged-in and connected brother. Trey reclined in a lounger, his goggled gaze on the ceiling, his capped fingers moving data through the blue-lit air as he searched for the information she'd requested: A search for Elroy Jordan's movements over the last three years.

Dante-angel?

Chloe tugs on the handcuffs, the chain tunk-tunk-tunk*ing against the bedpost. Wake up! Papa took the curtain away. Dante-angel, wake-upwakeupwakeup—*

Dante opened one eye. Light shafted in, piercing his already aching head. He shut his eye again. *In the MG.* Easing his head back against the headrest, he massaged his temples. The car's interior stank of blood, gasoline, and tequila.

"Fuck."

Something hard pressed into the small of Dante's back. Wincing in the fluorescent light, he leaned forward and reached back to the waistband of his leather pants. His fingers wrapped around a smooth, cylindrical shape and tugged it free.

Dante stared at the gun—*nine mil*, a voice whispered—in his bloodstained hand. His breath caught in his throat as images strobed through his bruised mind. The sudden rush of violence—vivid, stark, intoxicating—slammed his heart into overdrive.

"The tavern . . ." he whispered.

Another dizzying montage of images: A broken pool cue spinning through the air; a knife plunging through his hand; a black-haired woman crouched behind the bar, terror on her face; an iridescent rose tattoo.

The taste of LaRousse's bitter blood.

The gun tumbled from his fingers to the floorboards. Dante squeezed his eyes shut. Touched his fingers to his temple. Shaking, muscles taut, he pushed past the pain, but the images whited out. No matter how hard he tried, he couldn't stop the flood of broken memories; couldn't control them, couldn't even hold onto them.

Dante opened his eyes. Fluorescent lights buzzed overhead. He breathed in the smell of wet concrete and mildew and soap. But beneath that, he caught the stench of old slaughterhouse blood.

Pain ice-picked his mind. CUSTOM MEATS. Ronin and Étienne. Jay, bound and hanging from a meat hook. Ronin's fangs piercing his throat. Heather kneeling beside Étienne, her gun pressed against his chest.

I knew you'd come.

You can still save him, True Blood.

Liar. Liar.

"Liar!" Dante screamed. He screamed until he was scraped raw inside, until his mind was empty and no more sound would come. He slumped back against the seat, drained, but still burning.

"Hey, little brother."

Dante glanced at the now opened driver's side door. Von knelt on the concrete, one knee in a rainbowed puddle of oil and water. He cupped a road-rough hand against Dante's face, pushed his hair back with long fingers.

"It's good to get that shit out," Von said, voice low. "Festers if you leave it inside."

"Yeah?" Dante whispered, looking into the nomad's green eyes. "How come I ain't never heard you screaming?"

Von snorted. "Nothing inside, man. I travel light."

"Bullshit."

Von's hand dropped from Dante's face to his chest. He pressed his fingers against the latex shirt. "You got a good heart, little brother. That's why I stay. No regrets."

"How can you know that when I don't?"

Von touched a finger beneath the crescent moon tattoo under his eye. Tapped it. Arched an eyebrow.

"Yeah, yeah, *llygad*. Got it."

Von lifted his hand from Dante's chest, but Dante caught it and folded his fingers between Von's. Dante leaned forward and kissed him. The nomad tasted of smoke and road dust. He listened to the steady thump of Von's heart and his mind flashed back to Lucien, to the taste of his blood, to the sound of the song thrumming through him—Dante tried to block all thought of Lucien, but it was too late.

You look so much like her.

Rage rekindled, bonded with the fire burning deep inside.

You knew all this time? And you never said anything?

Sliding his hand from Von's, Dante eased out of the MG. He took in his surroundings, realizing for the first time he stood in a car wash. Glancing down at his blood-caked clothing, the location suddenly made sense.

"Gotta clean up."

"Good idea," Von said. "That hot little FBI darlin' is at the house. She sees you like this, she's gonna think you shower in blood."

Dante went still. "Heather's at the house? Is she . . . okay?"

"Fuck, yeah. She's wiped out, like you, but fine. Sleep'll do you both good."

Dante nodded, then shrugged out of his leather jacket. He tossed it, metal jingling, into the MG. Spotting his shades on the passenger seat, he grabbed them, then slid them on. The fluorescent glare dimmed. His headache toned down a shade. He unstrapped his latex shirt, then walked to the car wash controls.

Patting his pockets—an image of dollar bills wadded up on the tavern's counter popped into his mind—Dante glanced at Von. "Got any money?"

"Yeah," the nomad said, digging in his jacket pocket. He

looked at Dante as he pulled a spike free, lifted his eyebrow. "So what was your plan? Wait for someone to overlook your sorry-ass state and load your palms up with quarters?"

"Fuck you. Twice." Dante pulled the wand from its metal sleeve.

Grinning, Von slid the swipe through the price slot. "Choose your poison."

Dante clicked the dial over to light rinse and pressed the on button. Water sprayed from the wand. Turning the wand around until the high-pressure stream hit his torso, Dante edged it up and down, washing blood from his clothes and skin. The cold water stung.

"Listen to me," Von said, stepping out of spray range. "You're exhausted. You're fevered. You need Sleep."

"Ronin's waiting for me."

"Let him wait. Dawn's a few hours away. He's gotta Sleep, too."

Sudden weariness coiled through Dante and he leaned a shoulder against the smooth concrete wall. Bloody water swirled into the grated drain in the stall's center. His temples throbbed with dull pain. He scrubbed at a stubborn stain on his leather pants, the water sluicing past his fingers. Setting the wand on the floor, he peeled off his latex shirt. Tossed it onto the MG's hood.

A small voice whispered his name—

Dante-angel.

Shutting his eyes, he leaned a bare shoulder against the wall. His right hand pressed against the concrete, the touch tentative, seeking . . . what?

Behind his closed eyes, a corona of light surrounded a key, puzzle-fractured and spider-webbed with black lines.

Is this the right one? Will it work on the handcuffs?

"Hey, Dante." The sharp sound of snapping fingers. "Hey, little brother."

Dante opened his eyes and looked up into Von's concerned gaze.

"You okay?"

Nodding, heart pounding, Dante picked up the still spraying wand and started washing himself again.

"What happened between you and Lucien, man?"

Dante looked at Von for a long moment, then resumed washing. "Are you asking as *mon ami* or *llygad*?" He suddenly thought of Heather—her gorgeous face half-shadowed in the club as she said, *I'm both, Dante. Friend and cop.*

"Friend."

"He lied to me." The spray slowed to a trickle, stopped. Dante straightened, shaking his wet hair back from his face. He slid the wand back into the sleeve.

Von whistled, then reached into the MG and grabbed Dante's jacket. Tossed it to him. "If Lucien lied to you, there musta been—"

"He knew my mother. All this time. He never said one word. Never said shit." Dante tugged the jacket on over his wet skin, leather creaking, metal clinking.

Memory flared one more time, Lucien's face, dark wonder in his golden eyes, his finger reaching up to stroke Dante's hair.

Genevieve . . .

The world spun suddenly—cathedral, car wash, slaughterhouse, gleaming pews, wet concrete walls, swaying hooks—and Dante grabbed the open car door to keep from falling. Pain spiked behind his eyes. His vision grayed out for a moment, then cleared.

He realized that Von had latched a hand around his biceps, steadying him. Dante glanced at the nomad. Von returned his regard, face troubled.

"Merci," Dante said.

Von released his hold, his posture tense, reluctant. "Go home, little brother. Sleep. Ronin'll still be waiting for you come evening. Go home. Please."

But Dante heard the thought behind Von's words, saw it in his eyes: *You're scaring me.*

"I plan on it, *mon ami*," Dante said, climbing into the MG. "I need to talk to Heather." *Need to make sure she's all right.* He keyed the engine on. It rumbled to life, the sound echoing against the concrete walls.

A smile quirked up one corner of Von's mouth. "So he *can* see reason." With a gentle push of his fingertips, he swung the driver's side door shut, then strode away.

Dante shook his head, amused, and shifted the MG into first. His amusement faded as darker thoughts circled through his mind. *Why the hell don't I remember my past? And why has that* never *bothered me?*

And darker still: *What if it's never bothered me because it ain't supposed to?*

Darkest: *What if it's never bothered me because I don't* want *to remember?*

Again he heard Ronin's knowing voice: *What are you afraid of, True Blood?*

Fingers clamped around the steering wheel, Dante drove the MG out of the stall. *Not you, Peeping Tom. Or what you know.* But he wondered just how Peeping Tom had come by his knowledge.

Troubled, Dante hit the gas, shifting into second, then third. He was missing something, forgetting something important, but the memory—like so many others—refused to come.

25

DEVIL IN THE DETAILS

HEATHER SAT CROSS-LEGGED ON the hardwood floor, examining the printout Trey had provided. Her exhaustion vanished in a buzz of excitement. Elroy Jordan *was* from New York, but before that he'd lived in Seattle—born and raised—during the time of the first two murders. He'd even lived close to the first victim, Karen Stilman. Credit receipts pegged him in Portland, Oregon, and Boise, Idaho during the times of the murders in those cities. In fact, Elroy Jordan could be placed at each kill site.

Paper rustled as Heather flipped to the page on Ronin. Nothing placed the journalist in Seattle until *after* the second murder. Ditto for the murders in Portland, Boise, Salt Lake City, and Helena. She frowned, scanning the data for parallels, for inconsistencies. She was positive Jordan and Ronin were working as a team. But, so far, the evidence dusted that theory.

After the Helena, Montana murder, Ronin's receipts and rental history placed him in New York—*before* the estimated date of Byron Hedge's death. Not after.

If what Stearns had said was true, that Moore had created

sociopaths to study, then was Ronin working with her? How else would he know how to trigger Dante? Why would he want to? What would he gain? Or was Ronin working *against* Moore? If so, why? Again, what would he have to gain?

Heather glanced at the sheet again, flipped back to the page on Jordan. The two couldn't be connected during the murders in Omaha, Chicago, or Detroit—Ronin didn't show in those cities until after the murders. But he *was* in New York prior to Hedge's murder. Shortly afterward, Ronin and Jordan had arrived in New Orleans together.

The next murder? Daniel Spurrell's.

For some reason, Ronin had intercepted Jordan, interrupting Moore's study of her wandering sociopath, and led him to New Orleans. To Dante.

So . . . maybe Elroy Jordan alone was the Cross-Country Killer. What was Ronin's role? Either he or Étienne had killed Jay. Jordan hadn't even been present.

Heather rubbed her face with one hand, her buzz fading. Nothing was making sense. She needed sleep, but she needed to find Dante first.

Leather creaked as Simone's brother shifted in his recliner. His fingers darted through the air, rearranging data and flipping it back into the net. The smell of hot circuits and ginger mingled uneasily in the room's close air.

"Thanks for your help, Trey," Heather said, easing to her feet.

Silence but for the creak of leather as the vampire's capped fingers blurred through the air. His dreads brushed the floor. Heather doubted that he'd even heard her. She wondered if Trey, in his own way, was just as lost as Annie. Maybe turning him hadn't worked out as well as Simone had hoped. Heather stepped out into the hall and quietly closed the door behind her.

Stearns's keys jingled in Heather's pocket as she walked and she thought of him cuffed in the kitchen; thought of the file in his car. *What're you gonna do, Wallace, keep him prisoner? For how long?*

She folded the printout in half. *He wants Dante. He thinks he's a monster.* Stopping in the kitchen doorway, she caught Stearns dozing, chin to chest, eyes closed.

What if he's right?

"I'm going to get the file," Heather said.

Stearns lifted his head, met her gaze, clear-eyed. Pretending, then. "Good."

"And after I do," she said, walking into the kitchen, "I want you out of here."

"Call me when you've read the file."

"No promises." She set the folded printout on the table.

Heather stepped to her chair and the trenchcoat flung over it, digging in the pocket for her Colt Super. Her fingers slipped past the cool shape of Stearns's Glock and locked around her .38. She pulled it free, tucked it into the waistband of her slacks; felt its hard, reassuring shape against the small of her back. She smoothed her sweater over the gun.

"Back in a minute," she said.

At the front door, as Heather grasped the doorknob, a hand touched her shoulder. She glanced into Simone's dark eyes.

"I'll walk with you," she said. A deep-red latex minidress hugged her curves, pale flesh visible through the side laces. Her long golden curls spilled down her back.

"Thanks, but I don't need a bodyguard."

Simone shrugged. "I could use the fresh air."

Nodding, Heather opened the door and stepped into the humid, rose-scented night. Rain misted against her face, beading on the front of her sweater. Walking the broken-stone path to the gate, she felt Simone just behind her, but the only footsteps she heard were her own.

When Heather reached the gate, she paused and looked back

at the house. De Noir hadn't moved. He still hunched on the roof, rain-glistening wings folded along his back.

"Did you get what you needed?" Simone asked.

"Yes," Heather said. "I have an address for Ronin in Metairie. Nothing for Jordan, but I imagine they're together. Custom Meats is owned by a real estate firm—"

Simone held up a finger, her gaze flicking inward. After a moment, a smile curved her lips. "Von found Dante. They're on their way home."

"Is he all right?"

"Mostly."

Relief curled through Heather, unknotting kinked muscles and pushing away her fatigue. She decided not to dwell on "mostly." Dante had been found and was on his way home. That was all that mattered. She slipped through the partially opened gate, walking with Simone to the road.

"You said you'd known Dante three or four years," Heather said, keeping her voice light.

"*Oui*. He is *mon cher ami*."

"Have you been friends the entire time?"

Simone looked at her, oak shadows twisting across her pale face. She opened her mouth to speak, but the sound of a car pulling up behind them on the gravel-edged road closed it again. She turned, lifting a hand against the glare of headlights.

Heather swiveled around, as well, reaching back with her right hand and sliding her fingers around the .38. A car idled in front of the gate.

"Excuse me," a woman's voice said from the passenger side. "Could you help us with directions?"

"*Oui*." Simone stepped over to the car. She bent down to look in through the lowered window. A point of red light appeared on her forehead.

Heather swung her .38 around, yelling, "Simone! Down!" She pulled the trigger and heard two shots crack through the night.

Simone dove for the ground, but hit hard, sprawling in the gravel and gasping in pain. *She's been hit,* Heather thought. The .38's bullet starred the car's windshield on the passenger side. The driver gunned the engine.

Heather dropped down to one knee and opened fire, pulling the trigger until she emptied the clip. "Stay down, Simone!" she yelled, hoping the vampire hadn't taken a shot to the head or the heart.

The car lurched toward her. Heather rolled toward the concrete and black iron-topped fence, then back up to her feet. Wishing she'd worn her trenchcoat, she sprinted for the dark bulk of Stearns's rental car, pulling the keys from her pocket as she ran.

Thoughts burned crystal clear in her mind: *Find Stearns's backup. Failing that, start the car and ram it into those motherfuckers.* Adrenaline fueled her muscles. Her heart triple-timed and the air burned in her throat.

She slid to a stop beside the Crown Victoria, gravel skittering beneath her shoes. Behind her, the sound of the car's engine deepened, picked up speed. She fumbled through the keys, their edges sharp against her fingers, until she found the alarm control.

The doors unlocked. Heather yanked open the passenger side door and lunged inside. Patting beneath the seat for any backup pistol Stearns might've planted, she squinted out the rear window into the blue-white glare of the headlights.

A form leapt onto the car. Simone stretched across the roof and reached in through the window for the driver. Brakes screeched. Tires squealed. The smell of burning rubber scorched the air. The car slid sideways and slammed into the Crown Victoria.

The impact knocked Heather shoulder-first into the dashboard. Pain lanced through her shoulder and down her right side. She bit her lip. The glove box flew open and several maps and a gun tumbled to the floor.

Bingo! Heather grabbed the gun and slid out of the car. Steam plumed into the air from under the hood of the car accordioned against the Crown Victoria. Flicking off the gun's safety, she cautiously approached her pursuer.

The female shooter was slumped to one side, a dark hole in her forehead. Simone lay across the car's roof, one hand latched onto the struggling driver's shoulder, the other twisting his hair. She'd pulled him halfway out the window. Blood trickled down his face.

Heather stepped around the rear of the car and walked up to the driver's side, the gun held in both hands. The driver squirmed in Simone's grasp, his grunts panicked, wild.

"Let him go," she called. "I've got him in my sights."

Simone yanked the driver the rest of the way out of the window. He skidded across the pavement, sliding to a stop next to the yellow dividing lines.

"Stay there," Heather said, stepping toward him. "Hands behind your head."

Cool air gusted through her rain-damp hair as powerful wings whooshed through the sky above her. A shadow darkened the road.

De Noir swooped over the driver, seizing him by the collar, and soared up into the sky. The driver's shriek, rising in terror and pitch, cut through the night.

"No!" Heather shouted. "Bring him back! De Noir!"

The shrieking ended abruptly. Something hit the pavement with a splat, something that steamed in the chilly air.

Heather's stomach lurched. She swallowed hard, tasting blood. She leaned against the car and lowered the gun. "Shit."

A figure blurred through the gate and raced up the road, dreads and cables snaking through the air behind him. Moonlight glinted from his fingertips. Trey stopped beside the car, his goggled gaze on his sister, panic etched into his face.

The car wobbled as Simone slid off of it. Blood glistened on her pale flesh. A hole marred her dress's left shoulder, just below the collarbone. Trey touched the spot with a net-capped finger.

Wincing, Simone said, "I'm okay." She lifted Trey's finger and kissed it before releasing it. She laced an arm around his waist, leaned against him.

A rush of wings drew Heather's attention. De Noir touched bare feet to the road, the driver's torso in one taloned hand, the man's lower half in the other. He walked to the car. Heather felt her gorge rise and jumped aside, not wanting a good look at De Noir's burden. He stuffed the remains in through the window.

"Why the *hell* did you kill him?" she asked. "I wanted to question him."

"He and his partner intended to kill you, Agent Wallace," De Noir replied. "And anyone near you." He stepped next to Simone and touched her face with one taloned finger. Simone's eyes closed. "Could you have trusted any information he might've given you?" De Noir's gaze flicked up to meet Heather's.

"Probably not. But I still could've asked." Shoving the gun into the waistband of her slacks, she marched back to the Crown Victoria.

After she tucked the gun back into the glove box, Heather discovered the locked briefcase on the floor behind the front seat. She tried a small key on the keyring, and the briefcase unlocked. She flipped the latches and looked inside. A computer CD, photos—her heart jumped into her throat when she recognized Dante's face—and manila folders. Shutting the briefcase, she eased out of the car.

De Noir waited for her, shadows and moonlight slanting across his body, his wings. "Go inside," he said. "I'll take care of things out here."

Heather nodded, deciding against asking for details and turned away. She trudged up the road to the house, heavy-limbed and weary. She'd burned off all the adrenaline and now she was almost dizzy with exhaustion.

She walked through the empty front room and into the kitchen. "I got the file and—"

Trey and Simone sat at the kitchen table. Silver stood at the sink, wetting a cloth. Stearns's chair was turned on its side. Empty.

"Where is he?" Heather asked.

Simone shook her head. "He was gone when we came in."

Heather sank into the trench-draped chair, setting the briefcase on the floor. She checked the trench's pockets; Stearns's Glock was gone. A glance at the table confirmed the printout was missing, as well.

Elbows on the table, Heather buried her face in her hands. "Shit."

26

SANCTIFIED

WITH THE DELICATE TWIST of a talon, De Noir worked the bullet out of Simone's shoulder. The compressed chunk of metal fell to the floor. Silver handed De Noir a wet towel, then bent to scoop up the dented and ruined bullet. He glanced at Heather. "Do you need this? For evidence or something?"

Heather shook her head. "Not now."

"Cool." Silver tucked the bullet into his jeans pocket. He looked at Simone. "Did it hurt?"

"*Oui*, a lot," Simone murmured. "I don't want to get shot again, *petit*." Trey, sitting beside her, squeezed her hand.

De Noir wiped away the last of the blood from Simone's pale flesh, then straightened. He tilted his head and a moment later Heather heard the rumble of engines out front.

Dante, she thought, sitting up, suddenly wide awake. She combed her fingers through her hair. Her pulse raced.

Smiling, Simone dropped the bloodstained towel she'd used to cover her breasts and pulled up her dress straps.

The front door opened. Heather heard the creak of leather

and the clink of small chains, but not one footstep. Dante walked into the kitchen, Von a pace behind.

Heather's breath caught in her throat at the sight of Dante—*when will I get used to seeing him?* He glanced at her, a question burning in his dark eyes, the irises no longer streaked with red or gold.

Then Simone stood and Dante went to her, wrapping his arms around her. He kissed her forehead, her cheeks, her mouth.

"You okay, doll?" Von asked, joining the pair, embracing them both.

Heather, throat tight, looked away. *He is* mon cher ami. And more, apparently. The excited beat of her heart altered to a furious tempo. Blood pounded in her temples. Scraping her chair back, she stood and strode from the kitchen.

She can have him. He doesn't need me for backup.

Heather raced down the hallway, fists clenched, not sure where she was going, just away. She stopped at the stairs, fingers hooking around the polished wood banister.

She closed her eyes. What was wrong with her? Hadn't she told Dante she was a friend, as well as a cop? Wasn't it her job to see him safe? Well, he was—home safe, at least. She needed sleep. Food. Time to think.

"Hey," a low voice said, sending shivers up her spine.

"Yes?" she said, opening her eyes. Her fingers white-knuckled the banister. She wouldn't turn around. Wouldn't come undone at the sight of him.

She tensed as Dante stopped beside her. His scent—falling leaves and dark earth, warm and close—enveloped her. His fingers brushed her hair from her face.

"Heather, look at me."

Heather released the banister and swiveled to face him, met his dark gaze.

"What the *hell* are you still doing here?" he said, voice strained. "I told you to run. I *meant* it. You're not safe here and I'm—"

"*You're* the one who's not safe here," she interrupted, cut by his words, his unexpected anger. "I know you're nightkind, but that doesn't matter. You're still in danger and you can't keep running off on your own. Maybe you need to be saved from yourself."

"I don't need to be saved," Dante said. "Don't *wanna* be saved." A muscle jumped in his jaw.

"Pigheaded," she muttered. "Y'know what? Don't worry about it. You want me gone, fine." Whirling, she strode away.

As Heather paused to pick up her overnight bag and laptop, fingers latched onto her shoulders and spun her around. She dropped the bag and swung her fist up, but Dante caught it and held it captive against his bare chest. Her left fist shot up, but he caught that one too.

"Dammit! Let go!" Heather said, body tensed, eyes burning. "What the *hell* do you want from me?" She tried to jerk free, but Dante's steel-fingered hands circled her wrists like handcuffs. Pulled her close. Pulled her into him.

"Let me fucking finish, *d'accord*?" Dante said, voice a near whisper. "I don't want you here because I'm scared of what might happen to you. Of what I *might* . . . what I . . . *could* do—"

"Shhhh." Heather shook her head. *Scared. For her. Of himself.* She looked into his unguarded eyes, shaken, throat tight. She realized in that moment that it wasn't sleep she needed. Or food. Or time to think.

Dante released her wrists and wrapped his arms around her, hugging her tight. His heart pounded hard and fast. His heat baked into her.

Sliding a hand up his pale, hard-muscled chest, Heather hooked a finger through the ring of his bondage collar. Tugged. But he was already lowering his face to hers. He kissed her and the touch of his lips, his tongue, ignited her, set her ablaze.

Yearning burned through her as the kiss deepened and a whisper of betrayal, hurt, and loneliness echoed in her heart; all the things she'd seen in his dark eyes when he'd breathed her name at the slaughterhouse.

I won't walk away from you, she thought, hoping he'd hear her.

Dante's breath caught in his throat. He slipped a hand under her sweater, his fingers trailing along her skin to the curve of her breast.

She shoved the jacket from his shoulders. It hit the floor with a thud. Her hands glided over his hips, to his ass, then up along the hard contours of his back. His skin felt like sun-warmed silk draped over steel. Dante shivered as she touched him. She opened her eyes to watch pleasure steal across his beautiful face.

Fire flared in Heather's belly, flamed through her veins as Dante reached up to cup her breast through her sweater. She moaned into their kiss, her hands slipping back to his ass, pulling him closer still. Dante was hard beneath the wet leather. Hard against her belly. Her breathing quickened. She closed her eyes.

"Holy shit, you two, the pheromones!" An amused voice—Von's?—said. "Take it upstairs unless you seriously want an audience."

The hand caressing Heather's breast dropped away. Through half-opened eyes, she watched as Dante flipped off the nomad.

Von laughed. "Dawn's coming, man. Coupla hours."

Ending the kiss, Dante lifted his head and smoothed Heather's sweater down. He scooped her up into his arms. "What happens when dawn comes?" she murmured, lacing her arms around his neck.

"I Sleep."

Heather heard the capital S in his voice and her thoughts shifted back to that first morning—*was it only two days ago?*—and Dante's drowsiness, snoozing in the car until danger had awakened him.

Heather kissed his cheek, his mouth, his ear. A low sound vibrated up from Dante's throat. "Get going, gorgeous," she whispered. "No time to waste."

Dante *moved*, carrying Heather up the stairs like she weighed nothing. His strength amazed her—slim and wiry, five nine—until she remembered what he was: nightkind. She kissed his throat, wrapped up in the power of his arms, the heat of his body. Dante's hair brushed against her linked fingers, soft and damp, and framed his face with black, wavy tendrils.

Upstairs, Dante carried her into the first door on the left—his room. Kicking the door shut behind him, he crossed the littered floor with the surefootedness of a cat, then eased her down onto the unmade futon.

Heather unlinked her hands from around his neck and cupped his face. She kissed him again. She murmured against his lips, "Light some candles. I want to see you."

Dante walked to the bureau, picked up a lighter, then blurred around the room; candles winked alight like evening stars in his wake. Returning to the futon, he sat beside Heather. He looked at her, *into* her, candlelight sparking orange from his rings, along the hoops in his ears, in his eyes. He caressed her cheek with the backs of his fingers, his rings cool against her skin.

Grabbing his upper arms, she pulled Dante down on top of her. Rolled him over onto the slithering silk sheets and straddled him. His hands slid up her thighs.

"It's quiet when I'm with you," Dante said, voice low, husky. "The noise stops."

Heather thought of him kneeling in the slaughterhouse, dazed, whispering *sanctus, sanctus, sanctus*. She thought of the photo she'd glimpsed in Stearns's briefcase.

"I'll help you stop it forever," she whispered.

She pulled off her sweater, unhooked her bra. Flung them on the floor. Dante's flame-lit gaze swept over her.

"Très belle," he breathed.

Smiling, she trailed her fingers across his chest, traced the small bat tattoo above his heart. Then she bent over, flicked her tongue over his hardened nipples. Dante's breath hissed through his teeth. His fingers threaded through her hair as she kissed her way down his flat belly to the top of his leather pants. Heather unbuckled his belt, her fingers fumbling with the snap and zipper on his pants; wanting to tear them off with her teeth.

Finally she grasped him. Hard. Hot. Pale as milk. Satin-smooth. She traced his length first with her fingers, then the tip of her tongue. A low moan escaped him, and the sound of it stirred the fire smoldering within her. He shivered, muscles flexing, as she stroked him. His fingers twisted free of her hair and brushed against her cheek, drew her gaze up.

"My turn," Dante said, voice a low purr. His fingers slid around her arms and pulled her up. Rolled her over onto the sheets. Heather arched up against him, pressing against him, skin to skin.

Dante plucked off her shoes, then removed her trousers, her panties, Heather lifting her hips as he slid them off. He kissed her inner thighs, his lips burning against her skin. She moaned.

A gust of air blew across Heather. She heard two dull thuds. She glanced at the floor. Two unstrapped boots. Leather pants. Then Dante stretched over her, naked except for the collar around his throat, pale skin gleaming in the candlelight.

"You cheated," she whispered, gliding a hand over his chest, across his belly and down, exploring his smooth white skin and hard muscles.

A wicked smile played across his lips. "You can cheat next time."

He kissed her, biting her lower lip. She sucked in a breath, but the sting faded as soon as it began. His hand caressed her breast, brushed over her hip, tucked in between her legs. Heather gasped. Pleasure shuddered through her.

Dante shifted, his lips closed around her nipple—kissing,

sucking. He trailed kisses from her breasts, across her belly and down, his hair sliding like black silk across her skin, tickling and raising goosebumps. He licked her, and she arched her back as his lips and tongue set her ablaze, his fingers stoking the fire.

Burning up from the inside out. Dreaming.

For a moment, a doubt wormed into her dream: *He's not human.*

But she remembered the pounding of his heart, the sound of his grief, the prickly raw smell of his pain. Remembered him spreading his jacket over Gina. Remembered the devastation on his face as he looked at Jay.

If that's not human, what is?

Time stretched, endless, ever-dusk. Her body vibrated at Dante's touch, spasming in pleasure, burning with every flick of his tongue. She shuddered as she came, the orgasm's intensity stealing her voice and leaving her breathless.

Dante kissed his way back up Heather's body, blue flame glowing wherever he pressed his lips. He kissed her and she tasted herself on his tongue. As they kissed, she guided him inside of her, her fingers stroking, directing. He moaned as he entered her.

Sweat slicked their bodies as they began to thrust together, rocking, pounding. She smelled him, deep dark earth and burning leaves. His scent intoxicated her. Blue light flickered in her mind.

Wrapping her legs around Dante's waist, Heather pulled him closer still. His breathing quickened. Sweat-damp hair curled beside his face as he looked into her eyes, his own pleasure-dilated and flecked with gold.

Pinning her right hand to the mattress beside her head, Dante intertwined his fingers with hers. He lowered his head to her throat and kissed it.

Heather felt a brief sting as Dante's fangs pierced the skin at her throat, the pain vanishing almost before she registered it.

An image of Dante in CUSTOM MEATS tearing Étienne apart flashed through her mind—*Run as far from me as you can*—but pleasure racked her and erased all fear, all thought. She moaned as he suckled at her throat.

She dreamed a wordless song; heard the rush of wings.

Time stretched again, minutes spinning away, lost to twilight. Dante lifted his head from her throat and disentangled his hand from hers. Sliding his hands beneath her, Dante lifted her up, still upon him, then down as he knelt on the futon. Hands on her hips, he kissed her. Heather tasted blood on Dante's lips, in his mouth—her blood. A strange thrill curled through her: *he has part of me inside of him.*

Heather rocked down as Dante thrust up, pumping, creating a tempo of their own; a rhythm of heat and sweat and ragged breath. As Dante's lips caught her nipple, sucking it into the warmth of his mouth, Heather was certain nothing existed beyond this moment and that nothing ever would. Just Dante burning inside her, fitting against her like no other; the air thick with the smell of musk and candle wax and the sound of flesh slapping against flesh.

Sensation built within her, ring after ring spiraling up and up and up, until it toppled, plunging her into a depthless pool and sluicing away all thought. She gasped as she came, the orgasm's intensity rushing through her like a river, *increasing* with every ripple instead of fading.

Dante moaned, as though he felt it too. He shivered, but never paused in his pounding rhythm. Blue light filled Heather's vision. Her muscles quivered, taut. She clutched Dante, her fingernails digging into his shoulders, her face pressed against his head, buried in the autumn fragrance of his hair.

One hand on the small of Heather's back, the other still on her hip, Dante lowered her onto the futon. His tempo altered; he drove faster, harder. His eyes closed. His lips parted. Pleasure seemed to light him from within. Wrapping her legs around his waist again, she held him tight and released herself to his rhythm.

Just as dawn grayed the room, Dante opened his eyes and looked into Heather with gold-streaked eyes. His breath caught in his throat, held there, the sound a near sob. Orgasm surged through her again as he came and she cried out as he shuddered in her arms. Dante's movement gradually slowed, then stopped. Heather held him close, her heart hammering against her ribs.

Beyond the curtains covering the French windows, night shifted into morning. Dante eased off of Heather and she snuggled against him, head against his shoulder, his arm around her. His heart thumped strong and steady beneath her cheek, not thudding fast like her heart.

"Do you have any idea how many rules I've just broken?" she said, draping a leg across his.

"Mmm . . . all of 'em, I hope."

"Now I know *two* things you're talented at."

Dante snorted.

Heather tipped her head and looked at Dante. His dark eyes were absent of gold flecks, his expression relaxed.

"Simone said someone's gunning for you," Dante said. "Do you know who?"

"Someone high up, I think," Heather replied. "At least, that's what I've been told. Because I won't drop the investigation."

"I'm gonna find Peeping Tom and Elroy the Perv. *And* whoever's hunting you."

The quiet intensity on Dante's face, the whisper of barely restrained violence in his voice disturbed Heather. She squeezed his hand.

"You know he's waiting for you, right? Don't go to him this time." She touched her fingers to his face, drew his gaze down. "We can bring both of them in for questioning, DNA samples, whatever," she said. "The evidence will link Jordan to the killings. You're a witness to Jay's murder . . . We'll buy time."

"You'll never bring Ronin in," Dante said, " 'cause he's gonna burn first."

"Too dangerous."

"Ain't asking permission."

"Pigheaded."

"It's still quiet," Dante said, voice sleepy, fading. "Stay here, *chérie*."

"I will." Rising up on her elbow, she kissed him. His eyes closed, and she knew he was gone then, lost to Sleep. "Good morning and sweet dreams," she whispered, pulling up the blankets and tucking herself back into his embrace.

Heather closed her eyes and tumbled into welcome darkness.

27

PENANCE

"I'VE LOST CONTACT WITH my people in New Orleans," Gifford said quietly. "I'm afraid they may have failed."

Johanna's fingers tightened around the phone. "Finish it yourself. If you find Stearns and Wallace together, make it a murder-suicide." She glanced at the bedroom window. Dawn glimmered behind the curtains. Sleep pressed down upon her.

"Of course. Anything else?"

"Since E's gone off the grid, I think we need to conclude his part of the project." Johanna's head nodded. She jerked it up. Forced her eyes open.

"And S?"

"Let him be. For now."

HEATHER AWAKENED, HEART POUNDING, mouth dry. She stared at the shadowed ceiling as the nightmare's stark images faded: the recurring dream about her mother's last stumbling walk, and the ride she'd accepted. Or at least the way she imagined it might've been.

Suddenly aware of the arm around her shoulder, the body nestled against hers, Heather turned her head. Dante slept, lashes dark against his skin, black hair tousled, his breathing so low she slid her hand over his heart. After a moment, she felt a reassuring thump against her palm. She trailed her fingers up past the bondage collar, past his lips, to his smooth cheek.

No whiskers, she mused. *Can't be just a nightkind thing, Von has a mustache and Ronin a beard.*

Heather traced her hand down his chest, the skin cool beneath her fingers, to his flat belly. She longed for twilight, longed to awaken him with kisses, with her hands, her mouth.

Sighing, Heather glanced at her watch. 2 p.m. She had work to do. Bad guys to catch—without Bureau help or blessing. A file to read. And if it was bad? A knot formed in her stomach and she pushed the thought away. She climbed over Dante, pausing to kiss his cool lips.

"*Très belle*, yourself," she murmured before easing off the futon.

The floor creaked beneath her feet as she pulled the blankets up and over Dante. He didn't stir. Heather had a feeling she didn't need to worry about being quiet. He'd sleep no matter what.

Must be nice, she thought, half stepping and half skipping over the CD cases and clothes on the floor on her way to the adjoining bathroom.

She flipped on the light. The room was painted black and lavender. Several things cluttered the counter: eyeliner tubes and pencils, black lipstick, a brush, toothpaste, soap, an MP3 player.

Toothpaste? Weren't vampires immune to cavities?

Clean, plush towels hung from the rack, and shampoo and conditioner stood on a shelf in the shower. And beneath the towels, her overnight bag.

Who . . . ? Then she realized it must have been De Noir. The others would've been sleeping like Dante, hibernating in the daylight.

Turning on the water in the shower, Heather let it warm up while she looked at herself in the mirror. She glanced at her throat, touching the spot where Dante had bitten her. No visible mark, no tenderness. Fire flared within her again, kindled in her belly, as she thought of him drinking in a part of her. She closed her eyes.

Playtime's over. Focus on the case. Focus on keeping alive—if you're dead, who will speak for Jay and all the others?

Unbidden and unexpected, an answer disrupted her thoughts: *Dante would.* Somehow that felt right to her—heart-true.

Opening her eyes, Heather stepped into the shower and closed the door. As hot water sluiced across her neck and shoulders, she realized Dante had *become* the case, that in her struggle to keep him alive, she hadn't noticed that the game had changed; she no longer knew if the Ronin-Jordan team wanted Dante dead or wanted him to *join* them.

Her name was Chloe. And you killed her.

She's been creating sociopaths for years.

It's quiet when I'm with you.

Turning around, Heather braced her hands against the water-slick tiles and tipped her face up to the shower spray. She hoped the water would ease the sudden kinks out of her shoulders, would loosen the tightness constricting her breathing, melt away the fear frosting her guts.

She remembered the thought she'd *shouted* at Dante: *I won't walk away from you.*

Her breath caught, ragged, a sob. A fist closed around her heart. Her chest ached. She realized she was scared, scared of what she'd discover in the file, scared of what she might be forced to do.

* * *

DRESSED IN A ROYAL blue blouse and khaki slacks, Heather walked down the stairs, shoes in hand. The house was silent, hushed. Feeling like she was in a church, she resisted the impulse to tiptoe. Dante's whispered words circled through her mind: *Sanctus, sanctus, sanctus.*

Treading down the hall, she paused beside the computer room. The recliner was empty, the computer off. Coiled cables rested on the table beside Trey's goggles. She suddenly thought of Annie, drugged and peaceful as she slept in a hospital bed, her restraints removed and curled up on the nightstand.

Shaking the image from her head, Heather continued down the hall, walking into the kitchen. She sat at the table and, bending, laced on her shoes. The briefcase still stood beside the chair; her purse and Stearns's keys rested on the cobalt-blue tablecloth.

She grabbed her purse, dug out her cell phone. She flipped through the caller log, noting several calls from Collins. She felt a pang of guilt. She'd left him pretty much out in the cold, no word, no explanation. Could she trust him? She didn't know where she stood anymore, and a few hours of sleep hadn't made the situation any clearer.

Rogue agents, Bureau-ordered hits, mad-scientist experiments in psychopathology, vampires and fallen angels and a slicing-dicing serial killer: the world and her understanding of it had spun one-eighty degrees in a few days time. The only thing she was certain of was her promise to the CCK's victims, the slaughtered dead—a voice and justice.

And her promise to Dante? Pain clenched around her heart again. She still felt him against her, inside of her, remembered the feel of him, hard muscle and hot skin, saw herself reflected in his dark eyes.

It's still quiet. Stay here, cherie.
I won't walk away from you.

Promises were made to be kept, not broken. She'd believed that as a kid and she believed it now. Nothing had changed. She'd do everything possible for Dante, keep him close and alive. And if the file proved Stearns right? If Dante was a voice needing to be silenced?

Was it even that simple anymore? She'd stepped into a world colored in shades of gray—a twilight world more layered and complex than she'd ever imagined.

You'll see him for the monster he is.

She knew that was a statement she'd have to examine and soon. But first, she had a pair of monsters—one nightkind, the other mortal—that she needed to stop before they killed someone else, someone Dante loved.

Highlighting one of Collins's missed calls, Heather hit send. He answered on the first ring. "Wallace, where the hell have you been?" Strain edged his words.

"Tied up. Look, I'm sorry. I know I should've gotten back to you—"

"We need to talk. In person. All kinds of shit's coming down."

Apprehension curled around Heather's guts. "What kinda shit?"

"In person. Didn't you say there were two bodies at that slaughterhouse?"

"Yeah."

"We only found one. The kid in the straitjacket."

Heather went still. She'd watched Étienne burn. "Can you pick me up?" she said. She gave Collins the address.

" 'Kay." He paused, then asked, "Is this Prejean's address?"

"When will you get here?"

"Twenty, thirty minutes."

"See ya then."

How could Étienne's body be *gone*? Unless nightkind had auto-recall in case of death, it meant someone had come for

his remains or he'd walked away. Either proposition was un-
pleasant.

Heather pulled her .38 out of the trenchcoat's pocket and,
despite the fact that she'd reloaded it last night, checked to be
sure the clip was still in place. It was. She didn't know who'd
emptied it before—Jordan, probably, after he'd awakened on the
sofa.

Slipping on her trenchcoat, Heather slid the .38 back into
the pocket. She slung her purse over her shoulder and, after a
moment's hesitation, dropped Stearns's keys into her purse. She
picked up the briefcase and walked into the front room.

"Anything you wish me to tell Dante?" a deep voice said.

Startled, Heather whirled. De Noir sat in the easy chair, back
straight, eyes closed, his body language alert and attentive. The
X-rune pendant gleamed at his throat.

"I thought everyone was asleep."

"And so they are," De Noir said, opening his eyes. His gaze
shifted to the briefcase, then back to her face.

"I left a message for him," Heather said. "Can you keep him
here?"

Gold glinted in the depths of De Noir's black eyes. "As I said
before, Dante does as he wishes."

"Then ask him to wait for me."

"Patience is not his strong suit, but I'll ask."

"I appreciate it."

Heather crossed to the door, pulled it open and stepped
outside into afternoon sunshine, the briefcase in her hand a
black-barred shadow across her thoughts.

E STOWED THE LAST of his gear into the new van, tucking his
satchel o' tricks beside the narrow air bed installed in the back.
Humming, he knelt and made the bed, smoothing a long section of plastic over the sheets. *Should keep the worst of the blood*

off the sheets. He folded the blankets at the foot of the bed. One pillow or two? E opted for one and placed it at the head of the bed. Sitting on his heels, he glanced at the black-tinted, UV-protected windows. Totally groovy. *Hope Dante appreciates the effort. All for you, bro.*

E strode into the house, sliding the van's keys into his jeans pocket. He closed the door and locked it. He walked through the curtained gloom, heart jittering, thoughts ping-ping-pinging through his skull. He grinned. He couldn't help it.

Tom-Tom still slept, the day not yet dead. E paused outside the bloodsucker's room. Golden light flared around his body, spiked the hall with his radiance. He touched the knob, twisted. Locked.

E's grin widened. Could it be that Tommy-boy was afraid? Of a god seeking retribution for the desecration of his altar?

That stocking was fucking mine.

Locked door. No problem. A god was always prepared. E tugged his lock-picking kit from his back pocket and opened it. Selecting a bobby pin, he inserted it into the knob's hole and pushed. The push-in button on the opposite side of the knob popped out. E's grin widened. Returning the bobby pin to the kit, he zipped it shut and tucked it into his back pocket.

E turned the knob, then stepped into the bloodsucker's darkened bedroom. Golden tentacles of light whipped through the room, illuminating Tom-Tom stretched out on his bed, hands at his sides, eyes closed.

E dropped into a squat and peered under the bed. No pretty blond toy curled among the dust bunnies. All gone. Except for the dust bunnies. Sighing, he rose to his feet, walked to the closet, and opened the door. The cardboard boxes and zippered black bag were missing.

E's heart thudded against his chest. Whirling, shivs sliding into his hands, he faced the bed. Tom-Tom slept, his position unchanged. E wiped at the sweat beading his forehead.

Motherfucker knows.

E's golden light ebbed to a dim glow. His fingers touched the Band-Aid on his neck. *He couldn't track me. Of course he knows.*

E circled the bed, wondering where Tommy-boy'd hidden the goodies. He studied the bloodsucker's snoozing form, his gaze stopping on the jeans. Keys. The Camaro. E bent over the bed and touched Ronin's left front pocket. His fingers slid across denim. Empty. Walking around to the other side of the bed, E bent again, his fingers groping the right pocket.

Score! A hard shape took form beneath his fingers. E wriggled a couple of fingers into Tom-Tom's pocket—*Don't mind me. Oops. Is that* it? *Guess I shoulda called you Tiny Tom.*—snagged the keys, and pulled them free. Golden light once again flooded E's veins as he straightened, keys in hand; he glowed, incandescent.

Time to say bye-bye.

A voice inside insisted—*No! Not yet! Make sure, first*—but E reminded it that a god didn't need permission. Bending over Tom-Tom, he slashed a shiv across his throat.

The bloodsucker's eyes opened.

HEATHER NEARLY CHOKED ON the last bite of her Cajun-blackened burger. "Dead?" she managed to say after swallowing the spicy mouthful. "LaRousse?"

"And his partner, Davis," Collins said. He looked worn and tired.

Heather and the detective sat at a picnic table set up beneath an aluminum awning beside a drive-up food place, the HERE 'N GO. They were alone, the other picnic tables empty. The aroma of hot grease and frying meat filled the air.

"What the hell happened?" Heather asked, dipping fries in ketchup.

Collins shook his head. "A fire—arson—at a tavern. There were three other bodies besides those of LaRousse and Davis."

"I'm sorry, Trent. I didn't like LaRousse, but the man didn't deserve to die hard."

A wry smile lit Collins's face. "Yeah, he was an asshole, but *man*, did he clear cases. He was a good detective. And he was one of ours."

"What do you know so far?"

"Not much," Collins said, running a hand through his hair. "The question is, was it something simple, like a robbery that went outta whack, or was it planned?"

"People lose their tempers. People panic," Heather said. "Shit spins out of control. Have the state cops checked employees and regulars?"

"See who didn't burn last night and why?"

She nodded. "Was LaRousse on or off duty?"

"On." Collins paused a beat before continuing. "In fact, they'd been out to Prejean's with an arrest warrant, but . . ." he shrugged. "Not home."

Heather pushed the remains of her meal away, appetite lost. "Arrest warrant? What the hell for?"

Collins held up a placating hand. "To bring Prejean in for DNA samples. LaRousse still thought he was good for the girl's murder."

"Gina," Heather said, voice level. "Her name was Gina Russo. LaRousse knew Dante had nothing to do with her death; I'd already vouched for him."

"I don't know what LaRousse's beef with Prejean was," Collins said. "I'm just laying out the facts."

"I know. Sorry."

"There's more," Collins murmured. He wadded up his burger wrapper and tossed it into the dark-plastic-draped trash can behind the picnic tables. "There's been another murder." He glanced at Heather. "Bad."

The detective's haunted expression surprised her. She leaned across the picnic table and touched his hand. "You okay?"

"Yeah. Just a long fucking day."

Heather squeezed his hand, then released it. "So tell me, how bad?"

"Victim had been cut apart. The killer placed parts of him throughout the room." Collins paused, swallowed. A muscle jumped in his jaw.

"Go on," Heather said, voice soft. She tensed. Waited for the guillotine to drop.

"I'm pretty sure it was the CCK," Collins said. "No anarchy symbol . . . fuck . . . mean, there *could've* been but we just didn't recognize . . . I've never seen . . ." He looked away. "There was a message. On the wall. In blood."

The day's warmth slipped away with the sinking sun.

"What did it say?"

"Does it matter?" Collins replied, looking at Heather. Anger burned the hollow look from his eyes. "That investigation's officially closed. Word from headquarters is 'copycat.' No contact with you is allowed."

"Trent, what did the message say?"

"'S is mine.'"

Heather fumbled her cell phone from her purse. She punched in Dante's number. The phone rang and rang.

Not recruitment, no. *S is mine.* Dante had been claimed.

SLAMMING THE MOTEL ROOM door open, Gifford lunged into the room, swinging his gun right, then left. The room was empty. He did the Bureau-standard enter and sweep: closet, bathroom, flipped on lights. Stearns was gone.

Gifford lowered the .45 to his side. He glanced around the room. Suitcase on the chair. Laptop on the desk. Bottle of scotch and a glass on the night table. Stearns intended to come back, given all he'd left behind. Wait for him?

A wastebasket beside the bed caught his attention. He

dumped the wadded-up papers onto the rumpled bedspread and smoothed the first sheet. The name ELROY JORDAN appeared. Scanning the sheet, he recognized the dates and places for what they were—CCK murder dates and scenes.

When he unfolded the second sheet, his mind shifted into overdrive. THOMAS RONIN. What was Johanna's *père de sang* doing in New Orleans? At the same time as E? Glancing at the address on the printout, Gifford decided not to wait for Stearns.

Gifford gathered up the papers and rushed out the door. He got inside his Hertz rental and punched the Metairie address into the car's mapping system.

Johanna had been right from the beginning. No coincidence.

Throwing the car into reverse, Gifford peeled out of the motel parking lot.

BLOOD SPRAYED HOT AGAINST E's face, spattered his shades. Tom-Tom's hand locked around his wrist; something snapped and pain shotgunned up to his shoulder. A shiv dropped into E's other hand.

Fucker broke my wrist!

That thought ended in colored bursts of light—blue, green, and purple—as a sledgehammer smacked into E's temple. He flew off the bed and slammed against the wall. Pieces of plaster rained onto E and the carpet. Vision graying, E glanced at his hand. The shiv was gone.

Done scared me shivless.

Dizziness spun through his mind. Tweaked his gut. But adrenaline kicked his pain, kicked his ass, and kicked him up onto his feet again. Bracing a shoulder against the wall, E tugged another shiv from the sheath at his calf under his jeans. Blinking his vision clear, he looked at the bed.

Rivulets of blood poured from the bed and pooled on the carpet. The room *stank* of blood. Tommy-boy choked on the shit, spasming on the bed, hands at his throat, attempting to stem the flow. Grinning, E staggered to the bed. The bloodsucker's gleaming gaze fixed on him, killing him a hundred different ways.

But not today. Today, E was a god, golden and powerful. The truest killer who'd ever walked the earth.

E raised the shiv into the thickened air. Air like honey. Like amber. The shiv plunged into Ronin's beating heart.

"Plans have changed, asshole."

LUCIEN CLIMBED THE STAIRS, Dante's pain flickering like a candle in his mind. His child still Slept, but fire and shadows had fractured his dreams, stolen his peace. Lucien stepped into Dante's bedroom. The mingled smells of sex and fading pheromones lingered in the air.

He knelt beside the futon and rested a hand upon Dante's forehead. Heat baked into his palm. Blood trickled from one of the boy's nostrils. Lucien closed his eyes and poured energy into Dante, icing his pain and strengthening his partially restored shields.

He is remembering. His past has set him on fire. Consumes him.

Dante stirred beneath his hand, pale face troubled. The bleeding slowed, then stopped. The fever faded. Smoothing Dante's hair back, Lucien bent and kissed his forehead.

Let him hate me. I will keep him alive and hidden.

And sane?

The muscles in his chest tightened. He stood. *I will do what I must.*

He crossed the floor to the French windows and drew the curtains aside. The last glimmer of sunset lit the room deep red; spilled blood. Lucien stood at the windows, listening to the others awakening in the rooms down the hall, listening to the night's primeval pulse, and listening to the rhythm of his own dark heart.

On the futon behind him, Lucien heard his child drawing in a deep breath of air. Heard the *anhrefncathl*—a Maker's chaos song—awakening within his son's soul.

Without looking, he knew when Dante opened his eyes.

"We've some things to discuss," Lucien said.

Dante stretched, silk sheets sliding beneath him, muscles uncoiling. Tattered dreams slipped past his recall. Before-Sleep images sparked in his mind—Heather beneath him, lips parted, face lit with pleasure; the tavern ablaze, LaRousse's sardonic smile; Jay—

Opening his eyes, Dante sat up, heart pounding. Reddish light poured in through the French windows, illuminating Lucien's tall form.

"We've some things to discuss," Lucien said.

Dante caught his breath as memory whirled through him—the cathedral, Lucien impaled, his whispered words: *You look so much like her.*

Untangling himself from the sheets, he rose to his feet. "No, we don't," he said. "Not ever again."

"That's where you're wrong, child."

Lucien unlatched the French windows and pushed them open. He stepped out onto the wrought-iron balcony. The deepening twilight shadowed his face.

Scooping up a pair of black jeans from the floor, Dante tugged them on and zipped up the fly. He strode out onto the balcony. Lucien's gaze was fixed on the last shimmer of light on the horizon.

"You can't go after Ronin," Lucien said.

"Can't? *You're* telling me I can't? Fuck you." Dante's fingers curled around the cold metal railing.

"Ronin will awaken your past. It will break you," Lucien said, turning his face to meet Dante's gaze. "Find another way to do penance for Gina and Jay."

"You no longer have any say in what I do."

"Did I ever? Does anyone? You're headstrong, child."

"I listened to *you*," Dante said, throat tight, aching. "You, more than anybody."

An image strobed into his mind: a little girl huddled in a corner, plushie orca hugged to her chest, her face tear-streaked and scared.

Dante-angel?

He staggered as pain lanced through his head. *Chloe. Penance for Chloe.* Strong arms wrapped around him. Supported him. "Let go," he murmured, pushing at Lucien's arms. "Leave me the fuck alone."

Stumbling into the bedroom, Dante made his way into the bathroom, shutting the door behind him. He sank to the floor, head in his hands, eyes closed. He struggled to keep the images of Chloe in his mind, but they slipped away from him.

He saw her huddled and scared, then lying in a pool of blood, but he never saw what happened in-between. The unseen in-between left him shaken.

Her name was Chloe. And you killed her.

Sweat trickled down his temples. He slid his hands up from his face and through his hair. Thumped his head back against the wall. The pain receded. Didn't leave, no, but backed off enough to think.

A thought pressed against his shields, a thought belonging to Simone. He opened to her touch. <*Heather is on the phone. She wants to talk to you.*>

<D'accord, chérie. *I'm on my way.*>

Rising to his feet, Dante turned around and twisted on the sink's cold water faucet. He looked into the mirror. In the twilight gloom, he recognized letters smeared across its surface.

WAIT FOR ME. In black lipstick.

Dante smiled and touched a finger to the message. Heather's scent clung to him—lilac and sage—and he didn't want to wash it away. Not yet. After splashing his face with cold water, he opened the bathroom door.

Lucien waited for him, golden eyes glittering in the dusk. "Are you going after Ronin?"

"None of your business," Dante said, walking past him.

Dante caught a glimpse of peripheral movement and side-stepped, too late. Lucien seized his shoulders, talons piercing his skin—the pain needle-sharp. He felt the warm trickle of blood down his back. He hissed, but Lucien refused to release him.

"It *is* my business," Lucien said, steel edging his voice. "It will *always* be my business. You are my son."

Dante stared at Lucien, stunned, mind reeling. *His son?* "Let go."

Lucien lifted his hands. Blood glistened on the tips of his talons. "I should've told you from the start—"

"Yeah, but you didn't," Dante said, voice husky. "And now it's too late." He whirled and strode from the room.

Dante sprinted down the stairs, muscles taut, heart pounding against his ribs. He struggled for air. He needed blood. He needed truth.

Penance. Maybe everything he knew and everyone he loved would be stripped away until he paid what was owed.

He found Simone in the front room, curled up on the sofa beside Von. Her eyes widened and the *llygad* straightened, brows knitted.

"What's wrong?" she asked, handing him the phone.

Dante shook his head. Tried to calm his breathing. *"Oui, chérie?"* he said into the phone.

"Wait for me," Heather said. Static crackled across her voice. "I'll be there soon."

Would she be stripped from him as well?

"Don't. I won't be here," he said. His thumb slid across the end button. The phone slipped from his hand, hitting the carpet with a muffled thud.

In the sudden silence, Dante heard the whoosh of wings, then the ceiling creaked as Lucien perched on the roof. His father. Fallen.

What are you afraid of, True Blood?

Rage burned through Dante, poured white-hot through his veins. "Not you, Peeping Tom," he whispered. "Not you."

28

CONVERGENCE

"Shit!" Heather stared at the cell phone in frustration. "Pigheaded . . ." She glanced at Collins. "We need to move it. Dante's heading over there without us."

The car surged forward as Collins floored it. "Hope you're right about the probable cause. If we take Jordan in for questioning, I don't want him getting off on a technicality."

"My research placed Jordan at each kill site," Heather said. "If we get a DNA sample from him, it'll match the evidence in every single case." She dropped the cell phone back into her purse.

The fire that'd been smoldering within her since she'd awakened beside Dante had flared to life at the sound of his voice. *Oui, chérie?* She could almost smell him—warm, earthy, and inviting. But underneath Dante's words, his voice had been strained. Migraine? she wondered. Or was it something else?

It's quiet when I'm with you. The noise stops.

I'll help you stop it forever.

Heather knew qualified hypnotherapists in Seattle who might

be able to coax Dante's subconscious into relenting, and help ease his past up from dark depths without pain. She trailed a hand through her hair. With humans, yes. But nightkind? Nocturnal blood-fed predators? The psychology wouldn't—*couldn't*—be the same. She sighed.

She looked at the briefcase on the seat beside her. Dante's past. Everything he couldn't or didn't want to remember contained in a slim black briefcase. *Dante's* past. *He* should see it first. The fist around her heart unclenched and she drew in an easy breath.

After they'd dealt with Elroy Jordan, she'd give the briefcase to Dante, tell him what Stearns had said, and then stay with him as he delved into the contents.

And if Dante was a monster?

Heather glanced out the passenger's side window, hands knotted in her lap. The road blurred past, black and endless. She remembered the taste of Dante's lips, the desolation in his voice at the slaughterhouse. Remembered her promises.

I won't walk away from you.

I'll help you stop it forever.

I'll never bury evidence no matter how much it hurts.

STEARNS PISSED INTO AN empty orange juice bottle, his attention never wavering from the house Thomas Ronin had rented. When he'd finished, he screwed the lid back onto the bottle and set it carefully on the passenger's side floor. He cracked his window for fresh air.

The tidy house was a block up and on the opposite side of the street. Stearns had watched it since noon. He'd watched as a man in his midthirties with thinning brown hair left the house in a Jeep, returning an hour later in a white van with black-tinted UV-protected windows. Elroy Jordan. According to the printout he'd swiped from Prejean's kitchen, Jordan was Wallace's prime suspect for the CCK murders. He was also one of Moore's projects.

No sign of Thomas Ronin, but a sleek Camaro parked in the driveway suggested that the journalist was inside the house. Stearns still wasn't sure where Ronin fit into the picture. An exclusive story deal? With a freaking serial killer?

And why not? Stearns had witnessed and participated in stranger, darker things.

Someone stepped out the front door. Jordan again, but something was spattered on his face and clothes. Hard to make out what in the deepening twilight. Then as Jordan tried several keys in the Camaro's trunk, Stearns realized the spatter was blood.

Whatever Jordan had going with the journalist seemed to have ended. In a messy but inevitable way. Playing with serial killers was pretty much like running with scissors; sooner or later you're gonna get skewered.

The trunk finally opened and Jordan rummaged around in its interior. After a moment, he straightened, then slammed the trunk lid down. He kicked the Camaro several times, then hammered one fist against the trunk.

Through the cracked window, Stearns heard Jordan scream, "Fuck!"

Stearns touched the Glock on the seat beside him. *Doesn't handle disappointment well.* Jordan stomped up the drive to the front door, then stopped. He paced back and forth as though uncertain. Afraid to go back in? Stearns wondered. After a minute, Jordan stopped pacing, squared his shoulders, and marched inside the house.

Glock in hand, Stearns slid out of the Buick LeSabre.

GIFFORD DREW ON HIS cigarillo, savoring the dark, vanilla-spiced tobacco taste, his gaze locked on the Buick LeSabre parked on the opposite side of the street three blocks down. He blew smoke toward his cracked window.

Stearns exited the LeSabre, his right arm down, his gun a black silhouette against his leg. He crossed the street, aimed for the house E had disappeared into. Gifford stubbed the half-smoked cigarillo out in the car's ashtray. Without Wallace he couldn't stage the murder-suicide gig, but he'd learned to improvise during his years with Johanna.

Gathering up a paper-stuffed grocery bag, Gifford climbed out of his Taurus. He strolled along the sidewalk, "groceries" crooked in his left arm. He reached inside his jacket with his right, fingers grasping the .45's grip.

Let Stearns take down E. I'll mop up what's left.

E THUMPED THE HEEL of his hand against his forehead. *Idiot! Shoulda waited.* Where could the bloodsucker have hidden the shit? Not under his bed. Not in his closet. Not in his car.

E walked toward the hall, heart pounding, knowing the goodies had to be in the house. Fucker'd been expecting Dante and woulda been ready for him. Striding down the hall, E paused by Tom-Tom's door and glanced inside. Blood everywhere. Even on the ceiling. But the bed was empty.

Heart hammering, E jumped past the doorway and ran to the hall closet. Yanked it open. Rummaged through the towels and sheets, flinging them to the floor as he did. E froze. Had he heard something *shuffling*? Lurching up the dark hall like a gore-oozing zombie? E whirled, shiv in hand.

He stood alone in the darkened hall.

Pulse racing, mouth dry, E returned to Ronin's bedroom doorway. The thick stink of blood rushed to his head—*Ah, smells like sex.* He stepped into the bedroom. As he did, he became aware of a scraping sound.

From the floor on the far side of the bed, dark, bloodstained fingers clawed for purchase on the wall. Bloodied gouges marred the paint.

E stared, heart leaping in his chest like it wanted *out*, thinking: *It's* Dawn of the Dead *time. The dead won't stay down. Don't wanna be torn apart and gobbled up by a zombie!*

A mewling sound drowned out the scraping finger noise. E clamped a hand over his mouth and the mewling stopped.

Shut the hell up. That's no zombie, just a blood-drained bloodsucker refusing to die. You're a god. Get a fucking grip.

E nodded. A god. He lowered his hand from his mouth and walked over to the dresser. Jerked open the top drawer. Gold light shimmered and an angelic chorus voiced a triumphant song. Nestled in the folds of silk underwear and pricey socks were the files. E scooped them up, then pulled open the next drawer. Nuthin'. He found the zippered black bag in the last drawer and grabbed it.

Nails scratched along the wall. E split, running up the hall, through the front room, and out the door.

When he reached the van, E climbed inside and stashed the bag and files beside his satchel o' tricks. Now all he needed was Dante. Where was the GPS receiver? E unzipped the black bag and searched its contents—vials of sedatives, trank gun, hypos, handcuffs—all designed with the fun-lovin' bloodsucker in mind, but no GPS receiver. How the hell would he track Dante without it?

E thumped his fists against his temples. Pain screamed up from his broken wrist. His stomach clenched. *Idiotidiotidiot!* Swallowing hard, he lowered his injured arm. Purple, almost black, bruises mottled his swollen wrist. He'd have to make a sling for it later. For the moment, he needed to find the GPS receiver.

E scrambled out of the van, then froze. A hard-looking man in a jacket stood in front of him, a serious fucking gun in his hand. The muzzle leveled with E's chest. E dropped to the concrete and rolled under the van. *Stop-drop-'n'-roll.* Something *tunk*ed against the side of the van. Bullet?

E glanced past his view of the man's polished black shoes, aware of a sound like an engine at high speed, redlining. On the street, a small black car jolted up and onto the sidewalk, peeled across the lawn, aimed straight for the house.

E narrowed his eyes against the glare of headlights. The car slammed into the front step. Bashed grill against threshold. The house shook.

Dante'd arrived.

STEARNS THREW HIMSELF AGAINST Elroy Jordan's new van as the sports car jumped the curb, tore across the yard and smashed against the house. Steam hissed into the air from the crumpled front end.

For a moment, Stearns hesitated, then pushed away from the side of the van. An accident? Deliberate? Then a slender figure in black slipped out of the car through the driver's side window and his heart kicked against his ribs.

Beautiful white face. Black hair. Leather jacket and chain-strapped black jeans. He jumped with ease over the car's buckled front end to the house's warped threshold, surrounded by spikes of blue/white light. Pale hands braced against the wood.

Stepping forward, Stearns lifted the Glock. "Dante!" he called.

He fired as the young vampire swiveled.

THE BULLET CAUGHT DANTE in the temple, the impact snapping his head to one side. He crumpled across the threshold.

"Stop the car!" Heather cried. Collins hit the brakes. She threw the door open and hit the ground running, yanking her .38 from the trench's pocket.

Stearns glanced up. Looked at her, then strode toward the MG. Toward Dante.

"Drop your gun," Heather yelled, .38 in a two-handed grip. She aimed it at Stearns. "Drop it! Don't make me do this!"

Stearns hesitated, then stepped forward, lifting the Glock. Heather fired. Stearns stumbled, dropping to one knee in the grass beside the MG. She ran from the sidewalk to the tire-ravaged yard, gun aimed at her former mentor.

"Drop it," she said.

The Glock tumbled from Stearns's fingers. Blood stained the shoulder of his jacket. Wincing, he linked his hands together behind his head.

"Let me finish him," Stearns said. "If you've read the file—"

"Shut up," Heather said, gun leveled with his forehead.

She glanced toward the house. Dante hadn't moved. He was sprawled across the threshold, haloed by the headlights, black hair spilled like wine across the carpet. A line of blood trickled from his temple across his face.

Heather looked away. Her breath rasped in a throat gone too tight. Not dead, she reminded herself, not dead. She sucked in cold air, pulled her handcuffs from her pocket. Kneeling behind Stearns, she ratcheted a cuff around one wrist, securing it.

Collins trotted past Heather to the doorway. "I'll check Prejean," he said.

"Heather, listen, you don't understand—"

"I understand that you shot an unarmed man," she said, voice low, tight. "Now shut the fuck up."

As Heather swung Stearns's arms down so she could finish cuffing him, a man carrying a bag of groceries stopped in the drive.

"Sir, please move on—"

The man dropped his groceries. Wads of paper tumbled onto the sidewalk as he drew a gun. Stearns jerked his uncuffed arm free from Heather's grasp and lunged for his Glock.

Heart triple-timing, Heather lifted her .38. "Trent! Look out!"

All three fired.

LUCIEN FLEW, THE WIND of his passage cold against his face. A different kind of cold rimmed his soul with ice. Through Dante, he'd experienced a brief moment of pain; then his child's consciousness had winked out. A faint thread of life force still pulsed through their bond, so he knew Dante wasn't dead. Injured, perhaps critically, but alive.

On the ground beneath Lucien, skewed headlights pierced the sky. Figures ran. Blood hunger, savage and blind and ancient, stabbed out into the night from the house below. Lucien spiraled down toward the house and its raging occupant.

Thomas Ronin would never be a threat to Dante again.

Lucien glided to the ground, bare feet touching wet grass as he landed. His wings folded behind him, then compressed down into their pouches. He strode across the lightless backyard and wrenched the screen door—metal screeching—off its hinges. Tossing it aside, Lucien battered the rear door inward with one fist and stepped inside.

FROM UNDERNEATH THE VAN, E watched as Heather knelt behind the motherfucker who'd tried to kill him, the hard-looking man who'd gunned down his Bad Seed bro instead. Then someone else joined the game. Suddenly, everyone was yelling, shooting, and leaping.

E rolled out from the other side of the van and, keeping low, crept around the front end; the sight of Dante slumped across the threshold drew him like a perv to porn.

He wished the best for his lovely Heather and hoped she wouldn't mind his taking advantage of her nasty situation. He preferred to think it was him she fought to protect and not Dante, since she'd come for *him*, after all, and not the party-crashing little bloodsucker.

But, hey, at least now he didn't have to worry about finding the GPS receiver.

E paused at the van's front end, gaze on the plainclothes cop hunkered down near Dante's body. He'd twisted around at Heather's warning and drawn his gun, but before he could fire a single shot, dark bloodstained fingers grabbed him by the shoulders and yanked him inside the house.

A creepy-crawly anthill feeling shuddered down the length of E's body. Tom-Tom had gained his feet. Just beyond the threshold, shadows jerked and jittered.

Bloodsucker or the restless dead?

E scuttled forward, hunched low, his gaze locked on Dante's pale face. In the yard, people screamed. Guns fired. Crossing mental fingers for Heather's survival—the game wouldn't be the same without her—E sidled up the side of the concrete step. Fluids leaked from the MG's ruined front end. Steam hissed and spat.

E reached a shaking hand for Dante's arm. Snagged him. Pulled. Dead weight. Sweating, panting, E dragged Dante down off the step. He hit the ground with a thud, metal jingling. He shifted his grip from Dante's arm to the collar of his jacket. Dante's pretty head lolled. Blood trickled from his right ear, streaking the side of his face.

Tugging and grunting and burning adrenaline, E pulled his bloodsucker bro to the front of the van. The side doors were still open.

Something flew out of the house. Heather yelled, "Shit!" More gunfire.

E partially pushed Dante into the van, then hopped inside and dragged him in the rest of the way. Rolled him away from the doors and eased them shut. Fetching the handcuffs from the black bag, he latched them around Dante's wrists. He didn't know how long Dante'd be unconscious, but best not to take any chances.

He hauled Dante's body to the rear of the van, lifted his arms, and slid the handcuff chain over a hook installed for that very purpose. The bloodsucker looked damned fine in hand-cuffs. A natural.

Grinning, E crawled one-handed to the driver's seat. He worked the keys out of his pocket. And waited.

HEATHER FIRED THE .38 as she threw herself to the side. Some-thing whizzed past her cheek, stinging. Glock in hand, Stearns rolled across the lawn and to his feet. He opened fire. The dark-haired man—*unknown subject*—staggered back, then fired again.

Stearns fell to his knees, his face blank.

Aiming for the unsub's head, Heather squeezed off a round just as the man ducked down behind the van. "Trent," she shouted. "Head him off!"

Heather lunged for the MG, diving behind it. She glanced at the house and her heart jumped into her throat. A blood-drenched figure bent over Collins. The detective's hands hung limp at his sides; his entire body seemed boneless. Thomas Ronin lifted his face from what remained of Collins's throat.

Heather swiveled and opened fire on the vampire. Grimac-ing, fangs bared, Ronin tossed the detective's body at her.

"Shit!"

The body hit, knocking the air from her lungs and taking her to the ground. Heather's head bounced against the wet grass. Flickers of light sparked through her vision. Trapped beneath Collins's weight, she struggled to breathe. She pushed at the body, sucking in the smells of sweat, blood, and shit; of death. Images of his shredded throat and lax face filled her mind. She shoved, frantic and gasping for air. Finally with one last thrust, she wriggled free of the body. She sucked in air, half sobbing.

Ronin now held the dark-haired unsub, his face buried in the man's throat. The unsub kicked, pounded, and squirmed. He emptied his gun into the vampire's gut. Ronin quivered with each bullet, snarling as he fed. Blood dribbled onto the concrete.

Climbing to her knees, Heather aimed at Ronin's head. She caught peripheral movement from the house and swung around, gun in both hands. De Noir, shirtless and shoeless, stepped out of the house, crossed the yard in two quick strides, and seized Ronin by the neck with one hand.

The unsub spilled to the drive, his body loose in a way that turned Heather's stomach. Ronin twisted in De Noir's grasp and slashed him across the chest with his fingers. Blood spilled, then . . . stopped. The gashes faded. Vanished. De Noir's wings unfurled. He carried Ronin into the sky.

The van started up. Reversed. Bumped up and over the unsub's body. Skidded out into the street. Heather jumped to her feet, heart pounding. Jordan! She raised her .38. Jordan puckered his lips, lifted his hand, and blew her a kiss. She fired. The bullet starred the passenger window. She squeezed off another round, but the gun clicked, the magazine empty.

Jordan hit the gas. The van accelerated down the street and into the night.

Heather tipped her head back and screamed, "Fuck!"

Jordan was gone. Dante shot . . . Dante . . . She whirled. The threshold was empty.

De Noir must've moved him or—She ran out into the street. The van was gone.

S is mine.

LUCIEN TWISTED IN THE sky, talons buried in Ronin's shoulders. The vampire sank his fangs into Lucien's chest, sucking in healing, life-sustaining blood. Lucien pummeled Ronin's head with his fist, distorting the skull and popping its fangs from his flesh.

The skull rippled, returned to its original shape. Ronin locked gazes with Lucien. "That taste," he said. "Like Dante's blood—unique."

"I hope you enjoyed it. It was your last."

Lucien gripped the vampire at shoulder and hip, then wrenched. Blood sprayed into the night as flesh and bones tore, separated. Torqued. Ronin screamed, eyes shut, his fangs moon-lit. His nails gouged furrows down Lucien's chest.

Lucien pulled Ronin apart at the waist. Organs dropped to the earth, a shower of gore. Below, the Mississippi snaked, glimmering beneath the stars, a black river crossing a black land. Lucien released the vampire's lower portion. Legs spasming, it fell into the river.

Winging through the night, Lucien slapped away Ronin's clawing, punching hands, fended off his snapping jaws. He hovered above a riverside factory smokestack. Sparks flitted into the sky from its dark mouth.

"I would lay the world to waste for my son," Lucien said and pulled his talons free of Ronin's flesh.

As the vampire fell, he grabbed the X-rune pendant. The chain snapped. Smiling, Ronin plummeted into the smokestack, the chain wrapped around his fingers. A shower of sparks flew into the air.

Lucien stared into the night, hand at his throat.

The pendant was gone.

29

ALL THINGS S

D ARKNESS.
     Music pounded, his own. Inferno.
Smelled blood, sour sweat, engine exhaust.
Tasted blood in his mouth, his own.
Something jabbed against his neck. Stung. Cold chemicals
flooded his veins. Dulled the pain in his head.
"Mine," a voice whispered. Unfamiliar. Fading. Fingers
touched his face. "I'll be your god and you'll love me."
Darkness. Drug rush. Dante fell, dreaming.

HEATHER SAT IN THE grass beside Stearns's body, her hand
frozen above his motionless chest, longing to touch the man
who'd been more of a father to her than James William Wallace,
yearned to say good-bye. But she couldn't force her hand any
lower.
He shot Dante in cold blood. And now—
A rush of cold air fluttered Heather's hair, drew her gaze
up. De Noir's black wings cut through the sky, flapping as he

landed. His golden-eyed gaze skipped around the yard. Desperation shadowed his face.

Sirens pierced the silence.

"Where is he?"

"Jordan has him," she said. "In the van." *S is mine.* Her eyes stung.

"I can't *feel* him," De Noir said, voice strained. "Something has obscured our link. Feels like . . . static." Fanning his wings, he lifted into the air.

"Wait!" Heather climbed to her feet. She looked around the yard turned killing ground. All dead. A pang of regret pierced her as her gaze fell upon Collins's body. She remembered their earlier conversation about LaRousse: *The man didn't deserve to die hard.*

Neither did you, Trent, she thought, throat tight.

If she stayed, she'd be busy making statements and doing debriefings for hours, possibly days. The CCK had Dante. Dante was nightkind, true. But Elroy Jordan was a sexual sadist who now possessed a victim who healed. One he could "kill" over and over again. She couldn't afford to lose time.

"Take me with you," she said.

De Noir hovered in the air, face cold and unreadable.

"I know Jordan's patterns, I can help. Please."

De Noir's taloned hands curled into fists. He dropped to the ground again. The sirens drew closer. Heather ran across the street to Collins's car, threw open the door and stretched across the seat. Grabbing the briefcase, she ran back to the yard and De Noir.

"Hold on," he said, wrapping an arm around her waist.

Heather draped an arm around De Noir's neck, heart kicking against her ribs. His wings flared, air gusted, and they rose into the sky. She looked down. Squad cars screeched to a slanting halt in the street before Ronin's house. Blue lights strobed across the houses, cars, bodies. A block down the street, an

ambulance waited, lights flashing, for the all-clear signal from
the cops.

The wind of De Noir's passage blew cold against Heather's
face, frosting her hair, her lashes. Shivering, she shut her eyes.
De Noir closed his other arm around her, held her tight and
without effort. His heat radiated into her, melting away the cold.
She tucked her face into his neck. His warm, earthy smell turned
her thoughts to Dante.

Heart aching, muscles knotted, Heather *shouted* her thought
into the night, hoping, somehow, that Dante would hear her.

I'm coming for you.

DARKNESS.

Pain throbbed in his head. His neck. Burned in his shoulders. Muscles twisted. He tried to lower his arms. Metal bit into
his wrists. Clunked against more metal.

Handcuffed.

Dante opened his eyes. Red laced his vision. He lay on his
side, arms stretched above his head. He smelled cheap tobacco
and plastic and the sharp scent of his own blood. A mortal knelt
behind him. Gripped his shoulder. Pain wormed and worried
into his neck, the base of his skull. Blood trickled hot down his
neck and under his shirt.

Papa Prejean's basement.

Dante jerked down with all his strength. Pain bit into his
shoulders again. Clunk-*tunk*. The cuffs held.

The hand on Dante's shoulder pinched. Hard.

"Hold still," an unfamiliar voice said. "You do that again, no
telling where this shiv'll end up."

Dante squeezed his eyes shut as the shiv dug and scraped.
More hot blood flowed down his neck.

"Got it! Hot damn!"

The digging stopped. Dante released the breath he'd been

holding and sucked in a lungful of stale air laced with the mortal's old smoke-and-bile stink; a stink he recognized, but couldn't name. Like an ice pick jabbing behind his eyes, migraine pain stabbed his thoughts, chipped away at his concentration.

The mortal wiped at his neck. Paper rustled. Then he slapped something across the wound. "Gotcha Batman Band-Aids. Thought you'd like that."

A fingertip shove to Dante's shoulder rolled him onto his back. His handcuffs clinked. And, beneath him, plastic crinkled. Dante opened his eyes and winced. A small covered light burned above him in the ceiling. Not a basement, no. A car? No sensation of movement. No engine hum. Not moving.

A shadow shuffled past, silhouetted against the light. *Kinda looks like Peeping Tom's assist—*

Elroy the Perv knelt beside Dante, a grin stretching his lips. A sling cradled his left arm against his chest. In his right hand, pinched between two fingers, he displayed a bloodied sliver of plastic. "See this?" he said. "A bug implanted at birth. So you could *always* be followed. Studied. Et cetera, et cetera. I had to dig mine out by myself."

Pain slammed through Dante's skull. Bugs? Implants? An image flickered behind the pain—a woman, short blonde hair, blue eyes, fangs—murmuring, *They're afraid of you, my little True Blood.* Pain shattered the image.

Ronin's low voice: *What are you afraid of, True Blood?*

A needle pricked the skin on his throat.

"Your nose is bleeding," Elroy said. "That's kinda sexy."

The Perv's lips, hot and tasting of tobacco, pressed against Dante's mouth; his kiss as gentle as a fist. As Elroy's hand glided over Dante's body, the drugs tumbled him back into the darkness of Papa Prejean's basement.

Dante-angel?

Let me burn, princess.

*   *   *

HEATHER OPENED HER EYES as De Noir descended, gliding, onto the wrought-iron balcony outside Dante's bedroom. She slipped her arms from around his neck and stepped down onto the concrete. Her hand felt frozen to the briefcase's handle. A quick glance revealed bright red fingers, cold, but not iced.

She walked into the unlit bedroom through the opened French windows. The air smelled of candle wax and crisp autumn leaves, smelled of Dante. The sight of the unmade futon, the rumpled sheets, twisted her heart. She closed her eyes.

Focus on finding Jordan. Focus on finding him fast—before he goes to work on Dante and learns he never has to stop.

Heather opened her eyes and strode across the room. As she rounded the corner into the hall, she saw Simone on the stairs, her pale face anxious.

"Lucien told us what happened," Simone said, stepping onto the landing. "What do you need Trey to do?" Her dark gaze shifted past Heather and up.

De Noir stepped past Heather, buttoning on a black shirt.

Lucien told us what happened. Of course. Heather swallowed back the words she'd planned to say, hard words—*Dante took a bullet to the head and now a serial killer has him, just as he said he would, just as he promised, in innocent blood.*

Heather said, "I need your brother to do another search for any kind of rentals or purchases recently made by either Ronin or Jordan. Have him do a vehicle search too."

"*D'accord.*" Turning, Simone trotted down the stairs.

De Noir glanced at the briefcase. "What's inside?"

Heather looked up and met his gaze. "Dante's past."

"Where did you get it?"

"From my boss," she said, voice low. "The man who shot Dante."

De Noir's jaw tightened. His gaze shifted to a point above and beyond Heather. Tendrils of his black hair snaked up into the now electrified air. The smell of ozone spiked the air. Heather's hair lifted. Her skin tingled. *Lightning strike.*

"Have you looked at what's in that case?"

"No. I'd hoped to give it to Dante."

De Noir's gaze dropped and swept over Heather. She saw nothing she recognized in his eyes, human or otherwise. After a moment, he nodded.

"Then we shall look at it together," he said.

ARM THROBBING, E STEERED the van into a rest stop off I-59. Needed a pick-me-up. He shut off the engine, glanced in the rearview mirror. Dante slept, head turned to one side, hand-cuffed wrists stretched above him.

E opened the door, slid partway out, then froze. Maybe Dante *wasn't* sleeping. Maybe he was faking it and planned some kind of kicking, yelling, rescue-me-bullshit. Better make sure. Climbing back into the van, E crawled past the front seats to the back, and scooted to the air bed.

Dante's breathing was slow and easy. Strands of black hair partially covered his face. E poked him in the ribs. Nuthin'. Doped and flying sky-high. He grabbed his shoulder, shook him. Nuthin'.

E's gaze scrolled down the bloodsucker's hard, yummy body— bondage collar; vintage black NIN T-shirt, rucked up a little, a line of flat belly exposed; chain-strapped black jeans, metal-studded belt, the belt and jeans unfastened at the moment.

E bent over Dante, a shiv sliding into his good right hand. He punched the shiv into Dante's chest. The bloodsucker's body spasmed. His breath caught, rattled, then released hard and fast. Blood bubbled up on his lips. But his eyes didn't open. Out cold.

Damned good drugs, E mused. *Wonder if he can heal with the shiv in his chest?*

Rummaging through his satchel, E dry-swallowed a handful of pills, then made his way up front again. He hopped out of the van and sauntered to the free-coffee stand. The image of Dante sleeping with the shiv buried in his flesh burned itself into his mind and left him trembling.

Heather sat at the kitchen table, the briefcase open on the cobalt-blue tablecloth, and switched on her laptop. De Noir drew up a chair and sat beside her, frowning. Taking a deep breath, she grabbed the folder from the briefcase, set it on the table and opened it.

Photos spilled out: some current, taken surreptitiously, Dante unaware; others showed Dante as a teenager, a child, a toddler; the boy's wary gaze, the toddler's fanged half smile, the teen's smirk and raised middle finger.

She handed each photo to De Noir. He studied every image for long moments, jaw tensing, wordless. One photo captured her attention: Dante laughing, his arms around a grinning girl with freckles and long red hair, her face half turned to him. Dante appeared to be twelve, maybe thirteen, the girl eight or nine.

Her name was Chloe. And you killed her.

Heather stared at the picture, at Dante's happy face, the only photo of him laughing—big brother and guardian angel for another child lost in the system of foster homes and state programs. Handing De Noir the photo, she slid the CD into the laptop's drive. When a menu popped up, she lined down to the section marked S AND CHLOE and clicked it open. Surreptitiously filmed footage filled the monitor:

In faded jeans and a gray tee, Dante sits cross-legged on the floor, his back against a neatly made bed, his attention focused on the book in his lap. Chloe sits on the bed in lavender cords and pink Pooh sweater, watching him, her sneakered feet kicking idly against the bed frame. A plushie orca is tucked under one arm.

"*Sound it out,*" *she says, twirling a strand of red hair around her finger.*

"*Kum . . . for . . . kumfor . . . tay . . . bull . . . kumfortaybull. Comfortable.*"

"*You got it!*"

"*Yeah?*" *A pleased smile lights Dante's face.*

"*Yup,*" *Chloe confirms.* "*Now finish the sentence.*"

"*Pooh's bed was comfortable and . . . warm.*"

"*You learn fast,*" *Chloe says.* "*I bet if you didn't sleep during the day and could go to school, you'd get straight As.*"

Dante snorts, then glances back at her from over his shoulder. "*I'd have all Fs.*"

"*For . . . ?*" *Chloe coaxes, gathering his hair into a ponytail and smoothing its black length between her hands.* "*What starts with F?*"

"*Fuck school.*"

She giggles, covering her mouth with her hand. "*Dante-angel!*"

A blur of motion, then Dante is suddenly up from the floor and tickling Chloe. She shrieks with laughter, rolling on the bed, her sneakers thumping the mattress. Laughing, he tucks an arm against his side and tries to protect his ribs from her retaliatory fingers.

He tugs free the plushie orca from under Chloe's arm and swims the toy through the air past her grabbing hands. He stops it at her nose. Leans it forward. "*Mmm-*wah *!*" *A big sloppy orca kiss.*

"*Can I brush your hair while you practice printing the alphabet?*" *Chloe asks.*

"*Sure,*" *Dante says, handing the orca back to her.*

"*Boy, you need to get your ass down to the basement and now,*" *a man's voice—bayou-bred and deep—says from off-camera.* "*Gotta visitor comin' and gotta cuff you up. You don't need none of dat school shit for the work you do,* petit *. Waste o' time.*" *The speaker laughs, a cigarette-raspy sound ending in a cough.*

"*Fuck you,*" *Dante says.* "*I'll be there in a minute.*"

Chloe's smile vanishes and she sits up, the plushie held tight against her pink sweater. "Leave him alone," she says, her voice sharp, her brows slanting down—defiant and pale.

"Hush, you. Or I'll put my hand upside your head."

Dante's hand squeezes Chloe's knee. She closes her mouth. He looks at the speaker, all expression gone from his face, but fire burns in his dark eyes, a fire the speaker must *feel, see.*

"You're gonna need more than handcuffs to hold me if you touch her," Dante says, his voice low and flat.

Another cigarette-raspy laugh. "Full of attitude, aintcha, boy. Move your ass or I'll just send little m'selle *feisty in your place—"*

Dante turns and kisses Chloe's forehead, smoothes her long hair back from her face. "Night-night, princess. I'll see you tomorrow."

Worry shadows Chloe's face. "Dante-angel . . ."

He shakes his head. "Shhh. Je suis ici. *Don't come down. Not tonight."*

She nods, unhappy. Dante blows her a kiss and walks from the room.

The footage ended. Heather paused a moment—how old was he? Twelve?—then she forced her fingertips from her palms, and clicked on the next section.

Later, eyes burning, she understood why De Noir had said that Dante's past was something better left unremembered. She understood it would break his heart. And she understood why Stearns had called him a monster.

CHOKING ON BLOOD, DANTE awakened. Darkness. Engine noise. Pain raked his chest. Blood filled his mouth. Turning onto his side, the handcuffs clunk-*tunk*ing as he moved, he spat blood on the floor until he could suck in a breath of air.

Dizzied, he listened to the engine's soothing, steady sound. He glanced down. A knife's hilt protruded from his chest.

"We've entered Alabama," Elroy said. "Don't it feel good?"

Dante caught Elroy's shaded gaze in the rearview mirror. The Perv grinned.

"Never mind the shiv," he said. "Couldn't resist. How does it feel?"

Dante coughed, spat, then said, "Fuck you. Take these cuffs off and I'll show you." He jerked his arms, rattling the cuffs.

Elroy laughed. "That's my Bad Seed bro."

Dante drifted off again as the miles rolled past, not really asleep, but caught in a twilight-zone haze created by drugs and pain. He opened his eyes as the van slowed down, then stopped.

The Perv keyed off the engine and stretched. He slipped between the seats, pausing to close a curtain between the front of the van and the back. He crab-walked over to Dante's side of the van. Grabbing a battered black satchel, he opened it and pulled out a file folder thick with paper.

"Time for you to learn a few things." Elroy dropped onto his knees and bent over Dante. "Like who and what you are." Grabbing the shiv hilt, he yanked the blade out of Dante's chest.

Refusing to touch his bond with Lucien, Dante tried his links to Von and Simone instead. Pain buzzed through his head as each attempt rebounded, unheard. Whatever the Perv was pumping into his veins had muffled his mind like a thick layer of gauze.

Elroy played with the shiv, twirling the blade up, over and around. Wet with blood, the knife glistened beneath the covered light. On his last over-and-under pass, he drove the blade into Dante's stomach.

Dante squeezed his eyes shut. Pain stole his voice. Another punch and the pain seared his chest, sucked away his air. He coughed up blood.

"Time to teach you all things S," Elroy murmured. "Open your eyes."

Fingers fluttered across Dante's eyelids. Whispered across his lips. He smelled blood on Elroy's fingers—his own. He opened his eyes and looked into Elroy's sweating face. The grin had vanished. His fingers still held the second shiv in Dante's chest. He pressed down on it. *Leaned* into it and twisted.

Pain corkscrewed through Dante's chest and black spots speckled his vision. He bit his lip, determined not to scream, determined not to give the sick little fuck the satisfaction.

Dante-angel?

Shhh. Not now, princess. Gotta wake up. Gotta quit dreaming.

"Listen to me," Elroy said.

Dante blinked until his vision cleared. Spat blood. Coughed. The handles of two shivs stuck up from his body, one in the belly and one in the chest.

The Perv held up photos. Dante stared. They were of him, but when he was younger, from the years he couldn't remember. Pain pricked behind his eyes, jabbed his temples.

"You're part of a project called Bad Seed," Elroy said. "Me too. In fact, we're the last surviving members. They got me when I was two or three after my parents did the ol' you-kill-me-I'll-kill-you routine." He held up a photo of a grinning toddler. "Wasn't I a cutie?"

Elroy picked up a folder, flipped through the contents. "Now you, you they had shortly after conception. They nursed your mama through a difficult pregnancy, then whacked her after you were born. Being a bloodsucker and all, they cut off her head and torched her body."

Heart pounding, struggling for air, Dante tried to make sense of Elroy's words. Pain scoured away his thoughts. He coughed. His mother . . .

Genevieve.

You look so much like her.

Wasps droned and his vision blurred. From a great distance, he heard the Perv say: "She named you before she died. And it amused Mommy-Bitch Moore to let you keep the name. Dante."

Something smacked hard across Dante's face, rocking his

head to the side. His teeth sliced into his lower lip again. White light sparked and flared at the edges of his vision. Narrowing his gaze against the light, he focused on Elroy's sallow face.

"I was losin' ya," Elroy said. "Your nose is bleeding again, by the way."

Dante coughed, a lung-tearing spasm that brought up gouts of bright blood. Elroy scooted back out of gouting/spitting range.

"Take out the fucking knives," Dante whispered after the spasm had passed. "Then go on. Read it to me. Hit me if I pass out. But read it to me."

The Perv lifted his shades and stared at Dante, hazel eyes full of wonder. "Read to you?" Crawling back over, he grabbed the hilt of the shiv planted in Dante's chest and pulled it out. Traced it across Dante's belly, blood trailing in its wake. "My pleasure."

Dropping his shades back over his eyes, Elroy read to Dante, pushing down on the shiv in his belly or backhanding him or both whenever the migraine threatened to drag him under.

> *Foster parents informed that subject has an illness that requires special attention and special nutrition, therefore earning them an increased payment. . . .*

DANTE REMEMBERED LAROUSSE AT the tavern, saying: *Sixty foster homes, two stints in the loony bin.* Light pinwheeled and fractured his vision. His head throbbed. His heart raced. He listened.

> *S's favorite "blankie" taken from him and burned. S forced to watch and informed the "blankie" was burned because he'd been "bad."*
>
> *Foster parents #10 punished S for defiance. They removed the curtains in a room full of windows and locked*

him in. He stayed in shadowed corners avoiding the sun-
light until there were no more shadows. . . .

SUNLIGHT SLANTING ACROSS THE carpet and hurting his eyes,
dust motes whirling in the air, fear creeping up his spine—
memory yawned wide and Dante fell. Sunlight blistered and
crisped his skin. The burned-meat smell curdled in his belly.

Dante sucked in air and coughed up blood. Pain scattered
the memory, swept it away. One little piece of knowledge clung
for a few moments: Loony bin stay *numéro un* had happened
right after that bit of punishment.

> *Foster mother #12 has developed a fondness for S*
> *and is forming a bond with him. S appears to enjoy her*
> *company. He will be removed from her care. . . .*
>
> *S increasingly defiant. His favorite toy, a plastic alli-*
> *gator on wheels, is taken from him and thrown away. He*
> *retaliates by throwing away the foster parents' cigarettes*
> *and beer. S beaten . . .*
>
> *S found or stole a guitar and is teaching himself*
> *to play it. He has an amazing ear and learns rapidly.*
> *Shows true musical talent . . .*
>
> *S drugged and brought into the clinic for examina-*
> *tion and study. Dr. Wells curious, as am I, to learn just*
> *how much a born-vampire can endure physically. The*
> *experiments will commence tomorrow. . . .*

FRAGMENTS OF MEMORY BUZZED up from below, carried on
the wings of Gigeresque wasps: A cold, steel table. Restraints.
Needles. Saws. A bloodied baseball bat held by a tech in a face
shield and blood-spattered lab coat. White-hot pain wiped the
images away. He wasn't *remembering*. He was *experiencing*. Elroy's
fist slammed Dante back into the here and now.

"Read to me," Dante whispered.

The Perv stared at him for a long moment, licked his lips, then continued reading.

> *Experiments shall be repeated once S reaches puberty . . . if vampires have a process like puberty. Shall be fascinating . . .*
>
> *S has developed affection for another foster child in his household, a girl named Chloe Basescu. He looks after her. She calls him "Dante-angel" for some reason, perhaps because he protects her from their foster father. S and Chloe often sleep together, but in a nonsexual manner.*
>
> *S showing signs of what I believe to be vampire puberty: night prowling, sexual promiscuity within his own age group, biting, fascination with blood, no longer satisfied with his daily dose of "medicinal" blood. He yearns to hunt. He seems to be both excited and confused by his feelings. Overwhelmed by his desires. He confides in Chloe. This troubles me. . . .*
>
> *Time to take Chloe away from S.*

Dante backs Chloe into the corner. "Get down," he whispers. "I won't let them have you."

As Chloe crouches, Orem the orca clutched to her chest, Dante stands in front of her. He hisses. Three men in black suits—bad fucking men like Wells, like Papa Prejean, like all the groping assholes who walk down the basement steps—spread out in the white padded room.

Hunger/want/need burns through Dante and their pounding hearts draw him. Their sweaty, hopped-up smell dizzy him. All three rush him and Dante drops low, spinning, slashing with his nails. Blood spurts hot across his face. Someone gurgles. Someone else gets behind him. Dante moves. Punching, kicking, biting. Whirls. The blood smell coils through him; he's lost to it. Drops to his knees and sinks his teeth into warm flesh. Blood pumps into his mouth, sweeter than licorice, headier than sneaked whiskey, and he can't get enough. He drinks until nothing's left.

On his knees, Dante looks around. All three bad-ass men sprawl on the bloodied floor. He swivels, wiping his mouth and reaching for Chloe. His hand freezes at his mouth. His heart thumps hard and fast; breaking.

Chloe . . .

Dante's princess, his little sister, his heart. He screamed as the in-between memory rammed past the pain. He screamed, yanking on the handcuffs, coughing up blood, choking. Something sharp jabbed his neck—stung. Cold curled through his veins.

As Dante slid down into drugged darkness, Chloe's image already fading from his mind—*No! Let me keep her!*—an answer to a question stood clear in his mind:

What are you afraid of, True Blood?

Not you, Peeping Tom. Not you.

Me.

Someone laughed and Dante didn't know if it was himself or Elroy. But whoever it was laughed and laughed and laughed.

HEATHER POPPED THE CD out of the laptop. Elbows on the table, she buried her face in her hands, weary and heartsick. Dante had been so caught up in the fight, in his rage and blood-hunger, that he'd struck out at everyone near him—including Chloe. She tried to blank out the images she'd watched, tried to forget the sounds she'd heard—too late. The stricken expression on Dante's face as he looked at Chloe's body, the desolate sound torn from his throat, would haunt her forever.

Like the scream in the slaughterhouse.

A chair scraped back. De Noir. Heather lowered her hands and looked up. He gathered up the reports, stuffing them back into the folder.

"I'll burn these," he said, his voice level.

"No." She sat up. "Dante needs to know . . . he needs to see . . ."

"This?" De Noir waved the folder. "No. He doesn't. No." He picked up the CD and closed his fist around it. Plastic cracked. Crumbled.

"What are you doing?" she cried, leaping to her feet. "We need that—"

"For *what*?" De Noir flung the CD pieces to the floor. "To hurt my child? To tear him apart again? The past cannot be changed."

Heather stared at De Noir. *My child?* It clicked then, the relationship between De Noir and Dante—watchful, sheltering, hidden. The sudden gold flecks in Dante's dark eyes. "Does he know?"

De Noir nodded, then looked away. "I told him tonight. I'd hoped—" He closed his mouth. Shook his head. He touched a finger to the hollow of his throat.

The X-rune pendant was gone. Heather sank back down into her chair. "No wonder he didn't wait when I asked," she murmured. "He was running from you."

"No," De Noir said. His gaze locked with Heather's, flared with gold light. "He thought he needed to do penance for Gina and Jay . . . for the girl he can't remember."

Penance. Everything Dante cared about had been taken from him since he'd been a baby. If he cared, someone or something suffered. Heather trailed a hand through her hair. He went to face Ronin alone so no one else would die. Or suffer in his place.

"I need this file to find Dante," she said. "Elroy Jordan has *claimed* him. The reason why might be in there."

"To torture him—just like you told me," De Noir said. "You warned me that I couldn't stop it. I refused to listen."

The regret in De Noir's gaze tugged at Heather. She shook her head. "Don't," she said. "You thought you could protect him."

She stood up, crossed to the counter. The faint smell of coffee lingered in the kitchen. Dumping out the old grounds into the trash, she rinsed the filter in the sink, then spooned in fresh coffee.

Elroy Jordan was the Cross-Country Killer. Maybe Ronin had been a part of that, or maybe he'd just pointed Jordan in Dante's direction. Ronin had known that both Jordan and Dante were part of Johanna Moore's sociopathology experiment. How?

She poured water into the coffeemaker, set the carafe on the burner, and tapped the on button. What had happened to Ronin? She glanced at De Noir. He stood motionless beside the table, folder clutched in one hand, head bowed. His black hair veiled his face. He appeared to be listening, his body almost quivering with effort.

"Dante," he breathed. "Ah, hush, child. I will find you." Lifting his head, De Noir looked at Heather. "I felt him . . . *heard* him . . . for a moment. He's . . ." De Noir swallowed whatever else he'd intended to say.

De Noir's expression told Heather that whatever he'd heard or felt from Dante was far from good. Cold twisted around her heart. "Ronin," she said. "What happened?"

"Dead."

So whatever Ronin had planned, exposé or blackmail, had died with him. How much had he told Elroy about Bad Seed? Enough, she figured, just enough to control him. Enough to whet his appetite for the whole story.

Heather listened to the coffee as it trickled into the carafe. So what was Jordan's plan? *S is mine.* One certainty iced her thoughts: No matter what, Jordan meant to possess Dante. Forever. And from Seattle to New York, graveyards sheltered the remains of all those Jordan had possessed in the past.

Where was he going? Where was he taking Dante? *S is mine.* Who had those words been aimed at? Ronin? The cops?

As the rich, roasted smell of fresh coffee filled the kitchen, the final piece of the puzzle locked into place.

Johanna Moore. The words had been meant for Johanna Moore.

Jordan intended to confront her with Dante—S—at his side and under his control.

Heart racing, Heather rushed to De Noir and grabbed the folder's edge. "I think I know where they're going," she said.

JOHANNA RETURNED TO THE hearth with a cup of brandied eggnog and sat down. Burning wood snapped, releasing the smell of pine into the room. Sipping at her eggnog, she flipped open her cell and speed-dialed Gifford again. His continued silence worried her.

On the third ring the call was answered, but Johanna didn't recognize the voice saying, "Hello? Hello? This is Detective Fiske. Hello?"

"Doctor Johanna Moore, FBI. How is it that you have Agent Gifford's phone, Detective?"

"I'm sorry, Doctor Moore, but Agent Gifford is dead."

The black, empty night seeped into Johanna, stilled her heart. "How?"

"We're still not clear on the particulars. We have several bodies at the scene," Fiske said. "Why was your man here?"

"Surveillance." The fire snapped the scent of pumpkin and cinnamon into the air. "Are the other dead identified? Perhaps our suspect is among them."

"Special Agent Craig Stearns and one of ours, Detective Trent Collins." Emotion laced Fiske's voice.

"I'm sorry to hear that, Detective," Johanna said. "Please keep me posted."

"Who were your people watching?"

"Thomas Ronin."

"House was rented under that name. I'll call you if I have any other questions."

"Fine, Detective. Thank you." Johanna ended the call.

She gazed at the fire, the dancing flames calming her, ordering her thoughts. She walked from the living room to her office and stepped behind her desk. She glanced at the GPS receiver. No signal. Like E, S was now offline. Were they together? Was Ronin with them?

Johanna walked to the window and pushed aside the curtain. Touching the pane of glass between her and the winter sky, she closed her eyes. She wished for snow.

Stearns and Wallace had cost her a good man, one she'd miss for years to come. What had happened in New Orleans?

Opening her eyes, Johanna turned from the window. She needed to find her beautiful True Blood child before Ronin corrupted him, twisted him. And if her *père de sang* was bringing E and S home?

Then she'd need strength. Johanna pulled on her coat and tugged gloves over her hands—a habit left over from her mortal life. She walked out into the night, her breath a pale plume in the air, and hunted.

DUCKING FROM THE COLD, damp wind, Heather pressed her face against Von's leather-jacketed back as the nomad gunned his Harley up the interstate toward Louis Armstrong International. She kept her arms wrapped tight around the nomad's waist, grateful for the gloves and helmet Simone had lent her. The wind blew through Von's hair, whipping its length from side to side.

Von steered the bike through traffic, swooping in, out, and between cars and semis with heart-stopping speed. The night blurred past, streaked with red and silver.

After Trey ferreted out Johanna Moore's address on the net, Heather had booked a seat on the next flight to D.C. She was gambling on the chance that Elroy Jordan was heading "home" to Moore, but it felt right.

De Noir had refused a seat on the plane, said: *I'll get there my own way.*

She wondered if he winged overhead even now, hair and lashes white with frost.

Trey had also discovered a purchase made by a C. K. Cross a few days earlier. A white Chevy van with customized windows and some interior alterations. The dealership had provided the temporary license plate number, but Heather hadn't passed the number on to the police. If Jordan was pulled over by cops, more people would die. Like Collins.

And Dante . . . Heather couldn't be sure of his reaction. She remembered the nightmare scene captured on the CD, remembered the cold fury on Dante's face as he'd murdered the Prejeans.

Dante sits cross-legged in a corner of the dining room, flipping through a music mag—Metal Scene, maybe—headphones in his ears. In his own world, but tensed, coiled, ready for hell in a moment's notice.

Dante removes his headphones when any of the other four foster kids in the house approach him, speaking Cajun with a couple, English with another; a quick, tilted smile. One teen, about the same age, maybe thirteen or fourteen, sits beside Dante for a time, putting his head on Dante's shoulder. Dante loops an arm around the boy and they sit on the floor together, looking at the mag.

Then, a heartbeat later, hell yawns open. Adelaide "Mama" Prejean smacks a blonde girl setting the table, telling her she's "doing it assbackwards." Cecil "Papa" Prejean, with an irritated grunt, backhands the girl and knocks her to the floor.

Dante rises so fast, even the camera can't capture his movement. The other boy sitting on the floor holds the fluttering mag, mouth open. Dante punches Mama Prejean, knocking her three feet across the room. He leaps on her, taking her to the floor. He pounds her head against the hardwood until the skull splits, blood and brains splashing across the grain, across Dante's hands.

Dante swivels, stands, and moves again. He pins a stunned Papa

Prejean against the wall and tears into his throat with his fingernails, ripping it wide open. Blood sprays onto Dante's ecstatic face. He licks it from his lips, his fingers.

Once Papa Prejean's done spurting, Dante lets go and the body slumps to the floor. Dante gathers the other kids and tells them they need to get out. He searches the bodies for credit spikes, cash, anything of value. Ransacks Mama Prejean's purse. He divvies everything up between the other four kids, keeping nothing for himself.

Once the others have gone, Dante sprinkles lighter fluid from the barbecue throughout the house, then fetches gasoline from the garage. Pours it over the bodies. He lights a match. Whoomf! *He lingers a moment before leaving the Prejean house for the last time.*

Dante watches the blaze from the street. Caught in the flickering shadows, his beautiful bloodstained face is rapt.

Heather remembered Dante standing in front of the anarchy symbol, saying: *Freedom is the result of rage.*

He'd won freedom for only four that night. Project Bad Seed had picked him up, then proceeded to fragment and bury his memory. Again. Wound him up, then turned him loose.

Dante had survived the streets. But would he survive his past?

Von swung the bike onto an exit ramp, downshifted. "Almost there," he shouted.

Stearns had called Dante a monster; but the real monsters were the people behind Project Bad Seed—Dr. Johanna Moore and Dr. Robert Wells. No wonder Moore had been so knowledgeable at the Academy, her profiles eerily accurate. She'd helped create the killers the Bureau profiled.

Had Bad Seed failed or succeeded with Dante? The murder of the Prejeans disturbed Heather, but knowing the torture he'd endured at their hands and at the hands of fifty-nine other pairs of foster parents—the worst Louisiana had to offer—understandable. Although she'd always believed there were no excuses for murder, there *were* reasons.

And in this case—a boy pushed to the brink and beyond—all she saw were shades of gray, even though she'd been trained to see *only* black and white; the law was either upheld or the law was broken. Simple. But was it?

Could Dante have just run away? Abandoning the other kids to their fate? If the project had been successful, Dante would've thought only of himself and used the others to his own gain. Never would have put himself in harm's way for a little girl. Never would have wept for her. Never would have walked alone into a slaughterhouse for a friend, willing to sacrifice himself.

I have a promise to keep.

But if the project had failed, he never would have murdered.

The bright lights of the airport glimmered ahead in the cold air. Heather looked over Von's shoulder as he opened the bike up again. Her thoughts shifted back to her conversation with Collins. Five bodies in a tavern. A fire. Arson. LaRousse and Davis, dead.

In fact, they'd been out to Prejean's with an arrest warrant. . . .

Shit spins out of control.

Bad blood between Dante and LaRousse.

Heather's muscles knotted. Her thoughts led her to a path she didn't want to walk. What if Jay's death and Dante's inability to protect him, his failure to keep him alive, had triggered the same impulses that'd followed Chloe's death? What if the project *had* succeeded, and Ronin had spun the right stressors into action?

What if Dante had been at the tavern? What if he'd taken his first step on the serial-killing trail? A trail he planned to keep walking?

Heather tightened her arms around Von's middle. For once, she hoped her intuition was wrong, her instincts false.

He murdered the Prejeans and torched their house.

Von eased up on the throttle and downshifted as he steered

the Harley into the departure/arrivals lane. The bike rumbled, the sound rolling back like thunder from the buildings. A few people glanced up, startled by the noise. Von eased the Harley up against the curb, then lowered the kickstand.

Heather swung off the bike. She unstrapped the helmet and handed it to the nomad. Von's windblown hair fell into place, gleamed like dark silk beneath the lights.

"I'll come with you," Von said, lifting his shades to the top of his head. "You need a bodyguard, darlin', and I'm willing."

Heather looked into the nomad's green eyes. The crescent moon tattoo glittered like ice in the light.

"De Noir's gonna be there. But thanks."

"Nothing against Lucien, but your safety ain't gonna be his prime concern."

Heather lifted an eyebrow. "And it would be with you?"

"For Dante, man," Von said. "I know he cares about you."

Heather swallowed. "He matters to me, too," she said. "But dawn's coming. You'll be Sleeping soon."

"Look, every time I doze off, just punch me. Hard."

"I've got enough to worry about without hauling your sleepy ass around D.C.," Heather said with a quick smile. "Thanks again, but I've been taking care of myself most of my life. I know what I'm doing."

Von flashed a wicked grin. "No doubt, darlin'. No doubt at all." He lowered his shades, settled them back into place.

"And we need someone here in case I'm wrong about Jordan."

"But you know you ain't," Von said, nudging the kickstand up and twisting the throttle. The Harley's rumble revved into a roar. "Good flight," he said. "And even better hunting. Bring him back, darlin'." Kicking the bike into gear, the nomad gunned it into the through lane.

Heather walked into the terminal, purse looped over her shoulder. Von's words circled through her mind—*I know he cares about you.* And she knew in that moment that *Dante* needed a voice—one that would deliver justice for his lost years and stolen, brutalized childhood, and for his murdered and discarded mother.

Dante's life had never been his own.

Dante had spoken when he'd killed the Prejeans; spoken to the monsters hiding in the shadows, watching and recording. Had Dante been a voice for Chloe?

And had Dante spoken again in the tavern, dazed, heartbroken, and lost to the past; spoken for Jay? Had he followed programming implanted by Moore? Or simply given in to his own dark nature?

Heather strode to the security desk to pick up a law enforcement permit for her .38. Pulling her badge from her pocket, she handed it to the bored guard.

Dante's mind had been damaged, but his heart was strong, compassionate. Having laid beside him, wrapped in his arms, Heather knew Dante could never be like Elroy Jordan, killing for pleasure, for power.

Oh? And when he fed? When he hunted for blood?

How about when he tore open Cecil Prejean's throat?

Would she have to speak for his victims? *Could* she speak for his victims?

Heather felt hollow inside, riddled with doubt. She'd tumbled head over heels for a guy who wasn't even human, and a killer. Yet, how could he be expected to answer for actions he couldn't even remember? She'd deal with that soon enough.

After she found him; after she saved him.

As E steered the van through Georgia, his gaze kept sliding up to the rearview mirror, sneaking peeks at the unconscious bloodsucker—drugged and handcuffed. A shiv still poked up from his belly. An electric tingle shot through E at the sight.

He rubbed himself through his jeans. *Soon*, he promised himself.

When Dante'd started screaming while he read to him from his file, E'd stared, more than a little freaked. The handcuffs had clinked and clunked and the van had rocked and shuddered until E'd been scared that Dante'd pull it apart. That was when he'd dropped the file and grabbed another syringe, filling it to the max with bloodsucker dope and jabbing it into Dante's neck.

Then Dante'd started laughing.

Dante laughs, the sound of it—low and dark and uncontained, broken somehow. Finally, E laughs with him, because it is *pretty funny, accidentally offing the person you're trying to protect . . . hilarious!* Hysterical, *even, and this thought sends E into another round of doubled-over-tears-in-the-eyes laughter.*

Dante's eyes close, tears sliding from the corners, as the drugs go to work. Laughed himself to tears too, *E thinks, enjoying their camaraderie. His Bad Seed bro lapses into silence.*

A blaring horn snapped E to the present. Headlights loomed in the rearview mirror. Busy eyeing Dante, E'd slowed to an old-lady dawdle in the fast lane. Although his first instinct was to slam on the brakes, then shiv the tailgating bastard, E slid the van into the slow lane. Last thing he wanted was the law on his tail.

The tailgating bastard blew past and E gritted his teeth as the bastard leaned on the horn one more time. E memorized the license number for future reference. He grinned. His gaze flicked back to the rear view, to Dante.

Read to me.

Those words from Dante's bloodstained lips had sent shivers down E's spine. Still did. E squirmed in the driver's seat, restless, aching. Hungry. Dawn was a couple of hours away and Dante'd Sleep with a capital S for the rest of the day. E'd catch a few winks then. Maybe a bite to eat.

And his Bad Seed bro? Would he need a bite, too? Could be fun, rounding up a tasty meal for Dante.

E squirmed. He couldn't, he *wouldn't* wait anymore.

He pulled the van into the next rest stop, parking as far from the other cars and semis as possible. He shut off the engine. Keyed it to AC and popped in Inferno's latest CD. Punched up the volume to mask the screams. The music pounded and shredded while Dante's sexy voice growled and whispered:

You try to kiss away my feelings / you need to change me / want to suck me dry . . .

E crawled into the back, yanking the curtain closed behind him. His broken wrist throbbed, but that didn't matter. He'd down some pills when he was done with Dante.

E knelt beside the air bed and brushed the hair back from Dante's face. His gaze lingered on the blood smeared under his nose and across his lips.

"Like an angel," E whispered, but the angel he pictured had black feathered wings and dark fuck-me eyes.

I only trust my rage / you mean nothing / maybe you never did / and that scares me . . .

Wrapping his fingers around the handle of the shiv in Dante's belly, he pulled it out. Blood oozed onto the bloodsucker's white skin. He slipped his hand under Dante's T-shirt, sliding it along his fevered, blood-sticky chest. The wounds in his chest were almost healed.

Golden fire filled E, set his body alight. His heart galloped, shaking his body with the intensity of its rhythm. He trailed his hand down across Dante's flat belly, past his unbuckled belt and into his unfastened jeans. The god indulged himself in another round of exploration.

Breathing fast, E pulled his hand out of Dante's jeans. He closed his eyes. When he opened them again golden cords connected him to his Bad Seed bro at the forehead, belly button and crotch.

E picked up Navarro's book of poetry and, sitting back on his heels, read to Dante.

I feel her there
in the dark
waiting to feed
upon my dreams
her tail, iridescent, coils
holds me prisoner
she sucks my breath
drinks me in
I burn beneath her
within her
a dying star

THE TASTE OF HONEY, sweet and thick, touched E's tongue. He closed the bloodstained book and set it on the floor. Knee-walking to the air bed, he straddled Dante. He leaned over and pressed his lips against Dante's. "I'm your god. I control every breath you take."

Dante's eyes opened, pupils dilated, ringed with brown.

"Name the one you love."

"It ain't you," Dante whispered, words drug-thick.

A flick of his wrist and a shiv dropped into E's right hand. He drew in a deep breath, savoring the smell of blood. Underneath, he caught a whiff of something sweeter. He frowned. A familiar scent. Leaning in, he sniffed Dante's throat. Pushed up his T-shirt. Smelled his chest. Blood and the faint scent of . . . lilac.

E's thoughts whirled back to the bloodsucker's house and the sofa he'd awakened on after plowing into the Big Guy. Whirled back to the woman nestled in the chair across from the sofa, tendrils of red hair across her lovely sleeping face. Whirled back to standing over her, shivs in hand, a benevolent god before a supplicant. Whirled back to bending over her and drinking in her scent. Warm and sweet—lilac. Like the scent that clung to Dante.

E straightened. Bitter truth wiped the honey taste from his

tongue, boiled and bubbled in his belly like fresh tar. E'd never been closer to his Heather than at that moment, hunched over her, smelling her, and he hadn't laid a hand on her—but Dante had, the back-stabbing little bloodsucker.

"You were with Heather," E said, voice low and full of righteous wrath. "She's mine. She's always been mine. She follows *me*."

"She's not *following* you. She's *hunting* you. She ain't yours."

"Name the one you love," E snarled.

"No."

"She's mine!"

E plunged the shiv into Dante's chest, then yanked it free and punched it back in. Blood flew and spattered. The golden cords linking E to Dante snapped, unraveled, spraying golden light into the air.

Stabbing and slicing, E went to work. Dante turned his face away, eyes closed in pain, blood foaming on his lips. He twisted, trying to dump E off, but E just grinned and squeezed with his thighs, enjoying the ride.

Had Dante *fucked* Heather? Drank her blood? Had she asked for more?

Breathing hard and fast, he parked the shiv between Dante's ribs, then grabbed his chin with bloodied fingers. E wished he had two good hands to lock around Dante's pale throat. As he forced Dante to face him, the bloodsucker's eyes opened. Gold and red flecked the thin ring of iris, glimmered in the depths of his dilated pupils.

"Enough," Dante said, voice bubbling with blood.

Pain shafted E's head, skewered his eyeballs, and lanced his ears. His hand flew up to his temple. He squeezed his eyes shut. Pain scorched his brain.

E screamed.

30

AWAKE

S NOW FELL IN WASHINGTON, D.C. Big flakes swirled down
from low-hanging gray clouds, hushing the city. Lucien flew
through the predawn sky, hair iced behind him, snow clinging to
his lashes and riming his wings. He listened, but static filled his
bond with Dante, buzzed and whispered—psionic white noise.

He hadn't felt anything from his child since that fleeting moment in the kitchen when Dante's anguish had pierced the static
and Lucien's heart. Madness had undulated in that cry, heartbroken and burning.

Loki's voice whispered: *You can't keep him from going mad,
brother. Not alone.*

How could he keep Dante's past from driving him mad? Let
alone his *creawdwr* gifts? The child was strong-willed, but he'd
been tortured since birth.

Genevieve . . .

The images from Wallace's CD burned behind Lucien's eyes,
images he'd carry forever. His beautiful little Genevieve, pale
and weak from blood loss, struggling to touch the son she'd just
birthed, hers and Lucien's. But strapped to the blood-smeared

metal table, she couldn't reach the black-haired, white-skinned, preternaturally silent baby.

"Let me hold him." Genevieve says. The scrubs-clad medical team bustle around the sterile, empty room like ghosts unable to hear her. "Let me hold him!" she screams.

The ghosts never pause. They wash blood from the newborn. The infant watches, golden eyes aware, awake. Vampire and Fallen.

And in that moment, damned.

"Dante." she whispers. "My Dante. Never give in. Make hell your own. Fight."

Genevieve closes her eyes. A tear slips out from beneath her dark lashes. "Pourquoi tu nous as abandonnes? Je ne sais pas ce que j'ai fait pour vous faire partir. je t'en supplie, sauve ton fils," *she prays. Her hands clench into fists.* "Éloigné le d'ici. Mets-le l'abri. Il est ma lumière et mon coeur—comme tu as pu l'être. Lucien, mon ange, s'il te plaît, écoute-moi."

Genevieve's words, her unanswered prayer, wrapped around Lucien's soul and burned, incandescent; a votive forever lit within him.

The report stated that Genevieve had been killed after they'd analyzed the milk contents of her breasts. No photos or filmed images of her death were included in the file. She'd become insignificant.

Gray shreds of moisture-laden clouds parted before Lucien. Snow shrouded the land below. Grief shrouded his heart. *If only . . .* He shifted his thoughts away from paths unwalked and unregarded. Even with eternity stretched before him, he'd learned there was still such a thing as too late and never again.

He could only focus on what was—and what might be.

Lucien tipped his right wing and spiraled down toward the awakening city. He'd agreed to meet Wallace at the airport. With or without her, he'd find his wounded child. With or without her, he'd take his vengeance on the woman who'd had Genevieve killed and who'd put his son through a hell beyond imagination.

A song pulsed within Lucien suddenly, chaotic and powerful. Dante's *anhrefncathl*, complicated and dark, crescendoed through Lucien's heart and mind. And chilled him to his core. Chaotic, Dante's song. Powerful. And mad.

Lucien closed his eyes. He heard Yahweh's weary voice: *Let them have me.*

Never.

Thousands of years ago he'd killed the friend of his heart—his *calon-cyfaill*—to keep the Elohim high-bloods from chaining the maddened *creawdwr* to their will and channeling his power to their own self-serving ends—including altering the mortal world. Yet again.

And if the Elohim knew another Maker—unbound and untrained and painfully young—walked the earth, they'd do the same to him.

But, without the balance he'd gain from psionic bonds, Dante would slip into madness, the fate of all unbound *creawdwrs*. And, unbound and insane, he could unmake the world.

You can't bind him alone, Brother.

Lucien swerved away from the snow-covered city below, angling upward, his wings slicing through the sky. He veered west. Dante's black aria wavered. Vanished. Lucien suspected his child had poured the last of his strength into that song.

Time to gamble. Time to transmute whispers into words and rumors into facts. Time to answer his Genevieve's prayer. Past time. He'd deal with the consequences as they came.

I would lay the world to waste for my son.

Wings flapping, Lucien hovered in the gray sky, snow melting against his heated skin. Blue light radiated out from his body. He burned like a star. Dawn faltered. Faded. Stars winked alight again in the renewed dusk.

Nightbringer.

Lucien voiced his *wybrcathl*, heart beating in time with his song, threading the music around his memory of Dante's chaos song; brilliant and pure, altering his aria into a duet of chaos and order. It rang, sharp and clear, through the returning night.

The Fallen in Dante would answer.

So would any Elohim within song range. Just as they'd answer Dante's *anhrefncathl*. Brief as it'd been, perhaps none of the Elohim had heard. Brief, true, but powerful.

A race, then.

THE PERV STRADDLED DANTE, his weight forcing the air out of Dante's lungs. A knife gleamed in Elroy's right hand. Fury contorted his face. He stank of tobacco and sweat and bitter lust.

Drugs still flowed through Dante's veins and his thoughts ebbed, low tide. His body thrummed, almost floated, but the handcuffs and the Perv's weight kept him anchored to the blood-spattered air bed.

"Name the one you love."

Dante met Elroy's narrowed gaze. "No."

Heather's face, flushed and beautiful, flashed into his mind. A fractured image of Chloe sparked behind his eyes, then vanished, snuffed, the image of Jay's pale face and lightless eyes overlaying it.

"She's mine!"

Elroy punctuated his words with his knife, stabbing it into Dante over and over and over. Punched. Slashed. Pain twisted into him, tearing him apart. Devoured him. He choked on blood. Drowned in it. It bubbled up from his lungs, trickled from his nose, gushed up from his stomach. White light flashed and strobed at the edges of his vision. Squeezing his eyes shut, Dante turned his face away. Pain ripped apart his mind.

Send it below or fucking use it.

The air reeked of blood and the Perv's sweat-sour odor. His

thoughts echoed in Dante's mind; mental shivs: *Had Dante fucked Heather? Drank her blood? Had she asked for more?*

Send it below or fucking use it.

The shiv slipped between Dante's ribs and stayed. Fingers grabbed his chin, forced his face around. Pain torched him. Dante stopped resisting and jumped into the raging flames. White-hot, melting, flesh burning, bubbling—shadows seared onto basement walls, a smoldering plushie orca—it consumed him. Ashed his control.

Ashes, ashes, we all fall down.

Here, hold my hand, princess. We'll go together. Forever and ever.

A song vibrated within him, chaotic, a strumming dark refrain. The melody blazed with rage. Hunger pounded out the tempo. Burned.

A shadowed figure uncurled from the ashes. Fire smoldered in his veins. He lifted his head. S opened his eyes. "Enough," he said.

Reaching into Elroy's mind, S funneled the pain the warped little fuck had dispensed with his shiv back into him; force-fed him his own shit.

Here. Have some. How does it fucking *feel?*

Elroy's hand flew up to his temple. Eyes squeezed shut, he screamed, the sound sweet to S's ears. The Perv tumbled off of S and crawled around on the van's carpeted floor, clutching his head and squealing.

Inferno's music poured from the speakers: *I'm waiting for you / I've watched and I've watched / I know your every secret.*

Coughing up blood, gasping for air, S yanked with his arms. The cuffs clunked against the van's metal back end. Sucking in a blood-choked breath, he yanked again. Poured what little strength he had remaining into his arms. Metal rended. Something popped. Black spots flickered through his vision. S lowered his handcuffed wrists past his head, wondering at the hook dangling from the chain.

The *cuffs* were nightkind-proof, but the *hook* welded to the van wasn't.

S moved his cuffed hands to the shiv in his side and tugged it free. Dropped it on the bed. He struggled to sit up. The van spun around him. His vision darkened. He lowered his head and waited for the dizziness to pass.

Voices whispered, clutched at his thoughts. Sweat beaded his forehead. Hunger spiked through him. He needed blood. He pulled his mental fingers out of Elroy's mind. The squealing stopped.

S slid off the air bed and crawled to Elroy. He shoved the Perv's head aside and sank his fangs into the mortal's sweaty throat.

I've stood in every room / of your house / and dreamed of you / wanting me.

Blood, hot and berry-sweet, spurted into S's mouth. He gulped mouthful after mouthful. Elroy's frantic heartbeat pulsed blood into his mouth almost faster than he could swallow. The Perv struggled. S slammed a knee between his legs. The squirming stopped. Fear and adrenaline spiced the blood pouring into S's mouth.

Musky pheromones and the pungent smell of blood—S's blood—laced the air. Elroy the Perv was hot and bothered and hard, even now, with S's fangs in his throat.

Like all that shiv-work and blood had been foreplay.

Something cold and dark curled around S's heart.

Très joli, *dis one, like an angel. Play with him all you want, but don't put nuthin' in his mouth. Boy bites.*

S ripped his fangs deeper into Papa's throat. The bastard squirmed again. Stank of desperation. Fucker sliced up Chloe. *Did he torture her like he did me?*

The image of a dark-haired, dark-eyed woman flashed behind S's eyes. *Gina.* The scent of black cherries wrenched him forward—*Elroy the Perv and . . . Gina. Not Papa. Not Chloe.* White light strobed at the edge of his vision.

Where am I? When *am I?*

A song vibrated through S, gleamed like moonrise. He pulled his mouth from Elroy's flesh and tilted his head, listening. He closed his eyes. The rhythm of his heart shifted to match the music resonating within his mind—Lucien's song.

Nightbringer. Friend. Father. Liar.

The tempo swirled through S, hooked his soul. Chaos and order. Compassion and fire. He shivered, and answered. S plucked dark chords, anger and longing and loss twisting through the refrain in equal measures. The song stabbed out from his heart like one of Elroy's shivs.

His own voice, low, snaked from the speakers: *I've watched you as you slept / I know you've watched me too / I've seen your footprints / beneath my window.*

Not mine. Dante's voice. Before he gave himself to the fire. I am after *the fire.*

<*No, child, no.*> Lucien's thought blasted through the drug-static blocking their bond.

Pain tore through S's mind. Blurred his vision. Darkness grabbed at him.

<*You are Dante Baptiste, son of Lucien and Genevieve. Not S. Not the child of monsters.*>

Wrong, S thought, head aching. *I'm S. Hafta be. Isn't that why Gina and Jay died? Isn't that how I'll keep Heather alive?*

Lucien's song ended with one last resonant chord, a promise ringing clear and full moon-bright across the sky: *I am coming for you.*

<*Don't. I won't be here.*> S's thought rebounded, blocked again by static, pain and blood loss.

S pushed himself away from Elroy's warm, huddled body. Hunger still gripped him. He glanced at the Perv. Imagined drinking him dry. Imagined ripping open his chest and squeezing his black, stunted heart until it pulped.

For you, Chloe.

"I can help you!" someone shouted. "You fuckin' need me! Dante!"

S's vision cleared. He sat on top of Elroy, straddled him, the mortal's chest bared, his shirt torn open. Bloody furrows scored the flesh above the Perv's thudding heart. Blood trickled along Elroy's throat, the skin punctured, torn.

The heady smell of adrenaline and fear filled the van. Sweat beaded Elroy's forehead, but his face was blank. Still.

S grabbed the Perv's shades and tossed them across the van. Hazel eyes met his. Something at-the-bottom-of-the-cave-dark flickered in those eyes. "You fuckin' need me," he repeated.

Do you know my *every secret?* Dante whispered from the speakers.

S leaned over the Perv, placed his lips a whisper away from Elroy's whisker-stubbled face. "No, I don't."

"I know shit you don't," Elroy said, his voice as empty as his face. "I know shit that's not in those files. Bad Seed made us brothers. You ain't in this alone. I want my pound or two of flesh—just like you."

S laughed.

Elroy swallowed hard. Looked away.

S pushed Elroy's head to the side with his cuffed hands and sank his fangs back into the mortal's wounded throat. Sucked down adrenaline-spiced blood. Listened to the frantic pounding of the Perv's heart.

Locks won't keep me out / words won't turn me away / I've long dreamed of this moment.

"I wasn't there when Ronin iced your boyfriend," Elroy said, his voice vibrating against S's lips. The Perv's heart rate slowed. Steadied. "But I was there for Gina. I know what happened, what Ronin did to her. I know her last words."

S froze. Remembered a black stocking washed free of every trace of Gina. Remembered another stocking knotted around her throat. Remembered her walking away with only silence as a farewell.

S lifted his mouth from Elroy's throat. Sat up and stared down into the Perv's muddy gaze. *Her last words.* A chance for Gina to live another moment. Pain sparked behind his eyes.

"I know what happened to Ronin, too."

"What's to stop me from ripping all that from your mind?"

"I'll make sure I die before you can get it." Elroy's gaze held steady.

"That's my Bad Seed bro."

Elroy's expression blanked again. "The Big Guy got Ronin."

S looked away, muscles knotting. *Bastard was mine.*

"Fucker was going for Heather too."

Heather. S shifted his gaze back to Elroy. "Is she—"

"Fine," the Perv said. "She even blew me a kiss as we hit the street. Well, okay, shot at me, but really, ain't it the same thing?" He grinned.

Relief trickled though S, unwinding the knots in his muscles. He slid off Elroy and crawled to the air bed. Dizziness spun through him. Spots flecked his vision. He leaned against the mattress.

"Looks like you need some of those Batman Band-Aids," S said, nodding at the blood-smeared tear in Elroy's throat. S's saliva would heal the wound, a few licks and it'd close. But . . . fuck 'im.

Elroy sat up and clapped a hand over the wound.

"Take these off," S said. He held up his cuffed wrists. The hook still hung from the chain like an urban legend—*and they found a hook in the roof of the car!*

The Perv wiped at his nose with the back of his hand. "We cool?" he asked, lifting his gaze to S's. "Still gonna kill me?"

S smiled. Elroy stared, mouth open, transfixed. After a moment, Elroy dropped his gaze. He glanced toward the front of the van. S heard his sly little mind planning to make a break for it, wondering if he could outrun his weakened plaything.

"Try it."

Elroy looked at him, then tilted his head to one side. Licked his lips. "Who are you?"

"You should know. You woke me up."

The Perv nodded. Wiped at his nose again. "Then you know we both got beefs to settle with Mommy-Bitch, right? *Both* of us."

"A pound or two or three of flesh, right?" S glanced at his cuffed wrists. "Take these off."

"Will you kill me?"

"Yeah. But not till after we settle the score."

Elroy the Perv sat back on his heels and considered. He trailed his hand through his hair. After a moment, he rose to his knees and wormed his hand into his front jeans pocket. Pulled out a key.

Scooting over to S, Elroy wriggled the key into the cuffs. He looked at S. "Not till after, right?"

"*Oui.*"

Elroy nodded and unlocked the cuffs. S shook them off his raw and bloodied wrists. The cuffs thudded against the carpet. He pulled up the bottom of his T-shirt and wiped blood off his face.

"Can we still play?" the Perv asked. Hunger edged his voice. He slid a hand up S's thigh.

Slapping Elroy's hand aside, S looked at him, fire smoldering behind his eyes. He smoothed a trembling hand over his slashed and bloodied T-shirt, over the wounds aching underneath. A memory nudged at his mind, a basement, then vanished. Pain coiled, waiting.

I am what you made me / no matter where you hide / where you run / I will find you . . .

S's hands dropped to the fly of his jeans. Zipped them up.

Buckled his belt. "Touch me again and *nothing* will fucking save you."

Elroy looked away, jaw tight, hand clenched. S bent, scooped up the handcuffs. Rattled them. The Perv glanced at him, hand still knotted. Without a word, S snatched his fisted hand and snapped the cuff around it.

"Hey, I thought we was cool," Elroy protested as S locked the other cuff around metal framework.

"Sleep's coming," S said. "And I don't trust you."

Elroy slouched against the wall. "Yeah, well. Same here." Pointing at the pillow, he lifted an eyebrow.

"You wanna get comfy?" S picked up the bloodied shiv. Lifted his gaze to Elroy's. Plunged the shiv into the Perv's thigh. "Fuck you."

Elroy sucked air in through his teeth, pain etched into his face. A vein throbbed at his temple. "Your ass is mine," he muttered.

"Yeah?" S said, climbing to the front of the van. "Don't think so." As he parted the curtain, he glanced back at Elroy. Easy meal. Hunger surged through him. He ached with it. But the thought of every drop of the Perv's bitter blood pouring into his veins, pumping into his heart and lighting his mind, left him cold. *And if he really holds Gina's last words?*

S slipped through the parted curtains, eased down into the front seat, then opened the door. He hopped out onto the concrete, the night cool against his face. Closing the door, he sucked in the night's smells: wet grass, diesel fuel and hot rubber, wild roses. An interstate rest area.

He half walked, half staggered toward a semi truck, his boots soundless against the pavement. Hunger drained what little strength he still had; the drugs fucked up his system, blurred his thoughts. Dawn brushed gray against the horizon and drowsiness seeped into him, like blood into dirt. He had to feed, then get back to the van.

S stepped up onto the running board of the semi. Checked the door. Locked. He crashed a fist through the window; shattered glass rained onto the pavement and into the cab. Then grasping the window frame, he slid into the cab, his movement so quick, the startled driver was still blinking sleep from his eyes when S dropped on top of him.

Pinned him. Tore into his warm throat. And fed.

31

WORDS SPILL OUT
LIKE FIRE

JOHANNA STRODE DOWN THE empty hall, buoyed and buzzing on her stay-awake pills. Her heels clicked against gleaming tile. *What happened at dawn?* The thought whirled through her mind and she stopped, heart pounding.

Snow falls, silencing the awakening world beyond her window. The sky lightens, illuminating thick flakes against the gray dawn, then . . .

Johanna resumed walking.

Then the light flickers, like a candle caught in a sudden breeze, gutters and goes out. Darkness sweeps across the horizon. The day reverses. *Power reverberates through the air. Power so intense, so strong, that even inside her townhouse, as she stands stunned at the kitchen window, it surges through her, leaving her weak-kneed and clutching the counter. Words form in her mind, blaze within her consciousness. They are words she doesn't recognize—like symbols, like ancient glyphs—and they spill like fire from her mouth. With a sudden inward rush of air, the power vanishes, clearing her mind and dropping her to the linoleum. Dawn returns. The sky lightens once again.*

Johanna punched her code into the keypad beside the door to her office, then tipped her face down for the retinal security scan. A thin bar of light skimmed her face. She blinked, vision dazzled. The door clicked open. She stepped inside, closing the door behind her.

What happened this morning? Why did she think it had something to do with Ronin and her missing experiments? *No, correct that*, she thought as she sat behind her desk. *With S.* And *thought* had nothing to do with it. It was a *feeling*, liquid and intuitive and impossible to analyze.

Johanna switched on the vid-phone, keyed in a number. Music. Something to do with music. She thought of S perched on the edge of a kitchen chair, guitar across his thighs, cradled next to his body, his long fingers slipping sure and fast across the strings, his pale face rapt. Just as it would be when he tore into his first throat. As it would be when he torched the Prejean house.

"Johanna, what a surprise," said a deep, familiar voice.

Startled, she glanced at the monitor and into Bob Wells's smiling face. Curving her lips into a smile, Johanna shook her head. "Not a pleasant surprise, I'm afraid," she said. Wells's smile faltered. "I'm sorry, but I have bad news."

Wells rubbed a hand along his chin. He glanced away for a moment. When he returned his gaze to the monitor, his brown eyes were emptied of all feeling. He looked at her, expression neutral, waiting.

"Both E and S are offline and together. I suspect they've been interfered with, fed information."

"By who?"

"Thomas Ronin."

Wells lifted an eyebrow. "Your *père de sang*? You've been careless."

Johanna stiffened. She leaned forward in her chair, the leather creaking beneath her. "I called to warn you," she said. "I believe they're coming here, given Ronin's involvement. But I think S will want you, as well."

"It's *you* he'll remember," Wells said. "And all the attention you lavished upon him. You never told me, Johanna—but, how *did* his blood taste?"

"Don't play this game with me, Bob," Johanna said. She smoothed all expression from her face, but her hands clenched into fists, unseen, on her lap. "You loved him, too. I'd be worried about the day he remembers that love. And you."

A smile touched Wells's lips. He inclined his head. "Touché."

Interesting reaction, Johanna mused. *But wrong.* She severed the connection. Bob Wells's image winked out. Had that been *amusement* lighting his eyes? She glanced out the window. Snow fell, thick and fast, the sky white.

Had *Wells* given the project information to Ronin? If so, why? To test her abilities? Or S's?

Johanna shifted her gaze to the chair in front of her desk. For a moment, the smell of dark tobacco and vanilla filled her nostrils. For a moment, Dan Gifford sat in the chair, his gray-eyed gaze calm, attentive. He leaned forward, fingers steepled together and said: *I see. What do you want done?*

Turn back time.

She had no regrets, save one—sending Gifford to New Orleans. She wished she'd kept him at her side and had sent lesser men to deal with Stearns and Wallace.

The phone buzzed. Johanna pressed the intercom button. "Yes?"

"Wallace's plane will land in a few minutes."

"Pick her up. Bring her to the lab."

"Understood."

Johanna ended the call. Time to prepare. The thought of leaving D.C. crossed her mind. More than once. Catch a flight anywhere. Why stay? By the time Ronin and the others found her again, she'd've had time to plan. To set things into motion.

But the thought of her little True Blood in Ronin's hands for any length of time knotted her stomach. She needed to reclaim him. And if he'd been awakened? His memories resurrected? Then she'd need to bury them again and lull him back to sleep.

Johanna rose to her feet and crossed the snow-lit room to a cherrywood file cabinet. She unlocked the top drawer, removed an unlabeled CD, then relocked the file cabinet. She returned to her desk and slipped the CD into a padded mailer. Sealed it. Addressed it to Dante Prejean.

If things went wrong, Johanna wanted to be certain Wells didn't walk away untouched. And if things went right, well, maybe Wells still needed to worry. But not about S. Perhaps he should worry about an unexpected visit from Johanna.

HEATHER WALKED THROUGH THE crowded terminal, listening to voices over the audio system announcing flights cancelled due to the storm. She scanned the faces of the people around her, of those waiting at the baggage carousel, of those hanging out in front of the coffee kiosks and souvenir shops.

Heather's stomach rumbled at the smell of fresh-brewed coffee and frying bacon. Realizing that she hadn't eaten since yesterday afternoon, she joined the line at Sunny's Breakfast 'n' More.

As the line moved forward, Heather's gaze skipped around the terminal, looking for suits with that authoritative FBI stride. Looked for a hand cupping an ear. Looked for comsets. Looked for De Noir. Watched for others *looking*, too.

Her gaze stopped. A man in a suit and parka spoke to a woman in a tan trenchcoat. Heather tensed. The man scanned the crowd behind the woman as they spoke and, Heather was certain, the woman scanned the crowd behind him. Moore's people? Airport security?

"Next."

Heather ordered a bacon, egg, and cheese sandwich to go and paid with cash. She'd told De Noir she'd meet him at the car rental counter. Maybe he was already there. Heather tucked her wrapped and steaming sandwich in her pocket and merged with the crowd. Her heart rate picked up speed. She unbelted and unfastened her trench.

Whoever Parka and Trenchcoat worked for, they wouldn't be stupid enough to start something inside the terminal. No, they'd wait for Heather to leave. Inside the terminal, she was safe.

Heather angled through the crowd, edging her way to the car rental kiosk. Several people stood at the counter, but none of them were six eight or possessed waist-length black hair. Where was De Noir? Had something happened to him? He'd assured her he'd be at the terminal by the time she arrived.

Unless . . .

Nothing against Lucien, but your safety ain't gonna be his prime concern.

Had De Noir finally reached Dante through their link? Before Sleep?

Hope sparked within Heather. If so, no need to confront Moore. Instead, she could build a case against Moore with the file, have her arrested. Blow the whistle? If she did that, if she took her evidence to the media, her career in the FBI would be over.

But wasn't it already over? Dead as Stearns? And what about Dante? Would he want his past—including his crimes—to be headline news and tabloid fodder?

Heather stepped up to the counter. A clerk smiled. "May I help you, ma'am?"

"Yes. I have a reservation. Wallace."

Heather turned, put her back to the counter. Beyond the terminal's windows, a blizzard raged, the falling snow a solid, slanting sheet. Cars and taxis huddled against the curb, barely visible dark smudges in a white swirling world.

Could De Noir have been caught in the storm?

She'd wait for a while, then call the house to see if Simone or Von had heard from him. Reaching into her pocket, she pulled out her still-warm sandwich and partially unwrapped it.

Suddenly feeling a presence behind her, Heather tensed. As she swiveled, a hand locked around her biceps. She looked up into Parka's clean-shaven face and blue eyes.

"Agent Wallace," he said.

"Take your hand off me," she said, voice level. Her gaze shifted, searching for his trenchcoated partner.

"No need to make a scene."

"I disagree." Dropping her sandwich, Heather swiveled into Parka and plucked his fingers from her arm. She locked his hand in an aikido defensive move—fingers to wrist, thumb to back of hand—forcing it down and back, driving Parka to his knees. He winced, pain etching his face.

Glancing up, Heather caught a glimpse of Trenchcoat pushing through the crowd. No time to wait for De Noir or search a parking lot for her rental car. Time maybe to catch a cab.

As Heather released Parka's trapped hand, she shoved him hard. He slid across the tiled floor. Whirling, she ran for the glassed-in front doors. Slipped her hand into her trench's gun pocket, wrapped her fingers around the .38's grip. *Not yet. Too many civilians.*

A shocked gasp rippled through the crowd. *Shit! Someone's pulled a gun*, Heather thought, diving for the floor. Something stung her back, low, as she rolled. *Hit? Shrapnel from a near miss?* She sprang to her feet, heart pounding, gaze focused on the main entrance doors and the taxis beyond. She'd lose them in the snow.

Something tingled through her veins. Burned. The automatic doors slid apart. She ran out into the storm. The cold bit into her, sucked air from her lungs. Her thoughts spun. Light-headed, she arrowed her suddenly rubber-limbed body to the nearest taxi. *Drugged*, she realized.

Slipping in the snow, Heather slammed against the taxi. She grabbed for the door handle to keep from falling, but her hand wouldn't work, just flopped at her side. She fell, the world spinning white-white-white. The brightness hurt her eyes. A man leaned over her, his face concerned.

"Miss, are you okay?"

From behind her, she heard a woman say, "Don't worry. She's fine. Just had a little too much to drink. Afraid to fly."

Snowflakes stuck to Heather's eyelashes, melting into her eyes. She tried to speak, but her tongue didn't work. Tried to shake her head no to the taxi driver, but her head wouldn't move.

Hands lifted her. Her head lolled. The white sky merged with the snow-covered concrete. "Relax," a masculine voice said. "Don't fight it.

"We're taking you to Doctor Moore."

Cold whirled into Heather's mind, icing it, shutting it down.

PAIN THROBBED, A GLOWING fireplace poker against the bone. E opened his eyes. His stomach lurched. Swallowing hard—*need my pills*—he looked around the van. The blood-smeared air bed was empty, the unused pillow a sudden reminder of the shiv in his thigh.

E glanced down. His leg burned beneath the blade. A rim of dried blood on his jeans surrounded the shiv. *Motherfucking bloodsucker bastard!* Something dark and excited coiled into him, lurking beneath his rage. The memory of the shivs buried in Dante's pale flesh sent tingles down E's spine.

A quick look over his shoulder revealed Dante sprawled on the floor. E scooted around to get a better look. The pretty little bloodsucker was belly down on the carpet, on the safe side of the curtains and the daylight burning beyond.

Head turned to one side, hair across his face, one arm under him and the other up, crooked at the elbow, Dante—*oops! Make that S*—looked like he'd dropped in his tracks. Or had taken another head shot.

E's gaze crawled over Dante, drinking in every detail. He wished S hadn't awakened until *after* he'd finished playing. Kinda wished he hadn't awakened at all. Really wished he had the key to the cuffs.

Teeth clenched, E eased his swollen and bruise-blackened wrist from the sling. Pain and nausea double-clutched his guts. Sweat popped up on his forehead. He swallowed back bile. Leaning his head against the side of the van, E rested and pondered the shiv. He doubted he could tug it free, not and remain conscious, anyway.

He glanced at Dante. Boy was down for the count. He could make all the noise he wanted—Dante wouldn't stir. Or S. E shuddered suddenly, remembered Dante throwing his own words back at him, all hard and cold, like the bloodsucker's voice.

That's my Bad Seed bro.

In that moment, E'd been sure he was going to die. Bad. Hard. Ugly.

But Dante wanted Gina's last words and only E possessed them. So the moment had passed and his heart still beat on and on and on. Would beat long after Dante's had stopped.

E's gaze skipped to the black bag and his satchel o' tricks beside it. Pills for the pain in one. Dope for Dante in the other. Just what the doctor ordered for both of them.

Moving carefully, E reached for the satchel. Grasped the edge. A lightning bolt of pain jolted up his arm to his shoulder and he screamed before he could stop it. But he'd been right about Dante—the bloodsucker slept on, undisturbed. Black spots flecked E's vision as he plucked at the Baggie of pills and slid a swollen finger along the bag's seam. It opened. Sweat trickled down his temples.

E's fingers scooped up pills, tucking them into his palm. Several spilled onto the carpet, bouncing and rolling every which way but toward him. Lowering his shaking hand, he dropped the pills he'd snagged into his mouth. Swallowed. His stomach felt tight as a fist. He leaned against the van. Breathed. In. Out. In. The nausea faded.

E closed his eyes. Wished he had his shades. Wished he had a smoke. Thought maybe *Dante* should be handcuffed and hurting and wishing for all manner of things while *E* snoozed. Like wishing he'd never been born. Fucker. Drank *his* blood.

Did it glow within Dante even now? If E opened his eyes, would he see his own golden light radiating from the Sleep-drugged vampire? E's heart skipped a beat, then resumed with a chest-vibrating thud. He opened his eyes.

Golden honeyed light slipped from between Dante's lips, streamed from his nostrils; starred out from around his slender body. Snaked around him in golden coils.

Bound him. Connected him to the handcuffed god.

E grinned. *Mine.* Once the pills went to work, easing the pain in his throbbing arm, he'd sneak a syringe and a vial of blood-sucker dope out of the black bag. Tuck them into his sling. Then bide his time with godlike patience.

And wait for the backstabbing little shit to turn his back.

LUCIEN LANDED, TOUCHING BARE feet to snow-tipped grass. His wings flared once, flinging droplets of ice and snow into the air, then folded behind him. Gray clouds hid the sun. Beyond the rest stop, cars rushed by on the interstate, tires hissing through the snow and slush. Two vehicles remained in the parking lot: a white van with Alabama license plates and a semi. The semi's shattered passenger's side window told Lucien that his child had fed—although his forced entry spoke of desperate need.

Wings tucking into their pouches, Lucien strode to the van.

He'd followed Dante's chaos song until it'd faded, but the song's rage and hurt and madness hadn't faded; it burned still within Lucien's heart.

Dante was lost within his own wounded mind.

An hour or so ago, the static blocking their bond had vanished and Lucien had followed it like an ethereal rope to his Sleeping child.

Lucien's fingers curled around the door's cold handle. Locked. Pressing his hand flat against the door, he flicked energy into the lock. Blue sparks showered to the pavement, melting tiny holes in the snow. He grasped the handle and opened the door.

Air reeking of blood and violence, sweat and stale cigarettes rolled out of the van like black smoke from a fire. Lucien caught his breath, for underneath, like coals beneath a pile of ash, smoldered the scorched and bitter stink of twisted lust, of evil.

Lucien listened to the slow, steady beat of Dante's heart. The sound soothed him. *I have found my son.* Climbing into the van, he parted the curtain and slid through, careful not to let the weak winter sunlight touch his child.

Lucien looked at Dante Sleeping on the van's floor. That burning-in-the-sunlight scream, that heart-wrenching sound of a child's agony—*his* child's—echoed within Dante's fragmented dreams. Reminded Lucien of what he'd felt . . . what he'd *heard* while standing in the kitchen with Wallace.

Chloe. My princess. My heart.

I won't let them have you.

Kneeling, Lucien gathered his son into his arms. Dante's heat baked into him. Heat when he should be Sleep-cool. Blood trickled from one nostril, streaking his lips.

Ah, little one, they took her anyway. There was nothing you could've done. Nothing. You were only a child, too.

Lucien brushed the hair back from Dante's face, touched the cool silver hoops in his ear.

His past devours him.

Lucien's gaze dropped. His heart constricted as he stared at the slashes in Dante's T-shirt. The blood smell—Dante's. He pushed up the blood-stiff material. Countless healing wounds crisscrossed his chest and abdomen. Cuts. Punctures. Knife wounds.

Are knives required equipment for a journalist's assistant?

Lucien finally gave his attention to the sleeping mortal handcuffed to the van. A bitten and purpled throat. One arm in a sling, the fingers swollen. A knife hilt stuck up from his thigh. Lucien's gaze flickered down to the boy cradled in his arms, paused, then returned to Jordan.

Across from Jordan was a mattress spattered and smeared with blood. Dante's blood. Blood also flecked the wall and the ceiling above. A book—poetry?—and scattered papers and photos littered the carpet beside the bed.

Lucien tensed. He recognized the photos. The same ones he'd looked at with Wallace. So, Dante's past had been given to him with blood and knives. Given without mercy by a dead-eyed mortal.

And yet somehow Dante had freed himself. So why was Jordan still breathing?

Had the wretch *bargained* for his life? Lucien's gaze shifted back to the papers and reports scattered on the floor. With what?

His first impulse was to gather Dante into his arms and fly home. Once his child was safe, he'd return. Then Jordan and Moore would endure a final reckoning, an Elohim judgment and an Old Testament–style death.

But daylight burned outside. He needed to wait until dusk to carry Dante home. Lucien bent and pressed his lips against Dante's, breathing energy into him, just as he'd done when Wallace had served her warrant. Urged his child up from Sleep. Up from the ashes he curled in, his arms around a little girl.

Pain slammed against Lucien's shields. Inhaling, he flexed it away. He touched his fingertips to Dante's temple. Poured cool light into his child's pain-ravaged mind and fevered body.

Dante drew in a deep breath. His eyes opened. He looked at Lucien, but no recognition sparked within the dark depths of his eyes. Shoving free of Lucien's hold, Dante rolled to his knees. Body coiled, muscles taut, he hissed.

Fear trailed a cold hand down Lucien's spine. Was Dante lost to madness? A *creawdwr* unbound and insane? Or was it simply Sleep refusing to release him? There was always a risk in awakening a Sleeper.

Lucien held up a placating hand. "Dante, child, you are safe. Hush."

"Not Dante," a low voice said. Jordan. "That's S."

"S doesn't exist," Lucien said. "Only Dante. S is a part of you, child. The rage you deny, the pain you ignore."

"He ain't exactly been *denying* rage lately," Jordan muttered.

Never taking his eyes off Dante, Lucien pointed a finger and snapped a whip of energy across the mortal. Jordan yelped. The smell of ozone cut through the air.

Lucien met Dante's red-streaked and simmering gaze. He saw it now. Sleep lingered in his son's eyes. "She can't rise with you. I'm sorry, but you must leave her behind and let her sleep."

"No." Dante's hands knotted into fists. Pain and Sleep shadowed his eyes. "I promised forever."

"Child, you've given her forever," Lucien said, voice husky. "She's always with you. But she doesn't need to be *here*. You are in a van with Elroy Jordan. He stole you. *Tortured* you. Dante, awaken."

Dante winced, his pale face drawn. He touched a trembling hand to his temple. "Chloe," he whispered. "I can still save her."

"It's too late, Dante."

Dante looked at Lucien, Sleep fading from his eyes. He swallowed hard. Looked away. After a moment, he nodded.

Lucien cupped Dante's face. "You are my son," he said. "You can hate me all you want, but that truth remains—you are the child of Lucien and Genevieve."

Dante jerked his head away from Lucien's touch and pushed fever-hot hands against his bare chest, preparing to shove away, then stopped. A single clear note rang through Lucien, reverberating through his flesh and back into Dante's palms. Wonder lit Dante's face. Gold gleamed in his eyes. Energy played back and forth between them; a *creawdwr* drawn by his creation, an *aingeal* captivated by his Maker.

Dante yanked his hands from Lucien's chest. Lucien saw the questions in his eyes as the golden gleam faded: *What was that? What just happened?*

"There are things I must teach you," Lucien said. "Before it's too late."

Dante shook his head, his hands clenching into fists against his thighs.

Lucien wanted to shake reason into his headstrong child even as he wanted to embrace him, hold him close and safe. "Yes, whether you like it or not."

"The Big Guy's your fucking *daddy*? Holy shit!" Jordan laughed.

Blue flames arced around Lucien, burned through his veins with a cool, cleansing fire. He turned. His hand closed around the mortal's purpled throat and squeezed. Jordan's eyes bulged. His tongue protruded. He kicked, but Lucien blocked each slow-moving blow with his arm. A shame. This would be an easy death compared to what he'd imagined for him.

"No!" Dante's fingers locked around Lucien's wrist.

"What bargain did he strike with you?" Lucien said, voice low. Jordan thrashed, eyes rolling up white. Spittle flecked his lips. "Dante, what?"

"He'll give me Gina's last words."

"In exchange for what?"

"A few more hours," Dante said. "I . . . S . . ." Confusion flickered across his face. "I . . . agreed not to kill him until after Moore."

"Ah, child," Lucien sighed. He relaxed his hold, but didn't release Jordan. His gaze shifted to Dante. "Her last words won't change anything. How do you know he's not lying to you?"

"I don't," Dante said. "But I'll know Gina's words from any he'd make up." Pain and loss shadowed his face.

Fragile, Lucien realized. *Dante's endured too much. He needs Sleep. Blood. Quiet.*

"There's nothing you can do for those already gone," Lucien said. "But *Heather* searches for you in D.C. *She* needs you. Not the dead. Their needs are over."

"Heather, *oui*," Dante breathed. His fingers slipped from Lucien's wrist. "Is she safe? Who's with her?"

Jealousy spiked from Jordan, black and bitter and sharp.

"She's alone," Lucien said, fixing his gaze on Jordan. Leaning in, he whispered into the mortal's ear, "She yearns to return to Dante's bed, his embrace. She's forgotten you."

Lucien released him. The mortal slumped, gasping and retching, supported only by his handcuffed wrist. Hatred poured out of him, hot and greasy, shimmering around him like oil on water. Lucien smiled.

"What the fuck are you doing?" Dante said. Exasperation and anger edged his voice. He ran a hand through his hair. "This ain't the time for games. Someone's trying to kill Heather and she's alone. I gotta get to D.C."

Lucien shook his head. "When the sun sets, I'll take you home—"

"No. I'm gonna finish this." Dante's eyes dilated suddenly. His body tensed. "Do whatever the fuck you want, but *I'm* going to D.C."

Pain whispered against Lucien's shields, pain and droning voices. *Why won't the past release him?* He reached for Dante. Lucien *felt* it as memory yawned open and swallowed Dante. Shook him. Lucien held him tight, heart hammering. His child's eyes rolled up white. His body arched. Convulsed.

Memory seizure.

Dante wasn't *remembering*. No, Lucien thought, that was too kind of a word for what his child experienced . . . relived . . . endured. A moment from Dante's past rippled, like the land during a quake, edging up, then sheering away into darkness. Gone.

Dante endured, yes. Lucien's throat tightened as he held his son's trembling body, brushed the hair back from his pale face. *But for how much longer?* He could hide Dante from the Elohim, protect him from nightkind and every other creature walking the earth—but he couldn't protect him from his past or from his own mind.

Dante needs to confront the past my absence condemned him to. Needs to confront Johanna Moore. Then, perhaps, he will heal.

Forgive me, my Genevieve. I failed to keep our son safe.

But I stand beside him now and will guard him forevermore.

"*Sa fini pas,*" Dante whispered. His eyes opened. Exhaustion shadowed his gaze, smudged the skin blue beneath his lashes.

"Shhh," Lucien murmured, touching Dante's temple. "It *will* end. I'll drive the van while you Sleep. We'll be in D.C. by nightfall."

Dante's eyes closed as Sleep took him.

Lucien eased his Sleeping child onto the bloodstained carpet. His gaze fell on the handcuffed mortal. Jordan glared at him with hate and jealousy.

Lucien moved beside him. Wrapped a hand around the knife hilt sticking up from his thigh, looked into Jordan's seething gaze, and yanked. The mortal sucked air in through his teeth.

Lucien tilted his head, listening. "A god? I've known gods. You're just rotting flesh needing to be buried."

A grin stretched Jordan's lips. "Yeah? Well, guess what? I've got Dante's protection." His gaze flicked to Dante's Sleeping form. "Ain't that an ass-kicker?"

The smell of pungent lust curled into the air. Lucien grasped Jordan's chin, forced his gaze away from Dante. "Touch him again and I'll peel that rotting flesh from your bones while you watch with lidless eyes."

Jordan jerked free of Lucien's hand. "I've got something he wants."

Lucien shrugged. "Your bargain is with Dante, not me. Remember that."

Jordan looked away. A muscle twitched in his jaw.

Half an hour later, Lucien pulled the van back onto I-75 and into Tennessee. Jordan sat in the front passenger seat, his right wrist handcuffed to the molded emergency grip above the passenger window. He stared straight ahead, face sullen.

Dante Slept behind the curtain on the rear seat Lucien'd unfolded, a blanket draped over him, head to toe. The bloodied air bed and protective sheet of plastic had been tossed into a Dumpster. Using the mortal's Zippo, Lucien burned the file on S, but kept the photos of Dante.

Snow drifted down from the gray late-morning sky. Lucien listened for trilling *wybrcathls*, but the sky remained silent. None of the Elohim winged overhead in answer to his *wybrcathl*, seeking the *creawdwr* who'd sang a powerful, chaotic response.

Yet.

32

A RISING STORM

VOICES PENETRATED THE DARKNESS—quiet voices, terse. "Traffic's finally moving," a man said. "We'll be there in fifteen."

A radio crackled. A car, then. A heater purred warmth into the air. A lurching forward motion.

"This is some storm," a woman said. "I hope we don't get snowed in."

"Check Wallace."

Fabric rustled. Vinyl creaked. A whiff of sweet melon. Perfume?

"Still out."

Heather's heart double-timed as memory awakened. Parka and Trenchcoat. The airport. Falling. Snow cold against her face.

We're taking you to Dr. Moore.

Images flashed through Heather's mind, stark and vivid—Dante slipping out the window of his smashed MG; Dante sprawled across the threshold of Ronin's house, blood trickling along his temple; Jordan grinning as he drove away in the van—and her heart sank.

Have I failed again?

Heather felt herself sliding toward darkness once more. She bit the inside of her cheek. Tasted blood. The gray morning light and bright swirling snow hurt her eyes, lanced pain into her head. She shifted her gaze to the seat in front of her, focused on the beige vinyl. Ignored the hypnotic *whoosh-shoosh* of the windshield wipers. Her entire body tingled, like she'd taken a massive shot of Novocain.

Glancing down, Heather saw her purse on the floor behind the front passenger seat. No doubt she'd been patted down and her .38 confiscated. She tried to move her hands. The index finger on her right hand twitched. A quick look confirmed that her hands were cuffed in front. Easier to slide her onto the backseat with her hands in front instead of behind?

Heather closed her eyes in case Trench checked on her again. She struggled to keep her breathing even without slipping into the comforting embrace of sleep. Why did Moore want her? Did she suspect that Jordan and Dante were on their way to D.C.? If she'd tried to have Heather killed in New Orleans, why not now? What had changed?

If Moore wanted her dead, like Stearns had said, why weren't these two taking her to the woods or a field and putting a bullet in her skull?

Had someone intervened? Spoken for her? Her father, perhaps?

She suddenly flashed back to her recurring dream of the shadow-faced driver slipping out of the idling car, hammer gleaming in his hand.

No. She shoved the memories and images away. *Focus on now.* Vinyl creaked and she kept her eyes closed, counting to a thousand before she risked a glance through her lashes. Trench's blonde head faced the windshield.

The tingling intensified, shifted into a prickling vibration. Heather's hands clenched into fists. Hope ignited within her.

She relaxed her hands. The tingling and prickling faded to a pins-and-needles sensation. She lifted her cuffed hands, her gaze fixed on Trench's blonde head, and edged her awakening fingers toward her purse.

The wipers *tick-tock*ed across the windshield. The snow-chained tires crunched through the snow, the sound thick and muffled. Heather's fingers slipped inside her purse. Her pulse thundered in her ears.

Her fingers fumbled through the purse's contents, tracing shapes, seeking a slim edge, seeking the feel of metal, the grit of alley dirt. Her heart thudded hard against her chest as Trench moved her head, then glanced out the passenger window. Heather yanked her hands out of her purse and returned to her original position. Closed her eyes. Breathed in and out, slow.

"It's really coming down," Trench said.

"The commute home's gonna be a bitch."

"*If* you get to go home."

"I'm getting out of there if I have to snowshoe home," Parka said, voice low, tense. "Have you read any of those reports? Do you know what S is?"

Heather listened, eyes closed, her fingers inching back to her purse. *So Moore* does *know. But how?*

"I know," Trench murmured. "I'll admit, I'm curious. I kinda want to see him in the flesh, y'know?"

Heather's hands dove into her purse. Her fingers plunged to the bottom.

Parka snorted. "You know what they say about curiosity and the cat."

"Yeah, yeah. When did you get to be such an old maid?"

"I don't plan on being psycho bait," Parka said.

A finger tapped against a sharp point. Cool metal touched her palm. Heart hammering, Heather slipped the nail file out of her purse.

"Me neither," Trench said. "Maybe that's what *she's* for."

Parka grunted.

Heather froze. Moore couldn't know about her relationship with Dante. Unless . . . Dante was still being monitored, hidden cameras watching his every move at home and at the club. If so, it explained why she wasn't dead and buried beneath the snow.

And De Noir? Had he abandoned her to search for Dante? Intuition told her yes. The memory of De Noir's stricken face burned bright in her memory. *Hush, child. I will find you.*

Eyes burning behind closed lids, Heather wished it so—funneled every bit of awakening energy, every future birthday wish, into the image of Dante safe beneath De Noir's black wings.

In the meantime, she didn't need intuition to tell her she was alone and without backup. Her fingers curled around the nail file. She lifted her hands, raised them to her chest. Dropped the file inside her blouse. Tucked it inside her bra.

Saved my ass in the alley.

She hoped it would again. She dropped her hands, lay still. A moment later, vinyl creaked and she caught another whiff of Trench's sweet melon perfume.

The car slowed, then stopped. Cold air blew into the car as Parka rolled down a window. "Hey, Morris," he said. "Where is everyone?"

"Doctor Moore sent most everybody home 'cause of the storm," a gravelly voice answered. Security check? "I'm surprised you're coming in."

"Me too," Parka grumbled as he rolled up the window, sealing off the flow of frigid air. The car moved forward, snow crunching beneath the tires.

A moment later, it stopped again. Parka switched off the engine. Heather opened her eyes. Glancing up, she caught Parka's blue-eyed gaze in the rearview mirror. Caught the lift of his eyebrow. Heather tensed. Parka *knew*. While she'd been watching Trench, he'd been watching her.

"Looks like our passenger's awake," Parka said. He opened his door and stepped out. Cold air and snow whirled into the car before he shut the door.

Trench swiveled in her seat, looked at Heather. "Let's do this easy. Okay?"

Heather nodded. She pushed herself up into a sitting position with her elbows. White specks whirled through her vision like snow. She lowered her head until the dizziness passed. Another blast of cold air followed by a solid thunk told her Trench had gotten out of the car.

The passenger's side door opened. Parka reached in, grasped Heather's upper arm. Snow blew into the car. Heather looked at him. He held her gaze for a long moment, then helped her out of the car and into the storm.

The cold bit through Heather's trench, iced her fingers, stung her cheeks. She stared at the building ahead of them, at the sign half hidden by the blowing snow.

THE BUSH CENTER FOR PSYCHOLOGICAL RESEARCH

WHAT HEATHER HAD SEEN in Parka's eyes stunned her. He knew she'd taken the file, but kept silent.

Trench gripped Heather's other arm. They crossed the parking lot hunched against a whirlwind of stinging snow and ice.

JOHANNA WATCHED ON THE security monitor as Bennington and Garth escorted Wallace into No. 5 and stripped her of her trenchcoat and shoes.

"Tell Moore I want to talk to her," Wallace said, her voice surprisingly strong and level for a woman recovering from a dose of Down-in-Three.

Garth exited the room without a word, Wallace's black trench draped over her arm, her shoes in hand. Bennington paused at the door, and then looked back.

"Might as well relax," he said. "It could be a while."

"Do you know why I'm being held?"

Bennington shook his head. "Sorry," he said. "I don't." He walked from the room, closing the door behind him. Red light scrolled across the door panel as it locked.

Wallace walked the padded room's circumference, her sharp gaze flicking up to the ceiling. *No fool*, Johanna mused. After one circuit of the room, Wallace sat, her back against the north wall. Wrapping her arms around her drawn-up knees, she lowered her head. Red hair swung forward to veil her face.

Headache and lingering sleepiness—two aftereffects of the trank. Johanna swiveled her chair away from the monitor. She glanced at the file on the polished surface of her desk. Wallace's record was exemplary. She'd done well in the Academy, graduating at the top of her class at age twenty-five. In the six years since, Wallace had proven to be a dedicated, talented and intelligent agent.

And, if Johanna remembered right, intuitive and compassionate and tough.

Memory sparked. A test given to the recruits to determine their motives for wanting to join the FBI; the simplest question the most revealing.

Why do you want to be an agent of the FBI?

Most answers had been along the lines of *to get the bad guys off the streets* or *to help protect my country* or *to make a difference* or even *to have a career in law enforcement with decent wages*.

But Wallace's answer was the one Johanna remembered: *I want to be a voice for the victims. To be a voice for the dead, a voice of justice.* She wondered if Wallace still believed in justice, still yearned to be a voice for the dead. Or had the last six years in the real world sucked her spirit dry?

Johanna combed her fingers through her hair. She hated

losing an agent of Wallace's caliber and potential. She'd been sharp enough to question the Pensacola M.E. on the autopsy findings and had been ballsy enough to challenge Anzalone to her face, then had returned to New Orleans to seek the true CCK.

A sudden thought flared to life. She didn't have to lose Wallace. Could she *turn* her? Convince her to be a voice for justice—not for just a couple of decades, but for centuries? Millennia?

A better question: Was Johanna ready to be a *mère de sang*? Her first attempt had been during a vacation in New Orleans. In truth, she'd only meant to feast upon Genevieve. Not until she'd nearly drained the dark-haired beauty had Johanna heard the second tiny heartbeat. The mortal hadn't even known she was pregnant. Burning with curiosity, she'd forced her blood past Genevieve's pale lips.

What would happen to an embryo when the mother was turned?

The result was on his way home, guided by Johanna's *père de sang*, S's grandfather, in a way.

Unless—*was* Ronin on his way with E and S? Her heart said *yes, disaster runs behind the storm, blood-borne.* Did her True Blood Sleep within Ronin's embrace even now?

Did he whisper lies into S's ears?

Or worse, the truth?

Johanna turned to the monitor. Wallace still sat against the wall, arms around her knees, head down. Red hair hid her lovely face. *Red* hair.

Johanna stared at Wallace's image. *Chloe.* Could she use Wallace as a lure for her little True Blood? Get him away from Ronin? Turn him *against* Ronin?

Let Wallace mull her fate for a few hours. Then Johanna would offer her a choice.

*   *   *

HEATHER DOZED, HEAD CUSHIONED upon her arms. Dreams and images pulsed in the darkness behind her eyes like the pain throbbing in her head.

Pulse: *Pleasure lights Dante's face, gleams golden in his eyes as he enters her. She smells him—burning leaves and frost.*

Pulse: *She tucks her face against De Noir's neck as he carries her through the cold night sky.*

Pulse: *Elroy Jordan stands over her as she sleeps, a knife glinting in his hand. He touches a finger to her hair.*

Pulse: *Stearns fires. Dante falls and falls and falls . . .*

Heart pounding hard and fast, a cry caught in her throat, Heather grabbed for Dante. Her hand seized his; his pale fingers closed around her wrist. And they fell. Dante wrapped his arms around her, hugged her tight against him as they plunged through a starless night. He kissed her, and the touch of his lips set her ablaze.

She burned as they plummeted, entwined, a falling star. The wind of their passage streaked her fiery hair across the sky. Dante's black tresses coiled around her flickering strands.

A song pulsed into her, vibrating through her, *into* her, dark and intense and pounding; it burned within her heart, her soul—Dante's song.

I'm coming for you, chérie.

I'll be here, Dante. Right here.

Shhh. Je suis ici.

She heard the rush of wings.

Heather's eyes flew open. Her heart bashed against her ribs. Leaning back against the wall, she sucked in a deep breath of air. Her head still ached.

I'm coming for you, chérie.

Heather folded those words into her heart, kept them safe. Dante'd *spoken* to her. She didn't know how, maybe because he'd drank her blood and that linked them, maybe because she'd dozed in an altered state created by the drugs in her system. But her intuition, her gut instinct, told her Dante was on his way.

Closing her eyes, she smiled. Hope kindled warm and bright within her. Her headache lessened. Her exhaustion faded. If Dante was on his way, then he'd gotten away from Jordan. Maybe De Noir had found him.

A buzzing at the door opened her eyes. The door swung open and a tall blonde woman stepped in. Dr. Johanna Moore. She wore a Euro-stylish tweed skirt suit dyed a deep red, her blouse as white as the walls of the room. She held a gun pointed at the floor in her right hand.

"I remember you from the Academy," Moore said, her voice light and conversational, as though she was at a business luncheon instead of in a padded room. "I was impressed by your empathy for victims."

Heather stood. The throbbing in her head increased with the movement. "Really? I'm surprised you recognized it." She pushed her hair back from her face and met Moore's gaze. "Are you here to do your own dirty work?" she said, nodding at the pistol.

Moore's smile tilted. Her gaze seemed to turn inward for a moment. "If it comes to that," she said, voice soft. "If it makes you feel any better, I'll regret it." She stood in the center of the room, a rose petal in snow.

"Not even a little bit," Heather said. "Do you regret Rosa Baker's death? How about all the other victims of the Cross-Country Killer–Elroy Jordan?"

Moore's blue eyes brightened. "Sounds like you still long to be a voice for the dead. I'd wondered."

"That's never changed."

"For most, it does."

"What do you care?" Heather glanced at the door, estimated the distance. Wondered how many seconds she'd have before Moore spun and fired.

"I can give you E," Moore said.

Heather's heart thumped hard against her chest. She looked at Moore. Studied her pale face. Sincerity glimmered in her eyes, but Heather had a feeling she only saw the shallows; in the blue depths, dark things lurked.

"You can finally speak for his dead. Give justice to the families of his victims. All you have to do is say yes."

"Ah. The catch. Yes to what?"

Moore parted her lips. Heather stared at the revealed fangs, thoughts spinning, blood cold.

"To me," Moore said.

33

HOMECOMING

I'll be right here, Dante. Right here.

Dante drew in a deep breath and awakened. Behind his closed eyes, his vision of Heather fell away, her hair streaking the night with flames. Waiting for him. He still felt the soft, warm touch of her lips, tasted her on his tongue.

Dante opened his eyes. Darkness, warm and close. His heart jumped within his chest. Adrenaline surged through his veins. Before-Sleep images, fractured and random, strobed through his mind.

A knife hilt sticks up from his chest.

Someone calls his name. He turns.

The Perv reads to him, voice low, coiled with excitement.

A blood-grimed hand gropes along his body, unbuckles his belt.

Lucien looks down at him, gold flecks in his black eyes. My son.

"I'm still here," Lucien said. His voice rumbled from in front of Dante.

Dante reached up and pushed away the darkness. A blanket. Sitting up, he shook his hair back from his face. *Still in the van,* he thought, taking in his surroundings. But the air bed was gone and the Perv—

Dante touched a hand to his slashed and blood-stiff T-shirt. Felt the healed, still tender flesh underneath. His muscles tensed beneath his fingers. He remembered the shiv punching into him again and again.

Dante parted the curtain. Night smudged the sky. Lucien drove the van, his gaze fixed on the snow-covered road, on the glowing red taillights of the traffic in front of him. Dante glanced at Elroy, at his wrist cuffed to the grip above the passenger window. Breathed in his ripe odor of old sweat, blood, and bitterness. The smell stirred the embers of Dante's rage to life.

"Where are we?" Dante asked, his attention still focused on Elroy.

"D.C."

Elroy glanced at Dante. "Oh, goody. You're awake." Shadows cast by signs and streetlights flitted across the Perv's face.

Dante remembered the adrenaline-sharp taste of his blood. Hunger stirred.

"J'ai faim," he said, his gaze lingering on the Perv's bruised throat.

"Feast, then," Lucien said. "He has no other use."

Elroy went still. Dante caught the heady smell of fear.

"I've got Gina's last words," the Perv said. He pressed himself against the passenger door, his gaze fixed on Dante. "You promised. Not till after."

"*S* promised," Lucien said. "Not Dante."

"Hey, you said there was no S," Elroy protested. "No S, just Dante."

Lucien shrugged. "Believe everything you hear?"

Voices echoed, like words spoken across a chasm. Dante closed his eyes.

We cool?

A pound or two or three of flesh, right?

Still gonna kill me?

"*Oui,*" Dante said. He opened his eyes. Elroy stared at him. "But not till after."

The Perv nodded. "Yeah. That's right."

Dante pulled his gaze away from Elroy, tried to shut out the sound of the blood rushing through his veins. Wind buffeted the van, slanting snow across the windshield.

<I dreamed of Heather,> Dante sent to Lucien. *<I'm pretty sure Moore has her.>*

<Do you know where?>

Dante sent an image of a white padded room. His heart double-timed. Wasps droned. But memory skittered away from his grasp.

<Ah. The research center, no doubt.>

The city looked emptied and desolate. Traffic signals swung in the wind, flashing red, yellow, and green lights across the snow drifts. Icicles dangled from stark tree limbs, sparkled from the edges of buildings.

The van crawled along the street, tires scrunching across the snow. Dante glanced at the green-lit map screen on the van's console. Almost there.

<Hang on,> he sent, not sure Heather could still hear him, their link blood-forged and temporary. *<I'm coming for you.>* He'd said the same words to Jay. Would he fail Heather, too?

Penance.

Dante-angel?

Hush, princess. Go on back to sleep. I ain't gonna fail her like I failed you.

Promise?

"Promise," he whispered as Chloe slipped through the cracks in his memory and disappeared. He tried to summon her image, tried to remember her face. He hit a wall at light speed. Pain pierced his temples. He sniffed and tasted blood at the back of his throat. Watched it drip onto his hand.

Fuck. Not now!

Dante tipped his head back against the seat. As the minutes stretched past, his pain eased, edged into the background behind his thoughts. The van stopped. A hand grasped his knee.

"Are you all right?"

"Yeah. Why did you stop?"

"We're there."

Dante lifted his head and looked past Lucien to the window. Snow fell hard and fast. He made out a building hunched in the darkness beyond the snow. Light spilled from the windows.

Reaching into his jeans pocket, he tugged free the handcuffs key. He climbed up between the front seats and stretched across Elroy to unlock the cuff. He heard the Perv's heart rate pick up speed. Felt him shiver. Dante turned the key.

The cuff dropped free of the emergency grip. "I'll give you Gina's words when we're inside the building," Elroy said, lowering his arm. "Then may the best Bad Seed bad-ass win."

"This ain't a fucking contest." Dante slid across the rest of the way and opened the door. Icy air and snow gusted into the van as he hopped to the ground. The snow-covered pavement felt slick under his boots.

Elroy shivered again, this time from the cold.

Dante tucked the key back into his pocket. "Get out. You run, I'll catch you. I catch you, I'll kill you."

Elroy's jaw tightened. His brows slanted down. He looked away, but before he did, Dante saw the mask slip; saw the grinning monster, his eyes bottomless pits that sucked in every scream, memorized every etched line of pain, captured each second of fear and despair.

It was the face Dante had seen as the shiv had punched into him, over and over and over. Red flashed through his vision. Grabbing Elroy by his shirt collar, Dante yanked him out of the van and into the snow.

Elroy hit the snow-covered pavement on his shoulder. Grunted in pain.

Dante bent, locked a hand around the Perv's arm and hauled him to his feet. Wind whipped through Dante's hair, iced his skin, his face. He felt Lucien's heat-radiating presence beside him.

Dante remembered Heather saying that her killer was mortal, all DNA evidence human. Remembered Elroy's hands sliding along his body, groping, fondling; remembered the stab wounds on Gina's body; remembered the anarchy symbols cut inside her thighs.

"I fucked up," Dante said. "You lied to me. *You* killed Gina. Not Ronin."

"I still have her last words," Elroy managed through chattering teeth.

"Not anymore."

Dante shoved Elroy down into the snow and sat on him. Twisting the Perv's head aside, he bent and sank his fangs into the monster's bruised throat. Blood pulsed hot into his mouth. Elroy shrieked.

Dante plunged into his mind.

The Perv's thoughts and memories rushed into Dante's mind like a dark and dirty flood—corpse-ridden, sexed-up, spiked with sharp shivs and hard dicks. Diving deep, Dante searched for Gina.

Thunder boomed through the night. Thunder or a shotgun.

"I OFFER YOU A rare and priceless gift," Johanna Moore said. "Just think of what you could do with it. The justice you could render."

Heather kept her back to the wall and her eyes on Moore. "And if I say no, you'll give me the not-so-rare gift of a bullet to the head."

Moore's shoulder lifted in an apologetic half shrug. "I'll have no choice."

"Is that how you justify what you do?" Heather said. Again she measured the distance to the door. "Do you think you're aiding society by murdering mothers and twisting their children into killers?"

"Ah. Stearns gave you the file, after all." Regret flickered in Moore's eyes. "So you know what S is."

"I know *Dante's* willing to risk his life for his friends," Heather said. "I know you failed with him."

Amusement lit Moore's face. "Failed? I don't think so."

Heather tensed, preparing to run. *Better to die trying than not to try at all.* "You're a vampire. How could you do what—" An image spun into Heather's mind, slamming aside her thoughts. She saw Dante's face and words rang like crystal through her mind: *Hang on.*

The image vanished and she stumbled, dazed, heart pounding. Dante was close. She looked up into Moore's wide blue eyes, watched as comprehension took root.

"You didn't go back to New Orleans for E," Moore said slowly. "You went back for *S* . . . for Dante. You slept with him. He drank your blood, didn't he?"

Heather grabbed for the Glock, but even stunned and musing, Moore *moved*, yanking her gun hand out of reach and closing her free hand around Heather's throat, knocking her back into the padded wall. Gasping for air, Heather pulled at the fingers clamping into her throat and cutting off her air. Moore's fingers felt like steel. Spots flecked her vision.

"And now he's coming for *you*. Not me." Disappointment edged Moore's voice.

Moore's hand dropped away. Heather slid down the wall to a sitting position. She sucked in air, coughing. Tears blurred her vision.

"Should I let him have you?" Moore murmured. "Should I take you from him? Should he do it himself?"

"He's no longer a little boy," Heather said, throat aching, voice hoarse. "He won't fall for your tricks. He'll see through them."

"Will he?" Moore whispered. "I don't think so."

A voice issued from a speaker near the ceiling: "Doctor Moore. We've got guests in the parking lot."

"I'll be right there."

Moore hooked a hand under Heather's arm and hauled her to her feet. A smile twisted her lips. "I guess you have a little time to mull things over. Consider this—say yes and I'll give you back to Dante."

Heather jerked free of Moore's grip. "He won't listen to you."

Moore laughed. "He never did." She strode from the room, the door shutting behind her. A red telltale lit up. LOCKED.

THUNDER BOOMED AND ROLLED across the sky.

Suddenly, Dante's weight was gone and E gasped in a breath of cold air. Rolling to his feet, he risked a glance over his shoulder. The Big Guy held Dante by the collar of his leather jacket. Directed his attention away from E—*thanks, Big Fella! But it won't save you*—and toward the figures approaching. One figure lifted a long, dark thing. Fire erupted. Thunder rolled again.

Shotgun.

E ran.

JOHANNA HURRIED DOWN THE corridor to the security room, her heels clicking against the tiled floor. Her heart fluttered against her ribs like a wild bird in a cage.

My père de sang *and my beautiful True Blood have arrived. And E.*

I have long dreaded this night. Long looked forward to it.

Wallace and S. Johanna shook her head, amazed that she'd overlooked something so obvious. With Wallace's red hair, it was inevitable that S would want her. Did he think he actually *cared* for Wallace? *He wants to save her.*

And if he does?

Ah, but what if he doesn't?

She swiped her card through the security room's lock, yanked open the door, and stepped inside. Garth and Bennington, trapped by the storm, both glanced up from a monitor. Only two guards remained on-site, also trapped by the storm. Noting their absence, Johanna guessed they'd gone outside to confront the unauthorized guests. She sighed. Ronin would kill them, of course.

"Let me see," Johanna said, stepping past the two agents. She perched in the chair before the monitor. It showed the front parking lot. A van was parked in the center of the snow-buried lot. Three figures stood near the van, but the heavy snow and wind obscured Johanna's view. One stood much taller than the other two and all seemed to be Caucasian. She frowned.

"Where's Ronin?"

"Haven't seen him," Garth said. "Only those three."

As Johanna watched, one figure shoved another into the snow, then sat on him. As the figure's head dipped, the wind stopped for a moment. Gleam of leather and chains, long black hair, white skin; her beautiful child. And it looked like he was feasting on E.

A smile touched Johanna's lips. *Seems like I can't give Wallace E, after all.*

Then she realized who the tall third figure was—Lucien De Noir, S's wealthy friend and companion. *No shirt. Must be vampire as well.*

Two figures in hooded parkas entered the parking lot. Mc-

Cutcheon and Ramm. Johanna tensed. Just what were they planning on doing? Issuing a parking citation? Shooing them off the property?

"What—" Johanna's mouth snapped shut when one of the guards raised a rifle, no, *shotgun*, and fired. She stared at the screen, pulse roaring in her ears.

De Noir grabbed S by his jacket collar and pulled him off E, shielded the child with his own body. The shot went wide. Missed.

"Call them off," Johanna said through clenched teeth. "Call those idiots off before they get killed."

The door hissed as Bennington left. Johanna stared at the screen. E rolled to his feet, then staggered away into the storm, one arm in a sling, the other hand pressed against his bleeding throat.

Another shotgun blast. Johanna gritted her teeth. S ducked low, then *moved*. She gasped, astonished by his speed. Was it the True Blood? De Noir *moved*, as well, his speed equally astonishing. Then S stood over the body of one of the guards, hands clenched into fists at his sides. A puddle of blood, bright red and steaming, melted the snow. Johanna blinked. She hadn't even seen S kill the guard. And the other? De Noir dropped the second guard's broken body into the snow.

Apprehension rippled into Johanna. "We'll direct them," she said. "Lock down parts of the building and leave other areas open. We'll have the advantage."

Black wings flared behind De Noir. Johanna froze, mouth open, mind empty of rational thought. De Noir wrapped an arm around S and lifted him into the air. Into the storm.

Fallen. One of the Fallen walks at S's side. Guides him. And I feared Ronin?

Johanna pushed away from the monitor, looked up into Garth's stricken face. "Okay. Okay. I want you to shut down—"

An explosion echoed through the corridors. The power went out. The building plunged into darkness.

Johanna felt the icy touch of real fear.

LUCIEN DROPPED THE GUARD's lifeless body into the snow. His wings untucked and fanned out into the wind. Before Dante could take off on his own, Lucien locked an arm around the boy's waist and lifted them both into the air.

"What are you doing?" Dante automatically slipped an arm around Lucien's neck.

"Looking for their power source." The wind buffeted them. Ice edged Lucien's wings. He scanned the power poles, listened to the frozen land. Captured electricity thrummed. Lucien smiled. He flapped down to the building's rear. Touched bare feet to the snow-covered pavement and released Dante.

Dante saw the door marked FIRE EXIT and loped toward it.

<After I shut the power down, wait for me.>

<No.>

Lucien spiraled up into the savage sky, watching his son as he stood in front of the exit door, black hair whipping in the wind, his hand poised to grab the handle.

As he flew toward a transformer, Lucien wondered where Jordan had gone, wondered if the mortal would freeze to death and hoped he wouldn't. Lucien had a different death in mind for him, one that involved his own knives and his own skin.

Hovering beside the transformer, Lucien arced blue flame across the sky.

A LOUD EXPLOSION VIBRATED in from outside. The light went out. Staring into the darkness, Heather reached inside her bra, felt beneath the warm curve of her breast for the nail file, and pulled it free.

She padded to the door. No red LOCKED light. Any secondary systems? If so, she'd better move before they switched on. She pushed. The door swung open. Pulse racing, Heather slipped out of the padded room and into the dark corridor. She pressed up against the wall. Listened. Allowed her eyes time to adjust.

Red lights flickered to life and bathed the corridor in an eerie glow. Nail file in hand, Heather made her way down the corridor. She wondered who had arrived. Jordan? Dante? De Noir *had* to be with Dante. Was Jordan still alive?

She remembered Dante's words: *I'm coming for you,* chérie.

I'm here, Heather "shouted." *I'm here.*

An image of Dante poured into Heather's mind, washing away all thought, all worry. Dizziness whirled through her and she stumbled. Grabbing at the wall, she caught herself before she fell. She closed her eyes, breathing fast, fire searing her veins.

Dante'd heard and answered.

He was on his way.

E SHIVERED CONVULSIVELY. HIS hands and feet were numb, but his heart blazed, an inferno. An inferno he was *dying* to unleash on his betraying Bad Seed bro. He grinned, or tried to anyway, but his face was also numb. Maybe a grin *was* plastered across his face, frozen for all time.

Hunkered down behind a shrubsicle, E watched as De Noir— *wow. Wings. Holy fucking shit!*—rose into the sky, Dante clutched to his side. Something else Ronin had neglected to mention. Fucker.

E tasted bile at the back of his throat and swallowed. Thought of the hypo hidden in his sling. Thought about the sweet smell of dark cherries and Gina's last words. He knew Dante wouldn't leave without them.

Bam!

Heart thudding against his ribs, E glanced over his shoulder.

The research center went dark. Swinging around, he ran for the door and the warmth beyond. Ran knowing Dante was stepping inside at the same moment.

A contest, fuck yeah. May the best Bad Seed bad-ass win.

E grabbed the ice-slicked door handle and, yanking it open, darted inside.

DANTE THREW THE DOOR open and ran inside, then stopped. Uneasiness curled through him, snaked around his spine. He breathed in the scent of pine antiseptic and ammonia. Memory prickled.

A woman, blue eyes almost black with wonder as she slides a knife into his side—

No, that was the Perv—or—

Wasps droned, needled venom beneath his skin. *I've been here. Many times.* Dante pushed the thought away, tried to refuse the memory, but it pushed back. Hard. Fragmented images whirled through his mind: Restraints strapped tight and biting into his wrists, his ankles, his chest; a liquid bead hanging from a needle tip; white walls smeared and streaked with blood.

The droning faded and Dante shuddered. *Heather. Focus on Heather, dammit. Don't fucking fall apart.* Pain throbbed at his temples and behind his eyes; he shoved it below.

Red lights winked on. A fiery glow lit the corridor.

Heather's voice whispered into his mind: *I'm here. I'm here.*

Dante listened for her heart, her steady, quiet rhythm. *There.* White light strobed at the edges of his vision.

Dante *ran.*

JOHANNA STRODE OUT INTO the corridor. The emergency back-ups powered on, flooding the building with red light. Garth stepped out behind her, gun in hand.

"Don't shoot S," Johanna said. "I have tranks for him."

"What am I supposed to do if he comes at me in the meantime?" Garth asked, one eyebrow arched. "Throw my gun at him? Offer my fucking throat?"

"You wanted to see him. Well, here he is. Just stay out of his way."

"Great. What about the guy with wings?"

Good question. "I'd advise staying out of his way, as well." Johanna *moved*, leaving Garth alone. And cursing.

Her little True Blood walked corridors he hadn't walked in six years. He'd been seventeen the last time she'd had him drugged and picked up. Of course, he had no memory of that, just another blank spot in his mind.

But this time, S walked these halls because he *chose* to. Because he meant to rescue Wallace. Because he meant to confront Johanna. Her heart jumped when she remembered his speed.

Confront? No, he means to kill. That's what he knows. It's in the blood.

Heather glanced down the empty red-lit corridor. She still felt the heat of Dante's mental touch; his image-voice circled through her mind—*On my way.*

Pushing away from the wall, she ran down the corridor in her stocking feet, the green-cool glow of the EXIT signs her guide. She couldn't stay put and wait for Dante to find her. Couldn't risk Moore finding her first. Couldn't risk Dante sacrificing himself for her. Because she *knew* he would.

Shhh. Je suis ici.

Pain bit into the undersides of the fingers on Heather's right hand. She glanced down. Her hand, white-knuckled and stinging, was clenched around the nail file. As she forced her fingers to relax, she heard a soft padding behind her, moving *fast*—

"Freeze, Wallace. Hold it right there."

Heather heard the unmistakable sound of a round being chambered and smelled the faint scent of sweet melon. Trench. Parka's partner.

"I'm not the one you need to worry about," Heather said, tucking her fingers over the nail file. "He's coming for me."

"Psycho bait. I know. Turn around. Slow."

"Walk away," Heather said. She measured the distance to the corridor's bend. If she was needed as bait, would Trench risk killing her?

"Don't. I'll put one into your knee."

Heather stared straight ahead. Shifted her sweat-damp grip on the nail file. Slid the point between her fingers. Heard Moore saying: *Should I let him have you?*

Not for you to decide. Heather whirled to the left, her hand arcing up and over for a file-toothed shoulder punch. Then she froze.

Elroy Jordan jerked a syringe from Trench's neck. The agent gasped, her eyes rolling up white. Her gun dropped from her fingers and clattered against the tiled floor. His gaze met Heather's. Abyss-eyed. A shark's unemotional regard.

"Looks like *I'm* the one she needed to worry about," he said as Trench collapsed, limbs twitching against the floor tiles. He shook his head. "That was supposed to be for my Bad Seed bro."

Trench went still, eyes wide. Silent. The pungent smell of piss filled the corridor.

"Oops," Jordan said. He grinned.

Heather lowered her hand, tightened her fingers around the nail file. Her heart hammered against her ribs. Jordan, alive. But a little worse for wear—bruised and bitten throat, arm in a sling, disheveled.

Jordan's gaze dropped to the gun on the floor between them. "Faithful Heather," he murmured. "I knew you'd come for me." He looked up. "But S is still mine."

"Wrong," Heather said. And lunged for the gun.

Jordan dropped at the same moment. As his fingers wrapped around the pistol's grip, Heather stabbed the nail file into the back of his hand. Jordan screamed. She yanked the bloodstained file from Jordan's hand. Lifted it again.

But Jordan spun on his knees and slid the pistol down the corridor behind him. The gun skittered across the gleaming tile into darkness.

Jordan sprang to his feet. "Whoever finds Dante first can keep him." He locked gazes with Heather. The abyss kaleidoscoped open within each eye, endless and hungry. "Race ya," he said.

Heather ran.

JOHANNA REACHED THE MED unit. Her fingers curled around the door handle. A scream echoed through the center and she paused. Male—Bennington? E? A shadow jittered on the wall at the corridor's end. She yanked open the door and slipped inside. As she eased the door shut, she tried to calm her frantic heart. She sneaked a peek out the door's window.

Johanna *felt* him before she saw him—mingled pain and rage spiked against her shields. And desperation. He struggled for control. He burned.

She carefully removed her shoes, then stepped backward to the drug cabinets. S's shadow stopped, twitched against the wall in the red light. Sweat trickled between Johanna's breasts, along her temples.

As Johanna unlatched the cabinet, the door flew open and slammed against the wall, denting the plaster. She brought up the Glock. S stepped into the room and she couldn't breathe for a moment, dazzled, as always, by his beauty.

"Welcome home," she said.

S stopped, dark eyes perplexed. He winced, touched a hand to his head. Blood trickled from his nose.

"Dante!"

S spun. The red-haired agent grabbed the doorway's thresh-old as she slid across the tile in her stocking feet. She looked past S to Johanna.

He wants to save Wallace.

Ah, but what if he doesn't?

"Shit," Wallace said.

Johanna fired.

A GUNSHOT CRACKED DOWN the corridor. E's heart leapt into his throat. He edged around the corner. Hugged it. Dante knelt on the floor, *his* Heather cradled in his arms. She touched a shaking hand to the backstabber's pretty face. E tensed.

Had her eyes gleamed *golden*? For *Dante*? For his cheating/lying/backstabbing Bad Seed bro?

Looks like Heather won the race. Fire charred E's heart. He reached into his sling, his fingers finding the syringe. He regretted emptying the vial into the ponytailed blonde, wished he'd saved just enough for Dante. Hand shaking with cold, with rage, he pulled the syringe free.

Something on the floor glinted in the red light. A gift to an angry god?

The bad-ass bloodsucker bent his head and kissed Heather's lips.

E's cindered heart crumpled to ash. *Does she taste of honey? I bet she does.* Syringe full o' eye-pricking pain in hand, he stepped forward, back still pressed against the red-lit walls.

A dart suddenly sprouted from Dante's neck. The blood-sucker shivered, but continued to kiss Heather. Or was he giving mouth-to-mouth? No, *his* Heather's fingers were wrapped in Dante's black hair.

Where had the dart come from?

E went still and watched. Johanna Moore stepped from the

room behind Dante, leaned over him and plucked the dart free. Stroked his hair.

"You failed," she whispered. "Again."

Another shudder snaked the length of Dante's spine, then he slumped to the side, Heather still in his arms, her fingers still entwined in his hair.

Together.

A strange wailing noise filled the corridor, rising and falling, like a siren. E became aware that he was running, the syringe raised in his bad hand like a shiv, when Bitch-Mommy's head jerked up. Looked at him.

"Ffffuuuuccccckkkkkk yyyyooooouuuuuu!"

E scooped up the shining gift from the floor with his good hand. Metal, sharp and slender. A nail file.

Bitch-Mommy Moore lifted the Glock. Fired. Pain flowered in E's chest, hot and full of thorns. Grinning, he kept running. Bitch-Mommy fired again. Another pain-flower blossomed in E's belly. He launched himself. He flew, a golden arrow, a god of death, pure and terrible. Golden light starred from his body, piercing, white-hot, and unerring.

The god slammed into Johanna Moore, knocking her back into the room. The syringe broke off in her throat. The nail file punctured her gut. Choking, she shoved the god to the floor. The god's stomach heaved blood up into his mouth. The god grinned. Bitch-Mommy clutched at the broken syringe in her throat and pulled it out. Then she lifted her eyes up and up and up.

So she finally sees me, the god thought.

Bitch-Mommy's face turned fifty shades of white.

Pleased, the god closed his eyes.

SOMETHING HOT AND WET spread across the front of Heather's blouse. She glanced down. Blood, bright red. Arterial. Dante caught her as she fell, gathered her into his strong arms. She looked at him and tried to say, *I'm sorry*, but couldn't find her voice.

Cradling her against his chest, Dante dropped to his knees. She touched a shaking hand to his beautiful, devastated face and smoothed her thumb beneath his left eye.

"Not for me, Dante," Heather whispered, showing him the moisture on her thumb. "No tears for me. Not your fault."

Dante pulled her closer. His heat radiated into her. "I won't lose you." He lifted his wrist to his mouth and bit it. Dark blood welled up on his pale skin. He pressed the wound against her lips. "Drink," he urged. *"S'il te plait."*

Dante's blood smeared across Heather's lips as she turned her head away. It smelled of dark sun-warmed grapes and tasted like Dante's kisses, heady and tempting. Her throat tightened.

"No," she whispered. Her vision swam. "No. I want to stay what . . . I . . . am . . ." She shivered, suddenly cold. Sleepy.

Gold fire lit Dante's eyes. Lowering his head, he kissed her.

DANTE'S SONG STIRRED WITHIN him, layering chord upon chord. Bending his head, he kissed Heather's bloodstained lips and breathed his song into her. He filled her with his essence, kindling blue fire at her core. He imagined her whole, healed, and wove blue-lit thread through her wound. Heather's fingers twisted around his hair. Her faltering heart beat strong and fast.

Something stung Dante's neck.

"You failed," a familiar voice said. "Again."

Dante shivered as cold spread through him, crackling like ice through his veins. His song faltered.

"Not true," Heather murmured against his lips.

He tasted the salt of her tears. Fire flared for a moment, and he breathed it into her before they sank together beneath the ice, plunging through starless night.

PAIN AND GRIEF SLAPPED against Lucien's shields like twin tsunamis, receding to return in ever stronger waves, deadlier surges. He ran, following his bond to Dante. Loss reverberated within Lucien like a broken song. Power swirled into the air, buoyed by a *creawdwr's* energy. Then, Dante lapsed into unconsciousness.

As Lucien rounded the corner, he saw Jordan fling himself at Johanna Moore, a syringe in one fist, a bit of metal in the other. He saw Moore shoot Jordan twice before the mortal tackled her. They both hit the floor hard. Her gun skittered across the tiles, coming to a stop against Dante's back.

Dante lay in the corridor, his arms wrapped around Wallace. Fading blue flames sparked and danced around them. Lucien heard Dante's slow, measured heartbeat, smelled the chemicals flowing in his blood. Wallace's heart pulsed, as well, a rapid patter.

In one long stride, Lucien stood beside his drugged child and the woman he cared for—cared for enough to sacrifice his own safety to ensure hers—but hadn't that always been his way?

It was one of the things Lucien loved and treasured most in Dante—his compassionate heart. All the things Moore had subjected his child to hadn't stolen that compassion or broken his spirit. He was wounded, yes, and some of the wounds might never heal, yes. But he'd survive. And he'd love.

Lucien saw Genevieve in every act of love Dante performed, in every kindness he showed. In those moments, Lucien saw his laughing, dark-haired little Genevieve.

But, as for the woman who'd killed her . . .

Lucien swiveled and watched as Johanna Moore pushed herself free of Jordan's body. Her hand reached up, grabbing the broken syringe in her throat. She yanked it out, blood trickling from the puncture, then froze, her gaze traveling up the length of Lucien's body.

Johanna Moore paled. Her fingers froze around the sliver of steel in her belly.

Jordan's blood-frothed lips curved into a smile. His eyes closed.

"Do you remember Genevieve Baptiste?" Lucien asked, kneeling beside Dante. "My son's mother?" He picked up Moore's gun and tossed it down the darkened hall.

Shock blanched Johanna's face. Widened her eyes. "*Your . . .* son?" she whispered.

"*Oui, mon fils,*" Lucien said. He glanced at Heather; she opened her eyes. "But, I believe my question was—do you remember Genevieve Baptiste?"

Lucien slipped an arm around Heather and eased her up, helping her to sit against the wall. Her gaze remained on Dante, reluctant to leave him. Lucien touched a talon beneath her chin. Heather regarded him with shock-dilated eyes.

"It's all right," he promised.

Heather drew in a deep breath, then winced. Lucien brushed her hair back from her face. Her wound no longer bled, but she needed medical attention. The drugs had kept Dante from finishing whatever it was he'd started.

"I'm waiting," Lucien said.

"Yes, I remember her," Moore stammered, voice rough. She yanked the file from her flesh. It hit the floor with a sharp tink.

Lucien drew a talon across his wrist. Blood welled up. He looked at Moore from beneath his brows. "Say her name."

"Genevieve Baptiste," Moore breathed. "I didn't know. I wouldn't have—"

"Be silent," Lucien said, gathering Dante into his arms.

Moore closed her mouth.

Lucien pressed his bleeding wrist against Dante's lips. The blood smell roused Dante's nightkind instinct and he sucked at the wound, swallowing the healing blood. Lucien knew it wouldn't cleanse all of the drug's effects, but it would lessen them.

Looking back at Moore, Lucien said, "I've read the file. I've seen the CD. I know what you've done to Dante. To him and to his mother, my love."

Moore looked away. She trailed a shaking hand through her blonde hair.

Why have you abandoned us?

Lucien tasted the ashes of bitter regret. He deserved Dante's hate, perhaps.

My Genevieve, I am with our son. He is safe at last.

Lucien pulled his wrist away from Dante's mouth, then bent and kissed him, breathing energy in between his lips. Urged his son up to consciousness.

Awaken, child. Time to take your revenge.

Time to free yourself from the past.

Dante's eyes opened, revealing dilated gold-rimmed pupils.

"AVENGE YOUR MOTHER," LUCIEN whispered. "And yourself."

Pushing Lucien's arms aside, Dante sat up. The corridor spun. Colored flecks starred his vision. His head ached, but a different kind of pain knifed his heart.

Heather.

He looked for her, saw her resting against the wall, a smile on her pale lips. Rising to his feet, he crossed the floor and, kneeling, touched a hand to her face.

He breathed a little easier knowing she'd live. He'd flooded energy and song into her, seeking what was broken. He wasn't sure what he'd done, but it had worked. He hadn't lost her.

Heather laid her hand over his, her skin cool. Wonder lit her face. "I hear a song. It's dark and furious and heartbreaking. So beautiful. Is it coming from you?"

Dante nodded. Leaning in, he kissed her. Her fingers interlaced with his. "Don't listen," he said against her lips. "Shut it out. *D'accord?*"

"Let it go. I can build a case against Moore," Heather said. "Let it go, Dante."

Dante leaned back. "No." He squeezed her hand, then released it. He stood.

Heather closed her eyes. "Pigheaded," she whispered.

Dante spun on his heel and strode across the corridor, past Lucien, Heather's fear pressed like a rose against his heart. For him. She was scared *for* him.

<Guard her.>

<Of course.>

Elroy the Perv's body stretched across the doorway, his shirt bloodied, his eyes empty, his heart silent. Dissipating heat shimmered up from the body. Dante's hands curled into fists. *Gina.* Elroy had taken the last little bit of her to the grave.

"Name the one you love," Dante whispered, stepping over the Perv.

Tomorrow night?

Always, ma petite.

Dante walked into a room rank with buried memories and the smell of old blood and medicine. He looked at the woman standing at the opposite wall—tall, blonde, nightkind. Never taking her eyes from him, she reached for a dart gun on the counter beside her.

Images sparked: *She looks down at him, smiling. He smells Chloe's blood congealing on the floor, on the straitjacket wrapped around him. "You've done well, little one. You failed to protect her, but you protected yourself. No one can ever be used against you if you're willing to kill them yourself."*

Sparked: *She tightens his restraints, smooths a hand through his hair, then, smiling, steps back as a man in a white lab coat and a clear mask walks into the room, a baseball bat clenched in his hand. And goes to work.*

Wasps droned. Pain whispered through Dante's mind. White light squiggled at the edges of his vision. He watched her hand slide to the dart gun; he *let* her curl her fingers around it.

She's the one, Dante-angel.

I know, princess.

"My True Blood," she said. A smile brushed her lips. "Do you remember me?"

"*Oui,*" Dante said, voice low. "I remember you."

Dante *moved* and caught her wrist as she raised the dart gun, then slammed her against the wall. The dart gun tumbled from her fingers and *tunk*ed against the tile. Moore twisted, but Dante held her against the wall, his hands locked around her wrists, his body pressing against hers, his thigh between her legs.

Dante smelled the blood flowing through her veins, listened to the hard pounding of her heart, smelled her—cinnamon and cloves and cold, cold ice.

Smelled lust, smoldering and pheromone-rich.

Moore stopped struggling. She looked into Dante's eyes. Her breath caught in her throat and another memory-fragment tore through his mind: Moore curled naked and warm beside him, reeking of blood and sex, her fangs in his throat, her fingers in his hair.

Rage coiled through muscles already taut. "What makes you different from *him*?" Dante nodded his head toward Jordan's body behind him.

"I know what's best for you."

"Yeah, he thought so, too."

"No one knows you like I do," Moore said, voice husky. "I've explored your mind. Mapped your psyche. But it's only a beginning. There are secrets, S—"

"Ain't S."

Music twisted through Dante: an aria, thorned and dark,

prickling around his heart, rising, pounding, a crescendo of fury and chaos and loss. Chords strummed; chaos rhythm pulsed discordant and raw.

His song burned. Incandescent.

"Did my mother ask to be turned?" Dante asked. "Did she choose?"

"Yes. But, she changed her mind later, when it was too late. I couldn't undo—"

"Liar," Dante whispered.

"What's that glow?" Moore breathed as he lifted his hands and cupped her face.

Chaos rhythm plucked at vibrating strands of DNA, breaking, compressing, erasing. *Unmaking*. Johanna Moore screamed, a long undulating sound that pierced Dante's aching head. His song pulled her apart—divided her into elements, played an arpeggio with her core. Spilled her essence. Separated flesh and bone and blood.

Johanna Moore puddled on the floor, her scream ending with a wet gurgle.

Blue spikes of energy whipped around Dante, flamed from his hands. He shivered, caught in the song, the rhythms of chaos, the tempo of creation. Closed his eyes. He saw stars. Heard a rush of wings.

<*Silence the song, child. You've avenged your mother.*>

Dante opened his eyes. The song faded into silence. Pain scraped through his head. He tasted blood. He looked down at the moist strands that used to be Johanna Moore. Kicked them apart. Then he turned.

Lucien stared at him, eyes golden, wings arched behind him, his face both rapt and . . . scared? Dante wondered. Lucien, scared?

<*Creawdwr.*>

Dante walked to the doorway. He knelt beside Elroy's cooling body. Could he pull Gina from a dead mind?

"Too late," Lucien said. "You've chosen the living over the dead."

Looking up, Dante saw Heather sitting across the hall, face stark, eyes dark and troubled. "*Oui*. The living over the dead."

Forgive me, Gina.

Standing, Dante stepped over the Perv's body one last time. He gathered Heather into his arms and carried her down the corridor. His muscles tightened as he smelled fear on her, fear *of* him. He held her close, his heart pounding hard.

A man in a snow-dusted parka stepped into the corridor, his hands out and open; *Look, nothing hidden here!* "I can call an ambulance," he said.

"You can trust him," Heather murmured. "He helped me."

"Okay," Dante said. "Call one." He breathed in Heather's scent—rain and sage and blood, drew it deep into his lungs. Scared it was the last time.

34

ALL THAT
COULD'VE BEEN

"Hey."

Heather looked up toward the doorway. Dante leaned there in leather and latex, one hand braced against the threshold. Fluorescent light winked from the ring in his collar and from the rings on his fingers. A half smile tilted his lips, lit his pale, gorgeous face. He raised his shades to the top of his head.

He still stole her breath away. She suspected that he always would.

Beyond him, in the corridor, nurses and CNAs stared, wondering who paid hospital visits wearing leather and bondage collars, wondering just what had wandered in from the frozen night.

"Hey," Heather said.

She pressed her hands against the mattress, meaning to ease up, but then Dante was there, arms around her, helping her, his hands hot against her skin. Pain rippled through her and she caught her breath.

"What's wrong?" Dante asked. "Do you need—"

"No. It's okay."

Dante looked at her for a long moment, his dark eyes searching her face. Then he inhaled deeply. He pulled the chair close to the bed and sat. He waited. Heather was pretty sure he knew what she was going to say—or, at least, suspected.

Reaching a hand over the bed railing, she grasped Dante's hand. A smile ghosted across his lips. He rubbed his thumb over the back of her hand. She glanced out the window, at the room reflected in the black sky beyond, and the two people in that room, holding hands and keeping silent.

Heather thought of the mystified surgeons: the worst of the damage to her aorta and her left lung healed or closed off, or miraculously cauterized. She should've bled to death in minutes. She remembered the taste of Dante's lips, the amaretto taste of his blood; remembered the cool fire he'd breathed into her.

None of which Heather could tell the surgeons. Or the investigators from the Bureau dispatched to take her statement, debrief her and uncover the truth. Or at least an *official* version of the truth. She knew better than to mention Bad Seed; she only discussed her hunt for a serial killer and how she'd finally found him.

One thing she knew for certain—her career with the Bureau was over. Her decision, one she hadn't voiced yet. The powers that be would be happy to file her away at a desk in an obscure city; would, in fact, prefer it.

Heather kept Dante from all of them. He'd saved her life. Even without that, she'd never hand him over to federal wolves. Hadn't Johanna Moore been wolf enough?

Johanna Moore. What Dante had done . . . Heather couldn't wrap her mind around it. What *had* he done?

Dante cups Moore's face. His hands tremble. Glow with blue light. Blue flame. His hair snakes up into the air. Energy crackles. Heather's skin goose bumps. Her hair lifts. She smells ozone.

Blue light shafts into Moore's body, explodes from her eyes, her screaming mouth. She . . . separates . . . into strands, wet and glistening, mingled blue and red. Dante unthreads her, separates every single part of her.

Johanna Moore spills to the tiled floor.

Energy continues to whip from Dante, blue tentacles snapping into the air and altering everything they touch. A counter twists into dark, heaving vines thick with blue thorns. The dart gun slithers into the shadows.

Dante's beautiful face is ecstatic—like it had been when he'd torched the Prejean house.

In that moment, Heather had been terrified of Dante. Of what he could do. His potential. Yet . . . had Dante been a voice for his mother? For all of Johanna Moore's victims?

"Talk to me," Dante said.

Heather shifted her gaze from the window. Smiling, she squeezed his hand. He burned against her palm. Felt fevered. "Are you okay?" she asked.

"*Ça va bien.* I'm good." Dante held her gaze, his own open and unwavering. "Talk to me, Heather."

She nodded. Talk might help. "What you did to Moore . . . what . . . how . . . ?"

"Dunno," Dante said. He trailed a hand through his hair. "I've never done . . . *that* . . . before. The song you said you heard? It's tied to that. I feel it inside." He touched their linked hands against his chest, above his heart. "It's like fingering the strings on my guitar, like composing on my keyboards."

"Is it a nightkind or a Fallen ability?"

Dante stared at her, surprised. "How did you know?"

"Your father told me," Heather said.

Dante nodded, then looked away. A muscle flexed in his jaw. After a moment, he said, "I'm pretty sure it's a Fallen thing. I used to think it was nightkind, but . . ." He shrugged.

"Can you control it?"

"Not always. No." Dante looked at her, reflected light gleaming in his eyes.

"Were you controlling it then?"

"More or less."

"Meaning?"

"Meaning I didn't have an outcome in mind," he said, voice low. "But I wanted to finish it—end her fucked-up game." His thumb once again rubbed back and forth across the back of her hand, a soothing gesture—for them both, she had a feeling.

Dante was nightkind and Fallen, and a killer. More than enough to send most women—sane women, anyway—screaming into the night. But there was so much more to him—a boy wishing his princess night-night, then walking into a basement alone; a man struggling with his emotions as he spreads his jacket over a friend's body and sits beside her so she won't be alone; a lover fitting against a woman like no other ever has—body and heart—asking her to stay.

It's quiet when I'm with you. The noise stops.

Run from me.

Did either of those statements reflect Dante's true center? Or did both? Had his life ever been his own? Heather scanned his dark eyes, his beautiful face. In spite of all he was or, maybe, *because* of it, he'd somehow captured her heart. Not knowing which scared the hell out of her. She needed answers. She needed a chance to catch her breath.

"Where is this going?" Dante said, watching her. His thumb was motionless on her hand. "Heather?"

"I want you to go home," she said quietly. "I'm heading back to Seattle as soon as I'm released. There's gonna be a ton of shit to deal with."

"You don't hafta deal with it alone."

"Yes, I do." Heather slipped her hand from his, grasped the cool metal railing. "Dante, I do. I've got things to think about—

to sort through. I need a little distance. A little time. Nothing's what I thought—what I *believed* it was."

A half-smile tilted his lips. "Nothing and no one. Believe me, I understand."

Heather cupped a hand against his face. "I bet you do."

Closing his eyes, Dante leaned into her touch and closed his hand over hers.

"You need time, too," she murmured. "You more than anyone."

"Don't tell me what I need." Dante's voice was rough, raw.

"Pigheaded," she whispered.

Despite his denial, his life, his world, had been ripped apart—his hidden past, revealed. Did he know any of it yet? Would De Noir tell him? Should she?

"Has your father said anything about Bad Seed?" She slid her hand from his face.

Dante's eyes opened. Something flickered in those dark depths—pain, maybe grief, maybe rage—then vanished. "No. Elroy told me. But I can't hold onto it." He shook his head. "No matter how hard I try."

Jordan. That hurt. "Oh, Dante, I'm so sorry."

"Don't be." A smile brushed his lips. He pulled his shades from the top of his head, slid them on. "Not your fault." Standing, he bent over her and brushed his lips against hers.

"This doesn't need to be good-bye," Heather said against his warm lips. "I care about you, you know that, don't you?"

"I care about you, too," he whispered, tracing a finger along the edge of her jaw.

Heather closed her eyes. When she opened them again, Dante was gone. But the feel of his lips lingered upon hers; his scent hung in the room. She pictured him walking out into the snow-covered night, alone.

She had a feeling he didn't expect to see her again. She'd known his leaving would hurt, just not how much. And it did, heart-deep—sharp and unrelenting. Tears slipped hot down her cheeks, into her ears. Folding her arms across her eyes, she wept.

For all the voiceless dead Elroy Jordan had left behind.

For justice unrendered.

For Dante.

She thought of all that could've been—traveling between New Orleans and Seattle; Dante creating music, touring, putting his past together. She might become a victim's advocate, a PI, something to help those who could no longer speak for themselves, and—together—she and Dante could work to heal his wounded mind and help him find the redemption he sought.

Could still be. *Nothing's written in stone.*

Penance.

Could he be redeemed? She believed he was worth the chance. She just needed to find out if she was strong enough to give him that chance. And herself.

I won't walk away from you.

A song wisp suddenly curled through Heather and, for a moment, she thought she heard Dante's voice, smoky and low, burning like a flame in her heart: *Shhh.* Je suis ici. *Always.*

GLOSSARY

To make things as simple as possible, I've listed not only words but phrases used in the story. Please keep in mind that Cajun is different from Parisian French and the French generally spoken in Europe. Different grammatically and even, sometimes, different in pronunciation and spelling.

For the Irish and Welsh words—including the ones I've created—pronunciation is provided.

One final thing: **Prejean** is pronounced PRAY-zhawn.

Aingeal (AIN-gyahl), angel. Fallen/Elohim word.

Ami, (m) friend, (f) **amie. Mon ami,** my friend.

Ange, (m) angel. **Mon ange,** my angel. **L'ange,** the angel.

Ange de sang, angel of blood; blood angel. **Mon ange de sang,** my angel of blood.

Anhrefncathl (ann-HREVN-cathl), chaos song; the song of a Maker. Fallen/Elohim word.

Beau diable, mon, (m) my beautiful devil.

Bonne nuit, good night.

Bon à rien, good for nothing.

Calon-cyfaill (KAL-on kuv-EYE-luh), friend of the heart, usually bonded. Fallen/Elohim word.

Ça va bien, fine. I'm fine/okay. It's going well.

C'est bon, that's good.

C'est vrai, that's true.

Cher, dear, beloved. **Mon cher,** (m) my dear or my beloved.

Cher ami, mon, (m) my dearest friend, my best friend; intimate, implying a special relationship.

Chéri, (m) dearest, darling, (f) **chérie.**

Chien, (m) dog.

Comment ça va, how is it going?

Creawdwr (KRAY-OW-dooer), creator; maker/unmaker; an extremely rare branch of the Elohim believed to be extinct. Last known creawdwr was Yahweh.

D'accord, okay.

Elohim, (s and pl) the Fallen; the beings mythologized as fallen angels.

Enchanté, delighted, pleased, enchanted.

Et toi, and you.

Fallen, see Elohim.

Fille de sang, (f) blood daughter; "turned" female offspring of a vampire.

Fils de sang, (m) blood son; "turned" male offspring of a vampire.

Foute ton quant d'ici, get away from here.

Frère, (m) brother. **Mon frère,** my brother.

Gètte le, keep an eye on him.

J'ai faim, I'm hungry.

Je comprend pas, I don't understand.

Je sais pas, I don't know.

Je regrette, I'm sorry.

Je regrette, mes amis, I'm sorry, my friends.

Je suis ici, I'm here.

Je va te voir plus tard, I'll see you later.

Laissez les bons temps rouller, let the good times roll.

Le coeur, the heart.

Llygad (THLOO-gad), (s) eye; a watcher; keeper of immortal history; story-shaper. A Fallen/Elohim word originally.

Llygaid (THLOO-guide), (pl)

Loa, (Haitian) spirit; associated with voodoo.

Marmot, (m) brat.

Merci, thank you. **Merci beaucoup,** thanks a lot. **Merci bien,** thanks very much.

Mère de sang, (f) blood mother; female vampire who has turned another and become their "parent."

Mon Dieu, (m) my God.

M'selle, (f) abbreviated spoken form of **mademoiselle,** Miss, young lady.

M'sieu, (m) abbreviated spoken form of **monsieur,** Mr., sir, gentleman.

Nightbringer, a name/title given to Lucien De Noir.

Nightkind, (s and pl) vampire; Dante's term for vampires.

Numéro un, number one. (Cajun)

Oui, yes.

Père, (m) father. **Mon père,** my father.

Père de sang, (m) blood father; male vampire who has turned another and become their "parent."

Petit, mon, (m) my little one, (f) **petite, ma.** (Generally affectionate.)

Pour quoi, why.

Sa fait pas rien, it doesn't matter.

Sa fini pas, it never ends.

Sa vaut pas la peine, it's not worth it.

S'il te plaît, please (informal).

Tais toi, shut up.

Tayeau, (s) hound. **Tayeaux,** (pl) hounds.

T'es sûr de sa, are you sure about that?

T'est blême comme un mort, you're as pale as a ghost.

Très belle, (f) very beautiful.

Très bien, very good, very well.

Très joli, (m) very pretty.

True Blood, born vampire, rare and powerful.

Viens ici, come here.

Vous êtes très aimable, you are very kind.

Wybrcathl (OOEEBR-cathl), sky song. Fallen/Elohim word.

GENEVIEVE'S PRAYER

POURQUOI TU NOUS AS abandonnes? Je ne sais pas ce que j'ai fait pour vous faire partir, je t'en supplie, sauve ton fils. Éloigné le d'ici. Mets-le l'abri. Il est ma lumière et mon coeur—comme tu as pu l'être. Lucien, mon ange, s'il te plaît, écoute-moi.

WHY HAVE YOU ABANDONED us? I don't know what I did to send you away, but I beg of you, save your son. Take him away from here. Keep him safe. He is my light and my heart—just as you once were. Lucien, my angel, please hear me.